BACK HOME

Once, years before, someone had asked Kate how long she had known Cornelia Waggaman Fitzgerald, and she thought for a moment and could not truthfully recall a time when she hadn't known her.

They had been born within two blocks of each other and within two months of each other in West Mystic, Ohio, east of Cleveland but west of almost everything else, including the Connecticut town after which it was named. . . .

In high school, they took turns being class secretary; were both finalists as Homecoming Queen, though Neela won by several votes, at least one of which was cast by herself (Kate, on the other hand, had voted for her best friend, thinking it would be reciprocated); and were deflowered within twenty-four hours of each other.

By the same boy.

Girlfriends

A NOVEL BY
DALLAS MILLER

AVON
PUBLISHERS OF BARD, CAMELOT, DISCUS, EQUINOX AND FLARE BOOKS

GIRLFRIENDS is an original publication of Avon Books.
This work has never before appeared in book form.

AVON BOOKS
A division of
The Hearst Corporation
959 Eighth Avenue
New York, New York 10019

First Avon Printing, February, 1977

AVON TRADEMARK REG. U.S. PAT. OFF. AND IN
OTHER COUNTRIES, MARCA REGISTRADA,
HECHO EN U.S.A.

Printed in the U.S.A.

MEMORY and being had been stilled, as if she'd been anesthetized.

Neela was only vaguely aware of having left Robert Pino's apartment. One minute she'd been on the bed, trying to relate her head to the rest of her body—the former kept rising, as if it were about to sever itself from her neck; the latter hurt terribly in a couple places—and the next minute someone was helping her into her clothes. Robert did not object. He was sitting on the floor, his back against the wall, studying the carpet as if it were the most interesting thing he'd ever seen. The Italian boy grinned at her from the bed.

The black man called Ronnie helped her down the stairs and into the street, then walked her east toward Sixth Avenue, all the while carrying on a ceaseless conversation with himself. At some point they ran into an apparition, bald-headed, Van-Dyke-bearded, and wearing a scarlet poncho. Words were exchanged, then the apparition accompanied them down the street.

Neela knew that somehow she would have to extricate herself from her new friends, but at that moment the block appeared deserted and she was afraid what might happen if she created a scene. While they'd been in bed, and somewhere between the end of the lust and the beginning of the loathing, she'd heard Ronnie tell her that she was his old lady now. She hadn't agreed or disagreed, merely listened in horror. She had a feeling that he wouldn't take to it kindly when he learned that she wasn't buying, only looking, thank you.

He hadn't even allowed her to wash, and now she realized that she was wet at the groin where semen was seeping into her panty hose. Her mouth felt foul and abused, and she ached in the rear end where someone—Angie, the Italian boy?—had tried to do something unspeakable, and would have, too, if Ronnie hadn't stopped him.

Ronnie now asked a question, and by way of reply she said, "There should be something in my purse. Robert said he'd leave me cab fare."

But, of course, Robert had cleaned her out. Apart from some change, she had nothing. The man in the cape conferred momentarily with Ronnie, then disappeared into a telephone kiosk at the corner. "Hey, man," Ronnie protested while he dialed, "she don't do that shit."

Apprehensively, Neela said, "What does he want?"

"I take care of you," he said. "Don't you be afraid, man."

When the Poncho had finished, he told Ronnie that everything was all set, but Ronnie replied, "No, man. I take her home." To prove that he meant what he said, he waved down a taxi and, as soon as one stopped, helped Neela into the back seat.

"She don't do that shit," Ronnie repeated.

This time the Poncho appeared to be convinced. He said that he would share their cab uptown, as he was visiting someone on East End Avenue. Then he added to Neela, "Where you going, man?"

Neela didn't know what to say. She didn't want them to know where she lived. In the end, she said that the corner of 83rd and Lexington would do.

She felt that Ronnie was protecting her from the other man, but she didn't quite know what was involved. Someone on East End Avenue—which was by no stretch of the imagination a ghetto—was expecting all of them, Neela included. Had the Poncho taken her for a whore? Was that it? She was high on something, she was good-looking, and she was with a spade. Maybe it was all the evidence he thought he needed.

Fortunately, Ronnie had pushed her into the back seat of the cab first, so that he sat between Neela and the other man. From time to time the Poncho looked over Ronnie's lap at her. A more conspicuous fellow couldn't be imagined. When he spoke, it was in a high, shrill, nervous voice, his hands moving in and out of his garment as he did.

Ronnie, who found four dollars in his pocket, was the only one with money, so he gave it to the driver and instructed him to let them out when it was exhausted. Neela wondered how long it had taken him to earn four dollars and what he had to do to earn it. He worked in the garment center, he'd told her after he'd made love to her, and out of charity Neela hadn't dared ask what he did. Possibly he was one of those robots who pushed portable closets around the streets. Every time Neela saw one of them, she couldn't help but think how they must hate and despise the world that humiliated them so. Yet Ronnie, for all that, was surprisingly gentle. If they'd met in some other way than a gang bang—my God, that's all it was, she said to herself—she might have liked him.

The cab stopped in the low Seventies and they got out and began to walk, Ronnie holding her by one elbow, the second man holding her by the other. Something was wrong with her coordination and she found it difficult to control her legs. Several times she stumbled, but Ronnie held on tight.

"Look," he said to her, "you my old lady now."

"It look like you old lady snortin' shit, man," the other said, then laughed.

Had she been? She looked at Ronnie for confirmation, but he averted his face. Had Robert Pino let her sniff heroin? No wonder her mind had almost left her body.

Before the Poncho turned to go eastward, he repeated his invitation to join the party. "My fren, he let white pussy in the door anytime, man."

Ronnie quickly cut him short, saying once again that she was his old lady and didn't do that shit. After he'd left, Ronnie warned her never to have anything to do with Ratman. "He crazy, man. He ice a woman once, she didn't do what he tolt her. You stay away from him."

Neela didn't have to be persuaded.

At the corner of Lexington and 83rd, he asked her when he could see her again, and she said she wasn't sure but that she thought she was going out to the Coast in a few days.

Tomorrow would do. He would leave work early or wouldn't go in at all. What time could she get away? "I wait for you right here, this corner."

Neela knew that it would be impossible to tell him that she didn't want to see him again. Instead, she said that it would be hard to get away, but perhaps she could get out of the apartment for a little while around ten o'clock.

"I be standin here," he replied. He squeezed her arm. "I take care of you from now on."

Neela said that she would see him at ten o'clock, having no intention of keeping the appointment. She said goodnight, thanked him again for having helped her home, then turned and made her way down 83rd Street. She looked everywhere for the right kind of building to rush into. At last, she came to a canopy and saw a doorman standing on the other side of a glass door. With surprising composure, she walked toward him. He opened the door, and once on the other side, she said breathlessly, "Please help me. Someone is following me."

She then asked him to permit her to stand inside the lobby for a few minutes until it would be safe to leave. She had no money, she said, but showed him an envelope with her name and address. "I'll make it up to you. I'll send you twenty dollars in the morning. I promise."

He said that it wouldn't be necessary. He would be glad to help. Should he call the police?

She would be all right if she could get home safely, she said. If she could wait a few more minutes, perhaps he could stop one of the cabs going by.

Several minutes later, a cab discharged a passenger in front of the building across the street, and the doorman detained it. Neela rushed out and slid into the back seat. She'd just told the driver where she wanted to be taken when she heard someone yelling, and then she saw a figure running toward the cab.

"Please *hurry*," she said to the driver.

When a traffic light at the end of the street stopped them, Neela turned and saw Ronnie running down the middle of the street. She pressed the lock buttons on both doors, then told the driver that she would give him fifty dollars as soon as she got home if only he'd go through the light.

"You gotta deal," he said.

Almost the same minute that his foot hit the accelerator, Neela could hear Ronnie's fists pounding on the trunk of the cab, and then all three of them were moving down the great avenue—the cab, Neela, and Ronnie somehow holding onto the bumper—but by the time they reached 80th Street, he had either jumped off or fallen.

"Don't stop," she said to the driver. "I'll give you another fifty."

While the driver waited downstairs, Neela went up to the apartment for the money. The minute the elevator doors opened, she heard the unmistakable sounds of people partying—"Inane, stupid, self-important, posturing people," Quentin himself described his friends, "but they have their uses"—and it was all she could do to brush past them in the foyer to reach her bedroom.

She always kept emergency cash in a dresser drawer, but she was down to seventy dollars. She was about to make her way into the living room, even though she knew she looked like a wraith, when she heard a voice from the doorway say, "What are you on, Mrs. Fitzgerald? I'm on bourbon."

She turned and saw Quentin's new friend, whose name she'd momentarily forgotten. "Look," she said, "could I bum thirty bucks off you? I have to pay a cab driver downstairs."

He was in black tie now, and reached into his breast pocket to withdraw a slender wallet. He was about to hand her the thirty dollars when he said, "Are you in trouble?"

"A little bit."

"If you like, I'll attend to the driver."

What a relief not to have to go through the gauntlet in the foyer again. If she could collapse into a hot tub for the next twenty minutes, quite possibly she might be able to face Quentin's friends.

She handed him the seventy dollars. "I owe him one hundred. Please don't ask me why."

His eyebrows went up briefly, then recovered.

"And I'd also appreciate it if you didn't mention it to Quentin."

"It wouldn't be the first time. I mean, that I haven't mentioned something to him."

It seemed to Neela that he was almost inviting conspiracy. As soon as he'd left the room, she stripped out of her clothes, dropping them on the floor on her way

Contents

I. Education Interruptus   1

II. Continuing Education   133

III. Education Concluded   235

I

Education Interruptus

IN the summer, wives went to the Island with the kids, and husbands slept with old girlfriends in Chelsea or found new ones in the Village.

In the winter, wives left tidy houses in the suburbs two, sometimes three nights a week to squeeze into narrow desks at the New School or NYU, ostensibly to improve their minds or what was left of them after ten or fifteen years of marriage, secretly to find something to distract them from the real or imagined horror of being older than they'd ever intended to be.

Katherine McCabe hoped to do both, but she very nearly missed the train.

Had, in fact, missed it at Princeton and as a result drove in a frenzy in order to get to Princeton Junction before she missed the connection too. She could hear the New York train pulling in even before she'd parked the car—Buddy McCabe's cheerless Hornet, not her own VW, which was laid up in a garage—and didn't have time to lock it, which would have earned her a long, polemical scolding from Buddy, had he known, about how one should never tempt the weak and the vulnerable, of which there were plenty. Foxy hair flying, she rushed across the parking lot toward the platform, clutching a purse, an overnight bag, and the loose-leaf notebook she'd acquired just the day before, the first paper she had bought in years, it seemed, which wasn't meant to be used for wiping up or to be blown into, but to write *ideas* on.

It had taken almost two months of badgering even to get that far. First there was the probing after she'd seen the ad in the Sunday *Times*—"You think it's crazy for me to go back to school?" she'd asked Buddy, who privately thought that once a woman reached the age of thirty-five, you bought her a Hammond electric organ and told her to bang away at it whenever she felt funny in the head; and he'd replied, "You're too damned smart already," the implication being that smartness was a liability to someone who did nothing more intellectual than stuff dirty dishes into a dishwasher, and who could deny that?

Buddy, at twenty-one, had already been lugubrious. At thirty-nine, he was downright morose, and self-pitying to boot. He loved repose and repetition and hated surprises and neglect. Once before, when Kate had volunteered to work for a political campaign, he'd pouted for weeks because she was never around the house when he needed her. In the end, he sent her a telegram that read *I am a vet of the Cold War, holed up in New Jersey, waiting for the end of hostilities. Please advise.*

After she'd persuaded him that an educated wife was no more a threat to family concord than a stupid one, there was the request for a catalogue, the choosing of a course where she would not be called upon to talk, sending in an application and a check, and finally the onerous task of finding someone to look after the kids two nights a week when they got home from school, then fixing their supper, and Buddy's too.

The last almost scotched the plan entirely, because

if there was one thing Princeton lacked, it was an impoverished class of people who could be depended upon to perform domestic duties. "But I found this marvelous widow," Kate McCabe boasted about the woman someone had put her onto. "Husband had a coronary, she says—someone else says cirrhosis—and didn't leave her with much, so she's 'helping out' people till she knows what to do with herself. You're almost ashamed to mention wages, but she's not. She says she can cook. God knows, anything more sophisticated than wieners and beans is wasted on the kids. But Buddy is another story. If he gets a bad feed, he's wrathful."

The arrangement, carefully worked out with Mrs. Ellman, was that on Mondays and Wednesdays Kate would go into the city on the 3:15 train and Mrs. Ellman would arrive no later than 2:30 for a quick briefing on the supper menu, fixings for which Kate would already have bought. But today, the first day, Mrs. Ellman was twenty minutes late, which threw everything off schedule, and when she finally arrived, it took all the self-control Kate could muster just to be civil.

She'd taken a nap so that she could be fresh for the children, the woman said by way of apology, and she'd overslept. What were the dears' names anyway?

What were their names? Kate couldn't *remember!* All she could think of was the 3:15 to New York, which she was going to miss unless she hurried.

"Suzie and Dutchie," she cried at last, grabbing her coat. "Suzie's absolutely benign. She'll sit in front of the television set from the minute she walks into the house till suppertime, and she'll eat everything on her plate, including the flowers that Wedgwood put there." When her daughter's personality began to make itself apparent—or failed to—Kate was at first alarmed. The little girl was somnambulant most of the time, either because she was stupefied by television or because it was the way she was put together. Nothing like her had ever existed in Kate's family in Ohio, and neither had she seen hints of it in Buddy's, though she was the first to admit that it was far more acceptable, even desirable, to be eccentric in New Jersey than it was in the Middle West.

As for Dutchie, she said to Mrs. Ellman, "Feel 'im the minute he walks into the house to see if he's wet his pants again." If he were four years old, Kate wouldn't have been so upset, but Dutchie was going on eight. For a reason which no one could divine, he refused to use the restroom at school, where he was in the third grade. Instead, his bladder grew all morning long, breakfast cocoa seeping into it; then ballooned gigantically in the afternoons on milk and soup from the school cafeteria; and was near the bursting point by four o'clock when the bus stopped at the end of the street and he dashed like a rabid dog to reach the house and the first floor lavatory before his eyes popped out of his head. If he didn't make it—Kate herself thought that running was what unplugged him—he'd creep in, sopping wet, through the back door, slink into the utility room and there strip out of his corduroy pants and underwear, toss them into the dryer, and sit bare-bottomed on a stool in front of the circular window, watching them spin-dry, tears streaming down his face.

Why *wouldn't* he use the restroom in school? Mrs. Ellman wanted to know.

Who could say? Possibly because someone had made fun of him. "But we hope he'll grow out of it," Kate said optimistically, as she reached for the door, knowing that he damned well better, no bones about it, because Buddy wanted him to go to Dartmouth, and Dartmouth didn't accept incontinents, did it?

Mrs. Ellman began to give her views on child rearing, but Kate said she really must hurry. Otherwise, she'd be late for her first class at the New School.

Late for her meeting with Neela Fitzgerald at Bloomingdale's, which was infinitely more important, because if she didn't get the key to Neela's apartment, she wouldn't have a place to sleep that night.

Surprisingly, it was Buddy who had suggested that she stay overnight in New York after her twice-weekly classes, rather than trying to outrun the muggers to catch the last train, or chance waiting for a bus at the Port Authority bus terminal, which attracted the most exotically degenerate crowd of people in New York City, perhaps in the Western World. Kate had jumped at the opportunity. She knew scads of people in New York, she said, whom she hadn't seen in years. She would simply get on the telephone and say, "Look, this is Kate McCabe. Katherine *Ferguson?* Could you by any chance put me up on a sofa or someplace overnight, do you think? Maybe Monday or Wednesday next week?"

In the end, half of the scads of people she used to know weren't even listed in the telephone directory anymore, either because they'd left the city, had killed themselves, had been committed, or were now celebrities and had private numbers. Of the few she finally located, she dialed one, but at the second ring hung up, having decided that she probably no longer had anything in common with old friends. Of the hundreds of people one met in New York, only a few wore well enough to be tolerable fifteen years after meeting them —fifteen days after meeting them, fifteen *minutes!*—so instead she called two girls she'd grown up with in Ohio who'd come to New York about the same time she had in the Fifties. At least they had geography in common.

She'd got through to Neela Waggaman Fitzgerald before she'd been able to reach Julie Silverman, and Neela said that she'd be delighted, which was more or less what she'd been saying as long as Kate had known her. At thirty-nine, she still had the animation of a high

7

school cheerleader, which she'd been and would be everlastingly. She couldn't answer a simple question without playing it for Uta Hagen, whose acting classes she'd attended when Kate, Neela, and Julie had shared a fifth-floor walk-up on West 13th Street in the Village, the apartment having been chosen by Neela, who even then had a fondness for high places. Julie Silverman, who at that time was tremendously overweight and worried about it—still was overweight, but had given up worrying—would sometimes get as far as the third floor, then sit down on the stairs and burst into tears.

"Kate, that is too goddamn marvelous for words!" Neela had said when Kate told her she was taking a course at the New School and needed a place to stay overnight—say Monday?—for the term. "We've got heaps of room. The children aren't living with us, thank God. They're all downstairs with nanny."

A duplex? Kate wondered.

"Nothing doing. We took a separate apartment for them on the floor below. Quentin subscribes to the old-fashioned notion that children should be brought out with the cigars and the brandy after the meal, shown off for three minutes, then put away again. Nanny is perfection itself. She's breaking them. You know, like on dude ranches in Wyoming where the cowboys ride mean, black-hearted horses till one or the other is thrown? That's what she's doing. Quentin says he won't live with them till they've been trained to eat sugar out of his hand."

How *was* Quentin?

Her husband was on the Coast, Neela explained, as if being somewhere was sufficient answer to how someone was. Quentin Fitzgerald had started out as a novelist, but had switched to script writing because it was easier and better paid. "What he is," Neela had confessed a year or so ago during a long, rather drunken lunch with Kate in a midtown restaurant, "is bad, but to the bathroom. Once there, she drew a tub, then while waiting for it to fill, stood leaning against the wash basin.

It was late, but how late Neela wasn't sure. Possibly still shy of midnight, though she felt so used up it seemed much later than that. One thing she definitely was not up to was being charming to Quentin's friends. Inevitably, they would be an exotic collection of people who made their living off art of one type or another, or—more likely—they lived off people who made their living that way. Meeting one of the latter was to meet them all. She'd even developed a nose for spotting them. She could walk up to a sweet-talking fellow, dressed in Hollywood Modern, and say, "Don't tell me. You must work for MCA" and eight times out of ten, he'd reply, "How'd the hell you know?"

Neela had always been tempted to reply, "I expect because you seem so horrid," but had never had the nerve.

Quentin had once tried to explain to her that the difference between success and failure in movie-making was merchandising the product. If you wrote scripts and were opposed to New York parties and TV talk shows, you were guaranteed oblivion. "Okay, so I suck up to people even though I hate their guts. If it means I get three hundred thou for the next script instead of two hundred, to hell with my personal feelings. You can't put personal feelings in the bank, Neela."

So Quent had, at one time or another, befriended just about everyone who could be of help to his career. Whenever he was in the city, he'd lunch with a well-known drama critic he hated. "Who knows?" he'd say. "I may go back to Broadway someday, and if that old fruitcake is still reviewing, it could pay off. You see what I mean, Neela?"

If Neela would object to the terminology—whether or not the critic was a *bona fide* fruitcake wasn't the issue; the issue was that Quent was a congenital brown-nose—Quent would complain that she didn't understand the first fucking thing about it.

Despite his own sexual bent, or possibly because of it, Quentin rarely had anything nice to say about New York or Hollywood faggots. In fact, on occasion, he went out of his way to ridicule them. Once, Neela swore she heard him say to a group of very straight friends, "The main reason I got outta Broadway, see, and went into flicks was that there were just too goddamn many queers in the theater."

Neela had listened in astonishment. Afterwards, when they were alone, she said, "If you hate them, why do you sleep with them?"

"Hey, wait a goddamn minute, willya?" he'd protested.

"And even if you didn't, you've stood on their shoulders to get where you are. Don't you have any sense of gratitude, Quentin?"

"Look," he replied, incensed, "everything I've done, I've done myself."

"And how, pal. Does that include fornication?"

"What the hell do you mean by that?"

"You sleep with someone, Quentin, but you always have sex with yourself."

Neela had always hated it when Quent crawled into bed with her. With him always came his monumental ego, and often it seemed to her that the only coupling that took place was between two facets of Quentin's personality. When he made love to a woman, it was his own soft, rather feminine side he copulated with (though he would never admit that he had such a side), and when he made love to a man, it was his own unparalleled virility that gave him a hard-on. The partner—whether Neela, Jill Montgomery, or Amos Guard—was secondary. What he really needed was a mirror.

Neela plunged into the hot tub and wondered how far Quent intended to go with Amos Guard. Obviously, he's *expensive* bad. He talks people into giving him $200,000 for a script, and the only one in town who'll like the movie is Rex Reed, and he likes anything that Pauline Kael despises."

Neela was sorry as hell, but she wouldn't be in town on Monday night, because she had to fly up to Boston to talk to someone about a revival—"Edward Albee, I think"—but Kate could use the apartment anyway, because no one else would be around. "Except the kids," she said, "and they'll be downstairs. If they make too much noise, call up Emily—that's the nanny—and ask her to turn the fire hose on them." Then: "How will I get the keys to you?"

Kate replied that she planned to take the subway to Bloomingdale's because her New School class didn't begin until eight, and Bloomingdale's was open late on Monday. Actually, all she wanted to do was walk through the store, hoping that its sumptuousness would rub off on her, its *chic*, and beauty.

"So I'll meet you there!" Neela exclaimed. "I never have anything to do in the afternoons, and I don't leave for Boston till night. Bloomingdale's is one of my favorite places. I don't know why the hell they don't keep it open on Sundays and put deck chairs in the aisles, the way they used to on the *Liberté*."

Neela, whose second, third, or even possibly fourth telephone suddenly began to ring, said she had to run, but that she'd meet Kate at Bloomingdale's at five on Monday. The Place Elegante. Did she know where that was?

Of course Kate didn't, but she would find it. She didn't know where anything was. She'd lived in the country for almost fifteen years.

Now, on Monday, clutching her scholar's notebook, Kate stepped up to the train at Princeton Junction, amazed at what she was doing: the brazenness of it.

Thirty-nine years old, almost in her dotage, and going back to school!

Yet what had Julie Silverman said when Kate finally got through to her in her West Side—where else?—apartment? "That is so fucking like you, Ferguson. You're getting tired of being a wife already, aren't you?"

For the hundredth time, Kate was horrified at Julie's rudeness, at her perspicacity, her nose—nicely carpentered, original, and never bobbed—for truth, and her insistence that everyone else in the world be as unhappy as she was. In the end, she volunteered the use of the apartment on Wednesdays, but told Kate that the comforts were minimal. "You'll hate it," she said.

Kate could imagine how Julie lived. There would be books scattered everywhere, the refrigerator would be empty except for a container of chicken livers, and three or four smelly cats would be perched on top of her sofa-bed, ready to leap on anyone who came near.

Afterwards, Kate said to herself, Why *am* I going into a city I don't like to sit through tedious lectures on Great Issues of Our Times when the only issue of our time I'm concerned about is myself?

Why?

Because she was tired of being Buddy McCabe's wife and didn't know how else to tell him.

That was why.

"It's an Age of Schlock," Buddy said morosely by way of explaining his lack of enthusiasm for the present day. "It's an Age of Trivia," he added, to account for his children's adoration of unworthy heroes, Rock stars, Pop stars, and other nonentities, in preference to his own company.

Saving the worst till last, he concluded, "It's an Age of Cunt," by which he meant a certain restlessness and aggressiveness he'd observed in women in general, and now in his wife.

"Oh, Christ," Kate had replied, "I resent that. Just

he was attracted to his good looks, his youth, and his talent, if any. As for Amos, he was nineteen and just beginning a career, so he would be complaisant and accommodating. He would drop a piece of ass in the right place, as Quent himself would say. But just how long, Neela wondered, would someone like Amos put up with Quentin's inability to focus himself. Neela had been patient, but would Amos be?

Sexually, Neela took Amos Guard for what Quent himself would call, "Gay all the way. *Viscerally* gay." There was a sweetness and gentleness about him, despite the cowboy lingo and the superficial toughness.

All Neela knew with any certainty was that Quentin had never before invited a friend of his—"friend" being a euphemism for sackmate—to live in the apartment with Neela. Her next-to-last analyst had explained once that bisexuals were very probably homosexuals in drag, and that sometimes as they approached menopause, male or female, they grew tired of the deception and broke loose. Even if Quentin were to announce to her, after all these years, that he was going to live with Amos from now on, Neela knew that he wouldn't do it flamboyantly. His ego would have to be protected at all costs. At most, he might say, "I'm living with a queer, but of course that doesn't make me one."

Finished in the tub, she stood up, then turned on the shower spray to rinse herself. Done with that, she pulled back the shower curtain and was just about to reach for a towel.

Amos Guard was standing there, holding a terry-cloth towel in his hands. Wordlessly, he began to dry her. He went about his work as if he were wiping an expensive object he'd just acquired at Parke-Bernet. It was such a curious, such a *baffling* experience that Neela didn't resist.

"That's very kind of you, Mr. Guard," she said when he'd concluded. "But don't you think that cour-

143

tesy requires that you knock before you open closed doors?"

"Ordinarily, I would," he said, then rested his head on her bare breast, "but not on my birthday."

Neela couldn't see that she had any other option, so she said, "Happy Birthday, Mr. Guard."

All Neela Waggaman Fitzgerald needed in order to look like a million bucks, Quentin once boasted, was to slip into a little three-hundred-dollar dress from Bloomingdale's, tight and sheer enough to show off her bare nipples quivering beneath it.

Which they now did as she sidled into the living room and quickly scanned it for faces she might recognize.

"Most of my friends are celebrities," Quentin often described the people he liked to take his leisure with. What they were celebrated for was sometimes a matter of conjecture. Their creative output generally depended on the absence of mental blocks; the presence of expensive therapy; the success of their married life and their love life, it being admitted that the two were rarely the same; on the demands of the marketplace; and on just plain *chutzpah,* of which they possessed perhaps more than God ever intended anyone to have, even New Yorkers who needed it more than most.

Despite his claim, Quentin's friends were little more than second- and third-echelon celebrities, either on their way up from or sliding back to the bottom. Quent did not know Burt Bacharach, but he knew John Raynor—Neela waved at *him* as she made her way through the room—who wrote tunes for Broadway musicals, the sort no one could ever remember long enough to hum. Quentin didn't know Jay Cocks, the serpent-tongued *Time* magazine movie critic, but he knew Maggie Sawyer, who freelanced for the heavier magazines, writing about movies as if she alone held the key to understanding them, and whose *explications de texte* sometimes went on for five pages. Neela hated her, but Quent had instructed her always to be cordial, it being his contention that friendship often made a lousy book or a lousy movie, even perhaps one written by him, really quite tolerable. Quentin had never met Tennessee Williams, but he did know Jack Roycroft—Neela smiled at him now, hoping that he wouldn't take it as an invitation to pounce on her and begin one of his endless monologues—who had written one very good play five or six years ago, and had done nothing since but go to parties; he had a reputation as a gorgeous conversationalist, but, as Quent said, a little bit of gorgeous went a long way. He didn't know Norman Mailer, Mia Farrow, or Sam Peckinpah, but he knew Wilbur Gerrity, *who* knew Norman Mailer and had himself written a New York novel about Irish-Americans, except (as Quent complained) it was Jewish, not Irish, in tone, because the humor was un-Celtic and black; he knew Bunny Remsen, who had made a modest reputation for herself in low-budget films, then became the mistress of a Mafia hood until he got his head shot off, upon which she wrote a piece for *New York* magazine on gangsters and how beautiful and kind they were when they weren't killing people; and he knew Stevie Bruce, who was twenty-six and on his way to his second million, having made three flicks which, as Quent said, you couldn't enjoy unless you were copulating with someone at a drive-in theater while watching them.

Instead of heading toward any of them, Neela made her way directly to her husband, who was standing by the huge front window next to Amos. Amos saw her approaching but Quent didn't, so that by the time she reached them, Quent looked up, his face flushed with surprise, even embarrassment.

Amos (my God, what *did* a man think who had just dried one's pubic hairs?) studied Neela in an academic sort of way, as if to determine if clothes were an improvement or a liability. He nudged Quentin to warn him ("I don't give a shit anymore, Amos, what people think. It's how I feel," Neela imagined his having said seconds before), then broke into hearty laughter.

"Here she is," Amos said brightly, "the only reason I'm staying at your fucking party, Quentin."

"It's Amos's birthday," Quent explained, "and I guess everyone is entitled to a little depression on one's birthday."

"I'm almost afraid to ask, but how old?"

"Exactly one year ago tonight, Amos Guard was conceived in the fertile mind of Irving Diament," Amos said, "about the only thing that ever has been. Until then I was Dennis Burr, as in Aaron. Irv said it wouldn't play."

Irving, who managed talent and also produced, had met Amos shortly after he came down to L.A. from Palo Alto and had immediately taken a liking to him. He'd sent him to acting school and got him bit parts in bad movies.

"The more I see you, the more you look like James Dean," Neela said.

"That's what Irving says, too. He got someone to put it on tape and he plays it at my bedside while I sleep. I'm almost beginning to believe it."

"Come off it," Quentin interrupted. "Irv is on your side. He's doing what he thinks is best for you. He's one of the few guys in L.A. who doesn't have his head up his ass."

"That's because he generally has it up someone else's."

The more she listened to Amos, the more Neela liked him, in a perverse sort of way. He was the least fawning actor she'd ever met. Most of them, particularly early in their careers, limited themselves to keeping their mouths shut and their flies open. But Neela had the distinct impression that Amos was quite prepared to tell everyone to go to hell.

"Look," Quentin said to her, "Amos is a bad drinker. He's probably the worst drinker in the world. Don't pay any attention to him."

Neela said that Amos couldn't be the worst drinker in the world, because her mother back in Ohio was.

"She couldn't have anything on my old lady," Amos said. "She was drunk most of the time I was growing up. And when she wasn't, she had a boyfriend in her bedroom. I got to sleep on the couch in the living room and listen."

Neela reminded him that he'd said his father was employed at a nuclear installation in Idaho.

"He is. Where he isn't employed is in my old lady's bedroom. He lives in one part of the state and she lives in the other. He just took off one day."

Like Neela's own father, except that in Charles Waggaman's case it wasn't desertion but extinction. More than ever, Neela felt a closeness, a tenderness for the young man in front of her.

She wasn't sure of it, but it seemed to her that Quentin was aware of it. "Neela, darling," he said with impatience, "you've been missing all evening and now that you show up, you're not circulating. How about mingling a little bit?"

"Why, of course I'll mingle, Quentin, darling," she answered, her "darling" even icier than his.

The battle had been joined, she was sure of that. Quentin had just told her "hands off," and she wasn't certain that she was going to obey.

Neela was exceedingly cordial to five or six people, all the while waiting for Irv Diament to free himself from Bunny Remsen, so that she could talk to him. A good many of those present were talking about movies, either just released or soon to be released, and about talent, and about deals. Properties were being discussed, ideas and trends, and most of all, money. From time to time, Quent's name was mentioned, and even *Wiser, Wiser,* which just about everybody had read. It would be absolutely fantastic for Amos Guard—"I *see* him as John Wiser," someone said—if only they could keep Amos sober enough to finish it.

When Irving pulled free of Bunny Remsen, Neela bore down on him, and after the pleasantries came right to the point. "So what is it between Quentin and your new discovery, Irving, or isn't a wife entitled to know?"

"You notice something, too?" Then, when she didn't reply, he continued. "It's both business and infatuation. A little of this, a little of that. Amos will make rich men of us all."

"Quentin already is."

"So what's wrong with more?" He took Neela by the hand and led her into a corner. "Let me tell you something. Quentin Fitzgerald is one of my oldest, dearest friends. I would not knock him for the world."

Quite correctly, Neela took it to mean that he would now do just that.

"Quentin needs a big one this time. Two years ago, I persuaded my good friends at Paramount to put up money for one of Quentin's scripts I thought was going to be a winner. It did not make money, Neela. Critically, it was a disaster. Popularly, it was a disaster. What else is there? I ask. This time the studio is less inclined to take a chance. They see—and I think they're right—that Amos will bring this one in. They're willing to put up the cash if Amos likes the role."

Neela was astounded. "There's doubt?"

"There is doubt."

"It isn't any good?"

"Neela, it is very good shit, but it is shit. Let me put it that way."

Stunned, she didn't know what to say. "But Quent says he loves it. It's all he ever talks about."

"You should know your husband by now. He could write verses for the American Greeting Card Company, and that would be all he'd ever talk about. Quent has a blind spot when it comes to judging his own talent. He looks and all he can see is excellence."

Instinctively, she wanted to defend Quentin, yet then she remembered that he'd deceived her for the past six months, ever since he told her that Irving was wild about the script. Irving's enthusiasm, however, was something less than rabid. In fact, he was telling her now that *Wiser, Wiser* probably wouldn't be produced unless Amos Guard would star in it.

So poor Quentin was doing now what he'd done all his life: he was turning on all his charm, and there was plenty, for Amos's benefit. Amos was probably as ripe for someone to replace his errant father as Neela had been when Quentin offered to replace her dead one.

As much as she hated Quentin for selling himself that way, Neela also saw it as an act of survival.

"Amos is a good kid," Irving said by way of conclusion. "He doesn't like the role, but he will."

She looked across the room at the disheveled blond head that had rested on her bare breasts only a few minutes before, and she wondered if its innocent owner was capable of breaking up her marriage.

What would happen now? If Quentin's deal went through, it would no doubt mean that he'd be on the Coast for the next six months to pilot the script through its final revision—mutilation, he would call it—during which time he would nurse-maid Amos. Neela would be urged to remain in New York with the kids. For Quent, it would be a work assignment or a separation, depending on how you looked at it. For Neela, it could be nothing but abandonment.

At the moment, possibly because she was exhausted, Neela couldn't even begin to consider a course of action to follow. It all depended on Amos, really.

After everyone had left, the three of them sat in the smoky living room, unshod feet up on the coffee table, and did post-mortems on the people who had attended. Amos said that he'd been propositioned by three of them, for sure, and one more, perhaps, but he didn't go into genders. Neela said that someone had thrown up in the guest bathroom and urged neither of them to use it, adding, "It was probably Maggie Sawyer. It's just the odious sort of thing she enjoys doing."

Finally, Quentin said that Irv had told him that the next few days would be crucial. His friends on the Coast were very definitely interested in the script, but some details still had to be worked out. Tomorrow, in fact, Quent would be tied up most of the day with Irving and a man from Paramount. Maybe Neela would like to show Amos the city.

"If he's insured," she said.

Before they made their ways to their separate bedrooms, Quentin said, "Well, we're almost home, baby," and Neela, for the life of her, didn't know if he was talking to her or to Amos.

Neela had a hell of a time getting to sleep. Demons, snatches of dreams, and old griefs came marching before her eyes. She heard Amos use the bathroom, then return to his bedroom. In another five minutes, she heard Quentin make his way down the hall to the bathroom, but then instead of going back to his room, he went to Amos's.

Neela didn't know why she should be so upset. After all, she'd known all about her husband's predilections before she married him—had, in fact, married him at least partly because of them—and it was rather late in the game to be revolted by them now.

Somehow or other, she fell asleep, a deep, bottomless, Seconal-induced sleep. Hours later—two o'clock, three o'clock?—she was vaguely aware that someone was lying in bed with her, as naked as she was, sleeping against her shoulder, and even before she touched him, she knew it was Amos.

———◆———

"Look, you little shit," Julie Silverman said to the clerk at Avis Rent-a-car, who had just told her that he wasn't permitted to let her hire a car unless she had a credit card. "*Listen!* I pay cash for everything, see? I don't believe in credit. I have more money in the bank than you'll make in ten years unless you're stealing from the till, you lousy little . . ." She was so angry that the appropriate denigration momentarily escaped her.

He was sorry, but unless she had a credit card he wouldn't be able to let her rent a car.

"Just for the weekend? Just to get to Amagansett? Can I have it if I give you a $3000 *deposit?*" She closed her eyes so that she wouldn't have to watch him shake his head negatively. "I mean, *really!* Am I the only sane person in this goddamn city?"

It was not meant to be rhetorical. Instead of answering positively, however, the clerk obstinately repeated what he'd already said.

The rudest people in the world, Julie concluded as she sailed out of the office onto Broadway, were those just recently emancipated from ignorance. Find a benighted man, teach him how to write his name, put him behind a desk or a counter, and what you have is a tyrant.

The city was coming apart at the scams. Everyone intimidated everyone else. Julie was even afraid to use her branch of the Chase Manhattan Bank anymore because the minute she walked in someone inevitably yelled at her, "Lady, you want the Food Stamp line, you're in the wrong one." Or she would wait in line for ten minutes to reach a teller, and the minute she got there, he would blow cigarette smoke in her face, then

shove a sign that said *Next Window Please* into her
tits. It could give her cancer!

What to do now? She needed a car and Avis was not
even trying. She stood on the streetcorner and tried to
think of other ways of getting to Long Island.

How had she even got that far?

Just the day before, while she was in her office trying to think of a pitch to make to Pete Vassall in order
to get herself invited out to Amagansett, the telephone
rang and it was Lois Raum.

"Look, Julie," Raum said—she preferred to be called
by her last name—"did you get the book I sent you or
didn't you?"

Julie immediately knew what was coming. Before
her own last book was published, she'd sent galleys to
all her friends, including Raum, and had then solicited
comments which could be used in the advertising. Almost everyone responded, at least partly because Julie
had always obliged them with encomiums about their
books when they came out. The system was wide-
spread and even spilled over into reviewing. Once Julie
had written a review in the Sunday *Times* of a detec-
tive novel written by a fellow named Jake MacArthur,
whom she'd met at a party and taken a liking to, and
Jake, in return, had reviewed her second book for the
same rag.

As Julie said, you really did have to stick together,
as the only people who read one's books anymore were
one's friends.

So when Raum asked if Julie would be a dear and
commit to paper the Silverman reaction to her latest one,
then send the comments to a P.R. man at her publish-
ing house, Julie knew at once how she would be able
to get an invitation to Amagansett for the weekend.

Ten minutes later, she had Pete Vassall on the line
and was saying to him, "Pete, I wanted you to know
that I've just finished your new book, and I think it's
absolutely marvelous."

As soon as he replied, "Well, don't keep it to yourself, honey," she knew she was halfway to Amagansett.

He would need all the help he could get on this one, he said. "The guys at the *Times* gave it to Joyce Carol Oates, and you know how I clobbered that third book of hers. She wrote a letter to the editor that was longer than my review."

Some people were very bad losers, Julie said.

She would get her head together and send her comments over to his P.R. people by Monday. "I'll try to do it this weekend. I have to get out to Westhampton on Sunday, but otherwise I'm at loose ends."

"But that's marvelous! Why don't you spend Saturday night with us in Amagansett? We're having some people in—sort of a party—and we've got plenty of room. *Do,* Julie. Didi would be pleased as hell."

Didi Kravitz was Pete's live-in mistress. She had worked on the magazine with Julie and gone down to Vassall's apartment in the Village for an interview about four years ago. She moved in with him the next day and they'd been together ever since.

Well, Julie hated to impose—"You're sure I won't be a nuisance?"—but in view of the fact that she had to be in the area the following day, it would be foolish to turn him down.

"So okay," she said, "I'll fill a hamper with stuff from Zabar's and Bloomingdale's. Anything you and Didi would particularly like?"

Well, he confessed a fondness for caviar, but she was to make certain to *ask* at Zabar's if it was fresh. And not the red, please, which was fit only for cats. Beluga would be fine.

The cocksucker! Julie said to herself after she'd hung up. Caviar!

She tried to telephone David Harpur twice to warn him that she might run into him on Saturday, but each time, as soon as Julie gave her name, David's secretary replied in her Sunnyside, Queens, sing-song voice that

Mr. Harpur was out of the office at the minute and would-you-care-to-leave-a-message? On both occasions, she'd said, "Tell 'im Silverman called. And would you ask him to get in touch?"

Of course, he never did, which almost certainly meant that Lily Harpur, that Wasp bitch with the tiny little nose and the apologetic little ass, had given David an ultimatum.

Yet what did David hope to accomplish by not telephoning and failing to explain what was going on, unless he wanted Julie to know that he was pissed off at her for calling him the other night at the office while Lily was there? And now no doubt doubly pissed off because instead of retreating into penitential silence, Julie had called twice more.

Well, Julie had been around long enough to consider herself an authority on men, and one thing she knew with certainty was that all men, including David Harpur, were governed as much by lassitude as by passion and intellect. Lily had apparently made a fuss, had told him to make a choice, and he'd settled for the status quo.

Quite possibly if Julie hadn't already been a casualty of nine other separations within the last fifteen years—once at a party someone had asked if she were married or divorced, and she'd replied, "Neither. Just frequently separated"—and if she weren't now hell bent on forty, she might have accepted David's silent treatment, hoping perhaps that things would blow over in time.

But she had already been a victim of nine profound relationships—at least she had found them profound—which had all ended with more or less the same kind of telephone call: "Look, Jewel, I think we'd better call it quits, okay? I don't want to spoil your life. No hard feelings?"

Spoil my *life*? she'd wanted to say. I thought I was *happy*.

There may have been no hard feelings on the part of the married men who had deserted her to go dutifully back to their wives or to look for younger girlfriends who screwed better, but there were *always* hard feelings on Julie's part.

Hard feelings were what enabled Julie Silverman to hold onto life.

Several times she protested and told her lovers that she'd given them everything they'd wanted: devotion, companionship, total allegiance. Well, yes, they'd answer, but the wife has been around so long that to leave her now would be like putting the dog to sleep. Didn't she understand?

No, Julie did not. Would not. In the end, hating loneliness even more than being loved less than another woman, she would try to come up with a compromise. She would crawl. She would cajole. She would send letters to their offices. Telephone incessantly. She would wait on the corner as they passed on their way to the subway. And she would succeed only in getting them to hate her.

"Be generous with yourself, Julie," her last analyst had told her before he'd expelled her, "but don't be wanton."

It was just as well that Dr. Rappaport had given her up, as he would almost certainly advise her not to go to Amagansett. Just the year before, he and Julie had had a terrible scene over her behavior on the beach at Easthampton, where Julie had rented a house with three other girls from the magazine. The first weekend they'd gone out, the three girls had spent all day Saturday in the sand getting suntans, while Julie had sat by herself on the back porch, glaring morosely at their glistening bodies, almost screaming every time an alarm clock signaled them to turn over. She took it until four in the afternoon, then gathered up her belongings, said good-bye to no one, walked all the way to the station in ninety-degree heat, and returned to a sweltering city.

"Why did you do that?" Dr. Rappaport had asked.

She did it because her friends were all so shallow. Getting a *sun*tan was shallow.

"Look at it this way," he'd said. "Why did they want the tan? To look pretty, don't you think? Isn't that really very commendable?"

"It's sickening."

"There!" he exclaimed. "You speak the truth at last. They were trying to look pretty, and you were sickened. Why?"

At times Julie hated Dr. Rappaport more than anyone else she knew. "I don't know why I come here if you never say anything nice about me," she complained.

"You're changing the subject. We're studying your motives. Why did you leave, Julie, and forfeit a thousand dollars' rent you'd already paid?"

Almost in tears, she had at last replied, "Because no one paid any attention to me. No one talked to me all day. They were all down at the beach."

"And you couldn't have joined them?"

"No amount of suntanning will make me prettier. With a suntan, I look like a rug salesman from Beirut."

"And does that make the girls on the beach shallow?"

"No. It makes me selfish and foolish. Is that what you want me to say, you bastard?"

It was all so lacerating, analysis. She was almost relieved when he gave her her walking papers and banished her from Group. He would try to arrange for another man to take her in tow, he had said at the time.

What had she done? she demanded.

"You know what you've done, Julie. You've *hurt* Arthur."

Arthur had been in Group and was about to graduate, so Julie, who had a large apartment, volunteered to throw the party. She scarcely knew the fellow, though she'd listened to his outlandish fears and depressions for the last twelve months. She resented the fact that Dr. Rappaport felt that Arthur was provisionally stronger than she was and thus warranted graduation, and it may have been that which caused her to react the way she had when poor Arthur arrived at her apartment a half hour before anyone was due. Julie, who was still cleaning the bathroom, had gone to the door, still with the toilet brush in her hand, and as Arthur stood there, she yelled, "Can't you ever do anything right, you scumbag! I'm cleaning my *bath*room, Arthur. And then I have to clean myself. Aren't you old enough yet to know that you *never* arrive early for a party? Now go away and don't come back till seven."

The result of which was that Arthur, for whom the party was given, was so upset that he didn't attend at all. The next morning, Dr. Rappaport found him sitting in a closet in his apartment on East 68th Street.

And shortly afterwards told Julie that she was too abrasive for Group and had better try something else.

"You could be a sweet girl, Julie," he said during his valediction.

She could be a sweet girl. All the way home, Julie repeated it as if it were a prayer. She'd spent a fortune on the man and the best he could say about her was that she had the potential for being a sweet girl, but wasn't one yet.

When she got home to her apartment on the West Side, Julie was in tears. She picked up the telephone, dialed Dr. Rappaport's office, and when he answered, she said, "Sweet girl, my ass," then hung up.

Julie held her foot against the door of the telephone kiosk at Broadway and 70th until a sinister-looking fellow had passed, then called Neela Fitzgerald.

"Neela," she said, "where the hell were you on Wednesday? Kate and I were worried sick."

A little exaggeration was necessary, Julie felt, because people like Neela needed constant reminders that they were loved. For her part, Julie hadn't been all that disappointed when Neela didn't join them at the Oak Room, as she had a tendency to monopolize the conversation.

Neela replied that she'd meant to meet them for a drink but had got tied up. Whenever Quentin was in town it was impossible to make plans. How was poor Kate, anyway?

"Well, you know Kate. She never changes. When she's seventy-five she'll still be the same way she was when she was seventeen."

"She seemed . . . well, overwhelmed when I saw her Monday at Bloomingdale's."

"Kate has been overwhelmed since birth." Julie could not understand why people like Kate won everyone's sympathy, yet she got none. It seemed to her that she suffered a hell of a lot more. "Look," she said, not wanting to talk about Kate McCabe, "did you know that it's against the law to pay cash for anything anymore?"

Julie gave a word-by-word reprise of her conversation with the Avis man, even including a fair reproduction of his accent. She was a splendid mimic and raconteur. Like most people who were fattish and the butts of many jokes when they were growing up, Julie loved to tell stories in which she appeared to advantage and her adversaries appeared mindless and humorless. In the end, she had Neela howling.

"But that's not why I'm calling—just to tell you how much I hate Avis. I'm calling to bum your credit card. Isn't there a Hertz place near you on the East Side? Avis probably has me on a blacklist by now."

There was, in fact, a Hertz garage on 76th Street. Neela had once rented a car from them to go to the country, because she was afraid to drive Quentin's Rolls convertible through the Lincoln Tunnel. "I'm always terrified that I'm going to hit the walls and the river will come in. Aren't you, Julie?"

"I've never noticed the walls," Julie replied, at once establishing the difference between their characters, as if either needed reminding.

Suddenly Neela became very organized. She would call the Hertz people immediately and reserve a car. What time would Julie like to meet her there? It was eleven o'clock now. Would one o'clock be too late? If Julie needed it sooner than that, Neela would simply tell Quentin's actor friend that he could have lunch by himself. "Breakfast I mean, as he's not up yet."

"No, no, one o'clock is fine."

"It's no trouble, Julie." Something else must have occurred to her. "If you like, I could even pick it up and take it over to where you live. Would that help any?"

"Oh, *Neela!*"

Julie was on the verge of tears. Perhaps because everyone else had been rude and unkind to her—the whole world was rude and unkind to her—she saw the offer as an act of kindness from which Neela couldn't possibly expect anything in return. Neela was about to make a special trip to the Hertz garage—had even offered to drive the car over to the West Side, a foreign country to her—yet, Julie asked herself, when, *when* was the last time I've ever done anything for Neela or even had anything nice to say about her?

A telephone booth at the corner of Broadway and 70th Street is no fit place for a revelation, for a shock of recognition, yet something not unlike both swept over Julie now. It was all she could do to say that she would meet her old friend at one o'clock before the tears came in earnest.

If anyone passing Julie on that stretch of Broadway—a street where passers-by are inured to human suffering; a street where most passers-by are themselves sufferers—looked in and saw her, they wouldn't have known what to make of her. It wasn't sorrow, exactly, on her face. More like understanding.

Oh, dear God, she said to herself. Please let me not be selfish and absurd. Please let me just this once think of someone other than myself. Let me think of David. Please.

If only God were half as wise and competent as Julie Silverman, somehow she felt that this time she might even have a chance.

Julie had packed her good weekender from Mark Cross—she had a second one, acquired through unraveling thousands of Plaid Stamps which had stuck together in a kitchen drawer, but it looked so shabby that she used it only when she went home to Ohio—and now stood with it at the corner of Central Park West and 70th Street trying to attract the attention of a cab.

In the end, not having been able to get one to stop, she rushed up to the entrance of the apartment house at 88 Central Park West where a doorman had been genteelly blowing a whistle for the last five minutes, and where a cab had just halted. The doorman said, "I'm sorry, ma'am, but this cab is taken," to which Julie replied, "Hey, aren't you the guy who exposed yourself to me in the bushes across the street a couple nights ago?" Either he was so intrigued by the notion, or so shocked, that Julie was already seated in the back seat before he could protest.

As soon as the driver moved into traffic, Julie positioned herself dead center on the seat, hands at either side gripping the upholstery, bracing herself for a collision. She had lived long enough in New York City so that anticipating violent death was second nature to her now. Even at her office in midtown, on the thirty-fifth floor of a glass-and-aluminum structure, she had mapped her escape to street level in the event an airplane crashed into it, setting it on fire, severing the elevator cables. For her own apartment, she had a

Hammacher-Schlemmer emergency rope ladder to be used in the event she woke up some night to find herself surrounded by flames, and had even once practiced using it, dangling it from her bedroom window down the rear of the building into the garden on the ground floor, where a cocktail party was in progress. She'd jumped the last three feet into a clump of azaleas, upon which someone handed her a cocktail and said that he'd never before in his life seen anything like it, and was her name by any chance Peter Pan?

Julie was so sure that *someone-out-there-was-going-to-get-her* that she couldn't even walk into a movie without committing all the exits to memory and choosing the route she would use if the building were suddenly to explode or if a madman rushed onto the stage with a tommy gun and shouted, "I keel you all." All, that is, except Julie Silverman, because by then Julie would already be crawling under the seats, making her way through the carnage, toward the exit no one else had noticed.

As the cab pulled up for a traffic signal on Fifth Avenue near the Museum, she relaxed somewhat, as she was on the East Side of town where people more often died of ennui than machine-gunning. She quickly glanced up and down the avenue, hoping to catch sight of Jackie Kennedy, but she saw nothing but the most ordinary-looking people walking the most extraordinary-looking dogs. One of the pleasantly serendipitous things about living in New York was that often, suddenly and without warning, Julie would come upon famous film stars or statesmen at the curbside, holding onto a leash while a dog squatted ecstatically, defecating on the pavement. Dogs tended to humanize even the rich and pompous. Once she was sure she had seen one of the Rockefeller brothers with a shitting poodle, and it gave her a kind of glow for the rest of the day.

"We're here," Julie said to the driver in the event he

couldn't read the enormous Hertz sign under which Neela Fitzgerald was standing. She reminded herself that she would have to tell Neela about the hazards of standing beneath objects that might suddenly become airborne.

"Neela, darling," she cried as she left the cab and made her way toward her old friend. "How can I ever repay you?" Instinctively, she took Neela by the arm and moved her several feet away from the sign.

Neela looked so chic and worldly, so oozing with money. She wore sunglasses, not really to protect her eyes, but for anonymity—as if people would otherwise ask for her autograph. The fact that she attracted even more attention with the shades than without them had no doubt occurred to Neela herself. People passing on the sidewalk slowed down for a better look—"Now where have I seen her before?"—obviously exhilarating her.

The irony of it was that they were far more likely to have remembered seeing Julie on the Johnny Carson Show, where she appeared after her second book came out, if only they took the trouble to *look* at her. But of course no one ever did. Julie could spend the rest of her life on talk shows and no one would ever stop her on the street.

"I'm dressed for the weekend," Julie said apologetically about her outfit, knowing full well that she dressed for the weekend seven days a week. "But you look absolutely ravishing, Neela. Absolutely. I love you, do you know that?" She took her old friend in her arms and hugged her.

Neela knew Julie well enough not to be too impressed by the declaration of affection. Julie could as easily have said—and often had—"I hate you, Neela, do you know that?" with similar lack of preparation.

Why, anyway, was she rushing off to Amagansett? Neela asked.

"I'm about to do the damnedest thing." She began

to tell Neela more about her personal life than she ever had before. Not that she expected much in the way of sympathy or understanding. Julie had once said about Neela that she *had* no interior life at all, so how could someone who lacked one comprehend anybody else's?

She told her all about David and Lily Harpur. "I've been hurt so many times," she said, "and I don't want to be hurt again. I just won't take it anymore. I'm going to have it out with Lily Harpur, one way or another. If David won't leave her, then I'm going to make certain that she leaves him."

Neela looked crestfallen. "But I always thought you were so happy. I mean, you have that fascinating job, and you meet all those fascinating people, and you never have to worry about children or what to have for supper. And now you tell me you're unhappy." Neela's eyes were wettish. "Julie, I'm shocked!"

"Well, I'm sorry I even mentioned it," Julie said in a huff.

"I didn't mean it that way, Julie honey. I don't know what I meant. It's just that you always seemed so full, and I've always been so empty. Do you know what I mean? I've had to live through other people, people like Quentin. But you don't have to. You're so strong."

Julie hated it when people told her she was strong. How could she prove otherwise without going into a seizure on the sidewalk? She was weak. She was also getting old.

What *did* happen to forty-year-old unmarried women in New York? Were they issued licenses like dogs and was there a place like Bide-a-wee Adoption Home for those who couldn't cope? Did they carry neat, collapsible umbrellas even on sunshiny days, and go to the movies by themselves late in the afternoon? If Julie was lonely now—she scarcely needed confirmation—how could she bear the more terrible loneliness later on?

"I've never had it easy like you," Julie said almost

with animosity. "All you ever had to do was wiggle your hind end and you had all the boyfriends you wanted. But I never had any at all. Do you want to know what I did the night of the Christmas Ball in our senior year of high school. *Do* you?"

Neela looked at her incredulously. Christmas Ball? What Christmas Ball? What the hell was she talking about?

"Do you know where I was? I was home in my bedroom, listening to the radio and eating potato chips. That's where I was," Julie shouted angrily.

"Julie!"

Loudly, Julie sucked in the mucus from her nasal cavities. "I know, I know, you're going to say I'm being tiresome and self-pitying, but, Neela, this is my last chance, don't you see? If I can't do it this time, I never will. I'll be listening to the radio and eating potato chips all by myself for the rest of my life."

Neela really didn't think she could bear it if Julie broke down on the street. She hated to see people sad, almost as much as she hated to go to funerals. Quickly, before Julie could continue, she maneuvered her through the door into the Hertz office, which was certainly no place for *recherche,* and up to the counter.

Christmas Ball? Neela couldn't fathom why it was so important to Julie, now that she remembered the damned thing. She'd gone with Quentin and had been bored silly. The football coach had asked her to dance and his breath was sour under the Sen-Sen. Quentin was in a black mood because his mother had told him that day that she wouldn't have the money to send him to Harvard and that Ohio State would have to do instead. Afterwards, in the front seat of his car, they had masturbated each other, shivering even though the heater was on.

All her life, no matter what kind of party or ball she'd gone to, it had inevitably ended the same way: someone was always pulling at her pants and then, before she knew what was happening, a hand was resting on the bare flesh between her legs, and someone was whispering to her, "Can I go all the way, baby, okay?"

And Julie was supposed to be smart. Hell, Julie didn't know anything. The worst loneliness of all was to wake up in bed with a man who didn't love you, only the mound of flesh between your legs.

And Silverman thought she was smart.

Pete Vassall had written two rational, realistic, and phenomenally unsuccessful novels in his youth, and while writing his third, as he explained to an interviewer (Didi Kravitz, in fact), he was overcome by a madness, a frenzy not unlike Picasso's when he'd rubbed out Gertrude Stein's face in the famous portrait and substituted an African mask, leaving the rest of the body—it could have done with some improvement, too—incongruously intact. He then began to rewrite his book, annihilating reason and reality as he went along, and in time, though few knew what to make of it, it became a best-seller and Vassall became everyone's darling. Readers and critics especially, he said, loved to be confounded. To explain and enlighten was nothing. To worry and perplex was everything.

Julie didn't really know if he was good or bad, sane or insane. All she knew with any certainty as she drove up the long graveled drive toward the imposing white clapboard beach house was that a man who made as much money as he did couldn't be entirely out of his head.

Pete was in the sauna, Didi explained at the front door, and as these were modern times, Julie was welcome to join him if she liked. If not, would she rather have a nap and a wash? People weren't expected till seven-thirty or so.

Julie opted for the nap. Driving always left her dry-mouthed with fatigue and terror. Every minute on the way out she'd expected to meet another car head-on.

"How lucky you are," she said to Didi Kravitz as she was given a quick tour of the house. Every time she saw a piece of furniture she liked—a handsome highboy or a grandfather's clock or a cherrywood corner cupboard—she exclaimed, "But how gorgeous!" and Didi replied, "That's not ours. That belongs to Babs. She hasn't picked any of her stuff up yet. The junk belongs to Pete and me. We both hate and detest nice things."

Pete Vassall traded in old girlfriends for new ones as they aged or declined. Babs was a former friend, and several had preceded her. He hated to live with a burned-out woman, he said.

Behind the house was a tiny guest cottage with a small living room, a bedroom, a kitchenette, and a bath. A playwright friend of Pete's might wind up on the sofa-bed in the living room, "if he's too drunk to drive home," Didi said. "But he won't bother you. He's gay when he's drunk."

"And when he's sober?"

"Morose and married."

Didi leaned against the doorframe while Julie unpacked the few things she'd brought with her. When Didi was still on the staff of the magazine, they often had lunch together at one of the French restaurants in the Fifties and sometimes Didi had confided in her. Even asked for advice about boys she'd been dating, though she hadn't been able to get interested in any until Pete Vassall came along. He was scarcely a boy. In his late forties, Julie would judge. Worse than that, Didi, who'd been twenty-six when she met him, was now over thirty, and no longer a girl.

"So how are things going?" Julie asked. "You and Pete, I mean."

Didi attempted a smile, but it fell short of its goal. "We live from day to day. About once a week, he tells me he's had it, then the next morning he's forgotten he's said it."

It was inevitable, Julie said, that there were signs of fatigue after four years. Moreover, Pete was considered a seer, an interpreter of the age, and as a result was lionized by young people at the college campuses where he lectured from time to time. And Pete was partial to young girls.

So what would Didi do if they split up? Julie asked.

"Not if we split up," she replied. "*When* we split up. It's just a matter of time. I guess I've known from the beginning that he'd get tired of me sooner or later. *When* it happens, I expect I'll go back to work."

Julie said that if she heard of any good editorial jobs, she'd give her a ring.

"The advantage of having a profession to fall back on," Didi said, "is that a woman isn't entirely helpless when she's abandoned. At least she can pay her analyst."

"And the disadvantage?"

"Sure," Didi said, conceding the point. "The disadvantage is that it makes it easier for a man to leave you."

Julie didn't know how much Didi knew about her own affairs, but she had a feeling that everyone at the magazine must have divined that something had once gone on between Julie and Ed Arnoldson, who was Julie's senior editor, and had been Didi's, too. Someone once said that there was so much intramural sleeping-together at the magazine because everyone worked such a ghastly schedule that it was impossible to meet anyone outside of work. Ed Arnoldson had been Married Lover Number Nine, the one Julie was recovering from when she'd met David Harpur.

Before that, Julie had had a year-long affair with Sam Gold, an associate editor, and married of course.

Both relationships had begun so effortlessly. First, a head would poke around the door to her office late at night and complain about the rotten working conditions and the inept top brass. Then, the next time, the man would come in, sit down, and chat more amiably about whatever onerous task they were doing. And then, a week or so later, there would be an impromptu invitation to have supper at a Chinese restaurant down the block, just for an hour, of course, as both were working against deadlines, but it would last for three, and before it was over they would be surprisingly intimate. (The Chinese Ploposition, it was called by one of the back-of-the-book editors who worked in a corridor called Valley of the Drolls.) The next time they worked late, they would share a cab home, and both of them would be so tensed up by whatever they'd been working on that she'd suggest a nightcap. Then up in her erratic elevator, open the door, get the Jack Daniel's and Cutty Sark out from under the sink, and finally—like a soldier going into combat—Julie would poke around the bottom drawer of her dresser for her diaphragm, which had been lying forlornly there since her last affair.

Yet no matter how perfect and mutually satisfying the affairs were, they always ended. Perhaps it was the price one had to pay for emancipation. If Julie hadn't been able to look after herself, it was quite possible that she would be someone's wife by now.

As if Didi were now thinking along the same lines, she said serenely, "Do you ever see Ed Arnoldson?"

Julie's face flushed. Then she *did* know. Breathlessly, she said that he was now working for a monthly travel magazine and still living with his wife.

"Oh, I know that," Didi said with surprising ease. "I just wondered if you might ever run into him. We never see each other anymore, at least since I've been living out here with Pete. But he always sends me something for my birthday."

Julie caught her breath. "You don't mean . . . ?" She stopped because it was almost too absurd to suggest. "You weren't lovers, were you?"

"Didn't you know? I thought everyone knew."

Julie was overcome.

How *could* Ed? Hadn't he told Julie that she was the most important thing ever to happen to him? Hadn't he said that of all the people he'd ever met, Julie was the only one who—using borrowed words—rang a bell inside him? Hadn't he said that he loved her more than anyone else on earth?

And now to learn that he'd had an affair with Didi Kravitz, too. *When?* Before? After? *Concurrently?*

Somehow, Julie wanted to hurt her, but didn't know how to go about it without humiliating herself. Moreover—if what Didi had just told her about Pete Vassall was true—if Pete was getting ready to leave her, perhaps that was punishment enough.

Julie pleaded a headache and said that she was going to take an aspirin and lie down for a few hours.

After Didi had left, Julie lay on the bed, a wet facecloth over her eyes, and in the darkness she tried to conjure what she would be like in another few years. Would she move from affair to affair, never expecting any kind of permanence other than a yearly birthday present? Would there be a time when hope ran out, and it no longer seemed worthwhile even to begin a new affair in order to help get over the last?

In grief and horror, she thought, My God! What if three years from now, or four or five, someone tells me that she is David Harpur's lover? Could I bear it?

Could I?

Until almost eight-thirty, Julie thought that David and Lily were going to be no-shows.

By then, the twin living rooms had filled with convivial people, or odious ones depending upon one's point of view, who had come to commend or ridicule Pete Vassall on the publication of his new book. They were Pete's friends, Didi's friends, and as at least one young man confessed to Julie, no one's friend. "I can't relate to people," he said to her even before he introduced himself, "but hello anyway."

She also talked with a balding ex-editor at *Newsweek* who arrived with his wife and a girl described as a friend (whose was unclear) who said to Julie, "Don't I know you from the Johnny Carson Show?" Julie was thrilled until she realized the girl hadn't seen her on the show, but appeared on it with her while both were promoting books.

When Pete Vassall came up to her, he said to Julie, "You're a good-looking girl. How come I never made a pass at you?"

They chatted a few minutes before the guests began to arrive, but Didi was with him, which tended to inhibit him. Now, after Didi left, he said to Julie, "Hey, how do I get rid of that mean, selfish, carnivorous . . ."

Julie interrupted. "I figured things weren't going so well between you and Didi."

"Why is it that all women have to be jealous? Okay, so I'd expect it from some ignorant slob, but not Didi. I can't even go out of the house anymore to buy cigarettes without finding her by the door when I get back. 'All right, so where were you this time?' Those are the first words she says."

Julie waited, measuring his discomfort, then said, "Pete, I knew your wife, the one you always used to say was nagging you all the time. Well, kiddo, it's a rule of thumb that men with nagging wives always seek out nagging girlfriends."

"Now I know why I didn't make a pass at you. You would have driven me crazy."

At that moment, Julie watched as David Harpur walked into the living room with a striking woman. As David's eyes met Julie's, there was a look of apprehension, disbelief, even annoyance on his face, then he quickly recovered.

"So," Pete Vassall said to her, having observed what had happened. "There is more to you than meets the eye, as they say." Then, "David is a dear friend 'of mine. We play tennis together sometimes."

He was obviously amused. "That is David's wife with him, in the event there's doubt in your mind. The dutiful and beautiful Lily Harpur."

"Any bad habits?"

"Who? David? Thousands."

"Lily."

"She doesn't do much of anything that I know of. She's faithful, of course. She might drink a bit more than she should, but don't we all?"

Julie knew, in fact, that she drank a considerable amount. On more than one occasion, David had come home to find her close to stupefaction.

Why was it that rich girls carried themselves so much better than poor ones? Had their families been wearing shoes for a couple more generations or had they been taught how to walk, even stand while they were at the Brearley School? Lily must have been devastatingly pretty when she was in her twenties, because now in her forties, she still was: high cheekbones, a faint tan, small lips (bloodless?), and hair the color of champagne.

"It's funny you haven't run into them before," Pete Vassall said teasingly.

"Yeah." God, how Julie hated Lily Harpur. She would give anything in the world if only she could walk over to her now, pick up a table lamp, and crash it over her aristocratic head.

"You're a liar, Julie." When she didn't answer, Pete continued. "You know why I'm such a hot-shot writer? I know hundreds of guys smarter than I am. But I never let smartness get in the way of my intuition. That's why I knew, the minute you looked at him," he smiled now, "You're the girl David Harpur's been sleeping with."

For one of the few times in her life, Julie decided it would be best to keep her mouth shut.

"I knew there was someone, and now I know who."

With more composure than she thought possible, Julie said, "Does that mean the Committee Supervising Sex Lives in Amagansett gives you a gold star?"

"Don't misunderstand," he said suddenly. "I wouldn't dream of mentioning it to anyone. There is, however"—the faintest pause—"something you might be able to do for me."

Julie looked up with guarded interest.

"You might call Didi sometime early next week and ask her to have lunch with you in the city. She almost never goes into town anymore, and it would be good for her to get away for the day. Say Wednesday?"

Of course. Didi could spend most of the day in Manhattan while Pete diddled his latest girlfriend in Didi's bed. At this time of the year, it would have to be a local product: a clerk in a drugstore, a waitress in a drive-in, or someone else's wife.

No wonder Didi was alarmed when it took him so long to get cigarettes.

"Sure," Julie heard herself saying. "I think I could accommodate you."

"You're a sweet girl, Julie."

That's what a sweet girl was? Hell, if that's all there was to it, it was a snap.

Lily Harpur explained that they were late getting out of the city because she'd been tied up at a Morris Udall fund-raising gathering late in the afternoon. "I told everyone just to bring lots of money," she said, "and we would pass the hat. God knows, Udall is the only one anymore with any charisma."

Julie detested people who used trendy words. *Nitty-gritty, clout, charisma.* She had listened to their rise and fall at cocktail parties.

Someone who looked very much like Lily, except that her hair was darker, said that she would vote for anyone who closed the methadone clinic in her neighborhood on the East Side.

"Well, we're closer to it than you are, Suki," Lily Harpur said.

Soo-ki! How unbearably upper-class! She deserved to have marauding blacks and Puerto Ricans, high on methadone, overrunning her street.

"My objection to those methadone outfits," Lily Harpur continued, "is that they're all run by ... *dreadful* people out to make money."

By dreadful Jews, she meant to say, Julie knew. By dreadful, profit-making Jews, possibly even named Silverman.

"I'm just getting tired of sending the kids to school in a taxi," the first woman said.

Typical East Side liberals. Their grandfathers or great-grandfathers had got their money from the slave trade or making munitions for wars, and now they served chicken sandwiches to Morris Udall in their living rooms on condition that he would close methadone clinics that spoiled their view of the East River.

Julie needed air.

At about ten o'clock, someone touched her arm, and suddenly David was standing next to her.

With surprising gentleness he said, "Will you kindly tell me why the hell you came out here after I asked you not to?"

"Sure. If you tell me why you haven't called me in three days."

Just as Julie had thought, there had been a scene the evening she had telephoned David at the office and Lily answered. "I didn't bluff her," David said now. "She was good enough not to let me have it, then and there—breeding shows, Julie—because we were going out to dinner with some people. But as soon as we got home around midnight, she started screaming at me. She said she knew damned well what was going on. So

I figured that I'd better go underground for a while. I didn't accept your calls. Lily has a way of getting her hooks into everybody, sooner or later, and I don't even trust my secretary."

"She hasn't got her hooks into me, your precious Lily."

"You don't like her. I could have told you that."

"I feel like a sparrow to her peacock. But aside from the face and the nice tits, what a shit she is." Julie tried to control her rage. "Listen! I'm West Side Jew. She's East Side Wasp. There's a helluva lot more than Central Park between us."

"She means well, Julie. Like all of us, she's a product of her environment."

"Don't defend her!"

"Okay, I won't." Though there were people around them, he reached down and touched her hand. "Why *did* you come?"

"Because I love you."

There it was. She'd come all the way out to Amagansett just to say it, and David Harpur could believe or not, whichever he wanted.

"Can you get away from these people," he said, urgency in his voice. "Later on, I mean."

"I *am* away from these people, David. That isn't the issue. The issue is, can *you* get away? Don't you understand that yet?"

He would understand if she would do the same. Form still had to be considered, and feelings too. There was a chance, he said, that Lily would go home early because their daughter had a touch of the flu and she was worried. "She's very good about such things. If you ever get sick and need someone to nurse you, she's unbeatable."

"One more reason to stay healthy."

With luck, Lily should be able to hitch a ride home with someone leaving early. David thought he could stay another hour or two without arousing her suspicions.

When Julie remained noncommittal, he added, "I need you."

Well, that was better than nothing. Julie decided not to push her luck and ask for specifics. As soon as she told him that she was staying in the guest house, David said that he would meet her there a few minutes after Lily left.

"You'll be taking a chance, David."

"I take chances all the time. I'm a gambler."

So am I, Julie might have said, but didn't.

It was past eleven when Julie looked up and saw Lily standing with a couple by the front door, preparing to leave. She'd had compatible listeners for the last hour and a half—how could David, who loved silence, live with a woman who talked so much?—and Julie had almost begun to think that she would never leave.

After she was gone, Julie waited another five minutes, then made her way through the kitchen, onto the patio, and across the lawn to the cottage. Once in her room, she undressed, lay under the fresh sheets, and waited. A few minutes later, the door opened, and then David was standing over her.

"My God, I've missed you, Julie."

Don't tell me how much you've missed me, goddammit. Show me, Julie wanted to say.

It was one of the best.

Grade A. Prime.

Maybe because it was so daring or because both of them were trying to exorcise Lily Harpur, it went better than it ever had before. Afterwards, David asked her not to let him fall asleep, as he had to get home.

Yet when Julie finally heard his even, regular breathing and his mouth fell open, she didn't rouse him. He slept with his head in the crook of her arm, and rather than risk falling asleep and disturbing him, Julie lay with her eyes wide open, looking through the window, waiting for dawn.

It was already first light, and cars had begun to pass on the road in front of the house, when it occurred to Julie that possibly she'd made an error in judgment.

But then she heard something: the wheels of a bicycle moving over the gravel drive leading to the cottage. The wheels stopped, then a set of feet tread softly through the gravel toward the front door. A hand touched the knob and the door was open. Footsteps passed through the living room, into the small hallway, and stood outside the bedroom door.

Almost with relief, Julie watched as Lily Harpur opened the door and stood there, looking in. Not a word or a sound escaped her lips. Silently, impassively, she picked up David's trousers and went through them until she found the car keys. She went, leaving the door open, and in another few minutes Julie heard a car being started in front of the house.

"Was someone just in here or did I dream it?" David said, his eyes still closed.

"Yeah," Julie replied, overwhelmed by peace and joy. "It was Lily."

———◆———

Did all wives hate weekends as much as Katherine McCabe?

Somehow, it was almost possible to adjust to spending most of one's life with children—though Kate had known women who, through overexposure, themselves became childlike—and in time there was almost a truce with the stupefying tedium involved in looking after a house. As for Buddy, being with him for four or five hours at a stretch was also quite tolerable in its way.

But all three united—children, monotony, and husband—contrived to make weekends hell.

This one more than most.

Thursday morning when she got home from New York, there were two crises to be dealt with. First, Mrs. Ellman had left a note asking her to telephone, which Kate obligingly did, expecting a complaint about the children's rudeness or intractability. Instead, the woman told her that she would be spending a long weekend with her daughter in Pennsylvania, and could Kate perhaps find someone to fill in for her on Monday? Kate was in a rage—dammit, why do people enter into agreements if they break them a week later?—but she held her temper and said that she was sure she'd be able to come up with someone. In the end, having called almost every family in the neighborhood with a teenage daughter, she at last found a high school girl who agreed to come in on Monday, heat a prepared casserole for supper, wash up afterwards, and get the children ready for bed. Provided that her boyfriend could come too. Which, Kate knew from past experience, meant that the girl would be so busy getting herself felt-up or dry-fucked by some pimpled high school youth that nothing would be done right. Still, what else could she do, other than stay home herself and not see Ben?

Afterwards, Kate did the weekend shopping early in order to avoid the crush, had the VW done at a car wash so that Buddy wouldn't accuse her of never looking after it, and finally was about to shove a meat loaf into the oven when Crisis Number Two presented itself.

When she answered the door chimes, Kate at once recognized the woman and the boy on the stoop, but couldn't recall having seen the man before. He identified himself as a neighbor living at the far end of the next street—comprising small bungalows built before the area became fashionable—and said he owned a service station in Hopewell. Roy Crawford, his name was. How-do. After having got that much out, his voice almost broke with emotion as he asked Kate if he and Mrs. Crawford could have a few words with her son.

"My son?" Kate repeated. "You mean Dutchie?"

"That his name, Ed-wurd?" the man asked the boy next to him.

The woman squeezed his hand till he nodded. He was clearly retarded, Kate saw. He had a lopsided, largish head, with vacant eyes and an open mouth. Whenever Kate had seen him before, he was playing in the yard of a house she sometimes passed on the way home from the shopping center. Kate couldn't even begin to guess his age. Somewhere between ten and eighteen.

"Best call your son, ma'am," Mr. Crawford said. "We want him here, the missus and me."

Though perplexed and already angry at his tone, Kate did as she was instructed, then watched as Dutchie came down the stairs from his bedroom where he'd just changed his clothes.

"Now, Ed-wurd," the man said, "you tell 'er what he done to you."

The boy's face changed. Whatever confidence he might have had now drained from him.

Mrs. Crawford gave him a sharp slap on the neck with the back of her hand. "Now you tell, hear? Tell what the boy done to you."

He said, "Put his thing up'n my hole."

It was a few seconds before Kate could even make out what was being said—the mere words—and once she'd heard them, she couldn't fathom their meaning. Seconds later, when the meaning struck, she was appalled.

"Good God!" she exclaimed. "You must be joking. Dutchie isn't even eight years old!"

The Crawfords were not impressed. "Don't matter if

because I'm going back to school doesn't make me what's-her-name, Gloria Steinem."

"I liked you the way you were."

Not are, but were, as if the damage had already been done and was irreparable.

How had she been? Quiet, unobtrusive, and opinionless, a drudge with an absolute and implacable belief that she existed only in order to make life easier for Buddy McCabe.

And what was wrong with that? Nothing so far as Buddy was concerned. So far as Kate was concerned, what was wrong was that it seemed to her that unless she took steps immediately, she might lose her ego entirely, that it might disappear, like a negative left too long in the sun. Whatever it was—self-esteem, she supposed—that held people together and made their lives tolerable had in her almost washed completely away.

God knows, she was the least militant woman in the world and didn't care for long-haired, dirty-fingernailed girls telling her that she was being held in thralldom. She already knew it. She didn't mind being a woman, but she hated to share the condition with Women's Libbers, most of whom looked like the president of the Hockey Club back in college and said shit and fuck the way women of Kate's generation said please and beg-pardon. Kate didn't want them to be her spokesman (spokesperson, they'd amend it, proving Buddy's contention that it was an Age of Trivia), because they were so appalling, the kind of people no one in his right mind would want to sit next to at the movies.

Kate wasn't sure of many things—unlike Julie Silverman who gave the impression of being sure of everything, or Neela Fitzgerald who hated and deplored any kind of certainty—but one thing she thought she was sure of was that she had no intention ever of doing anything the least bit out of the ordinary. It was useless for people to tell her that she'd be happier as a biochemist or a nuclear physicist. Kate knew a number of

11

career women, and it seemed to her that they were no happier than she was, merely unhappy in a different way. She even knew several women who had left their husbands in order to emancipate themselves, and a year or two later were typing letters at insurance agencies at ninety-five dollars a week or serving as hostesses in restaurants. To be as bored at monotonous work as men were seemed to Kate an equal right she would just as soon do without.

All she wanted to do, really, was . . . well, she didn't quite know. She wanted to do something. Anything. Just to get her out of the house on Westminster Lane and away from the loneliness there.

The New School was a means, an avenue. Hopefully, the twice-weekly lectures would animate her, rouse her from her wifely torpor, and possibly help her make up her mind what she wanted to do next.

For the last five years, Kate had been sitting on the edge of life, almost waiting for it to be over, the way one looked forward to a summer vacation. Somehow or other, she wanted to get back into life one more time while she still had the flame, or whatever it was, that kept people from falling over that edge into the darkness on the other side.

The train was crowded for so late in the day. All the window seats were occupied, and Kate knew that she'd have to choose her seat with care to avoid spending the next hour listening to a bore: Princeton turned them out by the hundreds. Glancing down the coach, she gasped as she recognized a woman from the Garden Club bearing down on her. In a panic, she sank into a seat next to an elderly gent reading the *Christian Science Monitor*. She bent over her purse in fierce concentration, then stupidly began to count her change and even rearrange the pocket fuzz.

Rotten luck! The woman, whose name Kate couldn't recall, had spotted her.

"My, what brings us into the city so late in the day?" the woman asked when she was abreast of Kate.

What brings us is desperation, Kate might have answered. A hopeless marriage brings us. Loneliness brings us. The damned dog who starts barking every time I begin to talk out loud to myself, because no one *else* is around, brings us.

Instead Kate replied that she'd enrolled at the New School because her brains were beginning to feel a bit rusty.

"Isn't that astonishing?" the woman said. "I've just enrolled at Columbia. I'm taking a course in anthropology."

Minutes ago, just the thought of what Kate was about to embark on had seemed so cleansing and liberating, and now it was spoiled.

"Last year I took a course at Fordham in Operaplotz," the woman said—or at least it sounded that way to Kate—"and the year before I audited a course at NYU in pre-Giotto or post-Giotto, I forget which. My husband won't let me go to the New School. He says it's too . . . well, you know what." She narrowed her eyes and scrutinized Kate. "You're not Jewish, are you?"

"No," Kate answered. Not yet, she was tempted to add.

Before her marriage, Kate had lived long enough in Manhattan to know that if you weren't Jewish before you came to New York, you were after two or three years there. At least you felt Jewish. Because of the heat, because of the cold, because of the bad air, because of the crowds, everyone in New York felt that he alone was singled out for misery. The advantage of being Jewish, or feeling Jewish, was that you could almost bear it.

"My husband says that if I don't turn into a socialist after a semester at the New School, it's because I fall asleep in class," Kate said weakly.

13

"Well, do be careful. Especially on the streets. There is a war or something going on in New York. Never use the subways. Never talk to strangers. Never say hello to anyone. If someone looks the least bit suspicious, start screaming."

Kate was almost prepared to begin right then. Instead she opened her note-book, took a pencil from her purse, and stabbed the cover emphatically, explaining that she had some work to do.

As she left, the woman said to her that perhaps they would meet again during the semester.

Not if Kate could help it. Good God! And to think she'd thought seriously of taking a course at Columbia School of General Studies!

She was proud of herself for having remembered how to make her way through the underground maze of Grand Central to the Lexington Avenue IRT, though she hadn't used the subways for years.

The first thing she decided as she changed her easy rural shuffle into a fast New York gallop was that she looked suburban. So P.T.A. The young office girls rushing past her were dressed in ravishingly pretty clothes, designed to show off their sexuality.

Everything Kate had on was designed to apologize for it.

A month and a half ago, she'd bought a heavy tweed coat on sale at a Nassau Street shop, and it had seemed very chic when she wore it to the supermarket. Now, as she caught sight of herself in a window, she felt as if she should be getting out of a station wagon, carrying a casserole in her arms. The same shopping trip on which she'd bought the coat had yielded a neat little mink hat, which rode now on her head like a Cossack's cap. Yet apart from a hatted policeman, she seemed to be the only one in New York City who had anything on her head. Instinctively, she smiled at the policeman, who narrowed his eyes, leaned against a pillar, and looked at her as if to say, "Okay, lady, so what's your game?"

When the northbound express roared into the station, Kate inched herself away from the precipice so as not to be sucked down onto the tracks. She gathered her Nassau Street coat around her as the doors opened, then boldly made her way to a vacant seat. She was already seated and the train had begun to move when she noticed an arrow in electric-blue spray paint pointing directly to where she was sitting, and an inscription that so horrified her (*Sit here for blow job*) that she quickly rose, treaded through a field of morning newspapers, and half sat, half fell into a seat at the other end of the car. Stoney-eyed, she tried not to look at the graffiti on the wall across from her.

Yet at some point between 42nd and 59th Streets, Kate found herself reading what was written there in burnt orange.

I been here. Homer Jefferson.

Kate sat studying it, almost mesmerized.

I been here.

It was, after all, no more than what she herself was trying to cry out. It was why she was on an IRT train, which, if it wasn't exactly somewhere, was better than nowhere.

I been here. Katherine McCabe.

If only she had the courage to write it.

The train was certainly going too fast to stop at 59th Street, and it occurred to Kate that it was out of control. Perhaps the motorman had been shot. Hadn't there already been a hijacking, or was that something she'd read in a novel? It was impossible anymore to distinguish between fiction and reality. She jumped up from her seat and stood anxiously by the door, waiting for the conductor to come running through, shouting, "Run for your lives! There's a man here with an atom bomb!"

No one else in the car seemed to care.

At last, blood pumping wildly through her temples, she could feel the car slow down, and just in time she held out one arm to prevent herself from being thrown to the floor when it stopped. The motorman drove the way teenagers drag-raced on the Lawrenceville Road.

As she waited for the doors to open, the coach was momentarily silent, then suddenly it erupted with human sounds. The noise was stupefying. Mothers screamed at children in Spanish or Chinese. Black women yelled at children in Black. From out of nowhere, a gang of leather-jacketed boys came roaring up behind her, shouting at someone they'd left in the next car, or perhaps back on the platform on 42nd Street, or maybe even Brooklyn.

Why was it that the poor made more noise than the middle class? If she were to ask Buddy McCabe, she could almost predict his answer. A lack of self-control, he would say. Silence is not natural, he would say, any more than cleanliness is, or even kindness and civility. They all have to be taught, painstakingly.

The doors opened and Kate rode a wave of humanity onto the platform. As soon as she saw a sign pointing to Bloomingdale's, she began to breathe more easily. She was back on her own turf.

When she was twenty-one years old, and just arrived in New York, she often spent Saturday afternoons at the legendary store, walking up and down the aisles, choosing things she'd buy if she ever came into money. For her, Bloomingdale's had always been a kind of cathedral. Everything in sight was sinfully opulent, designed to lull you into the belief that life was splendid and everlasting and infinitely *good* so long as there was even a remote possibility that a Bloomingdale's box with your name on it might someday turn up in the foyer of your apartment building. If you were earning eighty dollars a week as a secretary, as Kate had been at the time, it gave meaning and purpose to life. The reason you worked was to buy things at Bloomingdale's. It was as simple as that.

It was shallow, of course. But who said that collecting clothes in New York was any more shallow than collecting babies in the suburbs? That charging a sixty-dollar cashmere sweater at Bloomingdale's was any more immoral than buying sixty dollars worth of junk groceries from the A&P, among them sugar-frosted cereal for the kids, Yummies for the dog, French onion cheese dip for Buddy, and for Kate herself, experimentally, a frozen Rock Cornish game hen which went into the freezer and slumbered uneaten for the next year, its wings folded over its breast as if it were in prayer?

Buddy, naturally, professed to hate what he called the Bloomingdale type. Useless, superfluous people, he called them, his index being that anyone who spent nine hundred dollars on an armchair was sinister and suspect, though someone who spent that much on a sit-down tractor-style lawn mower was very admirable and patriotic. People who went to cocktail parties in the East Seventies were mindless, frivolous parasites, though people who gave barbecues in New Jersey were really quite interesting. Actually, all Buddy was trying to say was that he was clever and commendable, and everyone else was ridiculous.

Especially Kate.

Kate even *felt* ridiculous. The only accomplishment in her life which she could be halfway proud of was giving birth to the two kids, and now, six years after Suzie's conception, Buddy said he was thinking of undergoing a vasectomy, first explaining to Kate that there already were too goddamn many children in the world, that starvation was imminent, and that he for one was not going to contribute to the mess any more than he already had.

But it's all I've done, Buddy! she'd wanted to say,

17

*and now you tell me that I haven't done anything but
contribute to a mess.*

The way out, she'd decided at last, was to shun her
body entirely, giving it up as a lost cause, and to culti-
vate her mind instead, in a small sort of way. She had
a degree in English from Ohio State, and with a few additional courses in Education she might even teach
school. Not that Buddy would hear of it. She belonged
at home with the kids, didn't she know that? They
needed her. It was no use trying to tell him that they
were both gone the greater part of the day, and generally she spent from eight-thirty in the morning till four
in the afternoon without seeing anyone but the dog. If
she pointed that out, she had a feeling he'd tell her that
the dog *needed* her.

Actually, it was the dog who finally got the message
to Kate that unless she got out of the house very soon,
she'd go crazy. About ten-thirty one morning, she'd
been sitting at the formica counter in the kitchen, having her fourth or fifth cup of breakfast coffee, and suddenly she was aware that the dog was growling at her.

Kate realized that the dog was growling because she
was talking to herself.

It scared hell out of her.

God knows, if she was truly going insane, the New
School would be of no help, and neither would Bloomingdale's. She saw sanity as a kind of one-track railroad
trestle over a deep valley; insanity as a train coming from somewhere, but which direction Kate didn't
know for sure; and salvation as running the right way
without coming face to face with an engine. What had
drawn her back to New York, frankly, were people.
Whether they were her salvation or the engine in dis-
guise, she was not yet prepared to say.

Still in the subterranean depths beneath Bloomingdale's, Kate spied an escalator and allowed herself to
be carried upward. It seemed to her truly an ascension.
From despair to hope. Meaninglessness to meaning.

Once at the top, she pushed through the doors leading to the store itself and found herself in the basement economy department. Looking neither to the right nor the left, so as not to spoil the elegance of the first floor, she boarded a second escalator which carried her to that great hall, everywhere about her stunning women who had obviously spent all day getting ready to go shopping. Suddenly, the Nassau Street coat she was wearing seemed to be the sort one used for shoveling out the driveway. Were there bouncers in Bloomingdale's? If so, Kate half expected to meet someone who would turn her out.

Neela had said the third floor, so Kate boarded still another humming escalator, and this time rose into a kind of Tiepolo sky, big-buttocked stone cherubs reaching out toward her from a field of Italian shoes. How could anyone not have illusions about oneself while shopping here? Somehow, she expected the clerks to break into song, something Handelian, the minute she reached the top.

There she was! Neela was sitting arrogantly on a velvet-covered chair, her spiked heels dug into a leopard skin just about where its genitals had once been. Predictably, as soon as she saw Kate, she raised her hands to her face in exaggerated horror, then exclaimed, "Kate! You poor dear!"

Did she look that bad? Catching sight of herself in a Rococo mirror, all she could see was her neat little mink hat, which now looked like a coiled raccoon tail slithering down her forehead. She would have cried, but instead tripped over the hoofless leg of the leopard and fell into Neela's arms.

Once, years before, someone had asked Kate how long she had known Cornelia Waggaman Fitzgerald, and she thought for a moment and could not truthfully recall a time when she hadn't known her.

They had been born within two blocks and two

months of each other in West Mystic, Ohio, east of Cleveland but west of almost everything else, including the Connecticut town after which it was named. The year was 1937, about which Buddy McCabe, also born that year, once said, "Lean and catatonic times produce a better than average kid." Kate and Neela had entered kindergarten on the same day (Julie Silverman was also in the class), shared each other's head colds and flu viruses, bled for the first time within two weeks of each other—Kate was horrified; Neela, characteristically, boasted to everyone—they had crushes on the same boys in junior high school, and always had more I's after *Swell* in Slam Books (Kate was generally *Swelllllllll;* Neela was always *Swellllllllllllllllll*) than any of the other girls in the class.

In high school, they took turns being class secretary; were both Homecoming Queen finalists, though Neela won by several votes, at least one of which was cast by herself (Kate, on the other hand, had voted for her best friend, thinking it would be reciprocated); and were deflowered within twenty-four hours of each other.

By the same boy.

It very nearly cost them their friendship, too. For Kate, what had happened between her and Rex Glotzbecker would always be one of the most devastatingly emotional experiences of her life; for Neela, it was a drollery. Years afterwards, at a cocktail party in New York City, Neela had turned to Kate and without preamble said, "Did I tell you or didn't I? I called home last night and Mama said that Rex Glotzbecker was killed. In a car accident. Do you remember him?"

Kate did the one thing she could do best, unexampled, and absolutely without parallel. Her eyes filled with tears.

"Do I *remember* him? Neela, how gross and insensitive can you be!"

"That *is* silly of me. You used to go around with him, didn't you?"

Used to go around with him, hell! Had been wildly, ecstatically in love with him. For one whole year, Kate couldn't even look at him without having her knees buckle. The courtship had started the September of her junior year after he'd kissed her on the way home from a dance in the gym. It took him from then till Thanksgiving to work up to a French kiss. From Thanksgiving till Christmas, whenever they were together, they were tongue and groove, and one night while thus engaged his hand accidentally brushed against her chest. He extracted his tongue long enough to apologize, but the next night he kept his hand there, and by the end of January he'd worked one breast free. By St. Patrick's Day, he was stroking both, even burying his head between them. By Easter, he'd coaxed her into the back seat of his secondhand Chevy and shortly afterwards had pulled down her pants. Toward the end of the first week of May, she could stand it no longer and let him go all the way.

The following morning, dreamy and euphoric, feeling a need to confess to someone, she confided in her best friend, Neela Waggaman. That night, Neela telephoned Rex Glotzbecker while he was doing his geometry homework, told him to be in her garage in fifteen minutes, and when he arrived, she said, "I hear you screw. Wanta do it with me?" Only a fool would have declined.

The next morning, as usual, Kate stopped in front of the large Victorian house where Neela lived so that they could walk to school together. When Neela ran down the front steps, her saddle shoes untied, her face was radiant with youth and happiness.

"You'll never guess what's happened, Kate," she said. "I've been known carnally, as they say."

Kate should have known better, but asked anyway. "By who? *Whom?*"

"Rex! He's asked me out again tonight, too. He's going to take me for a ride in his Chevy."

21

The same car in which Kate, after almost a year of struggle, had given up the only thing, apart from life itself, which was irrecoverable.

"I never want to speak to you again as long as I live," she said, walking away in a huff.

Neela ran after her and tried to patch things up. After all, she said, didn't she always save Kate a place in the cafeteria line? And who else would wait for her after school to walk home with her?

"Anyway," she concluded, "I don't think I want to see him again."

Kate was almost speechless. "But then, why . . . ?"

Neela turned on her cheerleader's smile. "I guess I just wanted to get the knack of things. Do you know what I mean, Kate? I was never able to get the knack of it till now."

"So now you have the knack. Congratulations."

"I still don't understand how they get it to grow."

Kate, who had read a medical book in her father's den and had a scientific bent anyway, attempted to explain. "It gets engorged, sort of."

"Did you see the picture Chester Channing's girlfriend drew of his thing?"

Kate scowled, then guardedly looked at her friend. "What picture?"

It was commonly known that Chester Channing, a classmate, threw a dimwitted girl named Barbara Lane into the bushes every day after school. People passing by could hear them squealing. "She drew a picture for me once," Neela said. "I'll get her to draw another one, okay?"

It took two 8x10 pages from Neela's English notebook to accommodate it. At lunchtime, when she laid it on the table of the cafeteria for Kate to see, Miss Ferris, the civics teacher, happened to be passing by and looked over the girl's shoulders. She very nearly dropped her bowl of chili.

Now, more than twenty years later, as Neela Waggaman Fitzgerald studied her old friend standing next to her on the third floor of Bloomingdale's, she said, "You're letting yourself go, Kate."

Kate wasn't letting herself go. She was simply going, ripening. To stop the process would be like stopping an apple from getting red or being eaten.

Scrutinizing her, Neela added, "What is that furry thing on your head? Is it dead or sleeping?"

Neela, of course, looked striking. She was wearing what looked to be a vicuña coat, lined discreetly with mink, only a tiny portion of which she exposed to the public.

Kate pulled up a second chair, tested it for strength, then flung herself into it. "Neela, there's no one to look nice for anymore," she said. "No one ever looks at me." In fact, on those few occasions that she'd taken more time than usual to fix her hair and face or wear something nice, the most she could expect was for Dutchie to look up from the TV set long enough to say, "Hey, you goin' to the doctor's?" which was very nearly the highlight of her social life. The way she was going, she figured that all she had to look forward to in the next ten years was a hysterectomy.

Kate had grown up on Hemingway and Scott Fitzgerald. When she was in college, she'd read books and watched movies the same way: always with the expectation of finding her own name on the next page, or her face in the next frame. If other people could live lives of dazzling beauty, engendering fanatical love, why couldn't she? All she needed was trial employment.

Yet at some time around the age of thirty-five, it occurred to her that she would never have been able to stand a rowing across Lake Como anyway, and that she had also been a fool to think she might have had a better time at parties on the Riviera than she did in New Jersey. It seemed to her that people who nourished the illusion that they deserved something special out of life were bound to live from hangover to hang-

23

over, or wake up some morning with a shotgun in the mouth.

So, she may have let herself go, as Neela put it. Or, from another point of view, she may have stopped letting herself go.

"It's what you get for living in the woods," Neela volunteered, having little understanding of New Jersey. "It may be all right for raising dogs, but it's no place for people. Why don't you sell everything and come back to the city where your friends can look after you?"

"Because Buddy likes the country."

Buddy was a teacher in a private school not too far from Princeton. He spent all day in classrooms, and in the evenings he enjoyed taking off his shoes and walking barefoot in the grass. As for being looked after by friends, it was what Kate missed most. Once a woman was married and had a family, she was expected to give up her old friends. To seek out new friends in the country was impossible. No one she knew had friends. Friends were what you had before you were married.

"What do you do out there anyway?" Neela asked.

What did Kate do? Well, she fixed breakfast, for one thing, then made the beds and tidied up. Then she'd wash a portion of the bottomless pile of clothes in the utility room. She made out grocery lists. Sometimes she'd bake a cake or a batch of cookies from a boxed mix. If the weather was nice, she'd putter around in the garden. In the afternoons, she went shopping. And, oh yes, yesterday she'd taken the dog to the vet because he'd swallowed a tulip bulb the day before and it was sticking half in, half out of his behind.

Neela pinched her eyes together. "And that's why you majored in English lit at Ohio State?—so you could take a dog to the vet's to have a tulip extracted from his anus?"

"It wasn't a tulip. It was a tulip bulb."

Neela bit her lip. "So what about the kids?"

"What about them?"

"Do you communicate?"

How could Kate communicate with them? All they did was grunt. They never talked to her except when there was nothing they wanted to watch on television.

Sacrifice, Kate didn't mind; a woman was expected to give up little things in order to make her children happy. It was the lack of gratitude that bothered her. When she was a very young girl, she had always been *nice* to her mother. Every chance she had, she would cuddle up to her for warmth and reassurance. But Kate's children, when they weren't eating or in bed, sprawled on the family-room floor, their feet up on the sofa, watching television. If she asked them to turn off the set and come help her in the kitchen—keep her *company,* she meant—they'd say, "Do we have to?"

If only they loved her, possibly she could forgive Buddy for not doing so.

"I just had to get out of the house," Kate heard herself tell Neela. "I suppose it's stupid of me to think I can go back to school, but I have to do something."

"I almost took a course at Barnard, but Quentin talked me out of it. He says that what's wrong with me, education can't cure. So now I'm seeing my shrink twice a week instead of once."

Kate, who probably needed analysis as much as Neela, had never been able to work it into the budget. Neela had been seeing pyschiatrists for the last fifteen years.

"Don't get me wrong," Neela said with animation. "It's not the same gent I was seeing back in the Fifties. In fact, it's about the seventh one. This time, though, I actually think I'm beginning to get my head together."

At the age of thirty-nine, she was getting her head together? If she didn't hurry, the only place she'd be able to put her got-together head would be on a mortuary pillow.

"You should try it," she said, as if she were recommending a new cosmetic.

Actually, Kate hoped that the New School would accomplish the same thing at less cost.

"How's Quentin?" she asked quickly, changing the subject.

"He's in Los Angeles. I've just sent him some shirts from Harry's Bar for his birthday. I looked all over Saks, but all they had was schlock."

"Is the marriage holding up?"

Neela's expensively vicuñaed shoulders shrugged. "We have an understanding. We've stopped being disappointed when we let each other down. We're very civilized about everything."

It depended upon what you required of civilization. Wasn't it Julie Silverman who almost knocked Kate out of her chair at lunch a year ago by blithely announcing that Quentin and Neela never slept together anymore? When Kate protested, Julie said that she had it straight from that horse's ass, Neela herself.

"Don't you know," she'd continued, "that beautiful women like Neela are attracted only to their fathers or to faggots?"

And which was Quentin?

"That I haven't worked out yet. I'm not sure he has either," Julie had replied.

Kate was truly perplexed. She couldn't imagine why Neela had married him if that was the case.

"Battle fatigue. By the time she met Quent, everyone else had just about worn off Neela's chest by rubbing it so hard."

Of course, it was useless to expect charity from Julie Silverman, though she demanded it from her friends. Whenever Kate would question something Julie had done, she would say, "You've never really liked me, have you? Because I'm Jewish." And then she would list a set of grievances dating back to elementary school: how Kate hadn't attended her birthday party in

26

the fifth grade, how she never answered the notes she wrote her in study hall, how she had poked merciless fun at her when she ran for class president and lost.

"Oh, Julie," Neela once said when faced with the same accusations, "that wasn't because you were Jewish. That was because you were such a stick in the mud. You were always reading Shakespeare. You were no fun."

"Life is not always fun," Julie had replied gravely.

"You wouldn't know what to do if it was."

"Neela, if only you knew how silly and superficial you are. I bet you haven't read a book since college."

"You're absolutely right. The last book I read was *Moby Dick* for a course at Ohio State, and the only reason I finished it was because I would have flunked the course if I hadn't.

"Reason is *that*," Julie corrected her. "Not reason is *because*. Reason is *because* is illiterate."

Neela looked up, struck by a blinding revelation. "Julie, you actually go out of your way to antagonize me. Why did you have to tell me that I'm illiterate? That is a . . . a gratuitous crack . . . just the sort of thing I'd expect from . . ."

"Go ahead and say it. Make some anti-Semitic remark now."

"No, I won't. Because if I do, you'll only continue to delude yourself into thinking that the only reason people get mad at you is because you're Jewish."

"Reason is *that*," Julie replied, having listened only to what she wanted to hear.

In the end, it was always Kate who served as peacemaker. Even-tempered, unexcitable, feet-flat-on-the-ground Kate.

"Have you seen Julie lately?" she asked Neela Fitzgerald from her chair on the third floor of Bloomingdale's.

"I see Julie every now and then in Fancy Foods. She comes over just to fondle things and salivate. You

27

know she's stopped eating professionally, don't you? She has a new life and a new job."

The last time Kate had seen Julie, she was reviewing New York restaurants for a chic magazine, doing what Neela said was the only thing Julie knew how to do well, which was to eat. Back in high school, whenever something went wrong, she'd go home and devour a whole chocolate cake. By the time she was ready for college—all three had gone to Ohio State; Neela had dropped out at the end of her junior year, telling everyone that New York City was all the education a girl needed—she'd slimmed down long enough to attract the attention of a married man, the first of many. ("I guess I have a weakness for other women's husbands," she said.) After she graduated, she, too, went to New York; wrote a Fat book, all about her experiences of having been fat; then wrote a Sex book, all about her experiences of having been an easy lay; and finally, when neither made her much money, she took the magazine job and began to eat for money, while continuing to screw for nothing. By then, she said, fat people in New York had bonded together and were calling themselves gourmets.

"But the trouble was," Neela continued, "she was getting fat again herself, and bored. So now she's eating people instead. She does those Profile things in the magazine. I never read them because they're so long. But Quentin says she writes in blood—never her own."

"I'm staying over there Wednesday night," Kate volunteered.

"You won't like it. She lives like a thirteen-year-old runaway." Neela paused, wet her lips, then added, "A thirteen-year-old Puerto Rican runaway."

"It's strange she never got married."

Neela arched her eyebrows. "Why should she get married when she can borrow everyone else's husband?

Poor Julie, I don't know what's going to become of her."

From Neela's point of view, most of the rest of the world could be described by the adjective "poor." Poor Princess von Furstenberg; doesn't she look a fright since her divorce? Poor Jane Fonda; did you see her walking down Fifth Avenue dressed like an unemployed Vietnam vet? Poor Jackie Kennedy; first that swinish foreigner, then that California tart.

"She'll have cockroaches, I warn you. When she came over to see us after we moved into the co-op—it wasn't cheap, Kate; it was $135,000, and that was before Sloane's and Bloomingdale's *did* it—she took one look around at all this gorgeous furniture I'd picked out, and do you know what she said? She said, 'So where are the cockroaches?' When I told her we didn't have any, she said, 'Neela, this is all so shallow.' "

Neela studied Kate's face. "Look, you really must do something with yourself. Buy some clothes or something. Fix your hair. Do you still have a charge account here?"

Kate wasn't sure. It was almost two years after she and Buddy were married before their application was accepted, and by then they'd moved to New Jersey. "I think it's probably inactive."

"*Kate!*" Neela exclaimed. "That is very rude. Tell them you're sorry. Tell them you've been out of the country. Maybe they'll understand."

In the end, Kate pleaded that she wouldn't have time to do any shopping today, but Neela insisted on introducing her to someone she described as "my woman" in the Place Elegante Department. "She needs looking after," Neela said about Kate as she introduced her to a fabulously dressed, languorously beautiful clerk called Miss Jenson or Miss Hansen or Miss Dawson. "Kate's a very sweet girl and one of my oldest, dearest friends," Neela told the woman, "but she has no taste."

29

Miss Jenson-Hanson-Dawson nodded in agreement.

Weakly, Kate said, "What time is it getting to be? I really must run."

It was getting to be sixish, and Neela had to run, too, because she had a plane to get ready for. "Everyone wants me to make a comeback," she said. "I'm almost beginning to feel . . . vapid, just like Julie says I am. So I might get a role in something. Quent says it would be good for me to get out of the house."

She was wasting her life, Kate said to her. After all, hadn't Neela got her picture on the cover of a national magazine the week she opened in a Broadway play back in the Fifties? Kate was sure that somewhere around the house she still had an autographed copy.

"Do you remember the magazine cover?" she said now. "Was it *Life?*"

"No, it was *Look*. It's defunct now."

"Well, maybe this time you'll get your picture on the cover of *Life*."

"*Life* is defunct too," Neela answered.

Kate was tempted to say that she herself was beginning to feel the same way. Instead, she said that she wanted to get down to the New School a bit early to reconnoiter the place before her class began. She wanted to make certain that she knew where she was going.

"Nowhere is where you're going if you stay in New Jersey," Neela answered solemnly. "At least I'm glad you're back in the city two nights a week so that your friends can help you renew yourself."

Next Monday, when Kate was due at the apartment again, Neela said that she would make a point of not going out. After Kate finished her class, they could stay up late and talk, the way they did at pajama parties in high school.

"It's so good to have you back, Kate," she said. "You must start life all over again. It isn't too late. Remember, we are still in our prime."

Who was she trying to convince? Kate or herself?

Speaking of "poor," poor Neela. She was almost forty years old, but still a cheerleader. Kate hoped that nothing would propel her from youth to middle age too quickly.

After Neela gave her a quick hug, Kate scurried away in the general direction of what she hoped was the Lexington Avenue end of the store. Somehow or other, just being at Bloomingdale's lifted the spirits enormously. Each woman had no more than a breathlessly brief period of beauty and grace before decay set in, but here, in this store, Kate had the feeling that it might be extended almost indefinitely.

It *was* good to get away from Westminster Lane. Even false hope was better than none at all.

As she made her way toward the escalator she saw a clock which read 6:25, and for a second she wondered what Buddy would be doing, and the children. More precisely, what would Buddy be thinking *she* was doing. Would he be worrying about her? Concerned that she was in a perilous city all by herself and perhaps wouldn't be able to cope?

"You're in the wrong pew, darling," a voice said to her now.

"Oh, so I am," Kate said to the rising figure of a woman. She then made her way to the Down escalator and at the bottom looked everywhere for Lexington, but had to settle for Third.

Why had Kate married Buddy McCabe?

Years later, it occurred to her that Buddy had finally proposed to her—circuitously; she had to ask him twice what he meant—because he was tired of living on fried eggs. Once when Kate had gone to visit him, when he first came to New York and was living in the West Eighties, she'd pressed her toe against the lever of his kitchen wastebasket and been horrified to see the cracked shells of three or four dozen eggs.

"Don't you ever fix anything else for yourself, Buddy?" she'd asked.

Sometimes, he answered, but more often than not he was in too much of a hurry. The apartment was always filthy. The john bowl was muddy. Pubic hair lined the bath tub. Rotting vegetables filled the refrigerator. Worse, he would sometimes wear the same pair of socks for a week and a half, till they were rank.

He was, in short, a man for whom a wife was not a luxury, but a necessity.

Kate had known him almost all her life (his family had moved to town when he was three), and she and Neela Waggaman had taken turns falling in love with him while they were growing up in West Mystic. At least until Quentin Fitzgerald had come along, at which time Neela directed her attention—insofar as she *had* any, according to Julie—toward him.

Socially and economically, the four of them couldn't have been more different. Buddy was third-generation Shanty Irish and second-generation Pennsylvania Railroad. Kate, whose father owned the local Buick franchise—"the Buick heiress" is how Julie described her still—was petit bourgeois. Quentin, whose father was an attorney, would have been Upper White Collar except that when Quent was fifteen his father overextended himself on the greensward at the Country Club and fell dead of a coronary; Quentin became former Upper White Collar, which is the most dangerous class of all. As for Neela, the Waggamans were what passed for gentry in West Mystic, and never let anyone, least of all Nell (she didn't become Neela till college) forget it.

Julie Silverman was a member of the gang only in a provisional sort of way—always would be provisional, by her own insistence—and socially no one knew what to make of her. The Silvermans had more money than the McCabes, even possibly the Fergusons, but Sol, her father, used a toothpick after meals. Worse than that, he always took five or six extra napkins from the diner on Main Street where he had lunch every day, stuffing them into his pocket as he left.

"What does he *do* with them?" someone once asked Julie.

"He saves them," she answered. "What else?"

Julie was the kind of person everyone said was the life of the party, but few boys ever bothered asking her to any. She had gone stag to the Junior-Senior Prom, the only girl in the class to do so. Buddy was gentleman enough to pick her up (his own date, naturally, was Kate), and Quentin, who was Neela's date, took her home. Afterwards, he said that he'd got a hand job from her at the front door, but Julie herself denied it, and Neela, who was watching, said that it was hyperbole. Also damned unlikely, because he came again about three minutes later all over her formal, ordered from Bonwit Teller in Cleveland, and though Quent was a virtuoso, twice in three minutes was probably more than he was up to, literally and figuratively.

With the exception of Julie, they all knew each other sexually by the time they were eighteen. Buddy and Quent had masturbated each other when they were thirteen or so; afterwards, Buddy pretended that it had never happened, though Quent quite enjoyed the experience and would have repeated it if given the opportunity. Once during a pajama party when they were sophomores—the year before Rex Glotzbecker corrupted them, and two years before they settled down with what would be their future husbands—Neela had run around her bedroom in the buff, then persuaded Kate to do the same, and both finally got so agitated that they ended up by rubbing each other off in bed. It scared hell out of Kate, partly because it was her first orgasm and partly because she feared VD, which she'd heard about and thought was compulsory rather than optional.

Rex Glotzbecker was the only man other than Buddy McCabe who ever got anything off Kate, as the saying goes, and Buddy never knew about Rex. She dated Buddy through her senior year of high school and her first two years of college before she let him do anything more than feel her up. At last, one weekend he drove her to Cincinnati where he persuaded her to spend the night with him in a motel. "We don't have to do anything, okay? You know what I mean?" Yes, she knew approximately what he meant.

Once in the room, they lay on top of the bed, fully clothed, and kissed each other till Buddy was so inflamed he could scarcely breathe.

"We better stop," he said. "I don't want to hurt you." Then he looked at her pathetically. "You want me to stop, don't you, Kate?"

What could Kate do? Could she be responsible for ruining Buddy's health—he'd said that he was sleeping badly and couldn't concentrate on his studies—or should she let him have what he wanted?

"Don't stop," she said out of kindness.

From then on, they slept together whenever they had a chance, though it wasn't easy because Kate lived in the Theta house and Buddy was then in the Phi Gam house. They made love outdoors when the weather allowed, sometimes in the back seat of a borrowed car, several times in Buddy's room, and even once standing up against a sycamore in the backyard of the Theta house.

Kate never thought in terms of the sociological reasons for love and marriage. All she knew was that when she was with Buddy, she felt less alone than she did when she wasn't with him. She wasn't sure, but it was altogether possible that the real reason people got married was that it was the only way one could guarantee that there would always be someone to talk to. Admittedly, with Buddy she listened more often than not, but even that was better than being alone.

Everyone who knew them in college said that Kate

and Buddy were the perfect couple. They were made for each other. Marriage was inevitable.

"But not just yet," as Buddy put it. "See, the way I figure it, we won't get married till I get my doctorate, okay? Maybe you can get a job with your old man and save some money while I wind things up in school. That way, honey, we won't have to begin at the bottom."

At the bottom was where Buddy had grown up, socially anyway. The McCabes of West Mystic were congenitally poor. Buddy was the first one in the family since the Middle Ages to get a university education.

"You think you can wait till I'm through school?" he asked her.

Of course she could wait. Women were accomplished waiters, weren't they? She would do just as Buddy asked. While he stayed in Columbus to begin work on his Ph.D., she would live at home, get a job at her father's showroom, and save every penny she made. If worse came to worse, and if after three years Buddy decided that they were no longer compatible— the smarter he would get, the duller she would become, writing bills for lube jobs and brake linings—she supposed she could always marry a car salesman.

In September of 1958, Buddy began work on his master's at Ohio State, having every intention of remaining long enough to finish his doctorate.

Instead, Kate got pregnant—if she was telling the story.

Or fouled everything up—if he was telling it.

The irony of it was that Kate had read *Anna Karenina, Madame Bovary,* and the sex manuals too, and had even personally known two or three girls who had got, to use the euphemism, "in trouble"—i.e., were trouble to everyone, including themselves. Yet despite that, she had let it happen.

She knew exactly when it happened, too. It was during the last week of April of their senior year, at a Saturday night beer bash at the Phi Gam house. Perhaps because school was almost over, everyone got very silly. Kate, who was a bad drinker, shared almost a pitcher and a half of beer with Buddy as they sat at one of the ancient, initial-carved oak tables in the dining room, Fee Gee's and their dates all around them in the smoky room singing rousing drinking songs, working themselves into delirium. Ordinarily, Kate wouldn't have opened her mouth to more than a whisper, but that night she was even persuaded to sing a solo. More than that, she climbed on top of the table to do so, everyone cheering her wildly, urging her on.

> Oh, it's beer, beer, beer
>> That makes me feel so queer
> In the COR-ner, in the COR-ner.
> Oh, it's beer, beer, beer
>> That makes me feel so queer
> At the Quar-
>> ter-
>>> mas-
>>>> ter's Ball!

Afterwards, everyone within reach hugged her, then they all chug-a-lugged their beer, and it seemed to Kate that she'd never been happier in all her life. She was among friends, and she was doing everything her parents had forbidden her to do: she was drinking, she was smoking, and she had her hand on the knee of the boy she was in love with. It was perfect bliss.

When she'd been a very little girl, her mother and father used to take Kate with them to the Moose Lodge on Saturday nights and allow her to watch the older people dance. Her mother would station her between the refreshment table and the wall, and say, "Now, Kate, you stay here like a good little girl. Stand behind the cakes and don't get in anyone's way." A scowl on her face, Kate would do as she was told, looking over the huge, five-layered cakes and wavy meringue-topped pies at the dancers suspended there, and no one ever came over to talk to her or keep her company. It seemed to her even then, because she was shyer and less aggressive than most girls, that she was a born spectator at life and that she would probably always have to stand by the cakes and watch other people.

But Buddy changed all that. In bed and out, he drove the loneliness away. And the next thing she knew—what *would* her mother say!—she was standing on a table belting out "The Quartermaster's Ball."

If only there could be an everlasting Quartermaster's Ball, at which no one ever died or became unhappy or even got older, and at which everyone was loved and admired.

So, later, when Buddy spoke to her over the din of the singing and said, "Hey, honey, you wanta come upstairs?" Kate didn't even attempt to remind herself that she'd been drinking too much and that Buddy had an absolutely wanton look in his eyes, and that it would be prudent to take a rain check. What was prudence anyway? Spinsters were prudent. And bachelors. Lonely, loveless people were prudent. Prudence never got you invited to a Quartermaster's Ball.

Girls were forbidden to go beyond the first floor of the Phi Gam house, but Kate didn't care. Buddy's roommates were away for the weekend, so what could possibly go wrong?

It went very well indeed. Between the beer she had drunk, Buddy inside her, and the rousing drinking songs drifting up the stairs, Kate gasped at the moment of climax.

Then, as Buddy came, she felt the warm surge of life essence shoot into her, and did nothing about it. It didn't matter. Life was too beautiful to fret about such things.

Later, she said, "Buddy, did you use anything?"

"What, honey?"

She repeated her question.

"Oh, hell," he said. "I forgot. You shoulda reminded me. You okay?"

Yeah, she was okay.

She wasn't, of course. When she missed her next period, she said nothing to Buddy about it, because she was afraid to. And then, before she knew it, they were home for the summer, Buddy had a job to help him with that fall's expenses in grad school, and Kate went to work every morning at the Buick showroom. She was sick a great deal, but since she was almost the only one around to use the ladies' restroom, no one seemed to notice.

By August, she knew that she could keep it a secret no longer, so she told Buddy.

"Oh, shit," he said. "You've spoiled everything."

What happened next, Kate would never be particularly proud of. In tears, she went to her mother and spilled the beans. Any other mother would have proposed a shotgun marriage—even a Buick marriage, free cars being more persuasive than guns to young men—but Mrs. Ferguson telephoned a friend of a friend, and that same afternoon Kate was in the home of a retired school nurse ("Why, I gave you your small-pox vaccination!") where she was aborted. For the next two days, she passed shreds of fleshlike material whenever she urinated.

When Buddy learned what had happened, he hit the ceiling. All men secretly hate being fathers, but what they hate even more is being deprived of the opportunity. He said to hell with everything and enlisted in the Army, to think things over, as he said. To punish himself, Kate thought. In any event, after two years in the service, spent mostly in Germany with the froylines, as he called them, he came home none the worse for wear.

Kate had by that time moved to New York into the

apartment with Neela and Julie. Socially, she was a flop. Weekends, Neela would spend with a fifty-five year old lecher on Central Park West, while Julie went to Fire Island. Kate would buy enough groceries to last two days, then hole up in the fifth floor walk-up on West 13th from Friday till Sunday night, reading books, listening to WQXR, and walking around barefoot so that the people on the floor below wouldn't know that she never had dates. When Buddy appeared, they started sleeping together again almost at once. She was grateful for the attention; he was so old-shoe and comfortable to be with. When he asked her to marry him, she couldn't see any alternative, except working as a secretary all her life, so she accepted.

After they were married, Buddy used the GI Bill to take his master's at Columbia, but then he petered out. The same week that he got his degree he was offered a job with a private school in New Jersey, doing hack-teaching as he called it, and he'd been there ever since. Now, fifteen years later, he was bucking for chairman of the English department, and would get it too, if only, as he put it, he could learn to kiss ass like the other guys.

And every time that Kate and Buddy quarreled—which they'd done with increasing frequency within the last year—he reminded her that he would have had his Ph.D. and would now be teaching at a college if Kate had not fouled things up.

Kate, the fouler-up.

Now, sitting next to a dirt-mottled window of the southbound IRT, at least Kate was able to remember that the Fourteenth Street stop was the closest one to the New School.

She was the only emphatically white woman in the car, very possibly, she was beginning to think, the only white woman underground in New York City. It appeared to her that there was an entirely new borough since she'd been in the city the last time. Manhattan still existed at ground level where well-dressed white people hailed cabs or rushed from place to place, while beneath them, in perpetual twilight, blacks and Puerto Ricans sat, ankle deep in newspapers.

Still, Kate rather preferred being with them than with the executive types at the street level—who were dashing about, making money, and ruining people. In New York, it seemed to Kate, there was a special kind of minority group, quite apart from race or religion, which encompassed a lot of unhappy people trying to stay alive, and frankly, at the moment, Kate felt more black and Puerto Rican than she did white, Anglo-Saxon, or Protestant.

As the train stopped and Kate tumbled out onto the platform, she felt her spirits soar. Quickly she made her way along the platform to a flight of stairs, passed a kind of underground street carnival selling spicy, ethnic foods, then walked up a second flight of steps to the street. Once at the top, she caught her breath, looked to her right and her left, then, noticing a Hispanic-looking fellow leaning against the Don't Walk sign, said to him, "Excuse me, but I've lost my bearings. Could you tell me if Twelfth Street is that way," she pointed in one direction, "or this?" and she pointed in the other.

By way of reply, he said to her—or at least she thought he said—"I wahd lock to fock you, baby."

Horrified—no one had ever said anything like that to her in New Jersey—Kate rushed headlong into traffic, despite the sign, and found herself hugging the center line as cars sped past. Two huge city buses fuming black smoke nearly knocked her over, then momentarily blinded her. Once the light had changed, she raced to the opposite side of the street, chose a direction that looked as if the Village might be at the end of it, then proceeded to walk.

If only Buddy had heard! Kate was almost tempted

to ask the man back at the corner to put his request in writing. Wasn't that the damnedest! Thirty-nine years old and she was still able to elicit something other than "Hey, honey, what's for supper?"

Incredible! If only Kate had the nerve to go back to the man and say, "Look pardner, it just so happens to-day is your lucky day." What would it be like anyway? God knows, it couldn't be worse than what Buddy provided her. She had come to hate weekends because of what she privately thought of as Buddy's Saturday Night Special. On several occasions, she'd even deliberately not renewed her prescription for the Pill, thinking that he wouldn't press, but at those times Buddy had merely rearranged his thrust, coming against her belly, her upper leg, and, once, very near her knee cap. Even if she cooperated fully, she got complaints.

"You didn't come," he would say dejectedly, all his artistry having been for naught.

Oh, yes, she did, she would lie, then add, "Sort of."

"Maybe you better see a doctor, hon."

See a doctor? Hell, maybe she'd better see a lawyer, she told herself.

Buddy thought that something was wrong with her engineering if she didn't appreciate his gift. Once when he was younger, he had boasted to her, "You know, honey, erections are a fantastic thing," and it had puzzled her for years. He hadn't said that the love act was fantastic or that Kate was. He said that erections were. Yet Kate knew for a fact that Buddy woke up with one every morning anyway—piss hard-ons, he called them—and if a bag of urine pressing against his prostate could evoke the same response as a woman did, where the hell did that leave Kate?

Well, it didn't leave her feeling very fantastic, that was for sure.

Thirty-nine, going on forty. What could she expect now? As Buddy's ardor, such as it was, would inevitably—providentially—begin to ebb, he would want to be mothered. She already saw signs.

"What kinda choker should I wear with this suit, hon?" he'd ask her, carrying in six or seven ties to show her. Or "Whaddaya think I should do about the lawn?—mow it today or wait till tomorrow?" Or "Kate, would you take a look in my ears and see if they're clean?" Or "Should I go downtown and get a haircut or shouldn't I? Or do you want to cut it again?"

Good God, there had to be more to life than looking into someone's ears. Kate was absolutely sure of it.

Deep in concentration, she stepped off the curb and was roused only by the furious honking of a taxi as it sped past her. She looked up at a street sign to see if she'd reached Twelfth Street yet, and instead saw she was at Sixteenth. As she had started on Fourteenth, she must have gone north instead of south. How stupid of her. If Buddy had been with her, he'd say, "I don't know anyone who gets lost easier'n you."

She turned now and began to retrace her route, hoping that no one was watching her. The advantage of being in New York was that eccentricity was commonplace and normalcy was an aberration, so that anyone watching probably wouldn't have cared.

Her feet and her ankles hurt from walking on the hard pavement after having spent fifteen years in automobiles. In New York, did people start dying from the top, as Swift suggested, or from the bottom? She was aware, too, that her eyes were smarting and running, possibly because of the automobile exhaust and the foul air, but she also wondered if perhaps she was in need of glasses. What if she found herself in the lecture hall at the New School and couldn't see a word the professor was writing on the blackboard?

"Excuse me," she imagined herself saying to the nineteen-year-old sitting next to her. "I am almost forty years old and am losing my faculties. What does that say up there?"

Would the youth look at her with adoration and say, "I wahd lock to fock you, baby," or would he see her as a geriatric monstrosity and change his seat?

By the time she reached Twelfth Street, her soot-filled eyes blinked spasmodically and her legs ached all the way up to the groin. Squinting at the end of the block, she was just able to make out the neo-Nazi architecture of the New School. As she approached it on the opposite side of the street, she felt a quickening inside her, then cold fear.

When she was directly across from the entrance, Kate stopped. From both directions, young people, faces rapt, made their way to the doors, books under their arms. They seemed buoyant and inspirited, as if they'd never once in their lives been hurt or disappointed. Kate listened to their cheerful voices, and as she did she could not make her feet work for her. She stood frozen on the sidewalk.

She didn't know for sure, but possibly she had waited too long. Maybe she already knew everything she would ever know, and a class at the New School would provide no more enlightenment than anything else in life had. Maybe there was something grotesque about a thirty-nine-year-old woman trying to change. The youthful people she was watching now would merely patronize her. She would be just one more pathetic suburban lady trying to horn in on their good times.

"Christ," she imagined them saying, "is that Mrs. McCabe asking another silly question? Why the hell doesn't she go home and snap beans?"

Oh, hell.

Kate didn't quite know how it happened, but she found herself walking south on a broad avenue. When she heard a bell somewhere toll eight o'clock, she was almost relieved, because it meant she couldn't go back.

In time, she found herself in front of a movie house. She bought a ticket, went in, and sat on the aisle, piling her coat on the next seat so that no one would sit there. She saw the movie twice through, and when the last show ended after midnight, she was surprised to find herself crying.

———◆———

For all that mankind did to prevent it, it was dawning once again. Just barely.

The air in New York City which yesterday had officially been described as "unacceptable"—though no alternative to breathing it was even hinted at—was this morning "acceptable to good," which meant that it could tolerate life for perhaps another twenty-four hours.

On the west side of town, toward which a sweat-suit clad figure now jogged through the park, rich slum landlords shared large-roomed, high-ceilinged apartment houses on Central Park West with Mafia overlords and the theatrical crowd. On mean streets leading westward from the avenue were poor clerk-typists in their first New York apartments, transvestites, muggers, and Jewish girls who were in group therapy.

Or had formerly been.

Of the hundreds of things that could be said about Julie Silverman—she was the figure jogging through the park at six A.M.—none explained her more readily than that she had been expelled from her group therapy sessions for reasons of truculence.

Truculence?

Now, as she made her way toward Central Park West and 70th Street, she rounded a bushy corner and very nearly collided with a jogger coming from the opposite direction.

"Don't you know enough to keep to the right?" the man said to her.

"Shut up, motherfuck," was how truculent Julie Silverman replied, continuing on her way, footloose in an Age of Schlock.

The Silvermans of West Mystic, Ohio, were one of three Jewish families in town. The easy way out—the least painful one—would have been for them to become less Jewish, but the Silvermans became more Jewish. Instead of buying cowboy hats, eating hamburgers, and putting pumpkins in the windows at Halloween, they resolutely affirmed their differentness. They sent all the way to Cleveland for kosher meat, delivered once a week in an old Ford pickup driven by a black-bearded, skull-capped old gent who set all the dogs in town barking. They celebrated suspiciously un-American holidays. ("Julie was unable to attend school because of a head cold," her mother, Rheba, learned to write on her attendance card on these occasions. Once when she'd written, "Julie was out for Yom Kippur," Julie's teacher said on her return, "Are you feeling better now?") And the Silvermans' Friday evening meal was a ritual that brought neighbors from blocks around to peer through their windows to see what sorcery was going on.

Julie was constantly reminded by her parents that the holocaust was only temporarily deferred. Everyone, her father, Sol, said, should anticipate the worst, Jews more than others.

"It is no sense trying to be happy, Julie," he'd say to her. "It is better to save."

As a result, the closets at home were filled with articles of survival. There were thousands of napkins from the diner on Main Street. Untold cans of sliced pineapples. Sardines, herring, and smoked fish. Candles of all sizes, colors, and shapes. Dates and figs. Matzos. And surplus Fourth of July firecrackers which were to be thrown in the goys' path should they ever attempt to storm the house during Friday evening's service.

"But Papa," Julie would complain, "this is America."

"Hah!" he would reply.

Sol Silverman had been enticed to move to West Mystic from New York City in 1940 because a cousin of a cousin, who had established a small store there, was getting on in years and needed first an assistant, then someone to buy out his business. It had begun as a kind of Army surplus store, but in time featured a general line of inexpensive clothing. What Sol offered was neither good nor bad; it was cheap.

Until Julie went away to college, she worked in the store every day after school and on Saturdays. Other girls (among them, Kate Ferguson and Neela Waggaman) met at the Sugar Bowl down the street and sipped lemon Cokes when they weren't giggling at boys, but Julie had to stand behind the counter at her father's store and say to people, "May I help you?" It was slavish and demeaning. Sometimes they were cross and rude to her, and she had to pinch her fingers to keep herself from telling them to go to hell. One Christmastime when the store was crowded, Julie waited on someone out of turn, and a woman said to her, "You little Jew," then walked out of the shop.

It was sobering.

Julie decided, there and then, that if there was one thing she wanted in life more than any other, it was to be in a position where she would never, *never* again have to be nice to people who didn't like her. It really didn't matter, so far as she was concerned, if they said it to her face—"You little Jew," she repeated to herself for days after the woman had uttered it—or if they kept it to themselves. The fact that most of them *thought* it was enough.

Sol Silverman's only concession to American life was a fondness for baseball and in particular the way it was played by the Cleveland Indians. Whenever there was a game, he would sit in the living room, his ear next to the radio. If Julie walked through, he would look up at her and say, "The Indians are losing." Or, on good days, he would say, "The Indians are winning."

Julie considered that being a Jew involved much the same kind of contest. If she got the highest grade in her class on a history test, or if a boy had talked to her in the cafeteria during the lunch hour, or even if Kate or Neela had confided in her in some special way, she would say to herself, "Well, the Indians are winning." But if the opposite occurred—if someone made a cruel joke at her expense, or laughed at her, or if she came in second or third in a test—she would say sadly, "The Indians are losing."

If Julie had been ravishingly pretty, as Neela Waggaman was, life might have been easier. Beauty defied prejudice. But Julie was neither homely nor good looking. Her face was utilitarian. It provided a site for vision, breathing, and expression. (In contrast, her brother Bernard, who was always called Brother, was loutish and ugly.) To her credit, it was never without animation. Teachers said, correctly, that Julie Silverman had the *cleverest* face they'd ever seen.

To a girl of fifteen who desperately wanted to be pretty, it was not much of a compliment, but Julie made the most of it. She was smart, there was no doubt about it ("A dumb Jew is a dead Jew," Sol reminded her), and in time she came to see smartness as a refuge, a sanctuary. Kate and Neela could be teachers' pets, but when teachers wanted something done that required dependability and good judgment, Julie was the one they always called on.

The trouble—and truly it *was* Julie's trouble—was that she sometimes volunteered even before she was called on. It was so very much her trouble that years later when Neela Fitzgerald was asked by her psychiatrist what she remembered about high school, Neela replied, "Good God, I don't remember anything except that Julie Silverman had her hand up all the time, and I mean *all* the time."

Julie did like to come out on top, even if it sometimes involved embarrassing teachers who knew less about a subject than she did. On occasion, she even took questionable steps to insure that she was champ. For three years running, she won first prize in a statewide essay contest sponsored by the Daughters of the American Revolution on the subject of the American Way of Life. Hers was about the only entry, year after year, that was not downright banal. The fact that she had sent drafts of all three essays to her cousin Sondra at Hofstra College for correction and emendation did not seem to her to conflict in any way with the American way of life, particularly as she felt that with a name like Silverman, her entry would have to be twice as good as a goy's.

Or as Julie herself put it years later in group therapy, using her racy, West Side New York voice, "You just beat the shitheels to the punch."

But it involved deception, another member of the group had said, someone who had earlier offended Julie by calling her a kind of Norman Mailer with a crack between her legs.

"Those motherfuckers in D.A.R. don't know anything *but* deception," Julie had replied, then looked at the faces around her, hoping to find at least one that was sympathetic, one that understood what it was like to feel besieged, but she saw nothing but the same old hostility.

The Indians were losing.

Until Julie went away to college, she never had a boyfriend. Her mother had tried to arrange romances with the sons of the other two Jewish families in town —Morton Friedman's father kept a shoe store and

Stanley Blickstein's father owned a jewelry shop—but her attempts failed.

"They are both good businesses," her mother had advised her. "And Morton has lovely red hair."

"You don't fall in love with businesses," she replied. "And Morton is an ass."

"You can be so choosy?" her father asked.

"My Julie is pretty. She is just big-boned," protested her mother.

Big-boned. Big-titted. Big-mouthed. Julie had heard it all before. If she had to depend on virtues other than those (wasn't it possible that some men actually preferred big girls?) she might as well call it quits.

But Ohio State was a revelation. For one thing, for the first time in her life, she was no longer ashamed of being Jewish. It was a perfectly natural condition and not an aberration. If anything, in the world of scholarship, it was desirable, because scholars, too, had always to keep one eye on enemies of light and promise. In college, to be smart was everything, and it no longer mattered that she wasn't as pretty as Neela Waggaman or Kate Ferguson. During the panty raid in the spring of her freshman year, twice as many boys yelped and squealed under her window as under Neela's, and when she was the first—what else?—to remove her brassiere and fling it over their heads, they roared the way they did at the Buckeye horseshoe stadium after a touchdown. And when, minutes later, they yelled for more, she bent over, stepped out of her panties, and sent them flying into the night air.

"*Hi, ho, Silverman!*" those in the crowd who knew her shouted as her panties floated earthward.

"Who else but a Jewish girl would have thought of it?" she said afterwards, somehow setting the tone of what was to follow, or refining a tone which had already been set, a kind of irreverence in the face of sacred institutions, indignation that society was so messed up that horny boys had to resort to facsimiles in order to get their pleasure.

Which was both silly and wasteful in view of the fact that Julie was theirs for the asking, and no one had yet.

Years later, her analyst said to her, "Let's try to understand it, Julie. There you were: eighteen years old and in Columbus, Ohio. You could have had your pick of boyfriends. So why did you choose a man who was already married?"

Julie didn't know. "Boys seemed dull and uninteresting. There was something about a married man that appealed to me."

"What is it, Julie? Say it."

"I really don't know."

"Yes, you do. Say it."

Painfully, Julie got the words out. "I protect myself that way. If I have affairs with married men, I know that they won't reject me because of some deficiency in *me*. They reject me because they already have a wife. I'm off the hook."

"Is it possible that you think you don't deserve happiness, Julie? And with a married man, you know from the beginning that it's going to fail?"

Wisely, Julie left the question unanswered.

While other freshman girls at Ohio State waited by their telephones for boys to call them, Julie stood in the hallway outside the offices of the English department, waiting to see Tom Rowlandson, in order to discuss a fine point of one of his lectures. Julie was the only one in class who had read and could pronounce Marcel Proust. The first theme she wrote for him was faultless, and he said to her after class one afternoon that it might be best if he exempted her from class attendance.

"Oh, no," she said. "I really am learning a great deal from you."

Tom Rowlandson knew better, but didn't put up a fuss. When she began to appear outside his office for impromptu conferences—"I was just passing by," she'd say by way of preamble—he knew that more than scholarship was involved, but he didn't exactly discourage her. In fact, he quite liked her company. After conferences, he often took her to a greasy spoon on High Street for coffee.

One day after they had compared notes on *The Marble Faun,* he turned to her and said, "You don't really want to talk about Hawthorne, do you?"

There were tears in her eyes. "No," she said.

"What do you want, Julie?" They had dropped the Miss Silverman–Mr. Rowlandson formality after the second week.

When she didn't reply, he said, "I'm married."

"I don't care if you don't."

"You probably won't believe me, but I've never done anything like this before."

"I'm the one who's supposed to say that."

He was still puzzled. "But why me, Julie? There are plenty of guys around here, better looking than I am. Probably a damned sight nicer than I am. And sure as hell younger than I am."

How could she say it? Other girls could be sucked in by football players and the fraternity crowd. But Julie found them tiresome. Quite possibly it would get her in trouble sooner or later, but she had a feeling that she could never love a man unless he was smarter than she was. Somehow or other—she didn't quite know how—a man's intellect and scholarship triggered in her the same reaction that sorority girls had to jock straps. Admiration very easily led to adoration.

"I can never leave my wife," he protested.

"I don't care."

Several weeks later, she happened to mention to her mother that she was seeing a man named Rowlandson.

Rowlandson? Was that a Jewish name? her mother asked.

"Not exactly, but he's nice anyway."

"Nice? So is Morton nice. So is Stanley. What's wrong with that kind of nice?"

What was wrong with that kind of nice was that neither of them was screwing her, and Tom Rowlandson was. Moreover—and no one was more surprised than Julie herself—he found her to be a frenzied and passionate lover, almost beyond imagining.

"O rare Julie Silverman," he'd say to her afterwards. "You are absolutely incredible. I have never in my life known a girl like you."

Maybe it was because she'd waited so much longer than most girls. But her gratitude was immense. While lying in Tom Rowlandson's arms, she showed it by abandoning herself, truly.

And thus discovered that mindlessness had a function as great if not greater than intellect. That the cause of it could not promise permanence—anything even beyond next week—didn't seem to Julie all that important.

Almost four years later, Julie graduated from Ohio State and from Tom Rowlandson more or less concurrently. He would see her from time to time, if that was okay with her. Whenever he got to New York, he would call. They parted the best of friends, both having been enriched by the experience.

When Julie announced to her father that she was going to New York, Sol said, "You mean you're going back to that shithouse? Haven't we been good to you?"

It wasn't that, really. For Julie it was a kind of pilgrimage. For most of the first twenty-one years of her life, she'd lived in Ohio, always feeling somehow as if she were little more than a guest overstaying a welcome. At Ohio State, she'd begun to think that Jewishness was, after all, a desideratum. There was no sense apologizing anymore.

"In New York," she said to Sol, "almost everything that's good is Jewish."

"For a little while maybe," he replied. "But don't kid yourself. If it's Jewish, it won't last."

During her first three months in New York, while she lived on West 13th Street with Kate and Neela, Julie tried to get a job with one of the women's magazines. She bought a neat little hat from Peck & Peck and borrowed a pair of nylons from Kate, but there was something about her style—the way she talked and thought—that made her interviewers uncomfortable.

That September, someone told her about a new magazine called *Central Park,* so as a lark and on the spur of the moment, Julie dropped by and asked the first person she saw if they were hiring.

"What can you do?" The man studied the girl before him, dressed in a sweatshirt and a pair of faded Levi's.

"One thing I could do is sweep up some of the shit you have all over the floor. Didn't anyone ever tell you about wastebaskets?"

Back in the 1950s, nice girls did not acknowledge excretory functions. At most, when they were very, very drunk, they might say bullshit, but to suggest that creatures other than bulls created such messes was unheard of.

"What else?"

"What do you need?"

"A food expert. We need someone to write a column on restaurants."

"I'm your girl."

In the end, she persuaded the editor to hire her on a trial basis and to pay for her dinner at "21." She turned in an arrogant, smart-alecky review, finding fault with everything from the headwaiter to the mousse.

The staff writer who went with her couldn't see any correlation between her appetite and the review. "She

53

ate everything, the way Hermann Goering collected art," he told the editor.

"But she didn't like anything," said someone else, who was to decide if she was to be given a full-time job.

"Look," the editor replied, "there is a very definite market for that. We are all tired of hearing nice things. Silverman writes mean. Give her the contract."

Even that first year in New York, while she was gaining a reputation as a writer—she also started her Sex book and her Fat book—she'd had time to have affairs with two men, both on the staff of the magazine and both married. It did not matter one goddamn that, as sometimes happened, she sat at editorial conferences, and that the man to her left was her former lover and the one to the right, her present one. During the affairs and after they were over, she was totally unembarrassed.

"Some people are made for it, I guess," she once said to her shrink.

"What is that, Julie?"

"To have lovers," she explained. "Some people are made to be wives—they can't help but be wives; it's in the blood—and some people are made to be lovers."

"That's fine as far as you went, but you didn't go far enough."

"Meaning?"

"Some men are made to be husbands."

"So?"

"It's a dead end. When a husband has a lover. It can't go anywhere. Don't you see that, Julie?" When she wouldn't answer he persisted. "You'll never be happy. You'll always be disappointed."

She shrugged her shoulders. "What good is being Jewish if I can't stand disappointment?"

Now, at thirty-nine, Julie had passed through eight, possibly nine affairs, the ninth being somewhat ambiguous. In Julie's circle, women counted affairs as suburban wives count children, and her toll was neither especially high nor particularly low. She never slept around the way Neela Fitzgerald did, though she probably had almost as many opportunities. After she appeared on the Merv Griffin and Dick Cavett shows, she was deluged by telephone calls from people she'd never met who offered to screw her. As politely as she could, she told her callers, "You misunderstand. I'm just an observer, not a supplier," even though her racy Sex book, *Screwing Around*, tended to suggest otherwise.

By this time, she was no longer food editor at the magazine. As one of her waggish colleagues put it, she moved from eating food to eating people, not (as Neela had told Kate McCabe), because of a bad stomach for the former, but a decided appetite for the latter. Every month, she was responsible for a Profile on a local celebrity or someone who passed for one.

It was through such an assignment that she met David Harpur, who was Number Ten.

After nine affairs, a woman tends to lose the sense of wonder and expectancy she once had upon meeting a man for the first time. She protects herself. She becomes guarded. Julie was very nearly rude to David Harpur during her interview with him.

He was an important man, and that was a strike against him. He was president of Lord & Knowles, one of the most prestigious investment houses in America ("Is that Lord as in *the* Lord?" was one of Julie's first questions); he was stuffy and rather pompous ("Do you always talk as if a couple hundred people are listening to you?" she asked, and he replied, "A couple hundred people generally are"); and he was very, very happily married, as he put it ("I think one *very* will do," she interrupted), to a member of a New York family that dated from the original Dutch settlement.

After he had charted his career for her, he said that if it hadn't been for the Second World War, he probably wouldn't be where he was. Using the GI Bill, he went to Harvard, and that awakened him. It was also where he met his wife. He indicated a photograph on his desk.

"And did she awaken you too, Mr. Harpur?"

He smiled, which was at least some indication that he might be human. "She held me together for about ten years. All through college and then when I was starting out on the Street. I don't know what I would have done without her."

"Yeah," Julie said, and he looked up sharply.

Julie had no tolerance anymore for listening to men talk about how good their wives had been to them. She had listened to it too many times while she was in bed with them. So she changed the subject.

After another hour's talking, she made arrangements for a photographer to visit him at his house on East 82nd and at the house in Amagansett, where he'd be spending the weekend. He was delighted to have talked to her. And, oh yes, could she possibly send the page proofs to his office before the article went to press? Just to make absolutely certain that he wasn't being misquoted.

"You don't have to be afraid of me, Mr. Harpur. I'm surprisingly benign." Nevertheless, she agreed to send him the page proofs. "There's one final question I'd sort of like to ask though." She waited. "You've been telling me that you're happily awaiting a merger with another firm, that you're happily married, and that you have three happy children. That is a hell of a lot of happy." She smiled ever so slightly. "So how come you're unhappy?"

Under the circumstances, he handled himself quite well. "I can't recall that I said I was."

"Neither can I, but you look that way. So I thought I'd ask."

He studied her as if she were just one more tough Jewish broad who had it in for men. Privately, he could never understand how the race had been able to perpetuate itself with every Jewess in the world walking around with a wisecrack on her lips.

"I guess it takes one to know one," he said at last.

Julie bit her lip, then decided to grin instead.

Before the article came out, she sent him the page proofs, but he never acknowledged them. About five weeks later, while she was working late one night, she picked up the telephone in her office, heard someone ask for Miss Silverman, then listened as a voice said, "Look, you probably won't remember me, but this is David Harpur."

"Sure," she said. "I was wondering how long it would take you to get up the nerve to call me."

He'd meant to thank her for all the publicity, he said, but hadn't got around to it for one reason or other. "I'm at loose ends tonight," he added.

It had seemed to Julie that he'd been at loose ends the first time she met him, five and a half weeks ago. Worse, that the ends were probably unraveling, and she had brought it to his attention. For that, a man could either hate a woman or love her.

"The family's out on the Island," he continued, "and I was wondering if you'd like to have dinner with me."

"Okay. Only there's one thing you should know."

"Yes?"

"I'm a very hard girl to get into the sack. It takes a hell of a lot more than dinner for two at a cheap restaurant."

He was unflapped. "I was thinking of Lutèce."

It was one of the best restaurants in town. And one of the most expensive. "I could be impressed," she said. "How much remains to be seen."

In fact, she was impressed out of her head. Not merely by Lutèce, where their bill for drinks and dinner came to over one hundred dollars, but by David Harpur. At some point during dinner, he said to her, "When you asked me that—why I was unhappy—it just about floored me. You'll never believe it, but I had

57

to cancel my appointments for the rest of the day. I *was* unhappy. But I hated like hell to admit it. It's taken me a month and a half to face up to it."

"So now you can answer the question." She waited. "Why are you unhappy?"

He let his breath out. Then with effort he said, "All my life I wanted to be a success. And now I guess I am. Except it's no fun anymore. I'd give it all up tomorrow if only I could *feel* something about someone again. I suppose I'm burned out."

"Wife?"

He shook his head. "Lily? There's nothing there. Except gratitude for sticking by me at the beginning. Otherwise, nothing. On her part or on mine."

"Kids?"

"Three, but only one's at home. Two are at school in New Hampshire. They're holding the marriage together. Without them, we would have been divorced years ago. Then you reach the age of forty and you say, what the hell. You're over the hump. If you've been able to take it that long, you figure you're good for another twenty or thirty years of unhappiness. Then you start waiting for a coronary to set you free."

Julie had never once begun an affair frivolously. She had turned down the half hundred or so men in New York who had at one time or another propositioned her (the same kind of proposition that three out of four times Neela Fitzgerald would accept). Flesh was something she didn't easily surrender. Of the nine men who had loved her during the last fifteen years, not one had gone to bed with her until she was ready for him. Whether it was good or bad, she didn't know, but somehow or other she had to have both an emotional understanding and an intellectual one before she went all the way.

Yet with David Harpur, possibly because he'd been so honest with her, she was ready even before the waiter brought the chestnut purée and whipped cream.

"A little while ago," she began, "you said you'd give up everything tomorrow if only you could feel something about someone again." She narrowed her eyes. "Would you consider tonight instead?"

Now, four months later, Julie slowed down her jog to a walk as she reached the curb at Central Park West. She'd left the apartment—and David Harpur, who was sleeping there—at shortly before six, dressed in her sweat suit and running shoes, and been jogging at a leisurely pace through the park ever since. Her morning run was about the only time she could be alone anymore, and she'd had a lot to think about in view of the fact that she and David had quarreled the night before.

David had just about lived in the apartment all summer long, from Monday through Friday, while his wife was in Amagansett. Sometimes, he'd go over in the middle of the afternoon, first telling his secretary that he wouldn't be available to anyone. Once in Julie's apartment, he'd put something soupy on the phonograph, often *Der Rosenkavalier,* then get a book down from a shelf and read himself to sleep in Julie's wingchair, where she would find him when she opened the door.

It was an incredibly close relationship because they didn't dare go out, after their first splurge at Lutèce. David simply couldn't risk being seen with her in any midtown restaurant, so at first they took cabs down to Chinatown or to Italian restaurants on Mulberry Street. One night, however, they ran into a lawyer who did work for Lily's family, and David was monumentally embarrassed until he realized that the other man wasn't with his wife, either. Still, it scared both of them sufficiently. From then on, Julie always cooked supper in the apartment.

But now that it was October, the house in Amagansett was closed and Lily Harpur was back in town. It meant that David could get away to see Julie only late in the afternoons—both of them would leave their offices early, make love hurriedly on empty stomachs, then David would have to rush over to the East Side—or on those occasions, such as the present one, when Lily was out of town for a few days.

After the wanton freedoms of the summer, Lily Harpur's presence in the city made for a certain strain. Sometimes David would start looking at his watch while Julie was still concluding her orgasm. Sometimes he would be out of the apartment five minutes after she came.

Even last night, when both of them should have been relaxed, things went badly. Julie had looked forward to it all week, and then David couldn't perform. It was the very first time it had happened.

So Julie concluded the worst, which was that despite what David had told her, he was still sleeping with Lily, and had in fact slept with her the night before.

"No, it isn't that," he said when she asked him. "Maybe I'm just beat."

Juile shook her head, denying that as a reason.

"Okay, so Lily and I had a fight last night before she left for Washington. I think she knows that I'm seeing someone."

"How? We've been careful."

"Who knows? Probably because I've been so happy."

His marriage, he explained, had reached the stage of resignation; neither he nor Lily expected anything of it anymore, not even much in the way of pleasantries. Since he'd been seeing Julie, however, David was aware that subtle changes were taking place in his disposition, and perhaps some of his kindnesses may have inadvertently been directed toward his wife.

"I suppose I haven't been as bearish lately as I used to be. So she's put two and two together. Or at least she thinks she has. But when she asked me point-blank, I said no."

Julie felt herself sinking.

"Oh, shit," she said. Then the tears came. A torrent of them.

David went to pieces when women cried. It was a cheap, melodramatic, un*gentle*manly thing to do, he said. It was what high school drop-outs who worked as waitresses at Howard Johnson's did. "What do you mean, anyway, *oh shit?*"

"Oh, shit, you're never going to leave her."

The truth of the matter was that they'd never really talked about it. They talked around it. David admitted that he no longer loved his wife, but that was not the same as hating her.

Julie had never seen her except in a photograph. She looked to be the sort of woman Julie sometimes passed at Bloomingdale's, where they charged two or three thousand dollars' worth of clothes in a half-hour shopping expedition, a big car waiting for them outside —illegally parked, but what difference did a twenty-five-dollar fine make?—with a blackamoor standing by the door.

"Look," Julie said once she'd recovered, "I know what you're going to say. You feel a sense of responsibility toward her. You've been through a lot together and she's the mother of your kids. You just can't tell her now that she's redundant and no longer needed. Right? Okay. I agree with you, David. I don't think we should hurt her. It's just . . . what the hell happens to me? Am I supposed to share you with Lily for the rest of my life to avoid hurting her goddamn aristocratic feelings?"

It wasn't as simple as that, David protested. "I know what *you're* going to say. You're going to say that it's my ego talking now, not my sense, and that I just can't stand the idea that Lily could function without me. But the truth of the matter is that if I leave her, Julie, I don't think she could start over. Do you see what I mean? I think it would just about wrap up her life.

She's forty-three, two years younger than I am, and when you leave a woman who's that old, their natural reaction is to become widows rather than divorcées."

A woman that old, Julie might have said but didn't, was only four years older than she was.

"I want to get her ready for it," he concluded.

Julie was astounded. "Get her ready?"

"Before we were married, Lily used to paint. She was pretty good, too. I'm trying to get her interested in it again, so that she'll have something to fall back on."

"You could always send her to the New School," Julie said in a smart-aleck sort of way.

"Pardon?"

Why was it that whenever people started feeling useless or coming apart at the seams they decided to enroll in night classes and become painters or potters or writers or composers? Could you put off a nervous breakdown by potting bowls and urns for all your friends?

"Well, that's just fine, David. You're going to stick a paint brush in Lily's hand and that's going to solve everything. She can paint her way out of her neuroses. But what am I supposed to do in the meantime?"

Julie had the uncomfortable feeling that she'd already had this conversation with someone. Who? Not Kate McCabe, who *was* going to the New School, so it must have been—group therapy! One night, one comment led to another, and before she knew it, she had blurted out most of the details of her affair with David. She'd grown sick of the seven tortured souls at group, each one trying to out-agonize the other, so when the opportunity arose for her to describe her own happiness, she let them have it, right between the eyes.

She concluded by saying that David would very shortly leave his wife.

Everyone in group looked at her doubtfully.

"I know the type," a woman named Ruth from Gramercy Park finally said. "They stay married to the same woman all their lives, but they run around with every girl who makes herself available. My husband was like that, the bastard."

"He's not that way," Julie protested feebly.

"You wait and see, honey."

It was inconceivable. Yet now David was hedging. He'd had the opportunity to confess everything to Lily, and instead he had chosen to protect her.

Still, somehow or other they'd managed to make love—possibly with more desperation than ever before—and for a little while afterwards, everything was the way it had been all summer long. Then Julie made the mistake of asking if David would be able to get over some time during the weekend, just for a few hours.

"We'll be out on the Island over the weekend," he'd replied. "A guy named Pete Vassall, who lives near us out there, is having a bash to celebrate a new book."

"But that's splendid!" Julie cried. "I know him. He used to freelance for us before he got so rich. I'll call him up and get an invitation, too." She turned toward David. "Is that all right?"

No, it wasn't all right. It very definitely, emphatically, was not all right.

"But, David, I didn't say I'd get *close* to her," Julie insisted. "I don't even have to meet her."

"Lily would know."

"There you *go* again! Protecting her!" Julie leapt out of bed. "Damn you all to hell, David! If you want to spend the weekend with that tired old cunt, then go ahead and do it, but, by God, this is the last time you've slept with me."

The result of which was that Julie slept—if it could be called that—on a blanket spread over the kitchen floor, while David tossed and turned all night in the loft bed. At five-thirty in the morning, she could stand it no longer, and that was when she pulled on her sweat suit hoping somehow that the poison from the night before would drain from her as she jogged in Central Park.

Now, as Julie made her way back into the building from the street, she could hear the seven-o'clock beep on WQXR. Two Mexican hairless dogs in the same apartment as the radio began to yap as she opened the door to the tiny elevator. As the elevator creaked to the top floor, she passed through ethnic and sociological smells: curry, chilies, tarragon, and grass.

Once in the apartment, Julie went directly to the kitchen and put water on for instant coffee. She stepped out of her sweat suit and running shoes and walked into the bedroom, then lay down next to David and began to stroke his hair.

"You're all sticky and wet," he said at last.

She ran her tongue over his forehead, his cheeks, then his lips. "We had a fight last night."

"I can't remember."

"There are some things we should never discuss."

David reached over for a cigarette, which meant that he was feeling tense and needed something in his hand to get him through the next few minutes.

"Like wars or politics," she said, and at once he relaxed. At the beginning of their affair, sometimes moments after making love they would talk about wars past (Vietnam: he was a hawk, she was a dove) and wars to come (Middle East: "But I'm more pro-Israel than you are," he'd once said, and she replied, "I hate war more than I love Israel"), and often they got into shouting matches that ended only when David crawled over on top of her again.

"I didn't mean that," she continued, "about wanting to go out to Pete Vassall's house. It isn't important. You were right; I just wanted to see your precious Lily squirm a little bit."

"You are so . . ." David couldn't help but smile, "combative. When you're out of bed. Always wanting to pick a fight." He laughed outright. "Out of bed, you're all piss and vinegar."

"And in bed? What am I like then?"

He pretended to ponder it. "All soft and fragile and vulnerable as hell."

Back at the beginning of the summer when they still went down to Mulberry Street to the Italian restaurants, David used to poke terrible fun at her for being so aggressive. If Julie wanted another roll or more butter, she would whistle through her teeth to attract the attention of the waiter. On the street, she would stop people who were littering and tell them to use the goddamn litterbaskets, please. Anyone at the other end of a leash from a dog defecating on the sidewalk got the tongue-lashing of a lifetime. Once Julie had even threatened to arrest a mild-mannered woman who had plucked a marigold from Battery Park. "That belongs to the *people!*" she'd roared at the woman.

"In bed," Julie said, "I don't have to prove anything. I don't have to be tough. I can believe anything I want to."

"In bed, what do you believe in, Julie?"

"In you," she answered.

So still another truce was called. They made love once again, this time fighting the clock. David had to be downtown by nine for a conference with people who would be talking about millions of dollars, and Tuesday was Julie's busiest day at the magazine. They should be having breakfast now, showering, dressing, then running out to the street separately to hail cabs, David first because he had farthest to go. But dollars were trivial and so were magazines.

Even Lily. It didn't make that much difference to Julie that Lily still held part of David's allegiance. By now, Julie knew husbands well enough to know that they rarely left their wives. They were too chivalrous, too weak, or too frightened. Wives left husbands.

"Look, David," Julie said once they'd finished, "I

65

want to tell you something. I guess this is the way it's going to have to be. I've been thinking about it. You've got a family and you don't want to give them up. I've got nothing but half of you, and you say that I'm selfish if I ask for more. Okay, I've decided I am. From now on, I'm going to be happy with whatever you give me. Whatever is left over is okay with me." She waited. "And if that's not crawling, I don't know what the hell is."

"I think you've hurt yourself," the man had said to Katherine McCabe when she entered the elevator in Neela's building at two o'clock on Tuesday morning.

She'd done just that, which proved incontestably Buddy's contention that she couldn't look after herself. After she'd left the movie in the Village, instead of being sensible and level-headed and getting a cab to Neela's place at Park and 64th, she had decided to walk.

Walk. The entire sixty blocks at twelve-thirty at night!

It was insane, she kept telling herself. Decent people simply did not use the streets of New York City after eight o'clock at night when only addicts, raving maniacs, and degenerates were at large. She expected every minute to be stabbed or pulled into a foyer and ravished. Yet after the first fifteen blocks, she was almost exhilarated by what she was doing, it was so absurd. She felt impervious to muggers and rapists. If anyone attempted to do her harm, she would pummel him with her overnight bag, kick at his gonads—wasn't a man tenderest there?—and yell her head off. She just *dared* anyone to make her more miserable than she already was.

Yet by the time she reached the Fifties, the novelty had begun to wear off and fatigue had set in. Added to that, she was now aware that she'd left her little mink hat—deliberately?—at the movie and her head was cold. She hurried now, no longer interested in shop windows or faces or architecture, and as she prepared to cross Fifth Avenue at 57th Street, she was careless and didn't wait for the light. Midway across, a gypsy cab materialized out of nowhere, bearing down on her, and she had to run for the far curb. Almost there, her heel caught in a manhole cover and down she went on the pavement, holding out her hands at the last minute to soften the landing. Even before she picked herself up, she knew that her hand was cut and bleeding, the shards of a broken Pepsi bottle—whose "generation" Kate had only this evening eschewed—glaring at her in the gutter.

Kate was made giddy by the sight of blood. In high school, she had fainted dead away during a Highway Department movie on automobile accidents and had to be carried to the principal's office. Now she sat on the pavement—several people across the street looked at her, but no one came to her aid—wrapped a handkerchief around her hand, gathered up her purse, overnight bag, and scholar's notebook, and stood up. Good Lord, how much farther did she have to walk? There wasn't a cab in sight except for the tail lights of the speeding gypsy cab which had almost run her over. Fifty-seven from sixty-four was what? Seven. And two wide blocks to the east.

Thank God she had the keys to Neela's apartment. In her present condition—bleeding, dirty-legged, tousle-haired—she doubted that the doorman would let her in otherwise. But as soon as she explained who she was, he said, "Oh, yes, Mrs. Fitzgerald said we were to expect you." Then he directed her to the elevator and asked her to wait momentarily while he opened the door of a taxi which had just pulled up in front of the canopy.

Kate was vaguely aware of watching a man in black-tie enter the lobby and make his way to the elevator. Before he reached it, however, she closed her eyes completely, hoping to make herself less conspicuous, but succeeding in doing just the opposite.

That was when he said, "I think you've hurt yourself."

Except for the exchange with the doorman, these were the first civil words directed at her since she'd left Neela at Bloomingdale's. Far from being the noisest city in the world, it seemed to Kate that New York was the most silent: millions of people walking around, never speaking to anyone.

She explained what had happened, aware that her voice was almost hysterical, then said, "When did they start breaking bottles on Fifth Avenue?"—the "they" a pronoun for all the enemies of nice and decent people.

"Better let me have a look," he said. When she was obviously reluctant, he continued, "You'll be relieved to learn that I'm not an ax-murderer. I live here. I also happen to be a physician."

The elevator had stopped at his floor, and he held the door open with his back while he removed the blood-soaked handkerchief from Kate's hand and looked at the cut. "You have glass in there, I'll bet you anything."

"I sort of figured."

"Also a deal of plain old New York dirt. I can clean it up for you if you like."

Kate was terrified. Not so much about her hand as being in an elevator at two in the morning with a man who, if she understood correctly, was inviting her into his apartment.

Oh, that-was-quite-all-right, she said breathlessly. She would see a doctor when she got home tomorrow.

"I'm really very harmless." This time he smiled.

"My name's Ben Purdom." Then, "You must be new in the building. I haven't seen you around before."

Kate explained that she was a houseguest of the Fitzgeralds on the fourteenth floor, just for the night. The Quentin Fitzgeralds. Did he know them?

"Is he the Hollywood character?"

Kate supposed that he was.

"Someone in the building drives a red Rolls convertible, and I've heard he has something to do with making movies."

Neela had once told Kate that the insurance premiums for Quentin's car each year came to more than what most people paid for a car itself. It seemed to Kate immoral that anyone should drive a car so expensive.

"As a rule," Ben Purdom continued, "I'd suggest that you turn down invitations to strangers' apartments in New York, but the truth of the matter is that I'm probably too tired to be dangerous. I've been at the hospital since seven this morning, then went directly from the hospital to a dinner party, and I've been trying to get away from the damned thing since midnight. My idea of hell is spending four hours at a party on Sutton Place South."

Kate was about to say that after fifteen years in the country, a party on Sutton Place South was her idea of heaven, but she thought better of it. In fact, she couldn't think of anything to say. She was suddenly aware that the silence was overwhelming.

"Do you have a name?" he asked. "Or should I think of you as Mr. Fitzgerald's houseguest?"

"Mrs.," she said by way of correcting him. Without really intending to, she found herself in a hallway where he opened a door and then she followed him as he led her into a long living room, leaning over to flick on lights at table after table. The largest Oriental rug Kate had ever seen covered the floor, one wall was given over to books in sumptuous leather bindings, and the furniture was either red leather or gold velvet. Kate could almost predict what Buddy would say about such a room and the kind of man who lived in it. To his way of thinking, any man who didn't sit in a vinyl-covered Barca-lounger was a faggot.

"I love the room," she said, standing at the entrance and looking in. "It's so . . . I don't know, masculine."

"It ought to be. My wife did it." He added as he disappeared down a hallway to turn on additional lights, "Ex-wife. Come with me. You still didn't tell me your name."

"Kate," she began, and then a madness overcame her. "Ferguson," she concluded.

"All right, Kate Ferguson. Let's take a look at that nasty cut now."

Kate didn't know what had made her say it, yet now that she had annihilated Buddy McCabe—and the last fifteen years of her life—she felt free and unbound.

"Whom are you running away from?" he said, waiting for her by the bathroom door.

"Did I say I was?"

"No, but women who fall down on Fifth Avenue all by themselves at two in the morning are generally running away from someone." Then, as naturally as if he'd known her all his life, "Who?"

"Myself, I suppose."

Until now, she'd thought it was Buddy McCabe she was trying to get away from, but the minute he asked the question, she knew that Buddy was only part of it. It was the uselessness, the triviality of her life that she hated, and Buddy was her enemy only because he'd helped make her that way.

"I just lied to you," Kate said, and was surprised by her own candor. "I just said my name is Kate Ferguson."

"And it's actually Kate McCabe."

"How did you know that?"

"That's what it says on your overnight bag. I read it coming up in the elevator."

"Then why didn't you object when I lied to you?"

He pondered it. "Because I thought, if I was right about you, you'd probably tell me the truth yourself." He grinned now. "Which, as you can see, is just what you've done. Come on in. We'll clean up that cut now and see if we can find anything spectacular down there."

He had a very gentle touch. He held her hand under the spigot till the blood had washed away, then swabbed the wound with alcohol from the medicine cabinet. He bent his head close to it, then with a pair of tweezers fresh from the alcohol he reached in and extracted a sliver of glass a quarter inch long. Kate had made up her mind that she would not say ouch even if he severed an artery. She sat on the closed lid of the toilet seat and watched his profile as he worked.

It was a good, lived-in sort of face, but nothing remarkable. His hair, which was light brown, was thinning on top, and he had what was left of a suntan. Kate was notoriously bad at guessing people's ages, but it seemed to her that he might be five to ten years younger than she was.

She watched with interest as he bandaged the cut—it would heal without stitching—then remarked, "Now you look like a proper victim. Welcome to New York, mecca and fatherland, Victim capital of the world."

When he looked up into her face, he saw that she was crying. "My God, I'm sorry. I didn't mean to hurt you."

It wasn't that.

Kate didn't know precisely what it was. It was being in New York, in the first place, because she didn't know where else to be. It was trying idiotically to go back to school when she knew damned well that she had the attention span of a month-old beagle puppy. It was spending four hours at an abominable movie, then

71

walking sixty blocks home because she couldn't bear the thought of being alone in Neela's apartment.

It was . . . she didn't know what it was.

"I guess I'm exhausted," she said at last, wiping her cheeks with her fists. "And also confused."

He broke into a smile. "Don't think that makes you anything special. I don't know anyone in New York who isn't. Come on into the living room and I'll fix you a drink, then we can feel sorry for each other. But if you think you've cornered the market on confusion, forget it, Kate McCabe."

He was, he explained to her, on the teaching staff at Columbia-Presbyterian Hospital, and also had a private practice that brought in twice the money and twice the problems. He was a neurosurgeon and people came from all over the world to see him. "Some of them wish they hadn't," he added. "Those who survive pay through the nose, if it hasn't dropped off by then. I am one helluva surgeon. If you ever have a brain tumor, I'm the guy to see."

He'd been married during his first year of med school, he said, to a girl he'd dated all through college, which happened to be Northwestern. She worked as a secretary while he finished school, interned, then served as a resident at Mt. Sinai in New York. She knew twenty different ways of making spaghetti, which was often all they could afford. As soon as he finished his residence, at the tail end of the Vietnam War, he was drafted and sent to Cambodia, where his wife went, too, and possibly because she hadn't anything else to do, she had a baby.

"Joanne hated it over there," he said about his wife, "the U.S. Army, the country we were in, and the people she was living with. A lot of the hatred finally rubbed off on me. The way she figured it was that she had sacrificed and gone without things while I was in med school, and now she was ready for the country club. Instead, she found herself in a jungle."

When he was mustered out, his wife wanted him to accept an offer at a clinic near Santa Barbara, but by then Ben Purdom was truly hooked on poor people. "Cambodia was really an eye-opener for me. My idea of being poor had always been eating spaghetti a couple times a week, but that's living it up in contrast to how some people have it. So when I got the offer at Columbia-Presbyterian, I knew I could also put some time in at a free-clinic in the Bronx, and I persuaded Joanne to come with me and give it a try for one year. A year, to the *day*, later, she left me."

He'd thought that all the money coming in might be able to hold the marriage together, but it wasn't half enough. "She really got very soured before it was over. The first half of our married life we had no money. And the second half, I was too busy and was never around. So she said I could either give up my free-clinic work or she would leave me, and I said that I was sorry, but that I had a lot of appointments for the following day. End of marriage. Can I do something to your drink?"

Kate wasn't drinking. She was listening. Apart from the contradictions—why was someone who worked part time at a free-clinic in the Bronx living on Park Avenue if he loved poverty so much?—it seemed to Kate such an incredibly admirable way to live one's life. Possibly even the path toward salvation.

"Why the attraction?" she asked at last. "For Cambodians and for people living in the Bronx."

Ben Purdom shrugged his broad shoulders. "Guilt, no doubt. Also I happen to think that in time self-interest corrodes. In a marriage, a friendship, or a profession. It's a peculiar sort of thing, but I don't think people can do without service. Unless we feel useful—and it has to involve more than merely making money—there's really no reason to stay alive."

That was what Kate herself had been trying to say. She lacked utility, both as a wife and as a mother. Buddy could exist quite nicely without her, though he would be annoyed by the inconveniences at first. As for the children, they'd depended on her when they were babies, but now they were more than content with the kind of mothering they got from CBS.

"We've all become so impossibly decadent," Ben continued. "I suppose I go to the South Bronx in order to cleanse myself. Life is so elemental there. People are struggling so hard just to stay alive that they don't have time for decadence."

The South Bronx? Wasn't that the most horrendous of all New York ghettos, and the most perilous?

"Sure. I've been mugged three times in the last year."

Kate was astounded. It was so contrary to reason. He was there in order to help the people. Why in the world did they set upon him?

"I didn't say I was mugged by people I treat at the clinic. It was outside on the street. And why not? I'm dressed in a nice suit, walking toward a nice car, and I look comparatively prosperous. So I lose my wallet one more time. Joanne could never understand, either. But hopelessness is really worse than cancer. If you have no hope—if you're the wrong color, if you're broke, if you're in need of a fix—there's no one to be indebted to. It makes wild men of us all."

"Where I live," Kate began tentatively, "we're all so insulated from that. Then when we hear about a twelve-year-old in the slums dying from an overdose of heroin, it's incomprehensible to us."

"Bodies and minds are abused as much, if not more, on Sutton Place South as they are in the South Bronx. Pot gets passed around after dinner and cocaine is snorted by beautiful women in five-hundred-dollar dresses. But people who live on Sutton Place and have habits don't have to mug people in order to pay for them. They pass the price along. Lawyers charge more, businessmen cheat more, entertainers get $200,000 a week at Las Vegas hotels. Muggers don't offend me, but those other worms do."

Despite the seriousness of what he was saying, Kate couldn't resist a smile. "And in the meantime you sit in this lavish apartment waiting for the revolution."

"No, in the meantime I sit in this lavish apartment waiting for the lease to run out. I've got four months to go. I'm buying a tiny house up near Nyack, on the Hudson. It's close enough to commute."

Somewhere, a clock struck three. Except while child-bearing and child-rearing, Kate couldn't recall having been up so late since the high school Junior Prom. She would have to get up from the sofa at once, she told herself, and make her way to Neela's apartment. She placed her drink on the coffee table in front of her, but that was the extent of her effort.

"So why are you in this maniacal city when you should be home in bed in New Jersey?" he asked.

Kate tried to explain what had happened outside the New School. Had she been telling it to Buddy, she would have told it differently, omitting the parts of the story that made her look like a fool. But to Ben Purdom she told the truth.

"I just stood across the street, watching the kids go in, and I couldn't move. I saw myself the way I was twenty years ago, and the way I am now, and I just couldn't understand what had happened. I never intended for things to turn out the way they have."

"And you don't think that anything can make a difference in your life anymore?"

"I didn't say that. All I said was that the New School wasn't going to make the difference." She looked at him half antagonistically, as if she'd decided to offend him—to repay the world for having treated her so shabbily—then excuse herself and go up to Neela's apartment. "I'm an utterly superfluous thirty-nine-year-old woman, so mixed up that I wasn't even able to run away from home with any success." Suddenly she stood up. "I really better go now before you ask me to leave."

He stood also. "I was going to ask you to stay. What would you say if I told you I needed you even more than you need me?"

Needed her? Someone needed Kate McCabe?

"I've been standing in front of the New School for the last year and a half," he said to her now. "Do you understand what I'm saying?" Then: "Will you stay?"

"Dear God," she heard herself answering, "yes."

Ben Purdom was only the third man who had ever made love to Kate, and she accepted it with the abandon of a woman who was starving. With Buddy McCabe, sex was something one engaged in on Saturday night for the preservation of health—his, not hers. It took him two minutes to prepare for penetration and another two minutes to polish it off. A few seconds later, he'd roll off and for the next hour and a half, or however long it would take her to get to sleep, Kate would look at the ceiling, eyes wide open, and listen to the sounds of cars passing on the street.

But Ben Purdom awakened something in her, one well-nigh unbearable sensation after another, until in the end Kate was aware that she was wailing softly.

Kate wanted to stay in his bed forever. If this were possible, she would require nothing else of God. In a kind of delirium, she fell off to sleep, holding Ben's penis in her hand, and when twenty or thirty minutes later she woke up, Ben was bent over her, looking into her face.

"You're beautiful, Kate."

"I feel beautiful." Everywhere Ben had touched her she felt beautiful. "I wish I could stay here forever."

"Then do it."

Suddenly Kate's hand was full again and Ben was loving her.

If only Buddy McCabe, snoring on his Simmons' Beauty-rest, could see her now. He often poked fun at the changes he saw or fancied he saw in her body. Her breasts sagged more now than they did when she was a young girl, and after he discovered what the condition was called, sometimes as soon as he opened the kitchen door and walked into the house, he'd say, "So how's the old Cooper's droop?"

It didn't matter if Kate reminded him that she was younger than Elizabeth Taylor, and no one went around asking *her* how her old Cooper's droop was. To Buddy's way of thinking, there was something preposterous about a woman's body anyway.

Kate and Ben woke up once more shortly after five o'clock, and his first words were, "What are you going to do now?" Kate knew immediately what he meant.

She would have to make some sort of decision. Earlier in the evening, as she walked north from the Village, she had decided that she would tell Buddy that her New School class had been canceled. Too few people had registered, she was going to tell him, so she would get her money back.

But now she knew that she wouldn't be able to tell him that.

"I was supposed to have classes on Monday and Wednesday nights," she said to Ben Purdom. "Could I see you on those nights?"

It went without saying. But he'd meant more than that. He repeated what he'd meant to say: "What are you going to *do*?"

She was unsure of herself. "That I haven't decided yet."

"But you've learned one thing, haven't you?" Then, persisting, "What have you learned?"

"That I can still love someone."

Okay, Ben would leave it at that for the time being.

What was important, he said, was that Kate knew now that she wasn't dead, burned out at the center. "And once you admit that," he continued, "you can't go back to living the way you used to."

"I know."

"Then leave him."

It would take time, she said.

"No, it doesn't. It takes about three seconds. All you have to say is 'I'm leaving you.' "

"After fifteen years, it isn't that easy."

"After fifteen years, most of them loveless, it should be very, very easy."

Well, why not? It was insane, of course, to think she should ask Buddy for a divorce just because she'd spent three and a half hours in bed with another man. That wasn't the issue. The issue was that she was happy now, and that she wasn't happy with Buddy. Whether or not she could still love Ben Purdom three weeks from now wasn't as important as being able to admit that she hadn't loved Buddy for at least half of the last fifteen years.

"You see," Ben Purdom was saying to her now, "we can't end our lives just because we've suffered a setback or two. Do you want to know something? When I saw you standing in the elevator with that bloody handkerchief around your hand, the first thing I thought was, This woman is going to start screaming any minute. It wasn't your hand. It was something in your face. A terrible sadness." He stroked it with his fingers. "And now it's gone."

He was right. The sadness *was* gone.

When the alarm clock roused them at six fifteen, Kate hurt all over, both from fatigue and from having been caressed. Her head ached from the lack of sleep, and she hoped that Ben wouldn't look at her till she did something to herself. It had never occurred to her before that doctors got up at such an ungodly hour, but Ben explained that doctors, like dairy farmers, did most of their important work early in the morning. Bodies were strongest in the mornings, he said, after restful sleep, and as a consequence he had surgery scheduled from eight o'clock on.

"How can you do it after you've had so little sleep?"

"A lot of caffeine and twice as much will power. In the O.R. you can't make the same mistake twice. As soon as I walk into the hospital, I'm wide awake." He slid out of bed. "Look, I'll get breakfast started while you shower and everything, okay?"

It was a kindness. No, it was a double kindness. For one thing, he was allowing her to use the bathroom before he did, and for another he was offering to fix her breakfast. Buddy never had. He didn't know *how*. Once, when she was ill, she'd asked him to put the coffee on, and he'd placed both the coffee and the water at the bottom of the pot. "What do you think the little device with the holes in it is for?" she'd asked him, and he had replied that he hadn't noticed it.

Kate had expected her face to look ravaged, but it glowed with something that hadn't been there in a long time. Ben Purdom had told her that she looked beautiful, and she believed him. Even now as she watched herself in the mirror, she did. For the last half dozen years, she had felt dumpy, and as a result she had looked dumpy. Was it unreasonable, now that she was feeling beautiful, that she should also look that way?

Ben would leave for the hospital at seven fifteen, he told her. She could stay in the apartment as long as she wanted. Forever, if she liked.

"There's a train at ten," she said.

What time could she be in on Wednesday?

"As early as five-thirty," she replied. She would be staying at Julie Silverman's apartment on the West Side, she added.

"Don't stay there. Stay here."

But what if something came up at home and Buddy tried to reach her?

"This Julie What's-her-name is a New Yorker, isn't she? Well, New York women are very savvy. They're not like suburban women. Tell her what's going on. Be frank. Also tell your friend upstairs. Mrs. Fitzgerald. She'll understand. Chances are, she's deceiving her husband."

"Neela? She's devoted to Quentin."

"Devotion in New York is different from devotion anywhere else in the world. It is a different style of devotion. Tell both of them that you'll be staying here, but that you'd like to use their telephones. Then if there's an emergency at home and your husband calls you there, they'll say you're not back from class, or some such thing. Then they telephone you here, and you can call your husband and say that you just got in. Okay?" He paused. "That is, if you want to keep him in the dark until you're absolutely sure of what you're doing."

Kate was awed by it all. "You'll never believe it, but when I was growing up, everyone thought I was a prude. At least Neela and Julie Silverman did. My mother wouldn't even let me go out for cheerleading because she said it was too bold, and I cried for a week. And now look what I'm doing."

Kate's mother had never been able to look her squarely in the eyes since the summer after graduation when she'd brought Kate to the retired school nurse for the abortion. Once, years later, when Kate had tried to talk about it, her mother had turned away, saying, "Kate, I don't want ever again to discuss our tragedy, if you please."

Our tragedy. Her mother's tragedy and her father's, had he been told, but not Kate's. Kate had merely been the bearer of dirt which had resulted in tragedy.

And what would she say now, Kate's mother, were she to see her daughter in the arms of a man who wasn't her husband? Would she understand it for what it was or would she misinterpret that, too? Would it be still another tragedy or would she see it as "our happiness"?

"I never thought I could be so happy," Kate said to Ben Purdom. "I hope it never ends."

From Grand Central, Kate tried to telephone Julie Silverman at her office, but she wasn't in yet, so Kate resolved to call her later in the day to tell her that she wouldn't be staying overnight at her place on Wednesday after all. As for Neela, if she was back from wherever she'd been—Boston, was it?—possibly Kate could get in early on Wednesday and have a drink with her, explain what was going on, then ask her to aid and abet.

Kate slept through most of the train ride home and was truly startled when she heard the conductor announce the Junction. She quickly picked up her things, dashed down the aisle, and onto the platform. Buddy's Hornet was parked just where she'd left it, but locked now, which meant that he had driven by the night before to check it—how *like* him to tuck in his cars but neglect his wife. On the steering wheel, he'd left a note that said, "Continuing education begins at home. Next time, how about locking up?"

A scolding, as if she were a child.

As soon as she got home, she took a nap for three hours, then showered once more and changed into comfortable clothes. She was in the kitchen, poking around the refrigerator—Mrs. Ellman had cleaned it damn her—to see what was available for supper when she heard Dutchie at the back door, then watched as he made a beeline through the kitchen toward the first-floor lavatory.

"You home already?" he said.

It was not designed to make Kate feel particularly welcome, and ten minutes later Suzie ambled in, looked around absently, then asked where Mrs. Mellman was.

81

"Ellman," Kate replied crossly, peeved that the woman had already won the children's affection.

More cheerfully, she added, "Mrs. Ellman will be coming back tomorrow." What had the woman fixed for supper the night before? she asked.

"Chicken Keefe," Suzie said, Irishing it.

"Chicken Kiev?" Good God, Kate had instructed Mrs. Ellman simply to drop the chicken breasts in Shake 'n Bake, but apparently she'd gone to the trouble to debone them, then had probably used all the butter in the refrigerator.

"Squirted everywheres when you bit it," Dutchie volunteered, coming into the kitchen, zipping up his fly.

"Well, she'll be back tomorrow."

"Neat," Dutchie said, then the two of them flung themselves onto the floor of the family room—what a misnomer that was—turned the TV set on to full volume, and Kate was alone again.

She probably should have stopped at the market, but she hadn't felt domestic somehow, or she was trying to put it off. Now she had to improvise for supper. No matter what she prepared, at least one person in the household would hate it. If she had pork chops, Suzie wouldn't eat them because once she'd watched a man carry an eviscerated pig on his back into the butcher shop. If she had lamb chops, Dutchie would say that they made him sick. If she had veal, Buddy would make faces while he bravely stuffed it into his mouth. About the only thing that met with more or less universal appeal was Swiss steak, so she force-thawed a large round steak now, then set it to simmering in tomato sauce in the oven.

She heard the VW in the driveway at shortly after six, and all the nerve ends in her body became alert. Would Buddy see a difference in her at once and know what had happened? Could men tell when their wives had deceived them, just as high school boys back in the

Fifties used to say they could tell if a girl was cherry or not simply by the way she walked?

"That goddamn car," he shouted the minute he walked into the kitchen. "You know what I paid those bastards at the garage? Forty-eight dollars, and it still runs like a truck." He yanked at the buttons of his coat. "I don't see why Volkswagen has such a hot-shot reputation. If you ask me, they've been making the same goddamn model for thirty years, and it's as lousy today as it was the day it first came out."

He threw his topcoat over the back of a fake Hitchcock chair, though Kate had told him a hundred times that if he didn't hang it up, she would only have to do it for him.

"I had to stay after school and listen to Old Fatass lecture everyone about how we're supposed to be teaching the whole boy. We are *not* supposed to be teaching them esoteric figures from eighteenth-century literature. That was a dig at *me,* Kate! No kid in his right mind wants to go to a private school anymore, so Old Fatass has to accept kids who can't adapt anywhere else. Then he expects the staff to coddle them. Well, nuts to him. The only thing those kids know how to do is break wind in class."

Buddy was in a rage. It seemed to Kate that teaching children must be the most lacerating profession in the world. Two or three times a week, Buddy would come into the house so agitated by something that had happened that he threatened to quit.

"You know what I'd like to do?" he said now. "I'd like to tell Old Fatass to take his job and stuff it."

Having got it out of his system for a few more days, Buddy added, "So how was school?"

School was fine, Kate replied. She thought it was going to be interesting.

"What's for supper?"

Without waiting for an answer, he picked up the evening newspaper and began to walk toward the stairs. Kate knew that he would sit on the john for the next twenty minutes, ruminating on world events.

Well, she was home again. No one had even asked her why she had a bandage on her hand. She could have stood in the kitchen with a severed leg and all Buddy would have said, after first complaining about the general tone of modern life, was, "What's for supper?"

◆

The doorman had told Neela that Mrs. McCabe spent Monday night in the apartment, but Neela looked all over and couldn't find a trace. In the end, she asked the day maid to change the sheets everywhere, including the convertible in the study. Upon completing this task, the woman reported, "She ain't been nowheres, Mizz Fizz-gerald."

Well, Kate was like that. Infinitely apologetic. An enemy of life. She had probably settled down on the floor for the night rather than soiling Neela's satin sheets.

Once when they were very young in West Mystic, Ohio, they'd been sitting on Kate's front porch and out of natural curiosity, Neela had turned to her and asked, "Kate, do you ever poop?"—because Kate never seemed to *have* to. Kate had burst into tears, run upstairs to her bedroom, and locked the door.

It had always seemed to Neela that Kate's unreality, or absence of earthiness, had repelled boys. No one was more surprised than Neela when Kate surrendered herself to Rex Glotzbecker in high school, then later began to go steady with Buddy McCabe. Buddy, of course, had hinted that one thing he liked about Kate was her innocence, and though Neela could have wised him up about Rex, she hadn't, just as she'd never told Kate that she and Buddy had slept together.

It was all the more surprising, then, when Kate telephoned from New Jersey on Wednesday morning and said that she hadn't spent the night in the apartment, but thanks anyway. There was something she'd like to talk about, however, so could Neela possibly meet her at the Plaza at about five-thirty for a drink?

"The Plaza?" Neela had said. "Today?"

"Julie was the one who suggested it. I'm meeting her there. The Oak Room."

Neela should have known. Julie Silverman never went into a bar unless she could integrate it. She'd even got her picture in the *New York Post* when she was the first woman ever to be served a drink at McSorley's in the East Village. The Oak Room, until recently, had been an all-male preserve, and Julie could be feisty and rude, would ask to be served Budweiser beer in the *bottle,* and if anyone put up a fuss she'd threaten to send him to jail.

"If you didn't sleep in the apartment, where did you sleep?" Neela couldn't resist asking.

That was one of the things Kate wanted to talk about.

Well, Neela would try to be there. She would be running here and there all afternoon, doing various little things, she said—"I am on a neighborhood antipollution watch, and I'll be out on patrol till three"—but there was no reason why she couldn't get away. Quentin had volunteered her services on the Dirt Squad, as he called it, saying at the time that it would be good for her to do something. All she had to do was keep her eyes glued on the sky, and whenever she saw smoke she was to report it.

"If we ever have another war, I'll make one hell of an air-raid warden," she said about her duties. In fact, she saw the job as one more manifestation of her expendability. While Quentin did important things, she was expected to occupy herself by looking at the sky.

After she spoke with Kate, she saw the children before they were taken to school. Despite her long friendship with Kate, Neela was not a woman's woman, but a man's woman, and often she felt uncomfortable even with the two girls. She saw them as rivals for Quentin's affection—it was cruelly ironic that her two children would also be Daddy's girls—and they, to punish her, worshipped their father, quite possibly because they saw so little of him, and when they did, he was always with glamorous people or doing glamorous things.

"When is Daddy coming back from Hollywood?" Deirdre had asked. Both she and her sister Ronan were envied by their classmates at school because they had once met Paul Newman.

"Daddy doesn't know yet," Neela told them.

Or, to be more truthful, if Daddy knew, he wasn't telling Neela, because she had called him at the Beverly Wilshire the first thing in the morning and was told that he'd already checked out. Yet Quent had said that he wouldn't be back till Thursday, tomorrow. So just to be on the safe side—she didn't want the girls to know that he didn't tell her things, or even lied to her—she left it in doubt.

For all his perfidy, Quentin still provided ballast for Neela's life. By mutual consent they rarely slept together anymore, but Neela genuinely enjoyed his company, when he allowed her to share it. He was tender, sweet, and affectionate. He was stronger than she was, supremely confident of himself, and most of all he was what Neela never was: he was busy. He was finishing scripts, he was making deals with agents, he was having lunch with actors, he was seeing this director or that producer. His conversation was laced with names of the famous, whether he knew them or not. He spoke of other people's money, often in the heady region of the millions, as if it were his God-given right to spend it.

It was a very modern marriage in that both Neela and Quentin agreed never to discuss each other's private lives.

"Private life?" Neela had said, years ago, when he first told her there were areas of his life where he didn't want her treading, and he would provide her with the same courtesy. "But if you're married, I didn't think anything was supposed to be private."

"You know what I mean," he answered, even then refusing to discuss it.

Of course, she did. And for fifteen years, only once or twice did she ever criticize him. "It is your father all over again," her analyst told her. "You and Quentin are father and daughter; you're not husband and wife. But he doesn't truly share himself, any more than your father did when he left you at the movies, then went on to visit his girlfriend."

Yes and no, Neela had replied. It was the same, and yet it wasn't the same.

"My father," Neela began, "did not . . ." She stopped, unable to betray Quentin this way, or to humiliate herself.

"Did not . . . ?" he tried to help her.

Did not swing both ways, she meant to say, but could not tell anyone, certainly not an analyst who would only accuse her of having married Quentin in the first place because she knew he would deny her sexuality.

Quentin had been true to his word and did, in fact, keep that part of his life private. If Neela had expected to find a pack of screaming queens around him, she was mistaken. For one thing, all his friends were celebrities, first and foremost singers or actors or composers or directors or screenwriters. Except for being smarter than most men, better looking, and more important, they were indistinguishable from any other men she might meet at chic New York parties. Some of them were so militantly male that Neela was shocked half out of her head to discover that they also played a role in Quentin's other life.

One of Quent's best friends was a former pro football player named Moe Rainey, who had a well-publicized reputation as a ladykiller. When he appeared at parties, he was always accompanied by at least two spectacularly beautiful girls, one of whom was living with him. Yet once Neela had overheard Quent telephone Moe at his East Side apartment.

"Look, Moe," he said, "I'm getting a party together. You interested?"

Moe, one hundred and ninety-five pounds of man, most of it dumb, must have asked Quentin who else was invited, because Quent replied, "Two chickens just in from Colorado. High school football types. They about flipped when I told them I might be able to introduce them to you."

Neela's mind reeled. "Christ," she said to her husband after he'd hung up, "Moe *Rainey?*"

"Neela," he began very patiently, "let me tell you something. If you're very good at something—it doesn't matter what—you don't have to take shit from anyone. You live life the way you want to. Don't you understand that yet? The only people who are afraid of what the world's going to think of them are the $10,-000-a-year salesmen who perform cunnilingus on their wives once a week and don't want the neighbors to know. If you're a big deal, you tell the world to go fuck itself."

"Like you and Moe do."

"Like Moe and I do."

Yet to his credit, Quentin had never once disgraced Neela. Perhaps because he traveled in a circle which permitted him to meet a great many new people, she never had to undergo the horror of public exposure after an arrest on a morals charge. Once after she'd read that an important government official, married and a father, had been arrested in a YMCA shower room, she handed the newspaper to her husband and said, "Comment?"

He read it. "What kind of comment would you like to hear?"

"What if it ever happened to you or Moe Rainey?"

"Moe can fight his way out of almost any kind of trouble he gets into, and I can buy my way."

"Even at gunpoint in a YMCA shower room?"

"But don't you see, Neela? I would never be there. And neither would Moe."

Yes, Quentin was very good that way. He would never disgrace her publicly.

Privately was another matter.

Because when Quentin pulled into the apartment shortly after noon on Wednesday, a day before he was due, he introduced Neela to a young Californian named Amos Guard and said that he would be staying at the apartment for a few weeks. Neela took one look at him and thought, Who is going to sleep with whom?

"We're going to make him another Robert Redford, Irv and I are," Quent said. Then, "We can put him up here, can't we? No one else is staying with us."

Certainly they could put up another Robert Redford. How could anyone not? Amos Guard couldn't have been more than nineteen, and he was using his age for all it was worth. He smiled boyishly at Neela, shook her hand when she offered it, and said, "Thanks, ma'am. I'm obliged."

My God, not only were they still turning out stunning-looking youths on the West Coast, but they were polite, too. It was such a novelty to hear civility again. As for comparisons, Neela was inclined to think he looked more like James Dean than Robert Redford, who, possibly because of close association with Paul Newman, was beginning to look rather Jewish in his middle age. There was a rural, farm-boy quality about Amos Guard which Neela found refreshing.

"I'm from Idaho," he said to her when she asked.

"And you grew potatoes?"

Well, not exactly. His father worked at a nuclear installation but they ranched part time.

"Isn't that hell?" Neela asked Quent. "You think you're talking to some sort of Huck Finn, and then you find out that his father works at a nuclear installation."

"Actually, Amos was at Stanford for a year," Quent explained, removing the last of the cowboy aura. "Then he dropped out, went down to L.A. to bum around, and that's where Irv and I met him." Then, "What room do you want to put him in?"

Perhaps sensing that there was something Neela wanted to say to Quentin Fitzgerald, the boy asked if he could use the bathroom.

After he'd left, Neela said, "Okay, so who wants another Robert Redford? Except you, maybe."

What the hell was she talking about? What was wrong with her now?

"What's wrong with me now," Neela said, rising to the argument, "is that you went out to the Coast with some whore named Jill and you came back with some stud named Amos. Quentin, you are going too *fast* for me."

Did she mean Jill Montgomery? If so, forget it. "Jill is Irving's new secretary. She went out to the Coast to do some work for us."

"Some screwing for you, you mean."

"Okay, okay. That's Irving's business, not yours. If you had to live with that hatchet-faced bitch he's married to, you'd cheat too."

Neela caught her breath, then said, "Am I also a hatchet-faced bitch?"

"What the hell is *wrong* with you? Why, all of a sudden, are you so fucking mad?"

Neela was so exasperated she could scarcely speak.

"Why am I so mad? I am so *mad,* Quentin, because you've been gone since last Saturday and you haven't even called to see if I'm alive or if the kids are all right."

"Neela, can I be honest with you?" He wrapped his arms around her and waited till her head was on his shoulder. "I *knew* you were alive. I called on Monday night and talked to Emily and the kids. They said you were in Boston. Okay, so you were in Boston. Did I complain? You didn't tell *me* you were going to Boston. Did I get excited? Did I rant and rave? Hell, no. You can take care of yourself, Neela. I *know* that."

Neela shook her head, even while it was on his shoulder. "No, I can't. You have no idea, Quent."

With one hand, he lifted her head till he could look into her face. "Tell me what happened."

"I was just lonely. I've never felt so lonely before."

"But the kids were here."

"No, it was a different kind of loneliness. I needed something else. I needed you. Then when I found you went out to the Coast with someone named Jill Montgomery, I guess I went to pieces."

"You went to Boston."

"No. Montreal."

"They said Boston."

"That's what I told them. But I went to Montreal."

"By yourself?"

"With someone."

He waited, then said, "But it didn't work out."

"I went with Robert Pino. Do you remember him?"

Quentin's expression clearly indicated that he did. "A scumbag," he said.

"You used to say he was a genius. Like Roman Polanski."

"He was a genius for about a month, then it was over."

Neela couldn't contain herself. "And how long is your Little Mr. Robert Redford, Junior, going to be a genius? For two or three weeks?" Not really expecting any answer, she continued, "Are you sleeping with him?"

Impatiently, he replied, "Amos is an actor. He's slept—at last count, he tells me—with about three hundred and twenty people. It's in the blood. He can't help it. All you have to do is look at him the right way, and his dick goes up. He's dumb, but he has class, and believe me, he can act. Pants on or pants off."

"You didn't answer my question. Have you slept with him?"

He was angry now. "Get off it, Neela. Of course I have. I'd be a goddamn fool not to see what he's like before he's famous. Irving and I have big plans for him. Don't spoil things. I'd also appreciate it if you could get the knife out of my back right now. Amos and I have an appointment in about twenty minutes with a guy who has a lot of money and is interested in *Wiser, Wiser*. Don't get Amos upset."

Wiser, Wiser was a script Quentin had been trying to peddle for the past year. It was about a Vietnam vet who goes back to college and falls in love with a girl, who in the end dumps him. It was wry and picaresque, except for the dumping, and it needed a twenty-year-old to play the role of John Wiser. The only people interested in the script so far wanted a package deal, something along the lines of Steve McQueen and Ali MacGraw. Whenever Quent pointed out that they were both middle-aged, he was reminded that they had box-office appeal, which was a hell of a lot more important than verisimilitude.

"It's a beautiful story," Quent said to her now, as if he were trying to popularize it with a producer. "Please don't give Amos a hard time."

Amos walked back into the room, aware somehow that he was the subject of discussion, and he looked bashfully at both of them.

"That's you on the cover of *Look* magazine in the

hallway, isn't it?" he said to Neela. "I thought you looked like an actress."

What did it mean, to look like an actress? Someone had once said about Neela that there wasn't a time in her life when she wasn't acting, and it seemed to her quite possible that even now, fifteen years after she'd done anything on the stage, she still *looked* like an actress, too.

"Should I know you?" Amos Guard continued.

It was the wrong thing to say. Somehow, Neela knew that she was obliged to say, no, you should not, yet that did not make it any easier. In the back of her mind she remembered now what Robert Pino had asked her: "So how come you didn't go all the way?"

How come I didn't do anything at all?

Maybe it was the juxtaposition—the fact that Amos Guard was just starting his career, and had at least stirred Quentin's enthusiasm—but suddenly Neela was depressed by the whole thing. Apart from the sexual hostility, she disliked the young man for his expectations, great ones if Quent was to be believed. She hated him for his youth and his promise.

"Look, it makes a beautiful story," she said, mimicking what Quent had said about his script, "and someday when I have lots of time, I'd love to talk to you about it, but I have an appointment of my own and I really must run."

"I'm having some people in tonight to meet Amos. Is that all right?"

Sure. That was all right. Neela was tempted to ask if she was invited, but thought better of it, for fear that he'd say no, she was not. She showed Amos which of the co-op's four bedrooms he could use and where he could find towels.

"I hope I'm not going to get in anyone's way," the young man said.

Absolutely not. She and Quentin were used to sharing the apartment with people who flew in from Los

93

Angeles or London or Rome, friends of Quent's mainly.

"What I meant back there," he began with embarrassment, aware that he'd upset her somehow when he asked about the picture in the hallway, "is that you're more beautiful now than you were back then. That's what I meant. You're probably the most beautiful woman I've ever seen."

Was she? Still? Neela felt warmed by the revelation. The fact that there were contradictions—if she was so beautiful, why was she rushing off to keep an appointment she'd never made, just so she wouldn't feel *left* at the apartment?—didn't seem as important as it had a few minutes ago.

Neela was smart enough to know that being beautiful was not everything, just as she knew that being homely could be no more than a small part of what a woman was. As for her career, or lack of it, possibly what had happened could be ascribed to what Quentin called "that indescribable quality." He once said about Neela that she was a hundred times more beautiful than Liza Minnelli, could sing better, and could act better, but that Liza Minnelli had "that indescribable quality." Naturally, Neela asked him to describe it.

"It's what you have if you can con people into wishing they were you," he'd said.

Well, only a lunatic would want to be Neela Fitzgerald. Not only did she have no life of her own, but she was being crowded out of Quentin's, too.

She was supposed to meet Kate McCabe and Julie Silverman later in the afternoon, but she just couldn't face them. Julie would talk about her work, Kate would talk about her family, and Neela would have nothing at all to talk about unless she lied a little bit more and invented still another imaginary reading of an imaginary play or a comeback that would never come to anything.

Once on the street, in a kind of hysteria, she headed toward a telephone kiosk and dialed Robert Pino.

"Robert," she said, "I have to see you."

"Yeah?"

"I want . . . do you remember you said you could give me something—remember?—to help me? Robert, I need something."

"Yeah, don't we all."

"Robert, I mean it. This time I mean it. I'm *with* you."

He waited, as if deliberating. "Okay, baby," he said at last. "Come on down. You got money, bring it."

One of Neela Fitzgerald's analysts (she'd been unlucky with them; three out of seven had propositioned her, and two had been successful) explained to her that it wasn't all that out of the ordinary for a very beautiful woman to have been a daddy's girl, and one of the purposes of analysis was to make her someone else's. It hadn't worked yet. Analysis, through the dredging of memory, served only to reaffirm her father's excellence and wealth of virtues, and the poverty of all other men.

To the union with Neela's mother, Charles Waggaman had brought stunning good looks and irresistible charm. Neela's mother brought a great deal of money and fragile health; the money came from Great Lakes shipping and steel, while the bad health came from a grandmother, Neela's great-grandmother, who had married the man who made all the money. Neela had known her great-grandparents only for a short while when she was very young. When her great-grandfather spoke of his friend Mark, Neela was led to believe that he meant Mark Hanna, and when he spoke of the man he'd helped make President, he meant Garfield.

Originally, the Waggamans had kept a horse farm outside of West Mystic, spending most of their time in a big house in Cleveland Heights. Neela's mother preferred the farm, however, so it was given to her as a wedding present, or, more properly, it was given to

Charles Waggaman for marrying her. It was thought that a pleasance would be a better place for her than a city house. A better place, as Neela often recounted to psychiatrists, for her to throw tantrums if she wasn't allowed to go slopping around the muddy fields on her chestnut gelding. A better place for her to fling a Royal Meissen dinner plate, laden with rare roast beef, across the dining room table at Charles Waggaman, hitting a Dutch genre painting on the wall instead.

A place for her to paint in watercolors, drinking herself to stupefaction as she did.

While Neela was growing up, her mother regularly, twice a year, entered a nursing home to take the cure. For a brief period after returning home, she would be affectionate and animated, then she would grow dour and self-pitying, and finally she would say incoherent or unprepared-for things, and the drinking would start all over.

Neela went to school in West Mystic because her father couldn't bear to have her out of his sight. He even encouraged boyfriends—Quentin Fitzgerald, for one—because he felt that the company of robust country fellows would be good for her. Neela was ravishingly pretty, and never lacked friends. "Nell," her father often told her, "you will never have to beg for anything."

When she was growing up, almost every Saturday afternoon after a painful lunch with her mother (sometimes a nurse would have to cut her mother's beefsteak for her), Neela would get into her father's Lincoln Continental—he never drove one of Mr. Ferguson's vulgar Buicks—and sit next to him while he drove to a town thirty miles away and deposited her at a Loew's theater. He had business to attend to, as he put it, so he placed her under the charge of an usher who, for five dollars, made certain that no one annoyed her and that she had as much candy and popcorn as she wanted.

Every Saturday afternoon, Neela would sit in her

seat at the Loew's in Painesville, raptly watching Errol Flynn or Jeanette MacDonald, Claudette Colbert or Tyrone Power, and they seemed to her such impossibly fine people that she couldn't imagine why her father preferred to spend his afternoon with anyone else. At a quarter to five, the usher would tap her on the shoulder to indicate that her father was waiting for her outside at the curb. On the way home, Charles Waggaman listened gravely as she described what she had seen.

"Oh," he would say almost as an afterthought as he brought the car under the porte cochere of the house, "if your mother asks, tell her I was with you, will you please, Nell?"

Once, when she was eleven, rather than sitting through a film she'd already seen twice, she told the usher that she had to use the restroom, and while his back was turned she rushed out of the theater. She walked up and down the side streets nearby, looking everywhere for her father's car. After some time she found it parked in the driveway of a small, neat bungalow. Across the street, several children her own age were playing, so she walked brazenly up to them and asked who lived in the house.

"That is where Mrs. Decosta lives," one of them answered.

"And whose car is that in the driveway?"

The children giggled. "Oh, that's her boyfriend's."

Neela sat in the front seat and waited. At four-thirty, she watched as Charles Waggaman appeared on the porch and a pretty woman kissed him good-bye.

He didn't ask her to explain why she wasn't at the movies. He slid into the car, patted her hand, and said, "When you're a woman, you'll understand loneliness the way I do, Nell."

Two years later, her father was killed in a freak accident while inflating one of the tires on his beloved Lincoln. It exploded and sent the wheel flying, almost severing Charles Waggaman's head. Three days after the funeral, Neela made a Saturday afternoon trip to Painesville all by herself. She parked the huge car where her father had always parked it, and knocked on the door that knew the knuckles of his fist. In a minute, a woman dressed in a blue kimono and wearing bunny slippers opened it. "If you're selling magazines, I don't want none," she said.

If seemed inconceivable to Neela that her father had been able to derive pleasure from the company of someone whose grammar was so bad. Still, she said, "I am Charles Waggaman's daughter. May I come in?"

"Charlie? Is something wrong. Has something happened?"

Neela walked down a hall, passing a bedroom with a huge unmade bed on the way to the living room. Once there, she turned to face the woman.

"Is he sick?" the woman asked. "He called me on Tuesday and didn't sound sick."

By way of reply, Neela asked, "Are you a whore or did he love you?"

"Do you know what your father will do to you when he finds out you've talked to me this way?"

Neela stepped toward her. "Did he leave any unpaid bills?"

"Something *has* happened!"

Neela opened her purse and withdrew a wad of money, part of the huge amount of cash she'd found in her father's safe at home. "There's five hundred," she said, placing it on a littered table. "Now will you please come here?"

"For what?"

"Just come here."

Neela waited till the woman was standing in front of her, then with one movement of her hand, she ripped off the kimono. The woman sucked in her breath.

Neela appraised the naked body. "He said when I'm a woman I'd understand."

"You get out of here!"

Neela saw the black mound between the woman's legs where her father had lain every Saturday afternoon.

"When I tell your father, he'll whip you."

"No, he won't, because he's dead."

Somehow or other, Charles Waggaman had tried to tell his daughter that if a man could bury loneliness in flesh, so could a woman. Neela wasn't quite ready to buy it—she was too young—but she decided to keep it in mind for later on.

In West Mystic, Ohio, she was thought to be a bit advanced, even bold, no doubt because she had seen so many picture shows. Before she was fifteen, she had a crush on one of the tenant farmer's sons, and she sometimes contrived to hide in the evergreens by the pond where the boy and his brothers swam in the nude. At times, she found herself stirred. Once when the boy was swimming by himself, she stepped from under the trees and hailed him, then sat on the bank watching his discomfort. She stripped to her panties and dove into the pond after him. Her breasts had only recently begun to enlarge and a darker color showed through the triangle of her wet panties. Under water, the boy held his hands in front of him in embarrassment, and when Neela came close, she saw why.

It was the first time she had ever seen a male member, that way. She tried to reconcile it with her father and the vulgar woman he had lain with while Neela sat by herself in the movies. When the boy asked if he could touch her—there, he said pointing—she nodded her head, and when he placed her hand on his erect penis, she felt herself quiver.

"Now I understand," she said.

Now, at the age of thirty-nine, Neela had lost count of the number of men she'd slept with, or the number of times Quentin had pissed her off by running away for a week or two with a girl he'd met or a boy he'd picked up at a casting call. All she knew about any of them—her own affairs as well as Quentin's—was that they wouldn't last for long, and there was always someone to come home to. Quentin was a good friend and a safe harbor. It was a new-style marriage, unbound by ancient rules, and if anyone in their set, a dazzling group of people connected with the theater or filmmaking, didn't like it, they could go fuck themselves.

What Neela really hadn't counted on was that at the age of thirty-nine there would be a diminution of passion and zest, even of interest in life, and while Quentin at least had a career that could carry him from girlfriend to boyfriend to girlfriend, Neela had nothing. Through habit, she still went to chic little parties with Quent, and over her dry manhattan scouted the room to see what was available in the way of after-hours entertainment, but lately she'd had to force herself. To make herself more cheerful, she'd drink too much. Drunk, she would meet terrible people and get into terrible messes.

Sometimes when she looked into a mirror and saw the face that had been on the cover of *Look* magazine when she was twenty-two, it seemed to her ugly and gross, bestial and carnivorous.

"You punish yourself, seeing the people you do," her new analyst had told her.

"I don't have much choice," she said by way of reply. "Everyone has to get through Saturday afternoon somehow."

"Saturday afternoon? I don't follow you."

"It isn't important," she said, it being her opinion that a fifty-dollar-an-hour psychiatrist deserved nothing but trivia, for fear that he might otherwise get to know what she was really like.

She'd met Robert Pino about a year ago at a Sutton Place party Quentin had taken her to. He'd walked up to her, appraised the other people in the room, then said, "La dolce shita."

He looked like something between a gypsy and a Sicilian, which was exactly what he was, and he drove a black Cadillac convertible with red leather seats, which should have put her off, but didn't. At that time he made his living filming TV commercials and waiting for someone to bankroll his first film. He took her to his place on West 11th Street, first stopping at a delicatessen for hero sandwiches, dripping with pickles and onions and ketchup. When he made love to her, legs and bread, salami and vegetables all entwined, his jaws were crimson, and Neela had taken an inventory of her parts and limbs for fear that it was more than tomato sauce.

Robert Pino went from ecstasy to ecstasy, in bed and out. He levitated over the rooftops like a Chagallian violinist, and invited Neela's own levitation—directly and unambiguously. When he telephoned her, he'd say, "Hello, this is Meat. You wanta get balled?"

Neela had tried to explain to her analyst her surprise when she discovered that Robert was on drugs, but he replied that he could have predicted it, just on the basis of her description. "No man can be that manic without help," he'd said.

Once, after they'd visited a friend on West End Avenue, she and Robert went for a walk in Riverside Park. Robert found a tennis ball in the grass and began bouncing it on the sidewalk as if it were a basketball. Suddenly it rolled onto the West Side Highway, and though it was the rush hour and cars were speeding northward in all four lanes, Robert dashed out after it. He swooped it up, held it like a football, and began to run with it up the highway, moving from lane to lane, tossing his hips like Joe Namath. All the while, horns were bleating, brakes were screeching, and Neela was screaming at the top of her voice. He was almost struck by nine or ten speeding cars before he finally turned, held out one arm as if to stiff-arm approaching traffic, straddled a white line, then played with the cars as if they were bulls and he a torero, yelling, "You hit me and I'll kill you, you cocksuckers!"

By the time he got back to the sidewalk, Neela was crumpled on her knees, sobbing. He walked up to her, handed her the tennis ball, then said that he'd be damned glad when traffic was banned in Manhattan because the air was so lousy. "So what time you have to be home to get supper for the bastard?" he added, the bastard being Quentin.

It was a galvanizing performance. Cars had pulled off the road just to get a second look at the madman who'd almost caused an eighty-car crack-up, and he was chatting amiably with a girl, as if nothing had happened.

"Why did you *do* that?" she screamed, rising to beat his chest with her fists.

He grinned. "That? I felt like it, is all."

He'd done other absurd things when he was with her. Once when they were passing a Woolworth's, he jumped on top of a plastic kiddie-ride kangaroo and wouldn't get off till she put a quarter in it. Once he hung from a single subway strap, his feet off the floor, all the way from West Fourth to Columbus Circle.

Then, at other times, he was zonked out of his head, pacificity itself. When she put it to him directly, asking him if he was on something, he readily admitted it.

"You're killing yourself, Robert."

"So who isn't?"

"What are you on?"

"Whatever I can get."

With the exception of pot, which was everywhere in New York, and poppers, which Robert held under her nostrils the second she began to come—they frightened her; each time, she thought she was only a heartbeat away from a coronary—Neela didn't share Robert's tastes or habits. She preferred booze, which was an old friend of the family. And she knew better than to mix it with some of the pills Robert now and then offered her. A combination of alcohol and barbiturates had killed Dorothy Kilgallen, hadn't they?

And if they could kill a nice Catholic girl like her, what chance did Neela Fitzgerald have?

Robert's building was on West 11th one block before it swooned into the desperate squalor around the West Side Highway. The front door was never locked and the mailboxes couldn't have been polished since 1890, though several showed signs of recent tampering. At the far end of the first-floor hallway, someone was either sleeping off a drunk or genuinely dead, and Neela was in no frame of mind to ascertain which. She scurried up the stairs to the third floor.

At the fourth or fifth knock, she heard the police lock sliding to one side, then the door opened to reveal a black face she'd never seen before. She stepped back instinctively.

"You want Bobby?" the man said, then indicated with a movement of his head that she was to come in. "He in the back, man."

Once, when Robert Pino was making a good deal of money grinding out TV commercials for ad agencies, the apartment had been elegantly and expensively appointed, but everything was now decidedly down-at-the-heels. Worn and abused, just as Robert himself was. No matter how badly he needed money, he'd never hock any of the furniture he'd bought late in the Sixties, when he was a Madison Avenue *Wunderkind*.

"Pardon the shit," Robert said to her, coming in from the bedroom, indicating plates and clothes and newspapers scattered over what had once been a good rug. "Some guys came over."

Neela could see. They were still there. Apart from

the black man, who had opened the door, someone else sat nodding in the corner.

"Ronnie and Angelo," he said by way of introduction, getting the attention of the former but not the latter. Then, "This is a cunt I know."

The black man looked at her as if he were about to say something, but apparently thought better of it.

"Ronnie's the spade. Angie's the one who ain't."

"Can't you get them to go home?" Neela asked on the way to the kitchen.

"This *is* home, man," the one called Angie said. Then, sourly, "Shit."

Of all things that annoyed Neela about Robert's set, none bothered her more than the "man" at the end of each sentence, and all the scatalogical data with which they peppered their speech. "Shit" was a word they could say a hundred different ways with a hundred different shades of meaning.

Robert indicated that she was to sit on one of the two kitchen chairs, then asked, "Your old man giving you a hard time?"

Neela couldn't even begin to explain what the presence of Amos Guard in the apartment meant to her. The agreement had been that the other part of Quentin's life was to be kept discreetly under wraps, but to have one of his friends actually living in the guest bedroom outraged her, humiliated her, *defeated* her.

"Everything is so goddamn hopeless, Robert," she said to him. "I used to be able to see a kind of future: what I would be or like to be a month from now, or maybe a year. But I can't see any future anymore. I can't even see . . . tomorrow."

What was it that Quentin, who was better read than she was, once said about getting old? Holden Caulfield at thirty-nine becomes Seymour Glass, he'd said. All the fun—assuming that there had been any in the first place—stopped with a bang, sometimes of a .38-caliber pistol.

"Don't your fuckin' shrink help?" Robert asked.

Neela's newest psychiatrist seemed almost as much a casualty of New York as Neela herself. Earlier in the month, he'd closed his office for an entire week when his pet cat died. Dr. Levenstein lived in a penthouse apartment near Beekman Place, and once when Neela walked out onto the terrace to admire the view from the twentieth floor, Dr. Levenstein stood far back from the edge. "I'm terrified of heights," he said in a good-natured sort of way.

In a city where even psychiatrists were unable to cope, how could anyone expect Neela Fitzgerald, with all her built-in deficiencies, to function from day to day?

"You know what's wrong with this fuckin' city?" Robert said suddenly. "You gotta be a Jew to get ahead. They stick together, man."

"Right on, man," said the black from the doorway.

New York was a paradise for haters. One of the dubious advantages of living with so many other people was that you could always find someone to despise. You could despise Jews. You could despise blacks. You could despise Puerto Ricans and Dominicans, not to mention Cubans. You could despise faggots. The Irish, the Italians, the Armenians. You could despise the rich, despise the poor.

"I'm not talking about that," Neela said.

"Well, what the fuck you talkin' about, man?" Robert inquired impatiently.

Neela exhaled all her breath. "I'm not sure but I think Quentin is getting ready to leave me, and I don't know what I'm going to do."

That was the message as she was beginning to read it. It seemed to her that Quent might be getting tired of the arrangement. If Neela was going to be bitchy all the time, why not live instead with Amos Guard? Obviously, there was a real attraction there, added to which Amos was an asset professionally. Neela was nothing but an extended liability.

"You'll get child support from that fuckin' pansy, and alimony, too. Hell, man, you'll be living."

She'd be living all right. Even more alone than she was now. At least now there was a kind of pattern to her existence: Quent flying out to the Coast, Quent coming home from the Coast, suppers at smart restaurants in the Fifties, parties on the East Side. Waiting for him to leave, waiting for him to return. Without that, what could there be?

"You should never of married a faggot in the first place. You were just asking to get your ass in a sling."

Neela shook her head. "It's not that. It doesn't really have anything to do with sex. It's something that has to do with two people, and one of them is getting bored."

"With a beautiful cunt like you?"

Quite possibly that was why he was getting bored. All Neela was, and ever had been, was a beautiful cunt. She wasn't smart, as a housewife and mother she scored zero, she had no talent to speak of, and at thirty-nine her once ravishing face was beginning to go and her traffic-stopping body was wearing out.

"So why did you come down here, man?"

She looked up at him in disbelief. "I don't *have* anything, Robert. Why the hell do you think I'm here? Do you think if I had an alternative, I'd be spending the afternoon with a junkie?"

"Okay, so why did you come? You want me to turn you on?"

It was a minute before she could answer. "I want you to turn me off. That's what I want you to do." She opened her purse and removed her wallet.

"How much you got?"

She didn't know. Whatever there was, he could have. All she needed was cab fare home.

"Baby," he said, "I like a woman who can pay her

own way." He got up from his chair and disappeared into the bedroom. When he returned several minutes later, he was carrying a plastic bag and a small spoon.

"Will it hurt me?"

"Man, it is to take away the hurt."

He carefully measured out the cocaine into the spoon, making certain that none of it spilled. When he was finished, he held the spoon up to her nostrils and told her to inhale.

Neela did, and almost immediately gave a shrill cry.

Her face was colorless. "I thought I was going to die. Everything started to go so fast. Like poppers, only more."

He held the spoon while she continued to inhale. Then, as she sat back in the chair, he brought the spoon to his own nostrils.

"How you feel now, man?" he asked in a minute.

How? It was impossible to explain. Excited was how she felt. She wasn't tired anymore. Alive was how she felt. Words began to spill out of her mouth.

"In junior high school," she began, "I was in *You Can't Take It With You,* and my father said I was better than Jean Arthur."

"Yeah?"

"He said I would never have to beg for anything, never in my life. He was such a fantastic man."

"My old man was a shit."

"I was Homecoming Queen in high school and again in college. I got my picture on the cover of *Look* magazine when I was twenty-two years old."

"Yeah, you already told me that, man."

"I could have married John Cowdrey, but Quentin told me, 'Look, when you're forty years old, he'll be seventy. Let me take care of you instead.' That's what he said to me."

"You should never of believed that faggot. I hate faggots worse than Jews."

"I always used to get home from school as fast as I

107

could—I wouldn't even wait for Kate or Julie—because my father would be there. But then when he died there was no one waiting for me at home anymore, and sometimes I used to stop in the woods with a boy."

"Yeah?" he said with interest. "Then whaddidya do? Put out?"

"There was no reason for me to go home anymore. Do you see what I mean?"

"Look," Robert said with animation, "you want Ronnie to ball you after a while?"

"I don't know where I am. It's like, where I am, I've never been before."

"Ronnie fucks like an animal. It'll do you good, man. Put life in you. There's nothing like getting balled by a nigger."

"He never even said good-bye to me. In the morning I went to school and that afternoon when I came home, he was dead."

"Aw, shit," Robert said in disgust, "whaddaya talking about? I'm talking about Ronnie."

Neela didn't know how she got there, but she was on the bed in the next room and someone was lifting her skirt. "Please," she said, "I don't do that. You misunderstand."

A head sank between her legs and soon she felt a tongue, then teeth, pleasure and pain. "Oh, God," she said, reaching down to hold his head.

"Baby," a voice said—it seemed to come through her abdomen, an echo—"gimme everything you got."

"Nothing. I've got nothing."

"Oh, baby, you got something."

"Help me," she said. "Please help me."

"I'm helping you."

In joy or terror, she didn't know which, Neela looked up and thought she saw her father at the doorway, but it was only Robert and his friend watching.

"Save some for me," Angie said.

For all her strident bravado—her ego would corrode bronze, someone had said about her—Julie Silverman could never walk into a place like the Oak Room at the Plaza without feeling a little too fat, a little too plain, a little too Jewish.

It was her peculiar style, however, never to cower or show lack of confidence, even when her knees were about to buckle, so instead of sneaking into that venerable watering hole, she walked in with an almost arrogant swagger, as if she had just bought the whole damned place and was about to announce loudly—her voice had almost no other volume—that she was having it torn down and replaced by a parking lot.

At the magazine, her colleagues made merciless fun of the way she spoke English—"A kind of Brooklyn College whine, like Barbra Streisand," someone had said about it, which was all the more perplexing because she had spent the greater part of her life in the Middle West. In fact, her speech was affected, an erected defense. In order to get the attention of a world which had something less than enthusiasm for girls like Julie, it was necessary to talk loud and to talk tough.

Julie made her way through the Oak Room to the long bar, boosted herself up on a bar stool, then thumped her fist on the richly polished counter.

"Would you perhaps prefer to sit at a table, ma'am?" a bartender said to her.

"No, I would not," Julie answered brightly. "What I would like is a very dry martini, which means about one-sixteenth of an ounce of vermouth, and no more than that. Wash your hands first, please. And don't get smart-ass with me and tell me to sit at a table."

She wasn't in the best of moods. After Kate McCabe

had called her to say that she wouldn't be needing a place to stay that night, Julie had tried to telephone David Harpur at his office to let him know that he could come over to the apartment if he wanted to, provided he could get away from Lily. But she hadn't been able to get through to him. He'd been in conference for most of the afternoon. Julie had given David's secretary the number of the Oak Room, but if David was still tied up in conference after five o'clock, his secretary would no doubt leave Julie's message with a pack of others on top of his desk, and he wouldn't look at them till tomorrow morning.

Which would mean that Julie probably wouldn't be able to see him until next week, as he had already made it clear that he didn't want her in Amagansett over the weekend.

Julie sampled her martini and looked at her watch, more or less concurrently, hoping to show the bartender her disdain for his skills. It was a quarter to six, which meant that Kate was already fifteen minutes late. It was so like her. She'd never been on time for an appointment in her life, either because she ambled or because she got lost easily. In high school, she'd always been the last one in her seat and the first one to raise her hand to go to her locker for a book she'd forgotten.

Julie had a premonition that Kate might be skidding into a decline, and she was not all that displeased. For the first five years of her married life, it had always seemed to Julie that Kate lorded it over her. It was always "Buddy and I have done this. Buddy and I have done that. We have bought the cutest little house. We've had the sweetest little baby." All Julie could ever talk about was the raise that she might or might not be getting or the sofa bed she might or might not buy. Not that Julie ever let on that she envied her friend. When Kate gushed about her house or her garden, Julie would reply that she hated houses—"I'm the kinda girl who's made to be possessed by rotten old landlords"—and as for gardening, if she got her avocado to grow, she considered herself lucky.

Still, at times Julie knew that it must be solacing to own something other than furniture or clothes. Recently, she'd begun to read the Sunday *Times* real estate section with something akin to lust, propping it up against the toaster on Sunday morning, then reading a page a day through the following Saturday. Dutchess, Putnam, Rockland, Orange, Ulster, Westchester, Nassau, and Suffolk: she recited the county names like a litany, imagining herself living in a carriage house in Tuxedo Park or a saltbox in the Hudson Valley. Well, what was wrong with that?

What was wrong with that, she would finally tell herself, was that the only advantage of living in Dutchess County rather than in Manhattan was that she would be living alone in a different place.

So, in the end, Julie always renewed her lease, scolding herself for not at least having the sense to invest in a co-operative.

Then, for the next month or so, she would prop up the Co-operatives and Condominiums section of the Sunday *Times*, reading each entry with interest and delight: "Sutton Place South. Is that where they have a view of the Silvercup Bread sign across the river?" Or "Do I know anyone in Fort Lee? Or what about going all the way up to Riverdale and getting away from these filthy streets?"

The leap from Riverdale to Nyack, from Nyack to Dobbs Ferry, from Dobbs Ferry to Tarrytown and points north was so logical and so unnoticed that before she knew what she was doing, she was saying to herself, "Well, if I'm going all the way up there, I might as well see what's being offered in Dutchess County."

And Putnam and Ulster and Orange.

She was halfway through her dry martini, wondering how she could possibly get through the night without seeing David, when something made her turn and she saw Kate McCabe timidly poking her head through the door.

Kate was as shy and bashful now as she'd been in grade school. When Julie waved, Kate looked momentarily apprehensive, as if she'd never sat at a bar before, then made her way toward it.

"Marvelous!" Julie cried when her old friend was standing next to her. "I love your hair, Kate. What have you done to it?"

Kate hadn't done anything. Someone at Bergdorf's had done it. "I came in early—I'm getting to be a shamelessly bad housewife—to keep a two-thirty appointment. Do you think he made it too light?"

Julie's own hair had started to gray in her early thirties, and at first she'd gone along with the notion that it was humiliating for a woman to alter nature in order to make herself a more attractive sex object. But in the end, she had to admit that it was even more unnatural to allow oneself to become ugly, so she'd been rinsing it ever since.

Kate studied the bar stool, touched it prudently, backed into it, then boosted herself up. "I've never sat in one of these before," she said.

"You could have fooled me."

Kate looked into Julie's glass, then asked, "What should I have to drink?"

Every time Julie met Kate after not having seen her for several months, it took her a few minutes to adapt. Julie wondered if ever in her life Kate had made a decision on her own. Was it habit or kindness that made her appear so helpless? Was she that way—were *all* wives that way?—because it made her husband appear stronger when he finally suggested something to eat or drink?

Julie would not play. If her old friend didn't have sufficient wits to think of a drink she might like to have, she could damned well go without.

"What are you having?" Kate asked.

"Martini. Dry. It's a little bit like sherry, Kate."

Then Kate would have one, too.

"Julie," Kate began, "I'm no drinker."

Julie cocked an eyebrow, brought her glass to her lips, then spoke over its rim, "Just an adulterer."

Kate was horrified. She looked right, then left to determine if anyone had overheard, and finally, and more or less predictably, her eyes filled with tears.

"People don't spend an hour on the train coming into this pestilential city just to go to the New School," Julie volunteered. "There has to be another reason. So last week when I talked to you, I figured you had a boyfriend here."

Last week she didn't have him, Kate protested. She'd just met him on Monday night.

"And you already think you're in *love* with him?"

"I am. Absolutely."

Julie made a face to indicate what she thought about such sentiment in other people. "Kate, you are so fucking innocent. You're going to break up a marriage just because someone has made a pass at you and you're afraid of menopause. Excuse me while I laugh. You're just going to make things worse than they are now."

Kate looked up in alarm. "How could things be worse?"

"You have no idea how worse they can be. Living out there in the suburbs, it's possible that your idea of unhappiness is when one of the kids gets the floor dirty. Well, let me tell you, there are plenty worse things than that."

Julie didn't understand, Kate complained. Julie had always had a life of her own. She did interesting and important things and she knew interesting and important people. All Kate had was ... well, she had nothing. Just the kids, the dog, the VW, and Buddy, and they weren't sufficient to tie her to life. Looking after her family had become as impersonal as looking after the car. Did Julie know what she meant?

If Julie did, she was not going to admit it.

"So what are you going to do? Leave Buddy?"

"I've already left him," Kate said emphatically. "All I have to do now is tell him."

She would be giving up everything. Was she aware of that? The security, the comforts, the calm predictability of her life. Was she prepared to start all over?

"I'm afraid, if that's what you mean, but I'm prepared to, anyway."

"Is he going to marry you, this other man?"

They hadn't even talked about it. It wasn't really all that important. What was important was that she could get away from Buddy.

"Horseshit," Julie said, then roared at the bartender to refill their glasses. "You'll end up at the age of fifty-five living in a one-and-a-half-room apartment in Tudor City. All by yourself. Some weekend, you'll open the window and jump out, and if you're lucky you'll land on a tourist looking at the UN, and if you're not, you'll land on New York sidewalk, which is extra hard."

Angrily, Julie said to the bartender, "Do we have to wait all day?" and then she was ashamed of herself, both for yelling at the poor man, and for saying what she'd said to Kate McCabe.

Kate was silently crying now, her face averted.

"Skip it," Julie said at last. "What I said, I mean. Go ahead and do it if you want to. I guess maybe I get pissed off when someone like you who's always had everything you ever wanted ..." Julie couldn't finish what she had been about to say. Suddenly, she covered Kate's hand with her own. "You know, back in high school, whenever I saw you and Buddy together, I wished that I was you. No, wait. *Listen!* Between classes, you two would walk around the halls, holding hands, and I thought—well, I thought it was the most goddamn beautiful thing I'd ever seen. I really believed if I really worked at it—listen to the reallys; I'm getting drunk—someone could love me the way Buddy loved you. And now you come along and tell me it's all over. Jesus, it leaves me empty. Do you see what I mean? If you can't do it, how can a slob like me?"

Predictably, Kate protested. Julie wasn't a slob. She was the cleverest person Kate knew, so sure of herself and self-possessed, and had always been that way. When Kate had had to make an announcement at a National Honor Society assembly in the high school auditorium, she was terrified for weeks before, and Julie had finally practiced with her. Did she remember? "Everyone said you were the best speaker at West Mystic High. Don't you remember junior class elections when you went out on the stage in front of seven hundred kids and gave that fantastic speech? Everyone else was so nervous that they forgot what they were going to say, but not you."

"Yeah," Julie said without enthusiasm. "And half the kids in the auditorium were making fun of me. Didn't you hear them when I walked out on the stage. *Big Mouth Julie*—that's what they were calling me. Except from where I was standing it sounded like *Big Mouthed Jew*."

"Julie!" Kate said. "I'm so sorry."

"Something like that," Julie continued softly, "makes you a very good speaker. Because you're fighting for your life. You've never had to, Kate. There's never been a time when I haven't."

Suddenly they were both subdued, each one reliving some private grief, and it was all they could do to fight back maudlin tears.

Kate was the first to recover. She said that she might as well have another drink because she wasn't expected at Ben Purdom's till almost seven. What exactly were they drinking, anyway?

"We're being consumed by dry martinis," Julie replied, then held up her index finger at the bartender, winked lewdly at him, and shouted for him to fill up the goddamn glasses.

While she was still sober, Kate enlisted Julie's aid. She wrote Ben's name and telephone number on a piece of paper, then stuffed it into Julie's purse. In the event that Buddy telephoned tonight, or any other Wednesday, when Kate was supposed to be sleeping over at Julie's apartment, would Julie call her at Ben's? For the time being, at least till she told him that she wanted a divorce, she didn't want to rock the boat.

"I'm asking Neela to do the same," she concluded.

"Where *is* Neela? I thought you said she was meeting us here."

Most peculiar. Neela was generally pretty good about keeping appointments; it was Kate who was forever being detained or getting lost. Could there be more than one Oak Room?

"At the moment," Julie began, indicating impaired vision, "it looks as if there might be two." Then, looking at her watch, "Dammit, it's after six."

It meant that David had almost certainly left the office by now and hadn't received her message.

"Maybe she got tied up at a rehearsal or something," Kate offered lamely. "She said she might be doing something pretty soon. Is there an Edward Albee?"

Yes, there was, so far as Julie knew, but she didn't know what that had to do with Neela. "I don't know what Neela could do for an Edward Albee play except kick up her legs and show off her big muff during intermission."

Well, it would be nice if Neela could do something, Kate suggested. She seemed so overwhelmed by Quentin. "You know, when I was talking to her, I felt something, and I don't exactly know what. She just about stood on her head, telling me how happy she is. But I bet it's hard to live with someone like Quentin. If it's hard to live with someone like Buddy, who's a failure, I bet it's almost unbearable to live with a success."

"He is the penultimate con man. I'm glad I'm not married to him."

Kate decided to seize the opportunity. "Aren't you ever going to get married? Every time I go home, I talk to your mother, and she says to me that you're seeing someone, and this time she hopes it's going to work out." She waited in vain for a response, then went on, "Your mother says that if you don't hurry up, you'll miss the right man entirely."

A brittle laugh escaped Julie's throat. "Hell, I don't have any trouble meeting the right man. So far, Kate, I've met about ten right men. The trouble is, they're always married." She turned toward her friend. "Am I worth getting unmarried for? Truthfully?"

Oh, dear, Kate had stumbled into something.

Emboldened by the martinis, Julie was suddenly telling Kate all about David Harpur. "I'm not sure," she concluded, "but it's possible that this time I'm going all the way. I mean, Kate, I think David is going to divorce his wife and marry me. I've got that—I don't know what—*feeling*."

Kate wanted to say, "But how wonderful!" but it seemed to her that it might not be appropriate. Instead, she said that David Harpur would have to be a madman to turn Julie down. "But married men are very lazy, Julie," she added. "They have to be prodded like children. They hate divorces for the same reason they hate moving from one house to another one: the mess and confusion. It's much easier for a woman to get divorced than a man."

117

Julie hated to admit it, but Kate had said what she herself had been trying to say since she had first met David. He would not do anything unless he had to. He might be forced into action, but he would never initiate it. Truly, it came as a revelation, but it seemed to Julie that perhaps Lily would have to leave David. Somehow or other she would have to be *persuaded* to leave him.

For her own part, Kate McCabe thought it was quite possible that Buddy would never give her a divorce at all. She would have to wrench it from him after a long, nasty, acrimonious battle. He would fight every inch of the way, first accusing her of moral turpitude, and he would almost certainly threaten to deprive her of the children.

With a start, Kate realized that Buddy McCabe, in all his wildest dreams, could never imagine that his wife would leave him. How could she possibly tell him?

It was six-thirty now, and Julie said she really had to make a telephone call. Kate said that she had to go anyway, because Ben Purdom was expecting her by seven.

"Look, we must keep in touch," Julie said. "Call me when you get into the city next Monday." At the door of the Oak Room, Julie stopped, then held the crook of Kate McCabe's arm.

"Isn't it strange what's happening to us?" she asked.

Kate couldn't say for sure what the strangeness was, but she, too, felt it.

What was it? That they were starting all over, both of them? Or that Kate's life had been as sorrowful as Julie's—was the knowledge sustaining to Julie?—and that they were closer now, because of that, than they'd ever been?

After Kate had left, Julie did what she'd told herself she mustn't do: she used a telephone in the lobby and called David at the office. She was certain that there would be no answer, and she could now take a cab home, open a can of tuna fish, and sit in front of the droning TV set till bedtime.

Just as she was about to hang up, a voice she had never heard before said, "Mr. Harpur's office."

Julie was so startled that she couldn't think of anything to say. At last she asked, "Is he still there?" From the other end, she heard the voice say, "David? Someone for you."

With absolute terror, Julie listened as David said hello. Although she knew what the answer was going to be, she asked the question anyway. "Just say yes or no, please. Was that Lily?"

"Yes," David replied emotionlessly.

"Oh, God, I'm sorry I called. I've probably got you in trouble. It's just—oh, hell, I missed you so."

David was a master at improvisation. "It's possible that Miss Wilkins, my secretary, would be in a better position to answer that than I am," he said. "Perhaps you can call in the morning."

"David, I'm so sorry. I didn't mean to mess things up. I love you."

"Sure thing," he replied. "No trouble at all." Then a click.

Now she'd done it.

What kind of woman *was* Lily Harpur? Would she accept the telephone call for what David pretended it was?—a business call at almost seven at night—or had she detected the surprise in Julie's voice? Was she on guard now?

It seemed to Julie that she had two options. She could let David artfully talk his way out of any embarrassment, and hope that he wouldn't be too angry at her for having been careless. If Lily bought the story, she and David could patch things up, and could continue as before.

Or, the other thing Julie could do was to take the offensive. If Lily's eyes had begun to open slightly, why not give her an eyeful?

119

It was a chance.

As Julie sailed down the steps of the Plaza into a cab, she felt absolutely buoyant.

"I think I'm going to Amagansett," she said out loud.

"*Where* you wanta go, lady?" the cabbie asked in puzzlement.

Julie corrected herself. Central Park West and 70th would do for the time being, she said.

———◆———

Ben Purdom had left a message with the doorman saying that he was tied up at the hospital and would be at least half an hour late. Kate was to go up to the apartment and wait for him there.

The doorman who handed her the keys was the same one who'd been on duty Monday night when she appeared with keys to the Fitzgerald apartment. If he saw anything out of the ordinary about it, he had the good manners not to let on.

Was Mrs. Fitzgerald in, by any chance?

The doorman replied that he'd rung the apartment several minutes before when a florist had attempted to make a delivery but no one had answered.

To the right of the lobby Kate saw a giant horseshoe-shaped creation, all red and yellow roses, with a banner across the top that read *Give 'em hell, Amos!*

"Mr. Guard is a houseguest," the man volunteered without being asked. "He is, I believe"—with a toss of his head he indicated what he thought of both the flowers and the profession—"an actor."

One of Quentin's oddball friends, as Buddy McCabe would say, it being Buddy's contention that no one but

120

an oddball could like Quent. Embittered by his own lackluster career, Buddy hated his old friends who had become successful. Once when Kate had taken him to see a movie for which Quentin had done the screenplay, Buddy had said afterwards, "You coulda fooled me. I wasn't aware that there *was* a screenplay."

Poor Neela. Despite the frantic cheerfulness, she had given Kate the most peculiar aftertaste, as if she were lonely to the bone. Somehow or other, one really did have to pity people who were as beautiful as she was. Plain people were prepared for sadness—even expected it as their due—but to people like Neela it must come as a stunning surprise.

Kate let herself into Ben Purdom's apartment, and this time she looked at it. On Monday night all she'd looked at, really, was Ben Purdom.

In addition to the living room, there were two bedrooms, two baths, and a small study. When she walked into the latter, she clapped her hands in delight. It was a kind of ghetto. Books were piled everywhere on the floor and copies of medical journals covered a sofa. Doctors must get a prodigious amount of mail, because heaps of it, unopened, lay on top of the desk. There were also two coffee cups and the sugary frosting from what might have been a Danish. In sum, it looked more like a student's room than a practicing MD's.

The other rooms were decorated to within an inch of their lives—in the case of one bedroom, it exceeded that inch—and though they were at once splendid and virile (Kate had never seen so many English sporting prints; where the devil had Ben's wife acquired them all?), they didn't truly reflect Ben's amiability. Only the tiny, impossibly lived-in study did.

Kate tried to think if Buddy McCabe had in any way left his stamp on the house he lived in. Perhaps the garage was his—with its oil stains, its two lawn mowers, its ladders, and paint brushes languishing in turpentine—but otherwise Buddy could leave the house to-morrow and there would be no trace of him. He never noticed the house. Several months ago, when Kate was about to have the upstairs hall repainted, she asked him if he had any preference as to color.

He'd looked up at her and said, "What color is it now?"

Almost *six* years since it had been painted light blue, and Buddy, who must have walked through the hall thousands of times, had never taken the trouble to notice it.

Ben Purdom's apartment contained no television set or radio, not that she could see, anyway. Yet in one corner of the study there was a music stand and on the floor next to it a case for, she was sure, a violin.

Was it possible that there was a man in New York City who came home from work at nights and played the violin?

Smiling to herself at her great good luck for having found such a man, Kate rearranged the *New England Journal of Medicine,* copies of which upholstered the sofa, until she had space to lie down. Reclining, she caught sight of an opened letter between the cushions, and when she picked it up to remove it to the end table, she saw the words *Dearest, Darling Ben.*

No, I won't read it, she told herself, then found herself doing just that.

I hadn't wanted to write again so soon after the last time—it was kind of you to get the check off to me right away; thanks ever so much for the extra dough—but I've just got a huge bill from Bloomingdale's I'd forgotten all about. Clothes and things for Jud, also for me. I must have got them the last time I was in New York. Also, I'm thinking of sending Jud down to your folks in Fort Lauderdale over Thanksgiving—maybe a week or so—and since I'd only have to put the bite on you later on, I might as well do it now. $600 should take care of Florida and Bloomingdale's too. Is that okay?

I know you have terrible demands on your salary, but so do I have terrible demands. The alimony just isn't enough. If it were, I wouldn't have to beg every fourth or fifth week. I also understand your objections to paying for my analysis, and, yes, I know damned well that you haven't made me what I am. The fact remains that I'm Jud's mother, and I'm having a hell of a time trying to adjust to being middle-aged and unmarried. I can't *decide* anything, Ben; I make a decision and fifteen minutes later I change my mind. Dr. Steingut says it's anxiety. If you could pay a share of the repair work, I'd be beholden to you.

Jud is in good health and loves you dearly. So do I, but I won't go into that again. When do you have to give up the apartment, and what will you do? Why don't you leave your horrid clinic and go up to Vermont, the way you were always talking about when you were in school? Really, Ben, there is more to life than treating cases of the clap in the South Bronx. Anyway, let me know your plans, and Jud and I will help any way we can.

Goodnight, darling!

Always,
Joanne

Most of the divorced women Kate knew spent the greater part of their time vilifying their former husbands. The loving tone of Joanne Purdom's letter was therefore confounding, even though the woman was trying to dun $600 from poor Ben. The letter was a testimonial to Ben's charity, gentleness, and love, yet it was written by a woman who had divorced him. There should have been at least some rancor, but if it was there, Kate was unable to detect it.

It was probably a good sign. Perhaps her instincts hadn't betrayed her, after all. One really ought to be wary of men who were hated by ex-wives, and one should be able to be at one's ease with those who were not. Ben was still loved by Joanne; *ergo,* Ben was very loving.

After she'd replaced the letter on the end table, she folded her hands in front of her and dozed off, supremely happy that she was on Ben Purdom's old sofa, waiting for him to come home.

Ben would not hear of eating in, even though Kate had poked around the refrigerator and said she could do something with eggs and cheese if he was too tired to go out. No, he was feeling gala, he said. "Damned if I'm going to eat at home on the first night that I've been in love for a long time."

What, exactly, did he mean? He meant, exactly, that since Monday night he'd been trying to convince himself that no man in his right mind could feel the way he was feeling about a woman he'd known for only a few hours. And then, after he'd just about persuaded himself it was possible, he'd walked into the apartment to find the selfsame woman sleeping on his sofa. He'd sat across from her on a chair and for the next five minutes committed her face to memory. Then, as he touched her and woke her up, he said, "Look, it's no use. I *am* in love with you."

Kate had told him what she'd been feeling and thinking since Monday. She'd been sure that the minute she stepped into her house she would lose her resolve. She'd even been thinking about sending Ben a note, telling him what a mistake it was.

"I actually thought that on the train going home. Do you want to know something else? While I was waiting for Buddy last night, I almost hoped—I don't know what—that maybe he'd *engender* something in me. I guess I wanted an excuse to stay away from you, because what we're doing is so damned impractical. But there was nothing. I mean, I gave him the chance, but there was nothing."

"How will he take it, Kate, when you tell him?"

"He won't believe it. He'll think it's a joke."

"And after he learns that it isn't a joke?"

Kate shook her head. "The first thing he'll do is get angry. Then he'll go to pieces. You see, he's such a disappointed man. When he was younger, and while he was still in grad school, he even thought that someday he might write books. Well, now he doesn't even read them, except those he has to in order to keep his job. He'll say that he's squandered his life and career on me, and now this is a hell of a way for me to repay him."

"And is it true, what he says?"

"Poor Buddy just doesn't have it, whatever you have to have to come in first place, the moxie or push or drive. He would have been a failure even if he'd never got married. It's built in."

"When are you going to tell him? About what's happened to you."

Kate didn't dare answer. She hated even to think of it. The divorce she wouldn't mind. But telling Buddy that she wanted one? Impossible.

"Tell him tomorrow when you get home."

"And then what do I do?"

Then she would see a lawyer, and Buddy would also see a lawyer. "They do all the messy work, the lawyers," Ben said. "All you do is sit back and wait for the thing to come to an end. First there'll be an agreement on separation, mostly to get your husband out of the house. Then if your husband doesn't contest the divorce—"

"But he will!"

Didn't Kate realize that husbands rarely did that? It was most unusual. Why would Buddy McCabe?

Why? Because at some point in his life, a badly beaten man will stand up and strike back. If Buddy couldn't punish the headmaster at the school where he worked for having, three years ago, passed him up as chairman of the English department—as he would almost certainly pass him up a second time, now that the post was vacant again—he would punish Kate instead. If he couldn't punish his son Dutchie for being lousy at baseball and always turning down his offer to play catch with him in the backyard, then, by God, he would punish the creature who had begat him.

"He'll want the kids," Kate said weakly. "Not because he likes them, but because he knows it would hurt me to be deprived of them."

If that was the case, they would have to make certain that Buddy was not provided with evidence that would result in his being awarded custody of the children. They would have to be careful.

Buddy McCabe certainly wouldn't be the sort to have her followed, would he? Ben wanted to know.

"Would he hire someone, do you mean? Hell, no, he'd do it himself."

"He could find out you're not enrolled at the New School."

"There's no law that says in order to be a fit mother I have to be."

"What about being in the building?"

"Neela's probably the only real friend I have, outside of Julie Silverman. I could say I come in to talk to her."

Ben didn't think it would work, then Kate herself admitted that she knew it wouldn't. "Damn it," she said. "I won't be able to see you."

Maybe, instead, two or three times a week, he could get away from the hospital early and try to meet her in

Princeton. Didn't she go shopping every couple days? What would prevent their meeting somewhere near her home while Buddy was working?

It was possible. Yes, Kate thought it might be best. She was pretty sure that she would have to give up coming into the city, once she'd asked Buddy for a divorce. If she stayed around the house and went back to her former schedule, it was more likely that they could get away with it.

"But what about the free-clinic?" Kate asked. "I thought you go there as soon as you finish at the hospital."

He did, but he would simply have to work something out.

To Kate, it seemed an indication of the depth of his feelings. His marriage had broken up because he'd been unwilling to give up his work at the free-clinic, and now he was proposing to do just that in order to see Kate.

"I like to be with you," he said suddenly, "more than anyone else I know."

It was absurd and unreasonable, but Kate felt that way too.

Most of the people at the tiny Yorkville restaurant where they ate looked as if they'd left college just the week before, and Kate realized with a start that she and Ben were probably the oldest ones there. It was sobering, to say the least. It was Buddy McCabe's contention that New York was composed only of outlaws who preyed on the decadent and the rich, and the decadent and the rich who moved from apartment to apartment—from security system to security system—trying to escape their pursuers. But he'd neglected to include the vast numbers of young people who, she supposed, merely preyed upon one another.

They sat at a table by the window, four tables away from a portly, scarlet-faced man playing the zither.

"How did you know I'm a sucker for this kind of place?" she asked.

"Because I am."

The tables were cheek-by-jowl, so it was hard to talk—shout, really, over the zither music—without being overheard at the next table, but after she finished her first stein of black Löwenbräu, Kate relaxed and felt less inhibited.

While they waited for the sauerbraten, Kate was surprised to hear herself say, "I read a letter of yours back at the apartment. It was from Joanne. I don't know what came over me."

There were letters from Joanne all over the place, he replied. It would be damned hard not to read at least one. Anyway, he didn't mind at all. What had she wanted? Money?

"Joanne never learned anything about money except how to spend it," he continued. "She's not mean or nasty about it. Just—well, improvident."

What had she meant about Ben's moving to Vermont?

"Oh, that. I guess I've been talking about it for the last couple years. Like everyone else who lives here, I love New York and hate New York. I'm afraid—I don't know what—if I stay too long, I'll be brutalized by it, like everyone else."

Brutalized, how?

"Driven to do desperate things. Irrational things. Let me tell you something. There's a park, Riverside Park, that runs along the river behind the hospital. Sometimes when I have fifteen or twenty minutes' free time, which doesn't happen often, I go down there for a walk. Anyway, a couple weeks ago I noticed that the park people had put a brand-new drinking fountain next to the tennis courts. Most of the broken glass had been picked up, and the rubbish, and the place really looked nice. It made me feel good. Do you know what

I mean? That someone cared enough about the poor people who use the park to remember that sometimes they get thirsty. Okay. Here it comes. Two days ago I went down there again, and just as I came over the hill I saw three kids *bombing* the new drinking fountain with big boulders. Chips of concrete were flying everywhere. They had the thing almost half gone. I was just speechless. It was like I was watching something out of prehistory. I wanted to ask them why they were doing it, since the damned thing was put there for them in the first place. I say, I wanted to ask, but I didn't. Because I already knew why."

Rage, Kate supposed. Feeling ineffectual and shat upon. Screamed at by mothers who were junkies and fathers who were pimps, hated by teachers, doomed forever to live in squalor and fear of one another.

"They don't have anything, Kate," Ben said, "so what difference can a drinking fountain possibly make? If the world hacks away at them, why the hell shouldn't they hack away at the world?"

Kate was suddenly ashamed of herself. "I've never ... in all my life ... known anyone who was poor. Really poor. Though I guess there must have been some back in Ohio. We lead such selfish lives, most of us. Not you, but I do."

Maybe, after the divorce went through, she might like to help out at the free-clinic from time to time.

"I don't know how to do anything."

"You can be nice to people. Talk to them. Sometimes we're so damned busy it's hard to do either." He waited. "Whenever I think how fine and beautiful it would be to live in Vermont, I remember that this is where the people are. In Vermont, there are only mountains. You can't talk to mountains or help them."

"Mountains—" how had Joanne Purdom put it? "—don't get the clap either."

Ben remembered the reference. "If a kid is thirteen

129

years old and has his first case of clap, it's as important to him as cancer. He's scared out of his head."

"But what if it's the same person you saw destroying the drinking fountain? Could you still love him?"

"Sure, I could. Twice as much, too, because he needs love more than other kids."

While they ate and sipped their heady German beer, they talked about the future. After the divorce, Kate would move into the city with the two children. She could get a short-term lease on an apartment till she decided precisely what she wanted to do next. Ben would not press marriage. It would have to be a decision made by four people, including Kate's children. If, once she was free of Buddy McCabe, the kids didn't actively despise Ben, perhaps she would consider it.

Somehow or other, the beer, the music, and the young voices around her stirred an old memory in Kate. She had been sublimely happy like this once before, but when?

Then the memory came, like death. Kate was in a dark bedroom of the Phi Gam house, and a young boy was on top of her. When the delirium came, it was all mixed up with the music from the party below: *Oh-it's-beer-beer-beer-That-makes-me-feel-so-queer-In-the-COR-ner-In-the-COR-ner. Oh-it's-beer-beer-beer-That-makes-me-feel-so-queer-At-the-Quartermaster's-Ball!*

She had wanted it to go on everlastingly, yet now it was over.

"What's wrong?" Ben asked, at once sensing a change in mood.

Nothing was wrong, Kate replied, lying (after the first lie, what was the use ever again of telling the truth?). She looked away from him, and as she did, she saw something outside the window so contrary to reason that she rested her knife and fork against her plate and stared.

"I think I just saw someone I know," she said. "Only it's impossible."

130

She'd thought she'd seen Neela. But it *was* impossible, because the woman who looked like Neela Fitzgerald was being helped along the sidewalk by two black men, one on either side, and she was walking in a stilted, artificial way, as if her legs didn't truly belong to her.

II

Continuing Education

he's eight year or seventeen. It's what he done. The wife and me wanted to talk to you before we get in touch with the police."

Lovely. They were suggesting, were they, that an eight-year-old boy be jailed for sodomizing an idiot. It was all she could do to ask someone to explain to her precisely what had happened, though she knew damned well that nothing at all had happened.

The man repeated what his son had told him. The day before, he had been sweeping out the garage, which he did most afternoons as a diversion, and Dutchie had run through the backyard on his way home from school, though Mrs. Crawford had often called to him and told him not to take a shortcut through her lawn. Afterwards, Edward had come into the house and his pants were all undone, but he wouldn't tell them what had happened. It wasn't till to-day, after his father had whipped him with a leather belt, that he finally told them. The boy who ran through the yard had done something to him in the garage.

"But it doesn't make sense," Kate protested. "Dutchie is just a little boy. There must be bigger boys who take shortcuts through your yard." Then she turned to him. "Did you do what they say you did?"

Dutchie was obviously frightened. He knew that he was being charged with something unspeakable, but Kate could read his face well enough to know that he didn't understand what the accusation involved. Both Dutchie and Suzie had been taught the correct names of their private parts, so Kate now said, "Did you put your penis in his—" here Kate couldn't think of the word "—his hind end?"

If previously Dutchie had been terror-stricken, now he was mad. "I throwed a *stone* at him! That's what I did."

"Why?"

Because he'd been running through the yard and the

boy had shouted at him, then began to chase him. Dutchie was afraid of him, so he picked up a stone and pitched it at him. Whether he hit him or not, he didn't know. "Suzie was with me. Ask her."

Suzie was in the family room, watching television, but she came as soon as she heard Kate calling her. Kate put the question to her directly. Had she and Dutchie run through the Crawford's yard after they got off the bus yesterday afternoon, and if they had, did anything happen?

Suzie looked at her brother for some clue as to how she was supposed to respond. Impatiently, Kate said, "Just tell the truth."

"Dutchie threw a stone at . . . at . . . *him*." As soon as she uttered the pronoun, she turned her head aside so that she wouldn't have to look at the boy.

"They're telling the truth," Kate said. "I'm afraid your boy has made a terrible mistake."

A mistake, no matter how it was resolved, that Dutchie would probably carry with him for the rest of his life. A mistake that perhaps, given his temperament anyway, would be remembered on an analyst's couch twenty or thirty years from now. He was so unsure of himself, anyway. What the hell would something like this do to him?

The man now removed his leather belt and held it before his son's face. "Was it this kid or not? Was it another kid? You lie again, Ed-wurd, and you won't be settin' down for a week."

The child trembled with fear. "Don't know."

"You don't know! You tolt us it was him! Now you change your mind!"

"Don't know." He held up one hand, preparing for a blow.

"Damn you, what did this kid do to you?"

The boy's eyes flashed with anger. "Hit me with a rock."

"Then who done this other thing!"

The boy couldn't remember. He didn't know. Some-one did. Then he broke into tears even before his father lashed at him with the belt and pulled him out of the hallway, through the door, and down the front steps.

Kate's breath came in short gasps. She could scarcely form the words in her mouth, she was so upset. "I don't want to hear anymore. Just go," she said to the woman.

Indignantly, the woman said, "Just keep your snot-nose kid outta our yard!"

Kate stood by the door. "*Go!* Right now before I say something I'll be ashamed of later on."

Kate slammed the door shut even before the woman was all the way through it. The door chimes began to ring wildly, and the woman on the porch was sobbing, "Damn snotnose bastards! Both of you!"

Kate sank into a chair in the hall and buried her face in her hands.

If Dutchie had been injured by this display of human degradation, what would he think when Kate tried to explain to him that she no longer loved his father and was getting a divorce? In a child's mind, would it be worse than sodomy? Would it be so unnatural and unreasonable that he wouldn't be able to grasp or comprehend it, and neither would Suzie? Would they both hate her as much as they hated this boy at whom they'd thrown a rock?

Even before she uncovered her eyes, Kate could feel Dutchie, his leg against hers for warmth and protection. He had taken it, this false accusation, more manfully than she'd thought possible. When at last she looked up at him, he was hurt, she could see, but not beaten.

"I won't go through there no more."

The grammar would have to be corrected later. To Kate, it was continually perplexing that Suzie, who was younger than her brother, would know the past tense of "throw" and would never think of using a double

181

negative. God knows where little boys picked up their version of the English language. Their ears were not tuned in to words. But somehow this was not the time to go into such matters.

"Okay," she said a minute later, wiping her cheeks with her fists, "listen to me, Dutchie. There are a lot of dirty things in the world and a lot of dirty people. Some of them don't mean to be that way; it just happens because of a set of circumstances. But you have to learn to live with everyone, so you'll have to learn to live with them, too." She waited, then asked, "So why did that boy come down here with . . . that awful story in the first place?"

Dutchie didn't know.

Yes, he did. All he had to do was think about it.

"I throwed a stone."

"Okay. And if you hadn't done that, he wouldn't have come down here and put us through all that. Do you understand? You hurt him, so he had to hurt you."

Was she asking too much? After such an outrage to his self-esteem, could he be interested in motives?

From the kitchen, Kate could hear Suzie loudly removing silverware from the drawer to set on the table. Hadn't even been asked, which made it something of a first for her. Yet somehow she had realized that the drama in the hall had upset both Kate and her brother, and such moments tend to inspire mature unselfishness.

"Tell you what," Kate said to her son, "I won't say anything to your father—if you promise never, never to go near their yard again."

Kate wasn't proud of the deal she was offering him. She was asking a boy who had been taught always to venerate the truth—even now, he hadn't lied—to ignore it temporarily, because if Buddy learned of it, she could almost predict his reaction: "Goddammit, I knew something like this was going to happen the minute you decided to go into that stinking city. Kids need a full-time mother, Kate."

At any other time she might possibly be willing to contest it, but not now because it would merely deflect her attention from the more important talk she would have to have with Buddy sometime this weekend.

"Okay," Dutchie said.

Kate went upstairs to her bedroom and sat on the edge of the bed, wondering if this was just the beginning.

By Friday night, Buddy McCabe no longer even pretended to like his job. If he ever ran away to the South Seas on the spur of the moment, Kate was sure he would do it on a Friday night, because by then, after one more grueling week, his spirit was gone. Or as he himself put it, "On Monday I go into that damn place thinking that I might make a difference, somehow, in those bastards' lives. But by Friday, forget it. Those loutish, fat-headed, overprivileged nitwits are killing me, Kate."

If it wasn't his students, it was Fatass, the headmaster. If it wasn't the headmaster, it was a parent with a complaint of one type or another. If it wasn't a parent, it was the heating system, or the cooling system. It was the midday lunch ("The garbage they feed those kids, Kate, and the fees over three thousand a year. No wonder the kids are fermenting all the time") or it was someone else's car in his parking space. It was his colleagues and his colleagues' wives.

Tonight, for a change, it was what he called the shaft.

"Goddammit," he said the minute he opened the door, "I'm getting the shaft again." He slammed his briefcase down on the kitchen table and sat down without removing his coat. "You know what I'd like to do, Kate? I'd like to quit that goddamn job tomorrow."

Kate, spreading frosting over cupcakes at the counter, had wanted to say it for years, but had never had the courage before. "So why don't you?" she asked him.

Buddy made the kind of face he no doubt made in class when a student came up with a wrong answer. It said Christ-how-can-anyone-be-so-thick?

"I'm serious," Kate repeated. "If you hate your job, why keep it? Why continue to do something you hate?"

Impatiently, he answered, "I can give you about fifty reasons, starting with mortgage payments, car payments, property taxes . . ." He lost interest in Kate's absurd suggestion. "Listen! Do you want to know what happened today?"

Quickly, Kate ticked off the outrages that had been heaped upon Buddy during the past year, wondering if today's was a repetition of an old one or an entirely new article.

"Fatass is giving the job to Henderson."

Henderson, who had joined the English department several years after Buddy had, was about to be named chairman of the department.

"Who told you?"

"Not Fatass, the cowardly bastard. Henderson himself! He knows how much I hate his guts, so he came into my office after lunch and broke the news. Kate, how can I work with that imbecile? The only reason he got the job is that he sucked up to old Fatass, and I never did."

Oh, dear God, if only he would stop. All his life, Buddy had maintained that virtue was never rewarded, and that the world did not appreciate the industry and pluck of Buddy McCabe. Only toadies got ahead, never the qualified and deserving.

"So what are you going to do now?"

Again the look of incredulity, then, "What am I going to *do*? Are you crazy, Kate? I can't do anything. I just have to accept it. What else can I do? I've got a *family*."

How many men used that as an excuse for their own ineffectuality? Kate wondered. For Buddy to think that he was sacrificing himself for his family somehow made it all very admirable.

"A hundred years ago," he began, "when a man got tired of things in one place, he hitched up the wagon and went west." Sadly he rose from the chair and made his way toward the refrigerator. "The hell of it is that there aren't any places left to go anymore."

He filled a glass with milk, then returned the carton to the refrigerator.

"I thought you weren't going to drink milk anymore," she reminded him. "Cholesterol."

"To hell with cholesterol." He gulped from the glass, leaving a milky moustache around his mouth. With the back of his hand, he wiped it clean. "I gave up smoking too, so I wouldn't get lung cancer. And now I get the shaft instead. I can die of humiliation in a classroom, instead of a heart attack." He laughed sharply. "Fuck it."

"You *are* in a good mood."

Kate tried to remember how he'd been when he was still in college before the world began to conspire against him. He used to read Baudelaire aloud to her and Rilke and Ezra Pound. Before he enlisted in the Army, he'd recited "Sestina: Altaforte" to her over the telephone, beginning "Damn it all! all this our South stinks peace." He had opinions about books and poems and ideas.

Why was it that some men, like Buddy, became diminished as they grew older and others, like Quentin Fitzgerald, became stronger and more cunning? A matter of disposition, Kate supposed. Even when he was in college, Buddy must already have had a premonition of failure.

What could he look forward to now, other than a providential early coronary? With each succeeding year, he would hate his job more, yet wouldn't think of resigning. In time he would become even more soured and dispirited, and the only thing that would keep him going would be the pension he was entitled to.

But by then, he would have forgotten how to form opinions or to read anything more complicated than newspapers or sophomore English themes. Cranky and contentious, he would roam the house—as a senile uncle of Kate's back in Ohio did—moving from one room to another, looking everywhere for the one thing he truly required more than he required a wife, children, or happiness, and that was the shaft. The beautiful, ever-present, indispensable shaft.

"I could have hit Henderson," he said to her now.

"Why didn't you?"

He threw up his hands in despair. "You think I'm crazy?"

Not crazy enough. That was the trouble. Too uncrazy.

If only Kate could say what she really meant. *What would you do, Buddy, if I changed my life? Would you change yours too or wouldn't you know how? What would you do if I asked you for a divorce?*

"A lot of people our age are changing their lives," Kate said optimistically, "and starting all over."

"And a lot aren't," he said with finality.

Well, she'd done the best she could for the time being. It was only Friday night, and somehow she had to live with him through Saturday and Sunday, so she didn't dare to be more explicit. She watched for the hundredth time as he took off his wet coat and draped it over the back of the fake Hitchcock chair, though it certainly must have occurred to him by now that *someone* hung up the coat for him, then cleaned up the watery mess on the chair with paper towels.

"If that bastard gives me a hard time," he added, mostly to himself, "I'm going to let him have it."

Kate had lost the transition. "Who?"

"Henderson," he answered with annoyance. "You weren't listening."

Neither were you, she wanted to say.

After supper, the kids sprawled on the floor of the family room and watched a TV program that must have been written for a class of ax-murderer trainees. Buddy sat in his vinyl armchair at the other end of the room and read the evening newspaper, fighting sleep all the way, and finally hit the dust when he reached the financial page.

It was almost nine, later than usual, when Kate herded the children up the stairs, Suzie in tears, partly because she wasn't allowed to watch "Bonanza," partly because she was running a temperature. The latter meant that she would come down with something in earnest either tomorrow or the next day. If her bug behaved like past ones, Dutchie would have it by Monday or Tuesday, Kate would acquire it by midweek, and Buddy would be felled by the following Friday. As soon as everyone began to feel well again, another virus would strike, this time perhaps beginning with Dutchie. It sometimes seemed to Kate that what living together was really all about was that everyone got everyone else's head colds and flu.

By nine-thirty, the kids had stopped whining, and Kate was able to sit on the sofa in the family room and read the front page of the paper. Tried to, anyway, until Buddy's sleeping face caught her attention, so she watched him. He was such a sweet, good-natured, helpless fellow, once you got used to him. If only Kate could hate him more, it would be easier to divorce him.

Afterwards, he would marry the first woman to come along who felt sorry for him, Kate concluded. A divorcee probably, also in her late thirties, because Buddy would lack the stamina to keep up with a younger woman. There were all kinds of women who needed to prop up weak men, so he should have no trouble.

Still, he was going to be hurt by a divorce; there was no question about that. Kate would become an enemy, like Fatass and Henderson.

"Okay," Kate imagined him saying, "so what did I do to deserve this shit? Haven't I always given you everything you've ever wanted? Don't I turn my paycheck over to you? Didn't I always drive a four-year-old car while you drove the new one? Haven't we always gone where you wanted to go on vacation? Didn't I break my balls to be nice to you? Haven't I . . . don't I . . . didn't I . . . ?"

"Yes, *yes*," Kate heard herself saying softly.

Buddy opened his eyes, saw her sitting across from him, and smiled. "What a dope," he said about himself. "I fell asleep. Hey, it's almost eleven. Turn on the news, will you?"

No, she wanted to say. I will not. We have to talk, Buddy. About us and about what's happening.

Tell him, Kate, Ben had said to her when she'd left his apartment, and she'd rehearsed on the train, in the car, at the market, and in the kitchen. It had seemed so easy then.

In the end, Kate got the channel Buddy asked for, then went upstairs and prepared for bed, leaving him absorbed in the day's doleful events. When, fifteen minutes later, he shuffled into the bedroom, he found her already in bed.

"Fucking rain tomorrow," he said to her in the darkness.

How many times she'd said it during the last fifteen years, she didn't know, but now she said it again. "Doesn't it always rain on Saturday?"

It *poured* on Saturday.

Which meant that no one got nearer the out-of-doors than was necessary to race to and from the car.

First, Kate drove Dutchie and Suzie to the junior high where they both took a swimming class, then went to the A&P to look at the roasts again, so that at least Buddy's last Sunday dinner would be memorable. After she found a standing rib roast (after the income was split and two households had to be maintained, no one could afford anything like *that* again), she stood in a long check-out line, howling children everywhere. A woman behind her blew cigarette smoke at her, but Kate decided not to make an issue of it.

Afterwards, she picked up the dry cleaning, a dozen doughnuts from the bakery for Sunday breakfast ("Why do you buy junk food like that?" Buddy would ask, then eat two or three of them himself), then dropped by an antique shop and told the woman there that she wouldn't be buying the Staffordshire tureen after all, as she'd be moving shortly and would have no need for it.

"Is Mr. McCabe leaving his position at the school?" the woman asked, and Kate realized with a start that she'd almost blown it. Of course, the woman knew that Buddy was a teacher, because Kate herself had told her when she put the ten-dollar deposit on the tureen.

It was just too uncivil for Kate to tell a perfect stranger that she was divorcing her husband even before she'd told Buddy, so she said instead, "Actually, we're just looking at other houses. We've been living in the same place for almost fifteen years."

Dutchie, who was promptitude itself, was waiting outside the school when she drove up, but predictably Suzie was ambling around the halls. They sat and waited for her for ten minutes, and when she came out at last—her face was flushed, her forehead was hot, and she'd probably left millions of bacteria in the pool—she said that she'd been looking at the trophies in the cases. Kate could have whacked her, but then it occurred to her that she was cross because she was hungry; one of the cardinal rules of motherhood was, never hit a child on an empty stomach.

It was past twelve-thirty by the time they started for home, and though she knew that it wouldn't possibly occur to Buddy to fix a sandwich for himself, even if he was starving, she remembered still one more errand.

"What for?" Dutchie moaned.

For something she'd almost forgotten.

Had deliberately tried to forget, in point of fact. She'd taken her last Pill the day before, she was in the middle of her cycle, and tonight was Saturday, which meant that Buddy would perform—or attempt to perform—his conjugal duties.

"What do you always get at the drug store in the blue box?" Suzie asked as Kate parked the car.

It had taken Kate at least half of her married life to be able to heap rolls of toilet paper brazenly on her shopping cart at the market, but she drew the line at sanitary napkins. She preferred instead to run into the drugstore, pay furtively, then dash out.

"None a your business," Dutchie said to his sister with astounding perspicacity, Kate thought, somehow divining that the blue box contained something personal.

Before she opened the car door, she rummaged through her purse for her prescription, half hoping that it wasn't there. When at last her fingers found it, she held on to it, not quite knowing what she was going to do. Then, surprisingly—at least Kate was surprised—she tore it in two, then in two again, and stuck the pieces in the ash tray.

"Whadid you do that for?" Suzie asked, and without answering Kate left the car and walked into the store, already anticipating what was going to happen, yet somehow she knew she had to go through it in order to make it more believable.

She strode to the prescription counter at the rear and waited for the pharmacist. When he appeared, she explained that she'd misplaced her prescription for the Pill, but could he perhaps fill it for her anyway?

"I'm afraid your doctor will have to okay that."

"But you know who I am," she replied. "I've been getting the same prescription filled here for the last five years."

"I'm sorry, Mrs. McCabe."

He even knew her name!

". . . but I'd be breaking the law," he continued. "You can use the telephone here to call your doctor, if you like."

No, Kate did not want to bother him on a Saturday, which was always a busy day for him. She would simply wait until Monday.

When she'd entered the drugstore, Kate had been depressed and uncertain. As she left it, she felt buoyant.

"You didn't get nothing," Dutchie said to her as she slid into the front seat.

"Anything," she corrected by way of reply. Then, "They were all out, honey."

Once, when Kate's mother was visiting from Ohio for several weeks, she expressed the opinion that Suzie's lethargy and Dutchie's intransigence both derived from the same source: eating nothing but sandwiches on Saturdays, which in time would almost certainly addle their minds.

Actually, it was Buddy who had originally suggested that Kate stay out of the kitchen at least one day a week, and far from considering sandwiches a punishment, the kids adored them. If the choice were theirs, they would eat all their meals at McDonald's.

After a soup-and-sandwich lunch, Buddy worked in the garage on one of his power mowers (he'd been tinkering with it for the last three Saturdays, and it was still inoperable), and the kids stretched out on the floor and watched TV until at last Kate yelled at them that it had stopped raining, dammit, and they were to go out in the backyard immediately and play, which they did for ten or fifteen minutes, then stood morosely by the sliding glass door to the family room, looking in at the blank TV screen. Kate did some washing, worked on a dress she was making for Suzie, then took a short nap late in the afternoon.

If, back when she was in college, someone had told Kate Ferguson that by the time she was thirty-nine she'd be spending her Saturday nights eating hamburgers at McDonald's, she wouldn't have believed it. Had Catherine Barkley? Daisy Miller? Anna Karenina?

Yet to suggest to Buddy that there might be something else to do invariably got the same response. Five days a week he ate out—lunch anyway. He spent half his life in a car. On weekends, he just liked to relax. It did no good for her to try to tell him that what she wanted desperately was to un-relax, to animate herself somehow.

At least, for a change, the kids didn't misbehave at McDonald's and no one had to be slapped. Dutchie, who had an alert and receptive mind, busied himself watching everyone who came in or left. Suzie, whose mind baffled Kate, watched only her Big Mac, and when she wasn't doing that, she looked at her French fries as if they were the most beautiful things she'd ever seen.

No one talked, of course, except to comment on the grub or to send one of the kids after extra napkins or to correct table manners. If McDonald's would only print injunctions on the wall, Kate thought, or for Suzie on the top of her Big Mac bun—*Don't chew with your mouth open. Use your napkin. You're going to spill your milkshake*—it wouldn't be necessary for American families to say anything at all.

So it came as a complete surprise when Suzie looked up from her feast and said to her father, "When did you ever have an eagle?"

Buddy chose to provide her with a pedantic answer, most of which no one listened to. The eagle was rarely seen in the Eastern states anymore, he said, and so far as he knew had never been domesticated. Moreover, some people had suggested that the eagle was an inappropriate symbol for democracy because it was a carrion eater and . . .

"Mrs. Rexroth said you had an eagle," Suzie interrupted.

Kate became apprehensive. Not merely because Mrs. Rexroth, who lived four houses away, was no great friend of hers—Kate had once complained about her dog—but because she had a feeling that Mrs. Rexroth wouldn't say anything pleasant about anyone if she could help it.

"What else did she say?"

Suzie recapitulated. Mrs. Rexroth had been talking to Mrs. Arvidson, who had just moved into the neighborhood, and Mrs. Rexroth said that Suzie's father was a schoolteacher and very nice, and that Suzie's mother was also very nice, but she herself pitied Mr. McCabe because it seemed to her that Mrs. McCabe destroyed his eagle.

"*Ego!*" Kate cried, and Suzie murmured, that's what she said.

Kate watched as Buddy's face turned crimson.

She almost knew why Mrs. Rexroth had said it, too. Early last summer, while Kate was out, Buddy had outlined the wood molding on the overhead garage door in the same shade of green as the shutters, and she supposed that Mrs. Rexroth had watched him. When Kate saw what he'd done, she made him repaint everything white. At another time, he'd bought and spent half a Saturday morning mounting a starkly modern mailbox on the post by the roadside, and the minute Kate drove into the driveway, she shrieked. The house was Early American. Hadn't he *noticed?* So why had he picked out a maroon-and-bright-silver mailbox shaped like a rocket? A mailbox wasn't supposed to hit you in the face architecturally.

In the end the same neighbors, including Mrs. Rexroth apparently, who had watched him mount the box so proudly in the morning, saw him sheepishly remove it in the afternoon.

Eagle destructive.

Yet he'd never once complained. Dammit, why hadn't he?

They finished their Big Macs in silence.

By the time they got home, it was seven-thirty and Kate began to feel as if she couldn't go through with it after all. While Buddy and the kids watched TV— thank God for the noise—she went upstairs and sat on the edge of the tub in the bathroom. If only she could telephone Ben, perhaps she'd be able to recapture her resolve, but he'd said he would be in Nyack over the weekend and she didn't know how to reach him.

Were there any distractions there? she'd asked him, and he replied, "Snoring dog, creaking roof, hissing fire: the usual country stuff."

Maybe usual in Upper Nyack but not in New Jersey. Even from where she sat, she could hear the TV roaring, shaking the walls of the house.

When at last she heard Buddy shout, "Hey, Kate, you okay?" she came downstairs, assuring him that she wasn't ill. It was Suzie who might be. "I'm not either," Suzie protested, preferring death on the floor while being entertained by whatever banality was transfixing her.

At about nine, Buddy suggested that she make some pizza, Dutchie said, "Neat," and Suzie wiped her 102-degree forehead and said, "Cool." At least it gave Kate an opportunity to get away. She was shaking by the time she reached the kitchen.

The heavy pizza dough gave her hands something to worry over (How many pizzas had she made in fifteen years? Did the Ford Foundation or the Guggenheims consider it sufficiently creative and important to warrant their attention?) and somehow or other between the baking, the eating, and the cleaning up, it got to be ten o'clock, which was weekend bedtime for the kids. Suzie was in tears because she wasn't able to see a movie and also because she was burning up with fever. Kate gave her an aspirin and sat with her until she was asleep, then stood by the window, looking out on the dark lawn till she heard the familiar voice of the weekend newscaster.

Kate checked the doors (leaving the front storm door open for the morning *Times;* Buddy always forgot), turned out the lights except those in the living room where he still sat, then said to him that she was tired and thought she'd go to bed. She heard a grunting response, but whether it was from him or from someone in the box, she couldn't say.

Wretchedly, she climbed the stairs once again. In the bathroom she cold-creamed her face and while she did it, she tried to summon up the courage to tell Buddy not to touch her, please, not tonight. The flu or something, she'd say. She got into bed and turned her back toward his half, hoping that somehow he wouldn't notice her.

In another ten minutes, she heard him mounting the stairs, then splashing urine in the bathroom, and finally brushing his teeth. Never, not even on their wedding night, had he gone to bed without doing the latter. Kate always knew that lovemaking was about to take place when a hand began to stroke her breasts, then the scent of Colgate toothpaste overwhelmed her.

He was in his pajamas when he left the bathroom, but Kate could hear him slip out of them before he got into bed. He crowded close to her, and she could feel his naked body against her nightgown.

"I forgot to leave the money out for the paper boy," he said for the thousandth time.

"I did it."

He bent over to part her nightgown—*"Tell him!"* she heard Ben say—then he climbed on top of her.

"I haven't been taking the Pill," she said weakly. "I lost the prescription and they wouldn't give me any at the drugstore."

She expected him to be angry when she explained what had happened, but he was very amiable.

"That's okay," he answered, then slowly began to rise and fall over her belly, high up, over her mound of hair (*"I am a mindless piece of flesh. I cook and clean and put the money out for the paper boy"*), till he came on her stomach, whimpering like a puppy.

"I'll get some Kleenex," he said seconds later, but Kate could no longer hear.

A sunless October dawning.

The cockcrow which awoke Kate was Suzie's terrified crying. Kate got to her just in time to help her to the bathroom and hold her head over the gaping toilet bowl while she fought for breath, then vomited everything but her tonsils: the pulverized Big Mac, snake-like-French fries, soupy vanilla shake, and spears of pizza, all in a swampy, impressionistic stew.

Afterwards, both were breathless, weak. Kate knew better than to try to call a doctor at six on a Sunday morning. If by ten or eleven things hadn't improved, she might risk a telephone call. If insurance firms could cancel policies on the accident-prone, she supposed that physicians could give up patients who became ill on Sundays, and it had taken five years of searching to find a doctor who was compatible. To be rejected by him now, because of a case of the flu, was something Kate would just as soon avoid.

Instead she helped Suzie to bed again, then sat in the chair across from her, closed her eyes, and drifted into a restless half-sleep. It must have been two o'clock when she'd finally been able to let her mind go limp—

she imagined it as a kite getting up into a windless sky—so she was tired and her eyes ached.

At eight o'clock or later, she heard feet scurrying down the stairs to the front door, and she knew that Dutchie was taking in the two Sunday papers. She listened as he went into the kitchen—to eat something he wasn't supposed to? candy?—then make his way up the stairs again. As he passed his sister's room and saw Kate seated there, he came in and wordlessly sat in her lap, draping his legs over the side of the chair, and opened the funnies. Not a sound. Not Good Morning. Not Hi. Not even Ugh. He stretched out with familiarity, against the very womb where he'd begun life, and started to scrutinize the comics.

One of Kate's hands was pinned down by his leg, but with the other she dug into his flannel pajamas till she found his buttocks, then caressed them, drawing warmth and comfort from the touch. He smelled of clean hair, chocolate—he *did* get into candy—and a vague little-boy smell of pee-pee. She watched him as he read and marveled at what she'd helped create. Someday he'd be grown up, would be in love, would marry, would have children of his own, would sit with them on Sunday mornings, would be happy or unhappy, and would die.

It seemed to Kate wondrous and absurd.

"They said in school there's no more Pogo," he whispered to her now, pointing at the comic strip as if in contradiction.

"Who told you that?"

"In school they said that." His finger rested on the creature, then drew a circle round his head.

Immortality possibly, but more likely clever henchmen. How could she explain? "It was the man who drew him, Dutchie," she said at last. "He died, but someone else must be doing it now."

"It looks like always, anyway."

It wasn't that hard to adapt to catastrophe, she

wanted to say. At times, life seemed insufferable and beyond sorting out, but in the end most people, like Pogo, learned to cope. Sadness was surprisingly forgettable.

Mostly because she wanted to share what he was doing, she, too, read the funny paper, finishing each page long before he did, then watching his lips move as he formed the words. "You finished?" he asked when he reached the bottom of the page, and once to make him feel an accomplished reader, she said, "No, wait."

Then Suzie was standing by the chair, out of her death bed, repositioning Dutchie's legs so that she also could be accommodated on Kate's lap. "You'll give us the bug," Kate said without alarm, knowing that she probably already had it.

"She's got cooties," Dutchie said accusingly.

"I don't either!"

Kate was warmed by their bodies, stirred by their smells. Would they hate her for what she was about to do to them? Bringing sorrow and disorder and confusion to the way they lived.

If the children loved their father so much, then why, dear God, can't I?

Because, she said, answering her own question, I am not a child. Buddy expects thralldom, and I no longer have a zeal for it. Somehow or other, I have to make something of my own life before it's all over.

"Your fever's down," she said, touching Suzie's forehead.

"Yeah."

"Don't say yeah. Say yes."

"Yes." She finished a balloon in the comic strip, then turned to Kate and touched her ear lobe. "When are we gonna have breakfast?"

If the body recovered so miraculously, why couldn't the spirit?

"As soon as your father gets up."

Kate would have to talk to him that minute, while

his mind was clean and unbeaten. She would tell him what was happening to her, and he would have a whole day, if he liked, to break down her argument. He would appeal to her sense of duty, her motherhood. He would accept all the blame and promise to improve. He would do anything to dissuade her. Or would he?

"It's all in your mind," he'd tell her. "You're brooding too much. Soon as spring rolls around, you'll be okay again, Kate."

But I don't love you anymore.

Would she have the tongue to form the words?

"Kids," she said at last, "how about getting down and putting your bathrobes and slippers on, and we can go downstairs and fix chow?"

God, one more thing she would be eternally indebted to Buddy for. *Chow.* He'd brought it home with him from the Army.

The kids scurried down the stairs, then Kate went into the bedroom where Buddy was still stretched out under the blanket. His eyes opened, and she must have appeared like an apparition: hair up in curlers, coldcreamed face, holding on to the Sunday funny paper.

"What the hell time is it?" he asked.

"There's something I have to tell you, Buddy."

He yawned, stuck his fists beneath his head on the pillow, and contemplated her, expecting perhaps to be told about one more correctable crisis: a hair brush down the toilet, a fist through the storm door, water in the basement.

"I'm sorry," she began, marveling at her strength, "but I want you to give me a divorce, Buddy."

———◆———

On the preceding Saturday, after Neela had left Julie at the Hertz garage—rather, after Julie had left her, not even offering to drop her off at the apartment, but then gratitude had never been Julie's forte—she'd walked west toward Park Avenue, and as soon as she passed Lexington she heard footsteps quicken behind her and someone call out her name.

"Hey, how you doin', man?" Ronnie said as he hurried up to her.

He must have been waiting outside the apartment building and followed her east to the garage. He'd obviously got dressed up for the meeting. He was wearing a modish dark-blue suit with a red-and-white floral sport shirt open at the neck.

"Oh, it's you." Neela didn't stop but continued walking and he fell into step at her side. "I'm really in the most awful rush." Then: "How did you know where I live?"

"Bobby got it wrote down. He in trouble, man."

"Robert?"

He'd been picked up with two other men in an apartment on Waverly Place, which had been staked out. Robert Pino had had heroin on him.

"He need bail, so I say I come see you."

Even without thinking, Neela said, "No."

"Bobby don't know no one else."

"He doesn't know me anymore, either. I won't even try to tell you how much money I've . . . thrown away on him. Just tell him that the supply has dried up."

"No one throw money away, man. People buy what they want. You know what I mean? Bobby help you out when you need it, man, so it your turn to help now."

200

Neela moved away from him, wondering if she should rush into the street and start screaming or continue walking toward Park as if she weren't afraid. "I'm sorry, but I have to go now. I really am in the most awful rush."

She felt his fingers dig into the crook of her arm.

"You and your fuckin' most-awful-rush. You lissen to me, man. You almost get me killed the other night. You doan even stop to see if I'm alive." He tightened his grip. "You like me when I'm in your pussy, man, but you doan like me no other time."

Neela stopped on the sidewalk and turned to look at him. He was a spectacularly good-looking man. Even standing next to him now, she felt his magnetism. "Look. I made a mistake. I should never have been with Robert Pino. He did . . . he gave me something so that I really wasn't responsible. I'm not that kind of woman. Don't you understand? I'm married. I have children." Suddenly she got angry. "And you can take your hand off my arm. I won't run away. I don't like to be intimidated."

"I know the feelin'." He let her arm fall.

She didn't understand, he began. All he wanted to do was to get to know her better, because she was all he'd been able to think of since he met her. He meant no harm. He wasn't like those other dudes in the garment center. He was studying part-time at City College.

"I won me a Carnegie medal," he said. "Bet you never knew anyone who done that before." He'd swooped down and picked up a child who had fallen onto the subway tracks, and he'd even got his picture in the papers. "Got a citation, too. You want to read it sometime?"

Neela said that she would like to, when she had a bit more time.

"I know all about you," he continued. "I ast Bobby and he tell me. You a famous Broadway actress."

Poor Robert. What had he told this man? Did it enhance his own ego to describe her as a famous actress?

"I haven't . . . done much lately."

There had been a dreamlike quality to his walk as they came down the block toward Park, and yet a kind of intensity, too. She was sure that he was on something even now. Flying. Possibly in order to get his courage up to intercept her on the street.

It was all so self-destructive. On the one hand he talked about college and medals for heroism, and on the other he'd already shot up—or whatever he'd done—for the day. There was absolutely no *way* he'd ever get ahead, no *way* he'd ever be a hero again.

Neela saw in him something which she also saw in herself: the same element of self-destruction. It existed in her own mother, too, now in her sixties, so severely brain-damaged by alcohol that she scarcely reacted anymore when Neela visited her at the nursing home in Ohio. Did this man named Ronnie recognize in Neela the same ineptitude for life?

Thank God I'm not black, Neela said to herself. To carry that burden along with all the other ones would be unendurable. Even now, as they walked south on Park Avenue, everyone who passed scrutinized Ronnie with suspicion.

"When can I see you again?" he asked now. "You know what I mean?"

Yes, she knew what he meant. As much as she hated herself for her weakness, she would have given anything to be in this man's arms even now. "I don't know," she replied. "Look. It's Saturday. I won't be able to get any money for Robert till Monday. Tell him that."

He would do that. But when could he see her again?

"Tell him that this is the last time. No more. Absolutely."

Neela tried to recall what Quentin had told her about his schedule. On Monday evening, he and Amos were flying back to the Coast, provided Quent could complete all his dealing and wheeling by Monday afternoon. Well, Neela was going along whether anyone liked it or not. She would take the kids out of school, rent a place for the winter, possibly in Encino, where they'd rented houses before, and forget that there was a New York City. If Quentin didn't like the arrangement, she didn't care. She would go anyway.

"Late Monday afternoon," she said to him now. "I should have the money by then. About four o'clock. How much does he need?"

The bailman would require a thousand.

An expensive friendship.

Where could he meet her?

"Come to the apartment. I'll have everything ready for you."

It seemed to Neela that she had several options. She would either have the money or not, depending on what decision she'd reached by then. But she knew one thing, and that was that she didn't dare see Ronnie again. If she decided to provide the bail money, she could leave it with the doorman. If not, she could tell the doorman to say that she had already left for Los Angeles.

"You and me, we can be friends now, okay, man?" There was a grin on his face.

Okay, they could be friends.

"I see you Monday, friend. Four o'clock. This time doan let me down." Ronnie squeezed her arm once more, turned, and walked east on 74th street.

Before he left that morning to keep an appointment with a producer, Quentin had extracted a promise from Amos Guard that he'd return to the apartment by two so that he and Neela could be at Tim Cassidy's place on Gramercy Park by three. Cassidy was, by his own description, a first-class drama coach, Method division, who had studied with the Strasbergs and later worked with them. When he was sober, that is. When he was drunk, he was not a mere drunk, according to Quent, but a mean, vindictive, dangerous drunk. The longer he was kept waiting by people who were late for appointments, Quent added, the drunker, meaner, and more dangerous he became.

He had agreed to help Amos with the script, first in New York, then in California.

At a quarter past two, Amos called Neela and told her that he was going to be delayed; she was to go down to Cassidy's place and he would meet her there. Quentin had warned her that Amos functioned only if someone were behind him, goosing him now and then, so she volunteered to grab a taxi, drive to wherever he was, and pick him up. Where was he anyway?

He was in the steam room at the Yale Club.

Was he a member?

He was a guest, he said. In point of fact, he enjoyed collecting steam baths and had visited at least a hundred different ones the summer he'd bummed around the States. Today, after having had lunch with Irving Diament at the Brussels, Amos had simply walked into the Yale Club, asked the first sympathetic person he came to if he minded directing him to the steam room, and—presto—he was soaking up a good grade of steam and sweating a very patrician class of sweat.

"Someone's been looking at my meat for the last fifteen minutes," he continued, "but I'm not sure anything will come of it. Here anyway."

"Cassidy expects us at three, Amos. Quent says he gets very upset if anyone's late."

"Tell him that I get very upset if I'm on time."

It was becoming increasingly apparent to Neela that drinking was only one of Amos Guard's problems. Before he began to drink for the day he was promiscuous—drinking was no pleasure, in fact, without it—the more outlandish and daring the promiscuity, the better.

But in the steam room of the Yale Club with all those bankers, diplomats, brokers, and lawyers? Neela shook her head sadly.

"Just try to be there by three."

Amos would try. A lot depended on how interesting his new friend was.

He obviously needed looking after. It was Quentin's hope, of course, that Amos would respond to fathering, but it now occurred to Neela that mothering would do almost as well.

It was a puzzlement to her that someone as dubiously sexed as Amos could arouse such expectations in women, as he did virtually everywhere Neela had taken him when she showed him the city. Teenage girls went gaga. Middle-aged women just stared. Yet if Quentin could, in fact, make a matinee idol (at least a drive-in movie idol) out of him, it wouldn't be the first time that a man who sent all the women swooning tended to eschew them in his personal life. Neela could think of at least five or six well-known Hollywood actors—one with a reputation as a tough guy, the others as handsome leading men—who were either full-time or part-time gay. On the West Coast, what one did in bed wasn't always what one did on the screen.

Quentin invariably explained it away by saying, "When you're really beautiful or really handsome, you go to bed with someone who reminds you of yourself."

"As you do?"

"As I do." He waited, then added, "You, too."

When Quentin was angry, he sometimes referred to Neela as a turncoat queer. During her twenties, she'd had a number of girlfriends—once, but only once, Quent had slept with both his wife and her girlfriend, but later said of it that that much *bonhomie* was too much for him—and she'd been attracted to a number of women since then. Yet the truth of the matter was that she preferred a man's body, when she preferred anything at all, that is. Lately, nothing had worked, neither the one or the other.

"You should have been a nun," Quent once said to her. "That or a fag hag."

"I might be one yet."

"Any preference?"

Neela had known at least one former actress who had entered an Italian convent at the age of thirty-two, after everything else had failed, but it was generally agreed that either she was crazy or the church was. As for fag hags, they were everywhere. Whenever she expressed disapproval of women who spent most of their time with queers, Quentin invariably reminded her of Marilyn Monroe. "Don't forget, kiddo," he'd say, "what most men wanted from Monroe was a piece of ass. The guys she went out with to *talk* to, the guys who kept her going between her shitty marriages, were almost all queers."

"So look where it got her."

"No," Quent protested. "The pieces of ass got her there. Talking to nice guys never killed anyone."

Maybe yes, maybe no.

Neela arrived at Cassidy's apartment shortly before three, and the first thing he said to her was that he was trying to give up booze. So instead he offered her a joint. Neela shouldn't have, but she shared it anyway.

From where he sat between two towering palm trees, he stared at her, then said, "Jesus, you look familiar. The face I mean. Where the hell have I seen it?"

Neela confessed that the only time her face had been anywhere was when it was on a magazine cover, but that was a long time ago.

"Jesus humping Christ, *Look* magazine!" he exclaimed. "Goddammit, that's where I know your face. Do you know I grew up with you? You're Neela *Waggaman!*"

When he was a kid in Indiana, he used to clip pictures of girls from the magazines and hang them on the wall of his bedroom. "Hey, look! Get this! I wasn't the only one. I'm from a *theatrical* family. My old lady had pictures of all the movie stars—she used to send away for them—in the kitchen and in the *living* room. There was this sorta wooden rail about a foot and a half from the ceiling, and she had it plastered with eight-by-ten photographs of the *stars*. And you were one of them!"

"The living room?"

"The living room. It was a beat-up old house, but once you looked up and saw all the pictures, you were in heaven." He looked at her fondly. "Neela Waggaman! So what have you been doing anyway? It's the craziest thing meeting you. I'm flattered all to hell."

She had been raising a family, she replied. She'd been busy being a wife and mother.

"Either I'm stoned or you're still beautiful. Your face has more—character or something."

It had something all right. Neela didn't know what it was either. When Cassidy passed her the joint, she drew on it as if her life depended on it. Cassidy got out his movie scrapbooks, and while they waited for Amos, he showed them to her. Most of them were from movie magazines back in the 1940s and 50s, and they were yellowed and smelled of dust. She listened to him recite scenes from *Casablanca* and *Remember The Day* and *All About Eve* and *Sunset Boulevard*.

He was going out to the Coast next week too, he said. He wanted to find a place to live not too far from Quent and Amos in Malibu.

"Quent didn't tell me he'd rented a house."

Cassidy must have realized that he had spilled the beans, because the next minute he was talking about movies again. Neela didn't press. Amos didn't show up at all. When she left, three joints and two hours later, she was stoned.

Quentin was pissed off because Amos hadn't even telephoned to say where he was. "I've got my career riding on his ass," he said to Neela when she explained the missed appointment with Cassidy, "and I just can't afford to let him have moods like this."

Annoyed, Quentin sat on the edge of his bed and pulled off his eighty-five-dollar Italian shoes. "Why the hell do people permit themselves the luxury of feelings?" he demanded. "Amos is deliberately giving me a hard time because he hates to have people tell him what to do. But at the same time, he can't function worth a shit unless someone's holding his hand. So the only thing he knows how to do is bolt. Well, dammit, I need him at the Ahrenbergs' tonight, and if he lets me down, honest to Christ . . ."

Neela decided that now was the time to talk it out. "What will you do, Quentin? Ask him to leave the house at Malibu?"

Quent paused momentarily, then continued to remove his socks. "I might," he said. "Who told you about that?"

"Does it matter?" She watched him walk to the closet, slide out of his shirt, then step out of his trousers.

"Not really." Out of deference to her sensibilities, he turned his back to her as he took off his briefs, then wrapped a robe around himself. "I had to have a place to sleep while the film is in production, and so did Amos. Stuart Faller—you remember him?—offered the use of his house while he's shooting a picture in Spain."

He was halfway to the bathroom when she said, "Okay, then this time I'm coming with you."

It stopped him cold. "No."

"Why not? And please, Quentin, don't give me any of that baloney about interfering with your work. I promise not to get in your way."

"No." He shook his head impatiently. "Amos is so goddamn high-strung all you have to do is look at him the wrong way, and he goes on a drunk. I don't want that to happen. It's going to be absolute hell working with him anyway. Living with him isn't going to be much easier, but I see no reason why I should invite disaster by having you around."

"But he likes me!"

Quentin took both her hands. "Like every actor I've ever known, Amos is fucked up, but he's just a little more fucked up than most. Like every actor I've ever known, he doesn't know who he is—why the hell do you think they act other people, Neela? Because they can't act themselves—and I don't want anyone giving him ideas that he's something other than what he is, which is weak, helpless, and dependent."

Neela should have known. Dependent on Quentin, he meant. No one else.

"You don't *want* him to like me."

"You'd only hurt him in the long run," he answered.

She pulled her hands away from his. "And you won't?"

"I help him. I listen to him. I tell him what he likes to hear."

It would have to be asked now, and she would not allow him to hedge. "Is there anything . . . *between* you and Amos?"

He shrugged his shoulders. "Neela, it's so damned rare for there to be anything *between* two people, as you put it, other than a sex organ that I suppose you won't believe it when I tell you I look upon him as a son. All his life, a stronger man has protected him. Without that kind of relationship, he's anchorless. Don't you see? He does stupid things which he later regrets."

Until he said that, she was almost prepared to buy the argument, but now she was incensed. "So where's my goddamn anchor!" she said. "Who the hell prevents *me* from doing stupid things which I later regret? God *damn* you, Quentin, *I'm* the one you're supposed to be married to!"

She rushed from the room, down the hall, into the

209

guest bedroom, locking the door behind her. Quentin begged her to come out. Hysteria would accomplish nothing at all, he said to her soothingly. It was already late, Amos still hadn't shown up, and they were due at the Ahrenbergs' at eight. Didn't she know that Ahrenberg was important? Without Ahrenberg, how the hell would he be able to get the dirty, unscrupulous, disgusting pack of nitwits who controlled the studio to finance his film?

"How can you take their *money*, Quentin, then call them—that!" she screamed at him.

Calm down, he said to her. She knew damned well what he'd meant. Among friends, a little prejudice heightened the competition. If only she knew what they called him. "Look, to them I'm a slick, opportunistic Irish bastard with a dick that can't make up its mind. I'll call people whatever I think of them, dammit. They would give me up tomorrow morning if I stopped delivering the goods, that's how much they like me. So why should I be grateful for that kind of shit?"

When Neela didn't answer, he added, "It's late, baby. I'm tired. I'm about to wind up something that's important to me, and honest to Christ, I could do without this fighting all the time. At the moment, Amos comes first. I know you don't like it, but that's the way it has to be. I don't want him to lose control."

Quentin caught his breath, then continued. "Amos is going to be polite to Ahrenberg tonight if I have to hold his balls in a pair of pincers and squeeze every time he makes a mistake."

Wearily, she said to him, "You people enjoy hurting each other."

"*Us* people? Oh, *hell*, when was the last time someone was nice to you in this goddamn city without expecting a favor in return that didn't involve getting hurt? Being *alive* is hurting yourself. Don't you know that much yet?"

"Thanks for reminding me that I'm dumb."

"A pleasure," he said. Truly. Then, contritely: "Neela, please open the door. I never promised you to be anything but what I am. In that respect, I've never deceived you, which is more than can be said for most husbands. I need you, baby. We need each *other*. Please don't let me down now, okay?"

Neela could feel herself weaken. She'd listened to the pitch before, and each time she'd come back to him after having told herself that living with Quentin Fitzgerald was impossible and demeaning.

But what else did she have?

Slowly, she dried her tears with a towel, then opened the door and surveyed Quentin's puffy face, lined and haggard in a way she'd never thought possible when she saw it for the first time, the day Quent had swaggered into West Mystic High School. Then, he'd not had to wear a harness on his back to keep his vertebrae from caving in. The smile was real and so was the handshake, and everyone had heaped love and favors on him. Life was simple and uncontrived. No deals had to be made. Only friendships sealed or love or whatever it was that Neela had felt for him.

Now, walking wounded both of them, they depended on each other for support through long-standing habit. They didn't have to sleep together anymore to renew whatever it was they felt for each other. But, by God, they had to be together, and it seemed to Neela now that Quentin's head was being turned—at *his* age—by a young actor, who needed him as much as Neela did.

"Look," Neela asked him now, "why do we live this way? Can't we go back and start over or something? Leave this awful city and these awful people and go somewhere else and ... I don't know what ... do *some*thing? What do you *want*, Quent, that you don't already *have?*"

Quentin took her in his arms, as he inevitably did each time she posed the same question. Maybe after this film, he'd call it quits, he said.

211

"Your father died when he was in his forties, Quent. What if you do? Then what difference will it make?"

"I won't, Neela!" It was a pledge, a promise.

"Do you think your father ever intended to die when he was forty-six years old? And didn't he drive himself right up to the end so that you and your mother could live at the country club? But what *difference* is a house at the country club if you can't live in it? Or if it has to be sold four or five months after you die to pay the bills you'd forgotten to pay?"

Hold on a little longer, he said to her. In another year or two, maybe they could put their money into some property in northern California and perhaps settle down and live like human beings. "I'm getting *old*," Quentin confessed suddenly. "I *feel* old. It's harder and harder for me to get excited over anyone or anything. I broke my balls writing *Wiser, Wiser*. I want to carry the thing through, baby. Give me a little more time."

She waited. "And Amos?"

"I like his company, I like his youth, I like the fact that he's going to help make me a half million bucks."

How could Neela compete with that?

"What about the house in Malibu?"

"I want to give it a try. See what happens. Get it out of the system, maybe once and for all."

That was the rub, of course. "What guarantee do I have that you'll ever come back to me? For all I know, you'll buy a little farm in northern California and live with Amos, not me."

No, she misunderstood. It wasn't going to last beyond . . . well, beyond the filming of *Wiser, Wiser*. Amos could go his way—better or worse for the experience—and Quentin could go his.

Quentin locked his arms around her. "Jesus," he said, "you've always been good to me. Be good to me now."

Whenever Quentin felt threatened or needed to persuade someone to his way of thinking, he did what he considered he was best at: he made love.

Neela faked it all the way, as she always had with Quentin, down to and including coming. Only a few times in her life had she ever had what seemed to her a true orgasm, and never with Quentin. To tell him, however—or even to be honest about it and not go through the simulation—would shatter his illusions, and in the end no doubt cause him to hate her. So she indulged him.

It was ruinous to have an ego like Quentin's, because when it broke, she knew, it would be catastrophic. People who have been unsure of themselves all their lives, as Neela herself had been, could take it when they woke up one day and nothing fit together or made sense. But Quent hated the truth unless it flattered him and sustained his fantasies. To be told that he was lousy at making love—or if not that, that he was unable to awaken anything in Neela—or that he'd written a script that was not universally loved, or that Amos Guard had spent part of the day being adored by someone else . . . well, first Quentin wouldn't believe it, then he would blame it on deficiencies in other people.

"We have to get ready now," he said to her once he'd finished. "Are you okay?"

Neela was okay. Just feeling a little tired and worn out. Was it absolutely essential for her to go to the Ahrenbergs'? If not, she'd just as soon stay at home, watch a movie on television, then go to bed early.

"I haven't been sleeping well."

Amos called while Quentin was in the shower, and Quent used the bathroom extension. Amos was a little tied up, he said, but he'd be at the Ahrenbergs' by eight-thirty. He'd see them there.

"Neela's not going," Quentin replied, "but, dammit, you have to be there. Don't fuck me up again, Amos."

What was wrong with Neela?

"She's feeling a little under the weather. Also she doesn't much care for Ahrenberg. But you have to like him, pal, or I'll kill you with my bare hands."

As soon as Quent had left, Neela began to drink. First a Scotch, then bourbon. After another bourbon, she told herself that it was the last, but then found herself pouring another one. Then she stopped counting.

At nine-thirty or so, the telephone began to ring, but Neela didn't answer it, because she knew her tongue would be too thick to carry on a civilized conversation. It rang for a good while, stopped, then rang again. In order not to listen to it, she turned up the stereo to full volume.

A fifth of booze a day: that's what her mother drank. It would be a while before Neela could catch up. A fifth of booze every twenty-four hours, before Neela's father died and afterwards. When she was very young, Neela used to hate to go near her late in the afternoons or the evenings, because by then she would be almost through her daily ration. Once Neela had gone into the third-floor studio and found her mother seated in front of her easel, her arms raw and bleeding from her shoulders to her fingertips, playing with the big tom cat, pitching him across the room, then waiting for it to attack her.

Oh, God, I will be just like her, and my father knew it, too.

Neela was feeling pleasantly relaxed now, almost ebullient. She heard a noise in the foyer and got up to see who it was, but found it difficult to make her way across the room. She stood still, holding onto the back of an armchair, and tried to focus on the figure she saw there.

"We're both drunk, Mrs. Fitzgerald," she heard someone say to her.

"I am congenitally drunk," she replied to Amos Guard. "It is the one thing my family excels at."

"I don't do so bad myself."

As he walked toward her, she saw that he wasn't exaggerating. "I am ... supposed to be somewhere, I seem to recall," he said with effort, then apparently lost the thread of whatever it was he'd intended to say. "It is a bad idea to drink by oneself, Mrs. Fitz. That is why God invented people, so that man would not have to drink alone."

"Didn't you go to meet Ahrenberg?"

"I've been visiting ... a friend."

"Quentin was expecting you. It was important."

Amos Guard shook his head in denial. "No, it isn't. Do you know what's important, Mrs. Fitz? What's important is that ... is that we go out and have ourselves a little tune. What do you say to that?"

"But what about the script? What about the movie?"

Gently he lifted the glass from her hand. "There is not going to be any movie," he said. "That is what Ahrenberg is going to tell Quentin. Okay? So let's get the hell out of here."

—◆—

"Hello, *David?*"

Julie knew damned well that it wasn't David Harpur on the other end of the line, but for the last half hour, ever since she heard the news—dropped like a bombshell right in the middle of lunch—her mind hadn't been functioning. Her reason, the one thing she'd thought would never let her down, had abandoned her.

The man who had answered the telephone at the house in Amagansett identified himself as a neighbor who was helping out just for a little while.

"I've just ... heard!" Julie cried. "I don't know what to say. Is David ... is he taking calls?"

David was already on his way back to the city. He'd

spent most of the morning with the police, then waiting at the coroner's office. He was now assembling the kids from their private school in New England and attending to all the melancholy details.

"Oh, my God," Julie said, "I just can't believe it."

It was the last thing in the world she expected. Lily was supposed to have been angry and disappointed and disgusted . . . anything but this!

Yesterday, Sunday morning, before David had got on Lily's bicycle and began to peddle home, he told Julie that he anticipated a row. Lily was high strung and puritanical as hell. To have found David in bed with Julie—well, it wasn't going to be easy going for a day or two.

Julie had returned to the city, expecting that David would call within hours to say that Lily had left him.

And now this, instead.

Julie had heard about it in a secondhand sort of way. She'd just finished having lunch with a colleague at a restaurant around the corner from the office when someone from the business staff spotted them and stopped to chat. Before she left, she said to Julie, "Say, you're the one who did that profile on David Harpur, aren't you? The most amazing thing has happened. I just got it from someone who knows him in Amagansett. He woke up this morning and found his wife dead in the bed next to him."

Julie almost blacked out.

Her colleague asked the questions, because Julie wasn't able to form words. No, no one had expected it. She hadn't been under doctor's care and there was no history of that sort of thing in her family. Of course, once you passed forty, anyone could have a coronary. There was also some talk . . . well, talk that perhaps she'd taken her own life, but there was no reason. She and David were divinely happy.

Julie listened in a kind of delirium, then said that she really had to get back to the office because she was expecting an important call. Once she got there, she shut the door, fell into her chair, and looked blankly at the Hudson River and the Jersey shore, wondering just how responsible she was for what had happened.

Death she hadn't bargained for. It had not even crossed her mind that Lily would . . . would *ruin* everything. And in such a vulgar, melodramatic way. How heartless and cruel to die in bed next to poor David. How had he discovered her? Had he spoken to her? Touched her? Given her part of the morning paper to read?

Of course, people *did* sometimes die natural deaths, and perhaps Lily had overextended herself the afternoon before. A tiny blood clot might have loosened somewhere and made its frenzied way to her heart, reaching it while she lay next to the beloved David.

Bullshit, Julie said. It didn't happen that way. She knocked herself off, the bastard!

To punish David. Julie could see it all. Lily must have realized that divorce required courage and stamina, and in the end she would have come out the loser. She would have been a scorned and discarded woman. But by killing herself, she could make life miserable for David. "This is how much I hate you," Lily Harpur must have thought. "This is what I think of you and that whore I found you with."

She'd made her point, too, because David should have turned to Julie immediately ("Julie, something has happened. I need you," he should have said), yet he hadn't even tried to get in touch. Not only was he accepting the guilt, as Lily had hoped, but he wanted Julie to share it.

Dammit, *no!*

Julie would have to get herself organized at once. She was not going to become a victim of someone else's suicide, no matter what Lily's intentions had been. She would have to consider matters carefully, weigh every move, and proceed with caution. David was a strong, resilient man, and there was no reason in the world for him to buckle during this crisis. First, as a widower and a father, he would solace and protect his children. Then, as a man, he would seek consolation from others.

From Julie.

Work was out of the question. Her desk was heaped high with matters demanding her immediate attention, but she was unable to concentrate. At last, she found Pete Vassall's Amagansett telephone number and dialed him. Perhaps she would be able to discover precisely what had happened. Novelists always knew everything about everyone's business except their own.

"I take it this is not a bread-and-butter call," were Pete Vassall's first cheerless words after Julie identified herself. "You've heard."

She had, but she was missing details. Was it a heart attack?

"She killed herself."

Julie felt the strength go out of her.

"Of course, David isn't admitting it. I heard it from someone who knows someone who plays bridge with the coroner. It was barbiturate poisoning, but David is saying that it was a coronary. I don't blame him. He's taking it pretty hard."

Had anyone seen him or talked to him personally?

"I haven't, if that's what you mean, and neither has Didi. I think one of the reasons he went directly back to the city was to avoid talking to people out here. We're all in shell-shock. She was such a . . . vibrantly alive woman."

Pete Vassall waited, then said, "The funeral services are set for Wednesday at St. James'. I guess that's where she was christened. Burial's in the Bronx."

The Bronx? Was he sure? Were rich people from the East Side buried in the *Bronx?*

"Sweetheart, they plant tulips on Park Avenue, but not bodies. Out to the Bronx they go."

The Bronx? My God, it was as bad as the West Side.

At least Lily couldn't pull rank on her anymore.

All afternoon she waited for the call. A half hundred times she told herself that he was too busy with family matters and funeral arrangements, and that she would simply have to wait until he had a few free minutes without weeping children or reverential morticians at his side. But knowing it didn't help any. She would succeed in quelling her doubts and fears, then two minutes later she'd be in a cold sweat again, looking at the telephone.

What if he thinks it's my fault?

Julie felt the walls begin to close in on her and even the dirty, smoky sky over New Jersey appeared to darken. She moved her chair away from the window and the perilous drop to the street. She was in the kind of panic she knew well from past experience, and through habit picked up the telephone and dialed Dr. Rappaport.

His receptionist said that he was with a patient at the moment, but perhaps she could ring back. No, Julie answered, she could not. It was an emergency.

In another few seconds, Dr. Rappaport said, annoyed, "So what's wrong now, Silverman?"

Julie explained that she had to see him. She was in a terrible bind. The worst crisis of her life, in fact. She was sorry she'd been so nasty and rude the last time she spoke to him, but—well, it was a reaction to her expulsion from Group. She apologized for all the insults. If only he could allow her an hour, say.

"Julie," he began patiently, "what good would it do? You resist improvement. You'll come over here, I'll listen to you for sixty minutes, then when I advise you, you'll call me a fool. You'll call me an ass. You'll succeed only in making me unhappy."

"When the hell did I ever get a full sixty minutes?" she complained. "You were always late to begin with, then halfway through you'd have to go to the bathroom or someplace. At fifty dollars an hour, you get restroom privileges?"

"You prove my point, Julie. You're already making me angry."

"Listen," she said more brightly, "I promise to behave. I really need to talk to someone. I don't ... know what to do."

"Julie, never in your life have you not known what to do."

"Please."

She could almost see him thoughtfully running his ball-point pen through his gray moustache. "Okay, so talk now," he replied at last. "It's easier to cope with you at a distance."

Julie drew in a breath and spoke slowly. "David's wife killed herself last night."

"David's wife?"

It wasn't so much a request for information as it was a code to activate that section of his memory bank labeled *Silverman's Affairs.* He was on a first-name basis with most of Julie's lovers, ex-lovers, their wives, their kids, their dogs; he knew where they lived, what kind of cars they drove, where they'd gone to school, and how much money they had in the bank.

"David was the lawyer?" he asked now. "Or was he the one at the magazine?"

"No, Frederick was the lawyer. Ed was at the magazine. David is in investments."

"Oh, *David*," he said with recognition now. "That means that Lily is dead."

Dr. Rappaport was plucking biographical information from his head. "Where did it happen? At the house in town or out in Amagansett?"

What a phenomenal memory! A gossip's recall.

Julie told him as much as she knew, then said, "I'm afraid David might blame me."

"Should he?"

"No." She waited. "I only met her once."

Silently his computer worked. "I wasn't aware that you'd ever met her. In fact, we talked about the inadvisability of that. Don't you remember?"

It had just happened. Quite spontaneously. Very recently.

"How recently?"

Damn him. *Always snooping.* "Saturday night," she answered at last.

"And she killed herself the next day?"

"No," Julie said, then added almost inaudibly, "the next night."

"And you're sure you did nothing to precipitate it?"

Absolutely nothing. She was sure.

"I don't believe you." He sighed resignedly. "You're lying, Julie."

Julie slammed her fist against the desk. "I am not lying! I am also getting damned tired of your accusations. You even said it once in front of the whole Group. Can you imagine how I felt? Don't you think I have feelings?"

Dr. Rappaport, who had strong opinions on the subject, kept them to himself. "Listen, Julie," he said, "you tend to withhold significant facts. From everyone. From me, from David, from Group, from yourself. You rewrite history. You're doing it right now. I really can't see that anything will come of this conversation."

Julie closed her eyes, then quickly said, "Lily caught us in bed on Sunday morning."

"Sordid details, please."

She recounted what had happened, omitting nothing. When she was finished, he was momentarily silent, then asked, "And when you heard the bicycle on the gravel, you didn't leave the bed? You didn't try to hide?"

"No." It was almost a relief to say it. The advantage of analysis was that it enabled one to crawl in one's own dirt.

"You heard her come into the house and you stayed in bed and did nothing. *Why*, Julie?"

"I don't know."

"Yes, you do."

"I don't *know*. That's why I called you."

His sigh this time was immense. "I cannot spend all afternoon talking to you, Julie, when you're unwilling to examine yourself. I have a patient waiting who needs me. You are as recalcitrant as ever."

It seemed unfair to Julie. A year before, when Rappaport had told her that she was parsimonious even with her dreams, hadn't she gone home and dreamed veritable sagas, then offered them to him? Didn't she nightly resurrect poor Sol and Rheba from the past to strut before Rappaport because he thought they might provide an avenue toward understanding her?

"Why didn't you warn David?" he asked now.

She bit off the words. "Because . . . I wanted . . . her . . . to see us."

Whether Rappaport was gratified at her confession or horrified, he didn't say. Instead he said to her, "Julie, you are a woman, a very modern and clever one. I shouldn't have to tell you, of all people, how a woman's psyche works. Suffice it to say that no matter who the woman is, how benighted or emancipated, nothing—I repeat, *nothing*—pains and humiliates her more than sexual rejection. It reaches the very nub of her. It must have been a crushing blow for Lily. I'm surprised that you weren't aware of it. Unless," he halted now, "you were."

Julie was outraged. Suddenly all her anguish was replaced by anger. "Listen, you motherfuck, what do you know about anything? David wasn't going to leave her, don't you see? He's weak and ball-less, like every man I've ever known. Someone had to propel him to make

222

a decision. You tell me that I was wrong. No, no, don't you dare interrupt me. After all the money I've spent on you, you can listen. It's easy for you to be critical, sitting on that perch of yours on Gracie Square, but let me remind you: *I* have been paying your rent for the last three years. Fifty dollars a session, twice a week, and another twenty to listen to those nitwits in Group, comes to almost five hundred a month. What do you get in your apartment for five hundred a month, Rappaport? You get heating, you get air conditioning, a security system, and snooty doormen. What do I get for my money? I get to listen to you call me a liar."

"Julie, we are not talking about money. We are talking about human behavior."

"Okay, so tell me something I don't already know. Listen! You've been married twice, divorced twice, and if you're not shacking up with that slut in the reception room, I'm no judge of anyone. But still you have the gall to try to tell me that I don't know how to live."

"Julie," he said weakly, "why did you call me? Just to tell me that you hate me?"

"*Yes!*"

"After I informed you that you couldn't attend Group anymore because you were an unsettling influence, I was ashamed of myself. I cried, I actually cried. I almost called you that night to tell you that you could come back, because everyone deserves another chance. But now I know better. You cannot bear to be happy, Julie."

"Goddamn you, I'm going to file a malpractice suit against you. I'm going to have you disbarred—is that what they call it?—hello! *hello!* Did you hang up on me, you motherfuck?"

She dialed again, but as soon as the receptionist answered and recognized the voice, the line went dead.

Julie rested her head on her desk and burst into tears.

Julie left the office two hours before quitting time, skipping an editorial conference at four because she was in no mood to listen to a pack of egoists lay out their views on weighty matters. She felt the way she had shortly after she'd given up smoking: her whole body ached, starting at her esophagus and reaching down to her toes. As in every other crisis in her life, she planned to eat her way out of this one, so she asked the cabbie to drop her off at Zabar's.

She bought enough pâté for a party of six, and a huge salmon flown in just that morning from Ireland. Around the corner at a liquor shop, she chose a bottle of Dom Perignon. At her pastry shop, she ran in for a Baba au Rhum.

Once in her apartment, she dropped everything on the kitchen table, kicked off her shoes, poured herself a double Scotch, and ate twelve pieces of Melba toast and most of the pâté.

Several hours and three Scotches later, the salmon still lay in all its splendor on the table, and Julie had just enough sense to know that she would incinerate herself if she tried to light the ancient oven in her kitchen. Instead, she cut the Baba au Rhum into eight pieces and consumed the entire cake, chasing it with Scotch.

By nine o'clock, she was still sitting in the dark, smacking her lips, when the buzzer in the foyer sounded, and she was so sure that it was David that she didn't take the customary precaution of calling down on the intercom before she released the front door lock. She stood in the hallway and waited for the elevator. Even before its door opened, she called into the cavernous hall, "David, I'm so damned sorry. Forgive me."

"It isn't David, darling," answered Neela Fitzgerald. "Lord, how can you live in this part of town? Amos and I have been followed for the last block and a half by a mugger, there's a rapist just outside, and we passed a transvestite in a red wig on the first floor."

"Neela! What are you doing here?" she demanded, then quickly added, "I'm drunk out of my mind."

"It's about time. You've been sober all your life." She hugged her old friend, then said, "This is Amos Guard," indicating a young man behind her, looking glassy-eyed. "He's the next Robert Redford. Amos, this is Julie Silverman, who is both the last Julie Silverman and the next one. I warn you: cover your testicles." She swept into the dark apartment. "Julie, it's morose to sit by oneself in the dark."

Julie said, switching on a light, "I've just had a terrible shock. Here, let me pick up the kitty litter."

Neela gasped. "Something has happened to your precious cats!"

No, it wasn't that. It was just that the trays needed emptying and some of her more fastidious friends objected to sharing a room with them. She now picked up an aromatic tray of sand and made her way to the bathroom.

"Why do you punish yourself, living here?" Neela declared, making a quick tour of the living room in search of objects of vertu, but finding none. "Why don't you send all this back to the Salvation Army and move somewhere else? Change your life. Start all over. Thirty-nine isn't old, Julie."

On her sally through the apartment, she found herself in the kitchen.

"Julie! There are cats all over the kitchen table! And a skeleton!"

It was only the salmon, Julie replied, flushing the toilet. "I think I must have forgotten to put it away."

"You need someone to look after you, Julie. Have you ever considered marrying someone who likes housekeeping? I think we have to redefine roles. Have you ever talked about that with Dick Cavett?"

"Does he like housekeeping?" Amos asked.

225

Julie placed a magazine over the empty box from the bakery so that Neela wouldn't know that she'd been piggish, then sat down on the sofa. "So what are you doing in the ethnic part of town?"

What they were doing was touring the bars. For Neela, it was a revelation. In New York, there were bars for every conceivable type of warped personality. They'd just been refused entrance at a place around the corner where someone had stopped Neela at the door and said, "Are you in drag or in leather?" Before that, they'd been in dike bars and bike bars, spic bars and mick bars. Everywhere they went, they were the center of attraction. It seemed to Neela that New York existed only to cater to alienated people.

Julie carefully scrutinized Amos Guard, wondering what his angle was. She'd always prided herself on being able to spot pansies—even those whom no one else could recognize—but she wasn't sure about Amos. He was the boy-next-door type. The kid-brother type. He looked as if he'd just come in from playing baseball. And yet . . .

"We've come to take you out to dinner," Amos said to her, eying the cake box, "if you haven't eaten yet."

Appetizer and dessert, but no entrée.

"I've been sitting here for the last four hours feeling trivial," Julie said. "I've been thinking of doing something terrible. Opening the window and throwing a potted plant out or something. Just to attract someone's attention. But on this street, no one would even look up. Unless I hit them on the head."

Julie then proceeded to tell them the doleful events of the weekend and her role in it. By the time she'd finished, she had to fight to keep herself from crying.

"Oh, dear," Neela said, "and I told Amos that if there's one person in New York who can cheer us up, it'd be you." Then, more brightly, "Listen! Do you know what he's going to do—this David Harpur of yours? He's going to turn to you now, Julie. He'll need you now more than ever."

"Do you really think so?"

It seemed to Julie that possibly Neela was right. If David were shallow and superficial, if he had no character—having no character was like having no entrails or bowels—he might misunderstand and blame Julie. But David was so wise and mature. Even now he must realize that Julie was suffering every bit as much as he was.

"I've made so many mistakes in my life," Julie now said. She rose from the sofa and began to make her way to the kitchen. "Can I interest anyone in champagne? At least the cats didn't get into that."

"I think we should all drink to our mistakes," Amos volunteered.

"Julie," Neela yelled into the kitchen, "do you honestly know anyone who grew up with us who's happy? I mean really and totally happy, without qualification. When was the last time you looked at our high school yearbook? *I* did about a week ago. And you know what I found out?"

"Yeah," Julie replied from the kitchen, "that I'm the only one who's unhappy."

"Julie!" Neela roared by way of protest. "Some of them aren't even alive! Do you remember Norma Lindstrom, the one who sat in front of me in senior civics class? She's been married three times and she's had a breast removed."

"But is she dead?" Julie asked.

"Well, being one-breasted in a two-breasted society can't be much fun, kiddo," Neela answered.

"No wonder I feel out of place," Amos said.

"And there's Kate McCabe. She's so unhappy, she's getting a divorce."

"Who said?"

"She did. She telephoned today."

An affair was one thing, but a divorce? Impossible. Not Kate.

Neela waited, then continued with her next disclaimer. "Quentin thinks that he's happy, but is he in for a surprise."

Julie brought the champagne into the living room, then slumped into the cushions of the sofa. "What's happened to Quent?"

"At the moment, he's being told that he's a failure."

Quent had spent the last year and a half writing and rewriting a script, Neela explained, which would make all other movies seem old-fashioned. But the trouble was that no one liked it. "Instead, Amos here has been offered a starring role in a flick about a man who gets caught behind the Iron Curtain while rescuing his girlfriend, who's dying of leukemia."

"What's going to happen to him?" Julie asked.

"He gets shot in the end," Amos answered.

"I mean Quentin."

Well, he would be broke, no doubt, for the time being, since he never made an attempt to save money. Felt compelled, in fact, always to spend more than he had. "Of course, that's no trouble, because I've got enough for both of us. I still get money from the trust fund."

Julie considered it. Quite possibly, it was what every woman secretly yearned for, but seldom accomplished. A good man who could be totally dependent on her was hard to find.

"Neela and I will look after him," Amos said.

Julie, who never allowed herself to be impressed by men's faces—she was partial to homely men, she said, because they were capable of deeper, fuller relationships—now looked into Amos's phenomenal eyes. "Who did you say you were?" she asked.

"You'd better call Irving Diament. He's in a better position to know than I am."

"We're all drunk," Neela said suddenly.

Well, it was better than not being drunk, Julie supposed.

Julie was torn between going out to dinner and waiting by the telephone in the event that David called. She even considered taking the initiative and telephoning him now, asking (as everyone asked of the bereaved) if there was anything she could do to help, but then she thought better of it.

David would have to allow the wounds to heal his own way, and to interfere with the process would only offend him. If he wanted to be alone with his sorrow for the time being, well, Julie would cooperate. She would keep to Silverman's holding pattern, as she described neither moving forward nor backward, neither gaining ground nor losing it, but just holding on for dear life.

As for the funeral on Wednesday, Julie supposed that it would be an elegant East Side do, and that no one would be smoking pot, as they did at West Side funerals, and as Neela and Amos were now doing, sprawled on the sofa. St. James' Church was such an eminently respectable place, Julie would probably have to wear a black dress, and of course she didn't own one. She had a nice pants suit from Bloomingdale's which might do. What did they think about ladies in trousers at East Side funerals?

Julie listened as Neela and Amos discussed the living arrangements at the beach house in Malibu where they would stay during what Neela referred to as Quentin's convalescence. If Julie understood correctly, Amos had already spent some time there with Quent and was explaining the layout of the place. There would be no need to take the children's nanny out to the Coast with them, as all one did was put the children out on the beach in the morning and pick them up before the tide came in. Neela would find it great fun to fiddle around

229

in the small garden. On days when she was bored, she could come into town with him and stick around the studio while Quent stayed at home with the kids.

A *ménage-à-trois*. Slightly out of the ordinary, but then these were not ordinary times.

When Amos excused himself to use the bathroom, Julie waited till the door was closed and she could hear him tinkling before she said, "So whose boyfriend is he? Yours or Quentin's?"

Neela's eyes opened wide. "You of all people! If anyone makes an anti-Semitic crack, you're on his back like a shot. If anyone says anything about the feminist movement that rubs you the wrong way, you let him have it right between the eyes. If I said nigger, you'd call the police. So what do you do, yourself? You make fun of Amos. *Look*, Julie, why do you, of all people— ex-Jewish princess almost every married man in New York has fucked—think you're in a position to be critical?"

Julie warmed to the quarrel. "You've never liked me, have you?"

Neela leapt up from the sofa. "If you want to know the truth, no! You're an arrogant, foul-mouthed, dirty-minded, insensitive . . ."

"God *damn* you! Get out of my house!"

"Gladly." Neela had already picked up her coat by the time Amos returned to the living room. Helplessly, he looked from one face to the other.

"You sit there drinking my expensive champagne, and all the while you've been thinking that I'm a dirty-minded, foul-mouthed . . ."

"There you go," Neela interrupted, "everything has to have a dollar sign on it. Do you think I give a good goddamn if your champagne is expensive or not? Really, you're impossible, Julie. You are now and you always have been. Do you know how long I've hated you? Since I found out you'd cheated in the Daughters of the American Revolution essay contest when we were in high school. Don't you think everyone in our class knew it? Why was it so *necessary* for you to win a D.A.R. contest, not once, but twice? I'll tell you why. Because you wanted to spit in our faces. Who wrote your goddamn essays, Julie? You used words in them that hadn't even crossed the Appalachians yet."

"That is a goddamn lie!"

"Julie, you don't know the difference between truth and lies. You're immoral. You're disgusting."

Amos was aghast. Minutes ago, everyone was champagne-mellow. Now two women stood looking at each other as if they had met the enemy they'd dreamed about all their lives.

"What about you, Waggaman!" Julie cried. "You've never in your life done anything more intellectual than spread your legs. If your family didn't have money, you'd be working in Woolworth's now. And why the hell do you think Quentin married you, anyway? Because you could pay the bills, that's why. You did when you met him, you do right now, and you'll be doing it at Malibu."

Amos quickly stepped between them. "Okay, girls," he began, "why don't we . . . ?"

He wasn't able to finish because the clenched fist that Julie had planned to rest somewhere on Neela's face landed in his eye.

"Jesus Christ!" he yelled, holding his eye. "Where'd you learn how to do that?"

"We're getting out of here," Neela shouted, making her way toward the door. "Come on, Amos. I never want to see . . . that odious creature again as long as I live."

Julie screamed at her. "You've *always* thought that! Ever since you first met me, you thought that. So why has it taken you so long to say it, Waggaman!"

Amos's eye was already closed and had begun to swell. He would almost certainly have a shiner.

"You should have a license or something for that," he said, indicating her fist. "Jesus Christ."

"Come on, Amos. The air in here is suddenly very bad."

"Get! Get! *Scat!* And take your pansy friend with you."

"At least I have friends. That's more than you have. No one but a masochist could like you."

"*Scat!* I said. Right now. This instant. I don't *need* friends. I don't *need* any of your simpering fairies around me. I don't *need* David Harpur. I don't need anyone, do you hear what I say, you mindless, decadent motherfucks!"

Julie sank to her knees, sobbing, as they fled to the elevator.

It was late, but Julie had no idea how late. Somehow the lights in the room had got themselves turned off again, and she was sitting on the floor by the sofa, listening to the telephone ring.

Slowly, she rose from her self-induced catatonia, looked around her in the darkness, then crawled toward the phone.

"David?" she said softly as she picked it up.

There was momentary silence, then a voice out of the past said to her, "This is Buddy. Buddy McCabe? I'm having the damnedest time trying to reach Kate. She's supposed to be staying at the Fitzgeralds' tonight, but no one is answering over there, so I thought she might have gone to your apartment instead."

Julie tried desperately to collect herself. She'd entirely forgotten what Kate had asked her to do in the event Buddy called. Somewhere there was a number where she could be reached, if only she could remember what she'd done with it.

Kate was in the shower, she said to Buddy. She'd stepped in just this minute. Could she call Buddy back in three or four minutes, say, so that she wouldn't have to track water all over the floor? Where was he, anyway? At home?

Yes, Buddy thought that would be all right. He was at home.

Was something wrong? Had something happened?

No, not exactly, he said. Just—well, Henderson had turned down the job, see, and old Fatass had offered it to him instead. He thought maybe Kate should know about it. It might ... well, he didn't know ... change her mind.

Bashfully, he added, "I guess it doesn't make any sense to you, but it will to Kate. I mean, I think it will." His voice broke, and it seemed to Julie that he must have been drinking, too, because it sounded as if he thought he was talking to Kate, even now. "Jesus," he said, "you don't know how long I've been waiting."

Waiting? Who wasn't? Did Buddy think he knew something about waiting that Julie didn't?

At last she remembered where the slip of paper with the telephone number was—still in the purse where Kate had stuffed it the day they'd had drinks at the Plaza—so she told Buddy that Kate would get back to him in a few minutes.

Waiting. What did Buddy McCabe know about waiting? What did anyone in the world know about waiting that Julie didn't know better?

III

Education Concluded

IT was almost eleven on Tuesday morning when the train pulled into Princeton station, and even from where she sat by the window, Kate could already see the note paper on the steering wheel of her parked VW, which indicated that Buddy had been in an instructional frame of mind when he drove by on his way to work.

It said: *Don't do anything stupid until I talk to you at lunchtime. Allow me that civility, please. Buddy.*

Allow me stupidity, please. Kate.

But fearing that she wouldn't have the courage to do anything at all, stupid or otherwise, once she'd been talked to by him, Kate folded the note and, because she'd been taught to be tidy even though her life was dissolving around her, dropped it in a litter basket on her way to a telephone booth at the end of the platform. When she got through to the lawyer whose name Ben had given her, she identified herself, then with far more serenity than she thought possible, she said, "I think I'd better talk to you about a divorce."

He was amiable, even jovial about it. He hoped, however, that she hadn't reached her conclusion during the heat of an argument, as sometimes happened. How long, exactly, had she been thinking about a divorce?

"About fifteen years."

Well, if that was the case, perhaps she would like to come in late in the afternoon. Four o'clock?

Just two weeks ago, she would have told anyone that four o'clock was sacred and inviolable, because that was when the kids got home from school and she was supposed to be in the kitchen whipping up culinary delights and naming them with a mixture of banality and college English (Meatballs Leopold Bloom, Salad of the Bad Cafe, Potatoes de Temps Perdu), in order to win the love and approval of husband and issue.

Four o'clock would be fine, she replied.

It was sheer luck that Julie had been able to reach her the night before, first having called Ben's answering service and being advised that he was eating at Luchow's. Kate's eardrums by then had been blown nearly into her throat by the oomh-pah band and she hadn't said any of the things she'd wanted to say to Ben when a be-moustached waiter leaned over and said, "Dr. Purdom? A telephone call for you." Ben, whose habit it was always to inform headwaiters that the hospital might call, said sullenly, "Oh, shit, I have to go to the hospital."

But it was Julie, so Kate talked, then immediately rang Buddy at home, expecting something truly catastrophic, but it was circuitous in the coming.

"Okay, listen," he'd said. "I asked around this afternoon and they need a typist at the administration office. Do you want me to tell them you'll take it? It would get you out of the house."

It would get her into a lunatic asylum, is where it would get her. "Buddy," she answered impatiently, "did you call me at eleven o'clock at night just to ask me *that?*"

Well, no, he just thought possibly if she worked outside the house for part of the day, and got her mind *off* herself (she imagined a huge and monstrous thing coupling with her), she would be able to . . . well, he didn't know what. Get back to normal.

To Buddy, Kate was a victim of approaching menopause, felled by forces beyond her control. Her mind, such as it was, needed immediate restoration, refocusing. If she typed forty or fifty words a minute—other people's words, of course; hers would be too stupid—she would not have to listen to the demons that had obviously taken possession of her faculties.

"Buddy, I really can't talk now. Can't this wait?"

Well, there was something else.

Kate should have known that she would have to pay for his magnanimity in finding her part-time employment. "What is it?" she asked in dread.

"Well, you know Henderson," he began. "The dumb fuck turned down the job. He's going out to Berkeley instead, at half the salary and all those dumb, hippie-types in his classes. So old Fatass—it almost killed him—asked me if I want the job. What should I tell him, Kate?"

Oh, *no!* Buddy didn't have to say another word. She knew exactly what was going on in his head.

Departmental chairmen and their wives were expected to live on campus. In fact, a stately pink-brick Federal house was available, rent free, which would mean that Buddy would be able to save money for the first time in his life. It would also mean, Kate knew, that Buddy would become surrogate father to every friendless and maladjusted child in the school while Kate would become surrogate mother. Departmental chairmen were required to hold a kind of perpetual open house, with little heads poking around corners from morning till night.

No wonder he'd suggested that she take a typing job. Being a den mother to hundreds of pimply-faced, sour-breathed, fermenting (Buddy's own description) boys would drive her over the edge, for sure.

Departmental chairmen needed wives; they were not optional, but compulsory. Buddy was trying to tell her that if she divorced him, he wouldn't be able to accept the job.

"I told old Fatass that I'd let him know by tomorrow afternoon," Buddy concluded. "I wanted you to think about it. That's why I called tonight."

Think about it? Worry herself sick about it, was what he wanted her to do. And, as always, she obliged, from the minute she broke the news to Ben ("Watch out. He's tightening the screws, Kate") till she telephoned the lawyer at the station.

Then suddenly she knew that no amount of importuning could alter her decision because she'd committed herself to a four-o'clock appointment.

"Don't let yourself be cowed by him," Ben had told her before she left his apartment. "Remember that you have a mind, too, and feelings and needs."

Buddy would try to wear her down, erode her confidence, reduce her to a cowering, shrieking, helpless ninny before the thing was over. He would appeal to her sense of fairness, duty, her compassion, her motherhood.

Oh, God, if only it were all over.

Already the house looked as if it had been abandoned moments before a nameless enemy had stormed the doors. Clothes were scattered everywhere, towels lay in soggy heaps on the bathroom floors, potato chips lined the upstairs hallway, a sweating Coke bottle rested in a water-mark on the antique secretary in the living room, and of course the beds weren't made. Kate knew better than to expect bed-making from Buddy (truly, he would profess not to know how), but she had hoped by now that she had reached some sort of Pavlovian understanding with the kids—or was it Skinnerian?—so that in return for making their beds, they would not be yelled at and reduced to tears.

Pavlov or Skinner. Kate's mind was clearly going.

Quickly, she went about setting the house in order, flushing an unflushed toilet (Suzie? Why would a child do that, again and again? Did Freud have an opinion?), snatching up the clothes from the floor and distributing them in the closets, and making the beds. In the kitchen, the high school girl who had covered for Mrs. Ellman had left the casserole dish from last night's supper soaking in the sink, because it would have required effort to clean it, and as Kate was about to drain the cold, greasy water, a humming in the background warned her that the radio had been turned down to no-volume, and had probably been going all night.

Did they teach slatternliness in high school home economics classes?

When Kate herself was young, it had seemed to her that what people had to fear most was annihilation. Now it was beginning to look as if survival was an even greater threat.

The world was revolting; people, habits, trends, and events were revolting. One would merely have to sit it out somehow. The only refuge man had anymore was his fellow man—or woman. If you lived to be sixty or seventy in an alien world, you were lucky if you'd been able to generate love in maybe two or three other people.

You could love someone—and show it—by making their beds, every bit as much as by sharing one with them. It was puerile and jejune (oh, those lovely Freshman Comp words Kate hadn't used since college!) to expect every woman to want the same things out of life as Lady Chatterley or Germaine Greer or even Mamie Eisenhower. You had to work with what you had and with what you could engender in others. If Lady Chatterley could be turned on by a gamekeeper stroking her back and purring, "This is where tha' shits"—how Kate had howled when she read her

241

smuggled copy in the Theta house—or if Germaine Greer never brushed her teeth because she considered it an offense against nature, well, credit to both of them. They were acting out their womanliness the best way they knew how.

But it wasn't Kate's way. Kate needed someone to talk to, to be sure, but he didn't have to catalogue her anatomical details. She didn't need an English game-keeper or his equivalent any more than she needed a cold-hearted, reeking-mouthed modern woman who felt compelled to tell other women that they did nothing right. Good God, Kate already knew that. But whether or not she brushed her teeth or used an underarm deo-dorant really wasn't the issue.

The issue was, well . . . the issue was . . . Kate didn't know.

That's what she was trying to find out. The issue was . . . somehow . . . to get through the next twenty or thirty years of her life and not be as ashamed and dis-appointed then as she was now.

When Kate heard the car in the driveway, her heart stopped. She hadn't even thought of Buddy's lunch—it would be the first thing he'd notice: the ultimate un-kindness on top of all others— so she now rushed to the refrigerator to see if the kids had left any sandwich meat. Two slices of baloney, one of pimento cheese, uncovered, and so hard it could shingle a roof. Kate at once felt contrite and guilt-stricken that she hadn't stopped on the way home from the station and picked up something. She would just grill a sandwich and count herself lucky if he didn't comment on it.

She busied herself at the counter spreading butter on two slices of four-day-old Pepperidge Farm wheat germ bread (Buddy had read that it was good for the bowels), and listened to him close the car door, then make his way along the brick sidewalk. The kitchen door opened, cold air blew in, and the next thing she knew, Buddy was saying, "Goddammit, Kate, I don't want to fight."

His face belied it. His forehead was furrowed and his eyebrows were almost merged with his lashes. His lips were set defiantly.

He yanked off his raincoat (button missing again; who would find a match and sew it on?) and flung it over the fake Hitchcock chair. Instinctively, Kate began to go to the closet for a hanger, but halfway there she decided that this time she would not.

"What have I done to deserve this shit, Kate?" he asked pathetically.

It was a puzzlement to Kate that all men looked at the world through the mind of Lenny Bruce while women were expected to see it through the eyes of Emily Dickinson.

"It's not what you've done, Buddy," she answered at last. "It's what you haven't done."

"Okay, so from now on I'll pay more attention to you, honest to Christ. I'll change." He was standing next to her at the counter. "I never said I was perfect. No one is. You aren't, either. I've put up with a lot from you, too, haven't I?"

Here we go, Kate said to herself. Had he learned it in the Army? When on the defensive, at all costs attack. He would provide her now with a numerical accounting of her faults.

"Did I want this damned house?" he demanded. "No, I didn't. But I went along with you because you wanted it. I knew right from the beginning it would be nothing but a pain in the ass, and it has been. The lawn's too big, the damned place has to be repainted every three years, the sewer backs up into the basement every time we have a rainstorm. . . ."

Some men would be happy if they could spend their lives in house trailers set on concrete blocks. She would have brought it to Buddy's attention now but for the fact that she already had, many times.

"Didn't I buy you the Volkswagen because you said you felt like you were in prison out here and couldn't even get out of the house unless you drove me to work in the mornings?"

"I didn't want a Volkswagen," she said, then regretted it, knowing she was playing into his hands. "I wanted a Chevy. You were the one who picked out the Volkswagen."

"*I* wanted the Chevy!" he yelled now. "You wanted the goddamn VW. You were the one who went on and on about the Krauts and what engineering geniuses they were. So a week after we get the fucking thing, the exhaust system falls off. *Falls off!*"

It was Kate's fault. There was no doubt in Buddy's mind. It would do no good to remind him that she had settled for the VW only after he said he would not have a Chevrolet in his garage.

"Please, Buddy," she said weakly, "we're not talking about cars."

"Okay, goddammit, if we're not talking about cars, what the hell are we talking about!"

Even if she could tell him, he was not going to listen. "I don't know what you want of me. I give you everything you've always asked for. How many men—I *ask* you, how many men—turn their paychecks over to their wives every second week and say, Here, spend it any way you want to. How *many?*"

She took a deep breath. "That's expedience, Buddy. You do that because that way you don't have to use your lunch hour to cash the check at the bank. You do it because paying bills and writing checks is a bore. That isn't a kindness."

His fist hit the Formica counter. "Okay, goddammit, from now on, I'll cash the fucking check at the bank myself, and I'll also pay the fucking bills!"

Kate began to feel the fight go out of her. It was no use even trying to finish making the sandwich. She rested the knife against the plate and closed her eyes.

"If this had happened ten years ago," he resumed, "I mighta understood. But it's so goddamn unreasonable. How can two people who've been married for fifteen years suddenly call it quits? That's what people do after two or three years, Kate, not after fifteen."

How many times have I wanted to tell you to go to hell? she said to him in her mind. Even during their first year of marriage, while they were still living in the apartment in New York. Even *then* sometimes she'd had to pinch her fingers together to avoid screaming at him. "Hey, honey, would you bring me a beer from the refrigerator?" he'd say to her from in front of the TV set, only ten feet away from the kitchen where Kate would be doing the dishes. Would you do this for me. Do that for me. Would you go down on me. Would you wrap your legs around my ass . . .

Yes, Buddy. Yes, Buddy. Yes, Buddy.

"Kate, you are such a yes-saying woman." Hadn't Julie Silverman, the most no-saying woman in the world, said that to her years and years ago?

"Look," Kate said suddenly, "we're not getting anywhere."

"Listen! I know a lota guys who wouldn't put up with this shit. I know guys, if their women give them a hard time, you know what they do? They go chasing after girls. Have I ever done that, Kate? Even once since we were married, have I done that?"

Oh, dear God, if only you had. Maybe then you would have appreciated what you had at home.

"Henderson!" he yelled. "Forty-six years old, a wife and three kids, and he has a twenty-one-year-old girlfriend in New Brunswick. Don't you think that happens all the time? Me, I'm faithful to you, I do everything you tell me to do, I give you everything you want. So what do I get for the favors? I get a kick in the ass."

Indolence was why he didn't chase other women,

245

Kate could have said to him. He was just too god-damned lazy to look.

"You spoiled things once before, Kate," he said now with passion, breathing heavily.

The Ph.D. deferred when Kate got knocked up in her last year of college! It would follow Buddy to his grave. His epitaph: Here lies a man who would have got his doctorate but for the perfidy and carelessness of a woman.

"You spoiled things once before," he repeated, "and I'm not going to let you do it again. You know what the job means to me. You'll leave me with nothing, Kate. Do I deserve that? I've waited all my life to do something I can be proud of, and now that I have the chance, you tell me you're tired of me and want a divorce. If you get married again, you'll get tired of him, too. Getting tired of people is immature." The burden of the request he was about to make was so great, he could scarcely form the words. "I've sacrificed for you, Kate. Can't you ... just this once ... sacrifice for me?"

Kate's mouth was dry and tongue-filled. "No," she whispered. Then the words were torn out of her. "I don't think I love you anymore."

Minutes ago, he'd looked defeated. Now rage filled his face and his temple veins were engorged with blood. He grabbed her by the arm.

"Okay, so who's fucking you!" he shouted. "I want his name, by God! I know damned well you wouldn't be doing anything like this unless someone made you. Who is he? *Tell* me, Kate!"

"Please leave me alone."

"You think you're so goddamn smart and liberated. You get tired of being a wife and a mother, so you go into New York and fall in love with the first guy who comes along and sticks it up you. Jesus Christ, Kate, I thought you had more sense!"

"Please *stop* it."

He tightened the grip on her arm till her face contorted with pain. "You're almost forty years old, Kate, and you're about to throw your life away like some fourteen-year-old kid. Goddammit, I won't let you do it!"

"STOP IT! STOPPPP ITTTT! I HATE YOU, CAN'T YOU SEE?"

In his fury, he struck out and she went flying across the room onto the floor. In the silence that followed, both were dazed and astounded. Blood trickling from her mouth, she looked up at him.

Buddy fought for air.

Oh, dear God, what have I done? Kate saw the hurt on his face and the disappointment. He looked so broken and defeated. His lip trembled the way Dutchie's did before tears came, and his breathing filled the room. Huge and elemental. He had never once taken a hand to her, or the children, or even the dog. It was so barbaric to strike people, he'd said. But to betray them was worse. Now as Kate looked at him, she saw his eyes harden, as if he were at last beginning to understand life.

"I'm sorry," she heard him say, then he rushed from the kitchen, leaving the door wide open. In another minute, she heard his car roaring out of the driveway and into the street.

———◆———

As she left the bed, Neela tried not to dislodge Amos Guard—they had slept together for animal warmth and human contact—then made her way across the room and into the hall, where the intercom was buzzing furiously. She was too disoriented to understand what the doorman was saying to her.

"I'm sorry," she said, "but who did you say?"

The doorman repeated that a Mr. Ronald Cheatham was in the lobby, and was she expecting him? His voice clearly indicated disapproval. All Ronnie had to do was open his mouth, speak a few words of Carolina English by way of West 125th Street, and most New York doormen would assume that he had the wrong address.

Neela tried to remember what she'd told him, anyway. Dammit, she'd said that she would have the bail money for Robert Pino by Monday afternoon, which was yesterday. She'd forgotten all about it. Her first reaction was to tell the doorman that she didn't know the man. Her next reaction was to stall.

"Would you tell him, please, to come back tomorrow," Neela said into the box imbedded in the wall. "Late in the afternoon. After six o'clock."

Neela remained standing next to the silent intercom, half expecting to hear a violent exchange erupt fourteen floors below, but the doorman didn't buzz again, so Ronnie had apparently left without a fuss.

She had a curious kind of aftertaste from his unexpected call, a sweet tingling mingled with fear. As she stood in the foyer, imagining Ronnie as he walked back to the subway, she was half tempted to ring the doorman to call him back. It wasn't merely because of the sensual response she'd felt—Neela hated clichés, but, dammit, he exuded sex—but also his strength. He'd said to her, hadn't he, that she was his old lady now and promised to take care of her? Well, the truth of the matter was that no one in the world needed taking care of more than Neela, and Ronnie was the only one who'd volunteered recently. Quentin was too preoccupied with his own destiny, and as for Amos, the best she could hope from him was companionship. Yet what really worried Neela about the black man who had just been turned away at the door was that he smelled of bad luck. A man could break under the strain of too much of that.

So it was just as well she hadn't asked him up. By six o'clock tomorrow afternoon, she, Amos, the kids, and Quentin, too—if he ever showed up—would be on their way to the Coast. Before she left, she would tell the doorman that someone might be calling for her later on, and she could leave an envelope for him. Twenty dollars ought to do it. No, during these inflated times Ronnie would need twice that to buy an ounce of marijuana, which would help him solve, temporarily, his major problem. Which was being alive. As for Robert Pino's bail money, Robert could bail himself out. Neela had all she could do to keep her own head above water.

"Hey," Amos yelled from the bedroom, "who'n the hell was that?"

"It was no one," Neela replied, and even she was struck by the aptness of the description.

Quentin hadn't been home since Sunday night, which gave some indication of the depth of his feelings at learning that Amos had a contract and that he himself had nothing but an option, soon to run out, on a script that Abe Ahrenberg, and maybe everyone else in the world, had told him had no commercial value at all. He would be holed up somewhere, trying to piece together a shattered ego, either by drinking up a storm or screwing till his penis fell off at the roots.

Amos, who was not half as dumb as he looked (could anyone beautiful ever look smart?), explained painstakingly to Neela why Quent had disappeared. It wasn't simply that he'd been humiliated, but humiliated in front of Amos, over whom he'd lorded it for the last two months—ever since he met him—in the sack, and whom he'd been telling that he had a fantastic script this time, by God (not *by* God, literally, but with his consent); that Irv Diament and everyone else who'd even got near it loved it to distraction; and that Ahrenberg was going to produce it, no matter what, so long as he could get the right kind of guy to play John

Wiser, someone who would induce everyone in America to cream in his/her pants at the very sight of him. "So I'm promoting you, Amos," Quentin had said to his protégé. "You're perfect for it. Stick by me, pal, and I'll make you another . . ."

Another Robert Redford.

In point of fact, Amos had won Irv Diament's love and Ahrenberg's backing—on another film—and poor Quentin was left out in the cold.

And in order to preserve himself, assert his masculinity, his *being*, Quent would pick up the first obliging girl he could find and screw her to within an inch of her life, beyond if she allowed. Whenever he suffered a setback, he inevitably acted out the maleness of his bisexuality. When threatened, anguish could be worked out of his system only through the sex act, right side up.

Amos had to be in L.A. by Thursday, so Neela was going ahead with her own plans on the assumption that Quent would show up in time to leave with them. By then, hopefully, his ego would be repaired, and after a painful sex-and-booze hangover, he would be able to start working again. All Quent ever needed to hear was himself saying, "Jesus Christ, this time I really have something. This time I've got a beautiful, *beautiful* idea," and believing himself, he would work like a man demented for the next four months.

Amos and Neela had been awake since ten, discussing how they were going to live on the Coast. Neela was really going to *do* something with herself, this time. It was already too late for this term, but possibly she could enroll at UCLA for the spring semester. Instead of merely draining her brain, year after year, as she'd done ever since she left college, perhaps she could restock it. Plant new ideas and outlooks. Get herself interested in something other than her own problems. Work with children who couldn't read, perhaps. Help people who lived in slums. Were there ghettos in California?

"There are ghettos everywhere," Amos replied. "There are ghettos in heaven."

Amos had a lunch engagement, so while he was in the shower, Neela called Irv Diament to see if he'd heard from Quentin, but Irv wasn't taking calls. Neela left a message with his answering service, and was looking for Abe Ahrenberg's number when the telephone rang. It was Kate McCabe.

The first thing she said was, "Neela! Listen to me! I'm so mixed up I don't know what I'm doing."

Neela said that she'd been that way herself for years.

"I've just had a terrible fight with Buddy, and he hit me. He's never done that to me before, Neela. He hit me and knocked me down."

Well, men did that sometimes, Neela had heard. Playing the caveman was what men were best at. Was she hurt badly?

"No," Kate answered. "It frightened me. Him, too. You should have seen his face afterwards. It was—as if he'd just done the most terrible thing he'd ever done in his life."

Well, that wasn't what Neela had seen on Julie Silverman's face after she'd taken a punch at Amos Guard. What had been on Julie's face was more like ecstasy.

Kate had called for a reason. She needed a place to stay overnight on Wednesday. "And this time I really mean it. I won't be coming into the city after that. I'm mortally afraid that Buddy will try to take the kids away from me, so I have to be very careful. That's why ... I'd better stay at your place tomorrow night. If you can put me up, that is."

Poor Kate. She was trying to confess that she'd been sleeping with someone, but given the upbringing she'd had, the words were slow in coming.

It was absolutely uncanny, Neela replied, but it looked as if they'd never be able to have their all-night, pajama-party talk fest. "We're leaving for the Coast,"

251

she continued. "But that's no reason you can't use the place. What time will you be coming in?"

Late in the afternoon, Kate said. She'd catch the same train she'd taken the afternoon they'd met at Bloomingdale's. What time had she got there? Five?

If that was the case, they would probably have a few minutes to chat. Neela would be running here and there, doing things that she'd put off for weeks, but she should be back at the apartment by then. The plane didn't leave till seven-thirty, but she liked to get to the airport early, because it was hard traveling with the kids.

"I want to see you, darling," Neela concluded. "I don't know what's happening between you and Buddy, but I know you're doing what's best."

"I hope so. I'm a little afraid of it, is all."

"Look at it this way. Your life is just beginning."

After she hung up, she went to the bathroom and talked to Amos through the shower curtain. She hadn't been able to get through to Irving Diament, she said, but she'd left a message. She hadn't found a listing for Ahrenberg, but maybe she was looking in the wrong place. How was it spelled, anyway?

"You might try M-o-n-t-g-o-m-e-r-y."

It took a few seconds to understand what he'd said to her. "As in Jill?"

"As in Jill. She lives on East 64th, the park block. A tiny little place, hardly big enough to copulate in, but the address is good."

"You've been there?"

"For a couple minutes."

"With Quentin?"

"Yes."

"The bastard told me that Irving Diament was screwing her!"

Amos turned off the shower, pulled back the curtain, then stepped out in front of her, dripping water over the tile floor. "Irving *is* screwing her." He grinned.

"But there is just too much girl in Jill for poor Irving." Then, "Do I arouse you?"

"Which way?"

"Is there more than one?"

"The answer is ... no. I mean, no, you don't arouse me."

"Good. That makes us even." He reached for a towel and began to dry himself vigorously. "Look, if Quentin shouldn't come with us to California ... I'm not saying that he won't, I'm just saying if he doesn't ... would it be okay if I brought a friend along?"

"I thought I was your friend."

"But you are."

Neela decided not to pursue it. Amos's friend—he'd just met him at the Yale Club—was at loose ends so Amos had invited him out to the Coast. What was wrong with that? Nothing, so far as Neela was concerned except that she didn't want the children corrupted.

"All babies conceived after 1950 were born corrupt," Amos suggested.

Still, she didn't want Amos and his new friend to be doing anything that would upset their little minds.

"Whose little minds? Neela, certainly you should know that children don't judge people sexually. Only adults do. I don't intend to make love in front of them, if that's what you mean. But then I wouldn't do that in front of anyone." He waited, then added—was it a pledge?—"Not even you."

Not to be hurt gratuitously, maybe that was all Neela could expect out of life anymore. Sure as hell, nothing else had worked out, and possibly the kind of relationship Amos was offering her was what she needed for the time being. A rain check, more or less, on life itself. Whatever was about to happen, she would sit it out, but in the company of someone who liked her. No more grabs. No more feels. No more gang bangs in Robert Pino's apartment. No more nights spent with a junkie in a Montreal hotel.

"I guess I've always wanted a sister," Amos said to her, finishing his drying, smiling wildly.

What the hell, it couldn't be worse than what had happened to her so far.

"A deal?" he said to her, holding out his hand.

"A deal," she answered, taking it. Then: "Go ahead. Invite your friend, Amos. I want you to be happy."

It sometimes seemed to Neela that she was extraneous to other people's happiness. At best, if she wasn't too demanding, they would allow her to share part of theirs.

"I know a lot of people on the Coast," Amos said. "You'll never be by yourself for very long out there."

Being by yourself wasn't quite the same as being lonely, but Neela knew by now that she couldn't ask for everything.

After Amos had left to visit his new friend, Neela called Emily the nanny on the floor below and asked her to get the children ready for a walk.

"They are helping me pack now, Mrs. Fitzgerald," the woman replied.

It would be months before the kids could adjust to a mother who wasn't dressed in a governess's uniform and didn't speak English with a Highland accent. Neela advised the woman that the packing could be completed later in the afternoon, but for the time being she thought the children might enjoy lunch at the Central Park Zoo.

"Oh, but we were there, the lambs and I, just last week."

The lambs and her. Damn her all to hell; she'd take them to the zoo anyway. Neela resented the fact that Emily was on better terms with the children than she was. When she'd been told that her services wouldn't be needed in California, she offered to go at half salary. "I'm so fond of the wee'uns," she said. (The *mon-sters,* Neela thought). In the end, Neela said there wouldn't be room.

Not for her, anyway—Scottish Presbyterian that she was—Amos, *and* Amos's friend.

Through habit, Neela dressed up to take the children to the zoo. It was unlikely, but there was always the chance that she might run into someone she knew, and she wanted to look her best. As she got older, it took increasingly longer to fix her face and her hair, and she would spend twenty minutes on her eyes, then the minute she stepped out of the building onto Park Avenue, she would cover her artistry with huge sunglasses. It didn't matter, really, that people passing her on the sidewalk weren't able to see as much of her as they might have liked. It was the impression she created, and Neela wouldn't have been able to carry it off if everything weren't done perfectly, down to her fastidiously cut and lacquered toenails.

Beauty wasn't in the eyes of the beholder so much as it was in the mind of the perpetrator. Neela always compared herself with Kate McCabe, who had good features, a nice body, and many endearing qualities. Yet half the time, Kate looked frumpy. She walked badly ("My feet were put on the wrong way or something," she would complain), often with her head bent downwards in order to avoid men's eyes, and always gave the impression that she was—or would shortly become—lost.

Neela, on the other hand, always walked down the street as if someone were following her with a movie camera.

Even now with the children, one on either side, she got stares.

"Are you excited to be going to California?" she asked Ronan, who was two years older than Deirdre. Both were dressed in navy-blue polo coats, patent-leather shoes, knee socks, and navy berets, which was more or less their school uniform.

"It's okay," Ronan replied, already world-weary.

"You'll be able to spend a lot of time on the beach. That will be fun."

"Yeah," Ronan replied.

Neela could never really get inside the children, the way some mothers could; whether it was because her children were more vapid than most or because she herself lacked the necessary warmth, Neela didn't know. When the two girls were with their father, they were easy and natural; with Neela they were stilted, uncomfortable, and very often just barely civil.

Well, some women were just not cut out to be mothers, and Neela expected that she was one.

"Do you like Amos?" she asked Deirdre.

"Yeah."

Neela had always fancied that children of hers would be wondrous, magical creatures who were bright, talented, and never did anything wrong. In point of fact, Ronan—despite the stirring Celtic name —was something of a lump. She got C's and D's in school and had no friends except her sister. She was pretty, however, so Neela knew that she would be able to get through life so long as she didn't open her mouth too often. As for Deirdre, she was plain-looking, but slightly more animated.

The hell of it was that if Neela had been given the choice—if God had brought out a hundred different babies in a hundred different bassinets—she probably wouldn't have chosen either of her daughters.

But, dammit, she would remind herself from time to time, who said you have to *like* your children? Children almost never liked their parents (some downright hated them), so why shouldn't parents, in these enlightened times, be able to confess that their children bored them?

"Listen," Neela said to them as they made their way

toward Fifth Avenue, "do you know what I used to love to do when I was a little girl?"

Ronan looked as if someone had just turned on a lousy TV program and it was impossible to change channels. Deirdre began to watch a dog defecating on the curb as if it were the most fascinating thing she'd ever seen.

Despite the lack of enthusiasm, Neela decided to press on. "I used to love to take long walks with my father. Just like what we're doing, right now."

"Is he dead?" Ronan asked bluntly.

The children scarcely knew their surviving grandparents. They'd visited Neela's mother several times within the last three years at her nursing home near Cleveland, but it was such a harrowing experience even Neela dreaded it. As for Quentin's mother, she'd remarried and was living in St. Petersburg, and even Quent said she was like a stranger.

"Yes," Neela answered, offended that her daughters cared so little about Charles Waggaman that they didn't know if he was alive or dead. What had he said to Neela herself years ago, after coming in from a walk on a glorious fall day? "Through his children, a man lives forever. Years and years from now, long after I'm dead, some child of yours will hear my name and a tremor will go through its heart."

A tremor. Yeah.

"Hey, look at that dog making poo-poo," Deirdre said to her sister.

Neela grabbed her hand and pinched it. Of all the things she'd thought her children might become, never in all her wildest dreams had Neela conceived of them as gross and insensitive. But children, she supposed, had to reflect the age, and the age was scabrous and scatological.

"When we get to California, we'll be able to spend a lot of time together." If the children were enthused, they contained it very well. "I've been so busy here,

257

I've relied too much on Emily to look after you, but things will be different when we're in Malibu."

"Can I get a hamburg at the zoo?" Deirdre asked.

"Don't you want to see the monkeys?"

The children said that they'd seen them last week. When she suggested that it might be fun to see them again, both made faces indicating what they thought of the idea.

"Oh, hell," Neela said, "so we'll get you your disgusting hamburg!"

Actually, Deirdre got two in the cafeteria line, then spent five minutes ornamenting them with ketchup, relish, pickles, and various pestilential dressings that looked as if they'd been out since the Fourth of July. On the way to the table, Ronan spilled her Coca-Cola all over her tray and also splashed the front of her coat and Neela's feet. It took all Neela's patience to clean up without losing her temper and yelling. By then, Deirdre had arrived at the table with her two by now cold patties, sat down in a sticky chair, and was halfway out of it again when her sister said to her, "There's a fly on your hamburg."

Deirdre used her hand to wave it away, and in so doing knocked over what was left of Ronan's Coke, this time spilling it over Neela's grilled cheese sandwich. Ronan said that she'd better use the restroom to wash her hands, and had pushed her chair back in order to leave when Neela said, loud enough to be heard four tables away, "You sit down or I'll kill you!"

They finished their lunch in total silence, both of the girls looking sour and unhappy.

By the time they'd finished, Neela could feel her underarms soaking wet against the coat of her Bloomingdale suit and her feet were sticky in her shoes from where the spilled Coke had run down her ankles. Her head felt hollow, raw, and aching.

On the way home, they stopped at the travel agency on Madison Avenue to pick up their plane tickets, and while they were waiting, Ronan suddenly pointed outside the window and said, "Look, there goes Daddy!"

Quentin Fitzgerald walked by, his face radiant with happiness, and next to him, her arm in his, was a long-legged, long-haired girl in a trench coat.

Deirdre was halfway to the door before Neela caught up with her. "Now you sit down, do you hear? I'm going to slap you if you don't sit down."

"But it's Daddy."

It was not. It was just someone who looked like him. It *wasn't* their father.

"It was, too."

Neela slapped her on the face, then watched her eyes fill with tears.

The two girls looked at her with undisguised hatred.

Christ, she hoped that Amos had left something in his bedroom to help her get through the afternoon. Pot. Cocaine. Anything. Something that would annihilate her senses, at least till Amos got home.

———◆———

Julie resurrected an ancient black cocktail dress from Altman's that she'd almost forgotten she owned, spot-cleaned and pressed it, and wore it to the office Wednesday morning with the intention of going to Lily Harpur's funeral as soon as she'd looked through the mail on her desk. She was delayed by telephone calls and by colleagues who leaned into her office to ask why she was all tarted up, but she got away shortly before eleven and hailed a taxi in the street.

Somehow, Julie was stirred simply by uttering, "St. James' Church, please. Madison and 71st." It was like saying Gracie Mansion, please, or "21." All the best people were married and buried there, and Julie personally knew more than a few Jewish families who had converted in order to make use of its elegant facilities and to rub elbows with the *ton*. The fact that it was also a good bit easier to arrive socially in New York by way of a St. James' communion than a bar mitzvah no doubt had something to do with it.

At one time, when she was in her twenties, Julie had spent hours going through the wedding announcements in the *Times*, substituting her own name, slightly altered (Miss Julie van Renasslaer Silvur) for those small-breasted, pert-nosed daughters of the aristocracy who had gone to all the right schools, had come out at Christmas cotillions or at dances given by grandmothers in Locust Valley, joined the Junior League and "did good" to prove that they weren't entirely superfluous, then married young Wall Streeters to prove that they were. At times, Julie would weep as she studied the Bachrach portraits accompanying the announcements, knowing that nothing short of divine intervention (and what chance did a Jewish girl have for *that?*) would make her as pretty as those Cynthias, those Vanessas, Alexandras, and Jennifers.

Yet here, after all those years, she was attending the last rites of one of them, which merely proved Julie's contention that it wasn't breeding that counted, but *chutzpah*. What difference did it make if you were the prettiest debutante photographed at Bachrach's that season if, in the final analysis, you were dead and all the homely girls were still living? On her wedding day, Lily Harpur had no doubt arrived at St. James' breathlessly expectant, assured that the life she was about to embark upon would be as rare and splendid as the one she was leaving. Yet now, twenty years later, it had been extinguished by her own hands because it had become unbearable.

Closed casket, too, probably, not to conceal disfigurement, but disappointment and the disappearance of hope.

While she was living, Julie had hated Lily because

she'd seemed shallow and spoiled. Dead, her character had vastly improved. It had taken resolution and courage to do what she'd done, and privately Julie admired her style and flair. A suicide, if it were handled the right way, could become a statement—extinction by barbiturates need be no less dramatic than immolation by fire—and the fact that she'd done it only inches away from the sleeping David (even *touching* him perhaps the second the flame began to go out!) showed that she hadn't been without invention.

There must have been more to her than met the eye, Julie heard herself thinking as the cab pulled up in front of a gray Gothic church. Had I known *that* about her, we might even have been friends.

The church was surprisingly crowded, and at first Julie was tempted to ask someone if she was at the right funeral. David had always maintained that Lily's "problem" was that she had no interests outside her own family. If that was the case, who were all these people? Julie estimated the crowd at over two hundred, possibly closer to three, most of them good-looking, flaxen-haired Anglo-Saxons. They sat morosely in their pews, concentrating on the air over the heads in front of them, as if they were watching a Pinter play. Now and then a comment was whispered, but so discreetly that Julie, from where she was sitting, was unable to get the gist of it. There were none of the wisecracks that were inevitably a part of Jewish funerals.

Wasps were apparently bored even by death. Jews always took an interest in it, possibly because the absence of it indicated that they had survived a bit longer than they'd expected.

Julie occupied an aisle seat midway down the nave, and as she scrutinized the people around her, she realized with a start that she didn't recognize a single face. So well had David Harpur insulated her from his other life that all of Lily's mourners were strangers to her. She saw herself as an observer, and worse, an interloper.

She wasn't even able to find David in the crowd, or Lily herself, for that matter. She had half a mind to leave her seat and scout around, but instead craned her neck to look over a pink and hairless head in front of her, then spied a kind of chapel leading off to the left of the altar. There, she was able to make out an immense bronze casket—good Lord, couldn't they have got her into a smaller number?—and David in profile, seated before it.

How often, during the summer, while Lily was on the Island, had Julie woke up first, then lay watching David's sleeping face, trying to commit it to memory? It had seemed to her the kind of face she could spend the rest of her life looking at, always with delight and discovery. Now as she watched it, she saw that his jaw was set somberly in grief. He stared at the monstrous object in front of him as if he were trying to get the attention of its occupant, possibly to beg her forgiveness.

On either side of him sat the children, his sons to his left, his daughter to the right. Julie felt that she knew them, though her knowledge derived exclusively from tales told in bed. One son hated school, she knew, but loved sports; the other was shy and introspective and read books; his daughter Betsy had recently, at the age of twelve, become a militant vegetarian, bringing her own concoctions of nuts, grains, and fruits to the dinner table where everyone else dug into bloody beefsteaks. Both boys were at Exeter and played guitars, which, as David said, made a father wonder why he'd bothered. Betsy lived at home and did poorly at Brearley, Lily's old school. "There is a kind of fissure in her personality," David had once explained. "She will run away to live in a commune by the time she's nineteen. What she is, I'm afraid, is all my faults enlarged, and all Lily's, put into one small, fragile body."

"Faults?" Julie had objected. "You?" It seemed to Julie that David was ineffably wise and understanding, sensitive, generous, and loving.

"I'm too damned ambitious and doubtfully talented. I work too hard and see too little of people I love. I'm a sensual animal, married to a woman who is not. I pretend to be strong, but in fact I'm as weak as the next fellow."

"Too weak to divorce Lily?" she had asked him.

"Too weak even for that. But remember, there are other things to consider." He would curse his bad luck. "If it weren't for Lily's problem, I would have left her long ago."

It was always Lily's "problem," really. She just didn't have enough to do, had no life of her own. If only she had done this, David would say—if only she had done that—then perhaps their marriage would have held up. David, in fact, was a champion of women's rights. If Lily had *done* something with herself, he would have left her long ago, as she would have been able to cope with living alone. But Lily was—well, all Lily was, was a woman, and that simply wasn't enough in these times.

Julie wondered what had gone through that Brearley-Vassar mind of Lily's the morning she'd gone home after having found him in bed with Julie. Had she gone to pieces or had she quietly announced that life with him had become insufferable and that she was leaving him? What had David said and how much had he told her about Julie?

When had Lily decided to punish him the way she had? At once? Even as she left the guest house, or much later, after her afternoon swim, after supper?

Had she said anything to him at bedtime to indicate what she was about to do? Had she left a note?

Dear God, Julie thought, the poor woman. I owe her gratitude. Julie didn't mean to, but suddenly she felt her eyes becoming wet.

Now, as a medieval-shrouded gentleman walked before the high altar, David turned momentarily and scanned the nave of the church. As his eyes found

Julie in the crowd, he started, looked at her with something between astonishment and relief, then concentrated once more on helping the three children get
through the ordeal. As the minister began the service,
David moved closer to his daughter.

At least it was a comfort to learn that religious services honoring the dead were as banal on the Upper
East Side as they were anywhere else in the world.
There was a sermon, a reading from the Scriptures that
was described as being Lily Harpur's favorite, and finally a painfully earnest account of her life. It sounded
like a job résumé. After college, she'd worked on *Vogue*
until she was married, had been a member of the Junior
League, and was active in voluntary work at Roosevelt
Hospital. (*I know, I know!* Julie cried. *While she was
wrapping bandages, David and I were making love!*)
Above all, she was a mother and a wife. Everyone
whose life had been touched by her, the minister said,
had been enriched. Lily Harpur was a rare and beautiful spirit who would be remembered for having brought
joy to the lives of others.

It was all Julie could do to avoid tapping her foot
impatiently on the floor, waiting for the man to con-
clude. It seemed to her unfair that at marriages, improvisation was allowed and guests were invited to
protest (though seldom did) the joining of two people,
yet at funerals no one ever asked for alternate points of
view.

I could tell you plenty, Julie said to herself. She
drank like a fucking fish, for one thing. She was such a
bad manager of household expenses that in the end
David had taken her checking account away from her.
She didn't like to cook, or even eat, for that matter.
She was a narrow-eyed, pinched-faced, tight-cunted
bitch, Julie wanted to tell everyone.

Suddenly, the pall was picked up and slowly borne
toward an exit at the side. David and the children followed, then other members of Lily's family, no doubt,

and David's, and finally a portion of those people who had been seated in the central nave. Others, like Julie herself, made their way up the aisle toward the Madison Avenue exit.

Outside on the steps, Didi Kravitz waved at Julie. "Pete wanted to come in," she said, "but he was tied up today."

Good Lord, it was probably just the excuse he'd been waiting for to get Didi into the city, while he stayed in Amagansett and frolicked with his new schatzi.

"Isn't it ghastly?" Didi exclaimed. "You never think that this is going to happen to anyone you know, and then—wham!"

It was going to be very hard for the children, Julie observed. The death of someone known and loved was always traumatic for young people experiencing it for the first time. It would be hard for David Harpur, too, in view of the circumstances of Lily's death.

"Hard for David?" Didi replied. "Nuts. The only thing that's ever been hard for that bastard is what comes up between his legs every time he sees a pretty girl."

Julie had to catch her breath.

"Poor Lily has had to put up with so much crap from that worm, it's a wonder she held off as long as she did."

"I don't understand," Julie said in confusion. "Do you mean David . . . do you mean that Lily . . . ?" Julie wasn't even able to finish.

"Look," Didi began, "I happen to be one of those oddities who's never been an admirer of David Harpur. I loved Lily. She was sweet and gentle and innocent. David is a selfish, craven, and cruel man. If he's taking this badly, he's getting just what he deserves."

Julie was confounded. She was sure that Pete Vassall hadn't mentioned to Didi that David and Julie were lovers, if for no other reason than because Didi wouldn't have spoken to Julie so bluntly had she known.

"Look," Didi began a second time, "he put the make on me the second time we were together, and Pete was no more than twenty feet away. I'll tell you one thing: David may be brilliant and he may be respected, even revered; but in my book, he's a shit. He and his girlfriends put that beautiful and wonderful woman where she is today."

Girlfriends? Had she said what Julie thought she'd said. It was all Julie could do to get the words out. "Do you mean . . . David has had . . . affairs?"

"Has he had affairs!" she exploded. "For the love of God, Pete and I have known him for three years, and he's worn out at least six or seven women in that time, Do you remember . . ."

And then she was off. Did Julie remember Chrissie Hollister, who used to work for the magazine? Well, David had been pronging her when Didi had met him for the first time. And then Trudi Steinway. Not the piano people, but the ones in plastic. David had moved on to her. Then, "Do you remember that revolting bitch named Alicia Ginsburg—David has a *thing* for Jewish girls—who wrote a West-Side-New-York-housewife novel about a year and a half ago, and John Updike—I wouldn't go into *that* even if you insisted—said it was the best thing since *Tom Jones?* Well, David and she almost got married, except that some former faggot named Donald Perkins got to her and took her off to the Canary Islands, and they've had a *child* . . . God knows, it must have been born light on its feet."

Julie's head reeled. She couldn't think.

Suddenly, out of the corner of her eye, she saw the long black hearse round the corner and begin its stately procession to the cemetery. As she watched, Julie couldn't hold back any longer, and the tears came streaming down her face.

"If you hear of anyone who has an apartment to

sublet for the winter," Didi said to the weeping figure next to her, "let me know. I'm coming into the city, I think."

"You're leaving Pete?"

Didi attempted a stiff-upper-lip sort of smile. "Some men need new women all the time, Julie. That's what keeps them young. If I stay out in Amagansett, I'll just have to watch Pete move in and out of other people's beds, like Lily had to watch David. And in the end, I'd probably do the same thing she's done. So I'm getting out now." She squeezed Julie's arm. "Keep in touch, will you?"

As Julie stood on the steps of St. James', watching the procession of black cars move northward, it seemed to her that Lily, once again, was drawing David away from her, even farther than the Bronx.

"Please don't leave me," she heard herself whisper.

Later, several mourners remarked about the dark-haired woman on the steps of the church, and they speculated about her. One of them suggested that perhaps she had gone to college with Lily, but another arched her eyebrows and said that she didn't *look* like someone who had gone to Vassar.

It was just as well—for everyone concerned—that Julie hadn't heard.

———◆———

Kate didn't even wait for Mrs. Ellman.

She relied instead on a lengthy note to explain the supper menu, thus avoiding any tiresome questions the woman might ask her. When she'd talked to her on the telephone, Mrs. Ellman had said, "Mr. McCabe seemed very upset when I ran into him on Nassau Street yesterday afternoon. I hope nothing is wrong."

Nothing at all was wrong except that Buddy was

more than upset. He was drunk. He'd just left the tap-room at Nassau Tavern where he'd been drinking ever since he'd left Kate lying on the kitchen floor. The headmaster—otherwise known as old Fatass—called at one-fifteen, asking if Mr. McCabe would be late for his afternoon classes, which was the first clue she had that he had no intention of meeting them.

Kate had done her wifely best, suggesting that Buddy had complained of feeling unwell and had no doubt stopped at the doctor's on the way back to school after lunch, and doubtless the doctor had detained him. Buddy *never* did anything without a reason, she said. Cheerlessly, old Fatass replied that he himself would have to cover Buddy's classes. Would Mr. McCabe please telephone as soon as he could? It *would* be con-siderate.

Kate waited all afternoon. She called everyone who might conceivably have run into him. Like Kate her-self, Buddy had few close friends since he'd left col-lege, so it was unlikely that he would visit anyone for consolation. When she went downtown to keep her ap-pointment with the lawyer, she was so agitated that she couldn't keep her mind on what he was saying. "Mr. Coxe," she finally said in desperation, "hold every-thing. Let me get back to you when I know what I'm doing."

He'd looked at her as if she were mad.

When Buddy still hadn't appeared by eight in the evening, she knew that he was out somewhere getting drunk. What else could he do after he felt so shat upon? At shortly after ten, the police called to report that he'd had a minor accident—a collision with a mail-box on Kingston Road. At the station, he'd been given a breathometer, and as a result was being charged with driving while intoxicated.

At first, Kate thought, Thank God he's in jail where he won't harm himself or anyone else. Then, with a sinking feeling, she thought, Oh, *no!* all the damage has already been done, and no amount of pleading or cajoling will erase it.

A schoolteacher could do almost anything he liked—beat his wife, fornicate with young girls, father illegitimate children, cheat and lie, and get drunk every night of the year—so long as he did it privately. But once it became publicly known, a schoolteacher was dead.

The damned thing would be in the newspaper, Kate knew. *Robert McCabe, 39, an instructor of English at the Mt. Morris School in Lawrenceville, was charged last night with driving while intoxicated on Kingston Road.*

Except that it would be wrong, and Kate knew it. It would have to read *former instructor,* because as soon as old Fatass and the Board of Governors got wind of it, Buddy would be without a job, contract or no.

Kate did the best she could. She got Mr. Coxe out of bed and asked him to meet her at the station. ("I don't quite understand, Mrs. McCabe. Am I representing you in a divorce case, or are you asking me to defend your husband?") Buddy would not speak with either of them. In the end, Mr. Coxe told her that he wouldn't be able to get him out of jail until the following morning, and in the meantime he was all right where he was.

No, he wasn't, Kate knew. Buddy was not all right. Never in his life had he been less all right than he was at the moment.

You spoiled things for me once before, Kate. All night long, Kate heard him speak the words to her, and she knew what he was thinking now: that she had spoiled things this time, too. If it hadn't been for her, he wouldn't have been driving down Kingston Road, in blackest, Lear-like rage.

In the morning, Buddy had a huge hangover and there was fear in his eyes. After he had appeared in court, he thanked Mr. Coxe, then without having said a word to Kate—the injury done to him was too great—he drove the Hornet home ahead of her, showered and shaved, changed clothes, and was about to leave the house when she said to him at last, "I'm sorry for you, Buddy."

His hand was on the door knob. He didn't even turn to look at her.

"Will they sack you?"

"What difference does it make to you?"

Then he was gone. Those were the only words he said to her. He'd been summoned to the school for a meeting with the headmaster and the Board, and by a quarter to three, when Kate finally left the house to catch the 3:15 to New York, he hadn't returned yet.

Kate sat abjectly by the train window, looking vacantly at the dullish countryside. She reminded herself that whatever happened to Buddy—defeated now to the very nub—was no longer a concern of hers. She'd coddled him, protected him, succored and defended him far too long. There were some men who had a talent—a lust—for failure and no amount of help from Kate would make him less a miscreant in the eyes of the Board of Governors.

Buddy McCabe: an enemy of decency, a corrupter of youth.

The divorce would have been cross enough for him to bear. But a divorced man who was also jobless was doubly emasculated, and for the first time Kate wondered if he would be left with sufficient will to recover.

Kate tried to imagine the interview he was having this very minute with the headmaster. The minds of children, he would be told, are tender and susceptible. Above all things, a teacher must command the respect of his students, and young people were merciless when they discovered a fault in a teacher. It was with regret, of course—particularly in view of the fact that he was about to be promoted—but the Board of Governors had unanimously decided . . .

"Okay, so get the shit over with," Kate imagined Buddy saying, his tongue having been emancipated by the U.S. Army long before dirty speech became fashionable.

If only he had the clear-headedness to see it as an opportunity, Kate thought. He had never particularly liked teaching—only someone with a child's intellect could possibly be happy teaching children, he'd always said—and there was no reason to suspect that he would have enjoyed being chairman of the department, except for the additional prestige. For years and years, he'd dreamed of quitting the job because he hated it, yet never dared because of the family, he said.

What would he do now? God knows. At the age of thirty-nine, was it too late to rearrange and redirect one's life?

Each time Kate tried to imagine Buddy working somewhere else and living somewhere else, she heard his cruel voice tell her, "What difference does it make to you?"

Kate was so lost in her own thoughts that she hadn't even seen the woman stop by her seat, then bend over to speak, shouting over the noise of the train.

"How are things at the New School, Mrs. McCabe?" she said.

Kate couldn't connect her with anyone she'd ever met before. She must have shown her ignorance because the woman added, "Don't you remember? I'm at Columbia's School of General Studies."

Oh, yes, Kate remembered now. The dreadful woman from the Garden Club who had taken a course in pre- or post-Giotto.

"I'm afraid I really won't be able to keep it up," Kate heard herself say. "This is my last day."

What a pity. Of course, it wasn't easy for a housewife to leave off baking cakes and start memorizing things again. Her course in anthropology had been over-subscribed, she said, so instead she enrolled in Chinese. "My husband asked me, *why* Chinese? Why didn't I take something sensible? And do you know what I told him? I told him that I'm fifty-two years old and I'm tired of being sensible. Don't you think I'm right?"

Yes, Kate did.

Well, she was sorry that the New School hadn't worked out. Columbia wasn't half bad so long as you didn't stray from the campus onto the streets. Perhaps Kate might give it a try next term. If she did, maybe they could have a late supper sometime. "There's a Chinese restaurant on Broadway not too far from campus, and by then, if I practice, I may be able to order in Szechuan." She smiled valiantly, touched Kate's hand, then continued up the aisle.

God, the poor woman was lonely. That was why she was taking her frivolous courses. Had she seen the sadness in Kate's own face, and was that why she'd touched her hand so reassuringly? Maybe, after all, there was a confederation of lonely wives who descended upon evening schools, and perhaps this woman was trying to tell her that it would work—Chinese, anthropology, or Giotto—if only Kate kept trying.

Strangely, Kate felt buoyed by it all.

She'd told Ben Purdom that she would fix supper for him ("All women screw alike, but all women do not cook alike," Buddy had once said to her, knowing that it would make her furious), partly so that they wouldn't have to go out, and partly to show him what a first-rate, top-drawer cook she was. After she left the subway at 59th Street, she walked eastward, then north, till she found a market with the kind of thin scallopine she wanted for veal Cordon Bleu. Going under the assumption that Ben's kitchen would be bereft of everything she'd need, she bought groceries that cost a whopping $21.63. Guiltily, she paid at the check-out, using Buddy's money.

How could she justify it in her weekly food budget, particularly now that Buddy would no longer be earning a salary, and knowing that if she went through with the divorce, he would be back where he started from: living in a tiny apartment that always smelled of fried eggs and dirty socks. He was proud of the fact that he'd been able to amass a savings account of six thousand dollars—"Money means freedom, kiddo; don't you forget it"—and often had said that they'd be able to weather almost any kind of storm, so long as they had a little dough in the bank. Six thousand had seemed like so much. Yet divided, if she went ahead with the divorce, it would buy almost nothing. A cheap car, maybe.

Fifteen years of working, and Buddy would have nothing to show for it but three thousand bucks and his share of the equity in the mortgaged house. My God, no wonder he'd driven into someone's mailbox on Kingston Road.

If she went ahead with the divorce, she'd said. *If.*

As she walked toward Park Avenue, groceries in one arm, overnight bag in the other, she tried desperately to think of Ben Purdom, but all she could think of was Buddy McCabe.

Kick a man when he's down. That's the way Buddy himself would put it. It didn't matter really that he'd been on his way down (Kate fancied that it was something like an incorporated village: Welcome to Down, pop. 1) for the last fifteen years.

If only he could be persuaded that getting fired was just the opportunity he'd been waiting for. For the first time since he married kate—felt *obliged* to marry her, though he'd *hoped* to marry true and perfect scholarship—he was without a job which he loathed. He could now do what he'd always wanted to do.

Dammit, he could go back to school and take his Ph.D!

It would be no trouble at all, really. They could sell

273

the house and most of the furniture, and move back to Columbus while he attended grad school. How long would it take anyway? Would they give him credit for the work he'd done before he enlisted in the Army? Probably not, but even so, it wouldn't take much longer than two years, as he already had his master's.

As she crossed Park Avenue, Kate tried to figure out the economics of it. They could use the six thousand for tuition and living expenses while he studied and later did his dissertation, and they could dip into the equity they had in the house, if necessary. Kate could get some sort of job in Columbus until he finished, then possibly she could take courses to get a teaching certificate. Buddy would be able to shop around for a decent job this time, one that would allow him to use his head (he loved eighteenth-century English literature; at the Mount Morris School, the century wasn't even acknowledged), and Kate herself wouldn't feel so goddamn frivolous. It would be an adventure for both of them.

Somehow, Kate wanted to run to a telephone and tell him.

Then, with a start, she remembered that she was divorcing him.

At the corner of Park and 64th, she stopped, uncertain of herself and what she was going to do. What had happened to her—still was happening—seemed miraculous. She had left Buddy in order to go to the New School because he had no need for her. She had no utility at all, no role anymore in his life. But now, because of what had happened, she was more vital than ever. She could hold the family together while both of them began a new life.

Kate was stunned. She stood on the curb while the *Walk* sign blinked green three times.

It was all so damned funny that Kate couldn't resist laughing. She'd gone to the New School, or attempted to, because she thought she hated Buddy, but in fact she hated herself. Her life had become moribund because she'd made it that way, not because of Buddy. There was a kind of sloth and a gradual relinquishing of hope that overwhelmed women in their late thirties, and Kate, too, had allowed herself to become a victim.

What a terrible, *terrible* mistake she'd almost made! Would Buddy ever forgive her?

Quickly, she made her way to Neela Fitzerald's apartment house. If she hurried, she would be able to see Neela before she left for the Coast, then go up to Ben Purdom's apartment and have a talk with him. Cooking supper was now out of the question. She would try to provide Ben with a rational explanation ("Buddy always says that it isn't that women are more susceptible to hysteria; it's that we show it more openly and honestly than men"), hope that he would understand, then try to catch the 8:05 to Princeton.

Adversity. That was what had been lacking, Kate knew now. Her own mother had told her that during the Great Depression families had never been closer. Hard times could bring people together.

To Kate, it seemed wondrous and fantastic that at her age she was still capable of self-education. On that gray Sunday afternoon when she first read the advertisement for the New School ("The Program That Recognizes Who You Are and Where You Are"), she had few illusions about it, privately feeling that she was the exception who would never recognize who she was or where she was. And yet somehow . . .

Kate wanted to crow out loud, she was so happy. She wanted to go up to a woman bearing down on her now on the sidewalk and say, "Look, you don't know me, but I recognize who I am and where I am." She wanted to take the doorman's hand, shake it vigorously, and give him a five-dollar tip for having helped, unknowingly, her education.

At first she thought she might be at the wrong building, as there was no doorman on duty. She backed up, looked at the address once again on the green canvas canopy, then waited inside the door. Doormen, she supposed, were not exempt from having to use the bathroom—she had read somewhere that New York policemen used plastic bags suspended between their legs when they directed traffic on wintry days—so she waited another minute or so, and then when no one came, and despite the sign which read *All Visitors Must Be Announced*, she walked across the marble lobby to the elevator.

She half expected someone to challenge her, but there wasn't a soul in sight. Kate tentatively looked into the elevator, hoping for someone to be there, but it, too, was empty. She stepped in, depressed the *Open* button for another few seconds, then pushed for Neela's floor. The doors closed, the elevator softly hummed, and she began to rise.

Neela's floor was a duplicate of Ben's: the same carpeting, the same expensive wallpaper, the same splendid crystal chandelier. Only two apartments opened off it, and for a moment Kate wasn't sure which door led to Neela's, but then remembered being told it was to the right of the elevator as you got off. Kate walked to the right, then rang the bell, and waited.

Neela had said that she would be leaving for Los Angeles later in the afternoon, but that she would certainly be able to see Kate before she left. Guessing that something had detained her, Kate decided to wait inside the apartment, as she still had the key which Neela had given her that afternoon at Bloomingdale's.

She inserted it in the lock and turned until she heard it click. When she tried the knob, however, the door was still locked, so she turned the key in the other direction till she heard another click. This time the door opened. It almost seemed to Kate that the door must have been open all the time.

The foyer was filled with packed suitcases.

"Neela? It's Kate. Are you here?"

When no one answered, she placed her overnight bag on the floor—far enough away from Neela's things so that it wouldn't be sent to California by mistake—and her bag of groceries on a chair. God knows what she would do with those. Make a gift of them to Ben perhaps, if he would have them.

She was just about to walk into the living room when she heard a sound, then stopped in her tracks. She didn't quite know why, except that it was a furtive kind of sound, unintentional, followed by deadly silence. Possibly one of the children, she concluded, or one of Quentin's houseguests. Kate stepped through the door into the living room and said, "Is anyone here?"

First confusion, then terror. The drawers in the huge secretary at one end of the living room had been pulled out and their contents scattered wildly over the carpet. Kate didn't dare even to move her eyes. Her skin had become icy cold. Slowly, with her heart thumping in her chest, she began to back out of the room.

There was a sudden movement to one side of her, and then a hand covered her mouth and an arm wrapped around her at her waist. Kate began to tremble uncontrollably.

"You won't get hurt none, you just keep quiet," a husky voice said to her. "Where'd she leave the money?"

He tightened his grip till she thought she couldn't breathe. Instinctively, she began to kick backwards at his legs with her heels. Then suddenly she was falling away from him and running into the hall.

"Help me! Please help me-someone-help-me-help-me!"

She flung herself against the closed door and her hand was on the knob when she felt him strike her. It was like a fist, but sharper. She gasped with pain as something tender deep inside her was pierced. She opened her mouth to scream, but nothing came.

As she slid down the door, she turned halfway and met the man's terrified eyes. He dropped the knife.

"I'm sorry, man," he sobbed. "I didn't mean to."

He moaned with a kind of revulsion at what he'd done, pushed her aside, and opened the door. Then he was gone.

Kate slumped to the floor, her back against the wall, and fought for breath. Pain came in shrill, excruciating waves, and she was afraid she was going to drown.

Neela's beautiful wallpaper, splattered with blood. My groceries on the floor. I'm so sorry. All I was trying to do . . .

Kate tried to inch her way along the wall toward the open door. If only she could get into the hall, someone would hear her.

Such a hash of things. I've made such a hash of things.

Buddy.

Ben.

Everyone.

Who would look after . . .

Must get out. Must go home.

With one hand, Kate pushed herself till she could see the hall and the elevator door. There was a humming from the elevator shaft, the sound of a door below opening and closing.

Scream now.

Kate tried, but nothing came. It hurt where sound should have been. She pushed herself once more—*Oh, dear God, I am coming all apart*—till she was at the door frame, then with all her strength threw herself out.

Her face hit the carpet, and she panted for breath.

God in Heaven.

A noise. A door sliding open.

Suddenly a scream came, but Kate didn't know if it was hers or someone else's.

Mouth dry, head pounding, Julie hurried down the long corridor, panicked by the faces she passed—the injured and maimed, the old and dying—her fist still around the message that had been handed to her during an editorial conference. *Kate in critical condition. Roosevelt Hospital,* it said, confirmation of her worst fears. Life could be terminated at a second's notice. The only mistake was that Kate had been the wrong victim.

And why, unless God meant to punish Julie, had Kate been brought to Roosevelt Hospital, of all places, where Lily Harpur had wrapped cancer bandages on those afternoons Julie had lain in David's arms? It wasn't fair. Julie didn't like it one bit. When, at last, she saw Neela, her face chalky white and devastated, she broke into a run, then wordlessly wrapped her arms around her old friend, forgetting their recent quarrel.

Predictably, Neela began to cry, for herself as much as Kate. When she had finished, Julie finally asked, "My God, what happened!"

Neela tried to explain. All she knew with certainty was that she had left Amos and the kids dawdling at Bloomingdale's while she returned to the apartment to finish her packing. The doorman wasn't on duty, and she had reminded herself to mention it to Quentin, who would certainly give someone a scolding. Once in the elevator, she'd leaned against the rear wall, tired from her afternoon of shopping, and she had just begun to rummage in her purse for her keys when the door opened. What she saw so boggled her mind—so defied reason—that she froze. Couldn't move. Couldn't even make a sound. The door had already started to close

279

before she was able to push the Open button, then run screaming into the hall.

Kate was lying on the floor, breathing more like an animal than a human being. Her eyes were filled with pain and terror. When Neela bent over to prop her up, her hand came away scarlet.

"I lost my head," Neela said to Julie. "The elevator was right behind me, but I started running down the stairs to the lobby, screaming all the way. Someone must have stopped me, because the next thing I knew, I was back with Kate, and people were trying to help her. She'd been stabbed."

Julie listened in horror as Neela repeated what the police had been able to piece together. The doorman said that a man with a package had asked for the Fitzgerald's apartment, and while he was ringing it, the man pulled a knife, forcing him downstairs into the boiler room. After the doorman was bound and gagged, the man had gone upstairs to ransack the apartment. Kate must have walked in during the middle of it.

"But why your apartment, for the love of God?" Julie asked.

It was what the police had asked, too, and Neela had told them what she now told Julie. She had no idea. Fate and bad luck, she supposed. Even when the police had given her the doorman's description of the man, and she knew at once who he was, she continued to say that she had never in her life seen such a man.

Neela was very sorry, but she was shallow and selfish, and to change now was impossible. Kate had always accepted her in the past in spite of her weaknesses, and she hoped Kate would do so once again. What difference, after all, would it make if Ronnie Cheatham were punished? It wouldn't correct what had been done, and it would succeed in making life even more intolerable for Neela.

She knew exactly what Ronnie would say to the police if they picked him up. He would tell them that he had balled Neela and had got high with her. She was his old lady, he'd say. It would make headlines in the *Daily News* and the *Post*, and all the squalid sex and drug-taking would be out in the open. Neela's life would be scrutinized, and Quentin's too. If they worked hard, reporters might even ferret out Neela's old *Look* magazine photograph and print it alongside Ronnie's as he was being booked.

Oh, no, not for Neela, thank you. Life was lacerating enough as it was. Neela had made a serious error in judgment in choosing friends, and poor Kate had had to pay for it, but damned if Neela was going to put herself on the rack, too.

If Julie guessed that her friend was telling only half the story—her old talent for smoking out the truth hadn't deserted her even now—she didn't accuse her. She knew enough about people like Neela and Quentin, however, to know that they were sometimes less than fastidious in choosing company. Quentin and Neela expected to be entertained all their lives, and frequently those who were willing to provide the entertainment were needy. And to tempt the poor was often dangerous.

As Julie listened to Neela's account, she felt the blood rush from her head.

"Is she going to die?" she whispered at last.

Kate was in guarded condition. She had undergone emergency surgery and was now in intensive care. Neela hadn't seen her since the surgery. Buddy had been notified and was due any minute.

Guarded. Kate had been in guarded condition all her life. The trouble with people like Kate was that they lived such protected lives that they were unprepared for evil when they met it face to face. What did Kate know about surviving? She was too meek and polite to contest for her own life. She was too non-assertive and non-combative.

Suddenly, tears came washing down Julie's cheeks. "I loved Kate," she heard herself say.

Both listened in horror to her use of the past tense, but neither corrected it.

In truth, Neela and Julie had loved being young when Kate had been, and being optimistic and unpoisoned by life. Kate's innocence had outlasted theirs, and she had been a life-line stretching back to their youth. Now, it seemed to Julie, even if Kate lived, she would never be the same. At thirty-nine, her girlhood would at last be over, her sense of wonder and expectations would be gone.

Under the burden of their emotions, Julie and Neela couldn't speak. Silently, they sat waiting for Buddy, marveling at what was happening to their lives. It was uncanny that they had been girlfriends for so long, their friendship held together by Kate's sweetness and good nature. Of all the people they had grown up with, they alone—and Quentin and Buddy—had wound up in New York. Had they recognized something in each other, even when they were little children, that no one else back home possessed? If so, what was it? Frailty or strength?

When Buddy finally arrived, incoherent with worry, they tried to comfort him, as they had in high school when a football game was lost. But he would not be deprived of his terrible feelings of guilt. He told them how he had disappointed Kate and denied her a life of her own. She'd had to feed only on the bits and pieces he spat up, and it wasn't enough. He was to blame, he said, for her having come back to the city. If only he had been kinder and more attentive, this would never have happened.

In grief, he said, "Dear God, if only she lives, I'll do anything, I promise I will."

Through the long night, they kept their vigil. From time to time, Julie and Neela called their answering services, and Buddy telephoned Kate's family in Ohio.

They took turns getting coffee, they walked up and down the quiet corridor, or they slept. Neela smoked incessantly, until Julie at last asked her to stop. Buddy whimpered and buried his head in his hands. Neela went to the restroom and came back smelling of marijuana. Julie stood by an open window, sucking dirty air into her lungs, and waited for the first pale light of morning.

At daybreak, they were permitted to see her momentarily, one by one, and Buddy went first. When he returned, his face was drained and he was speechless. He didn't rejoin them, but instead walked away to be alone. Neela was next, and when she came back, she said that Kate's color was better and her breathing more regular than it had been, which was a good sign.

At last, Julie was led down the aisle toward the narrow bed on which Kate lay, a screen on either side of her. Under a single sheet, she was naked except for the surgical dressing beneath her rib cage, and Julie watched with fascination as her breasts rose and fell. They had held up well under suckling children and fondling husband.

Brazenly, Julie rested her hand on Kate's breast, over her heart, hoping that Kate would feel its womanly succor and the communion of friendship. Silently, Julie prayed.

When she finished and opened her eyes, Kate was looking at her.

"Hello, Kate," Julie said. "What the hell are you doing in bed?"

———◆———

The telephone was ringing.

Neela told Amos to answer the damned thing and if anyone wanted to talk to her, to say that she'd already left.

"I'm gone. G-o-n-e. I don't want to talk to anyone. Period."

In a minute, Amos turned to her and said, "It's the moving people. They want to know if they're to come to start the packing today or should they wait till tomorrow?"

Neela had spent most of the morning tagging furniture. On some tags she'd written *L.A.* in red marking pencil; others said *Storage*. She stood now over a small Hepplewhite table which she'd bought years ago in London, where she and Quentin had gone to celebrate one thing or another, and she paused, tag in hand.

"Do they know about Hepplewhite in California?" she said to Amos Guard.

"They know about everything in California."

Suddenly, defiantly, as if she couldn't bear to consign it to a warehouse in a city which she'd come to loathe, she scribbled *L.A.* on the tag for the small table, told Amos to instruct the movers to stay away until the following day so that she wouldn't have to see them, then slumped into a chair.

Just when she needed him, Quentin had conveniently left for Rome where the snatch of the century, as Amos called Jill Montgomery, had taken refuge. Quent had stayed in New York just long enough to consent to the selling of the co-op, because Neela couldn't step into the hall without seeing Kate's twisted body there, the carpet crimson beneath her. In the end, the apartment was sold for a loss, but as Neela said, "When haven't I taken losses? I wouldn't know what a gain is."

Amos had stuck by her through it all, and to a lesser extent, so had Julie. After all these years, Neela was prepared to admit that she still couldn't fathom her old friend. That night at the hospital, four weeks ago, when Julie had returned from Kate's bedside, she had broken down completely. She had to be sedated, she was so upset. At first, Neela had thought that Kate had died in her arms, but, in fact, Kate had passed through the worst of it and was going to live. It was almost as if Julie herself had triumphed over death. Her face was exalted.

Since then, however, possibly because she had exposed her weaker side to Neela, she had been more abrasive than ever. Neela had seen her twice; once when they went to visit Kate, who was now back home, and once when they had met at Bloomingdale's, then gone out for a drink. Both times they quarrelled. The second time, Julie had called Neela an ass and a menace. How could Neela put up with that, even if it were true?

So yesterday, when she drove to New Jersey to say goodbye to Kate and Buddy, she went alone. She didn't even telephone Julie. If Julie was going to be offensive, she could damn well rent a car and drive out by herself.

Kate had aged; there was no denying that. She had put on weight, and her face was puffy. But she seemed happy at the prospect of returning to Ohio, where Buddy was finally—at the age of thirty-nine—going to begin work on his doctorate. Buddy admitted that it was insane, and that a Ph.D probably wouldn't be of much value when he was looking for a job.

"But what the hell," he said to Neela. "Money isn't that important, and neither is security. The important thing is that you're living with someone you love and doing what you want to do."

As soon as Kate mended, she was going to get a job to help with expenses. Once Buddy had his degree, she would try to get her teaching credentials. She was looking forward to it. It would make her feel important and useful, she said.

"What about the man you met in New York?" Neela asked Kate when they had a few minutes alone.

Something like sadness passed over Kate's face, but it quickly disappeared. "I talked to him," she said, "and he understood. The way I was, I would have reacted to almost anyone the way I did to him. I was so confused and so desperate."

Neela invited them out to California the following summer, but she doubted that they would come. Even in their little house in New Jersey, they had already become Midwestern again, and she had a feeling that once they got back to Ohio, they would never budge from it.

"But you'll like California. You're meant for each other," Kate had said to her optimistically, and Neela had pondered it in the car all the way back to the city. Had Kate meant that Neela was as glossy and unreal as California? As wanton and pleasure-seeking? As silly and superficial?

To Neela, it seemed quite possible that after all these years, she was ready to face up to the fact that she was meant to be a Californian, just as Julie was meant to be a New Yorker, and Kate was destined to return to Ohio.

Thank God there were places for people like Neela and Julie and Kate.

For the second time, Amos asked if it was too early to get the cabs, and for the second time Neela replied that she was almost ready, but needed a few minutes more.

Nick Lazenby, Amos's new friend, had been carrying luggage down to the lobby for the last half hour—he was proving to be a martinet about packing and being on time—and was waiting there now with the two children. He would be traveling with them to the airport in one cab, and sitting with them in the tourist class section of the plane, while Amos and Neela would follow in another taxi and travel first class.

Everything she was taking with her had already been removed from her room. She turned and once again surveyed the worn overnight bag which no one had noticed in the confusion, and now it seemed heartless to send it to Kate. It contained nothing of value: a night-gown, cold cream, a deodorant, toothbrush, a change of underwear and stockings. A loose-leaf notebook with Kate's name written on its cover, all its pages blank.

In the end, Neela decided that the best bet would be to place it in a kind of eternal suspension, consigning it to the warehouse along with those articles of furniture and *recuerdos* that had no place in California, a state, according to Amos, where no one had memories.

She quickly filled out a tag, then tied it on to the handle of the battered old suitcase—did it date from college days?—and as she did she was aware of the ar-omatic saddle soap Kate must have used on it to make it look more respectable before venturing into New York City.

"Hey, Neela, are you coming or aren't you? Nick has the taxis downstairs."

Finished now, Neela picked up two coats—what was the use of having a mink unless you could carry it on trips?—and a small jewelry case, then made her way out of the room. In the foyer, a chamber of horrors still, though it was recarpeted and papered, she closed her eyes momentarily.

Then paused.

"I'm holding the elevator," Amos said.

Now she was ready.

She stepped onto the waiting elevator. "I had to stop . . . to think something," she explained.

"And what did you think?"

She tried to smile. "I'm not sure."

"Good thinking."

She was saying good-bye to a lot of old things. In-cluding Quentin, at least temporarily. No one had men-tioned divorce, but she knew Quentin well enough to realize that his ego would not be able to bear up under her new living arrangement in Malibu. When she told him that he was always welcome, since, after all, he had chosen the house in the first place, he'd replied, "If you want to spend the rest of your life with a couple pansies, go ahead and do it. But don't expect me to be your token man."

It would be impossible for Quent ever to face up to himself. Every time he copulated with a woman, he expected the rest of the world to stand up and sing the *Star Spangled Banner*. He hated himself for having slept with Amos and people like Amos. He considered them contemptible. They were faggots. *He* was a man. He would follow Jill Montgomery around the world until he got bored with her, or she with him. Or until the night, once his masculine self-esteem had been patched together, he would get drunk and pick up a youth in the street. Then all the doubts would return. His penis would shrivel and he would come crawling back to Neela.

They had parted amicably. Quentin said that he had a great idea—absolutely fabulous—for a new script and that he'd be working on it in Rome. He would call her from time to time to see how she was, and the children. "Are you still my pal, pal?" he asked, then watched as she weakly nodded her head.

Maybe it was all she could hope for out of life. A relationship beyond friendship might tax her nervous system too much; to be anything more than someone's pal—God knows, she wasn't much of a wife or a mother—might be the death of her.

"All right, Quentin," she'd said to him at last, "you know where you can find me when you need me."

Now, as the elevator doors opened in the lobby, Neela saw the children and Nick Lazenby waiting on the sidewalk under the canopy. He had a way with children, Neela would say that for him. He also said that he was a passably good cook. He outscored Neela on both counts.

Standing at the curbside as the doorman stuffed the last of their luggage into the two cabs, Neela looked from face to face. First Amos. Then Nick. Then the children.

"We're a very modern family," she said cynically.

"There must be a wrathful God after all," Amos replied.

Behind the cabs, a huge moving van was double-parked, and two overalled men toiled with a sofa, carrying it up the ramp into the rear of the truck. A man Neela had never seen before hurried out of the building with a carton which he placed in the back seat of a gray sedan parked behind the van. Finished, he returned to the sidewalk to look at the collection of people at the curb, and it seemed to Neela as if he were about to step toward them and speak.

But the cabs were loaded now, and Amos helped Neela slide in, while Nick and the two children got into the other.

Thoughtfully, the man watched the two cabs move off into traffic, then when they were out of sight, turned and went into the building.

———◆———

When, five weeks after Lily's accident, as Julie euphemistically came to think of it, David Harpur still hadn't got in touch, Julie finally wrote him a blithely cheerful note. She didn't even allude to what had happened, but instead invited him over to dinner, or din-din, as she put it in West Side dialect. Two days later she picked up the telephone in her office and David's voice said, "Hello, Julie, I'm back. From wherever the hell I've been. I'm sorry I haven't called before now."

If there was a jet lag, he explained, there must also be a kind of death lag, and it had taken him the last three weeks simply to adjust to life.

He was trying to hang loose, he said. "I'm resisting

plans. Everyone has his own notion about what I should be doing, but I'm ignoring all the advice I get. I've thrown myself into my work, and that's been a help. I also try to spend as much time as I can with Betsy; she took things pretty bad. We have dinner together almost every night; otherwise I would have got up to see you. Do you understand, Julie?"

Sure, Julie understood. At a time like this, his children came first. Girls as young as David's daughter was were bound to be attached to their mothers (though Julie herself never had been), and it was only reasonable that he would want to spend every minute he could with her.

"Doesn't she have friends her own age at Brearley?"

Well, yes, she did, and everyone at Brearley had been most helpful. "But she needs her father, too."

Not half as much as I need her father, Julie might have said, but didn't.

In the end, he suggested that they have lunch toward the end of the week. "I've missed you, Julie. Do you know that you're about the only one in New York I can talk to? There are a million things I have to say to you."

Julie felt faint. She would have to confront him with what Didi Kravitz had told her, but that could wait. For the time being, it was enough just to be near him.

Afterwards, she considered the things he might want to say to her. He had once told her, at the very beginning of their affair, that he was the kind of man who couldn't live without a woman. For David Harpur, a woman was as necessary as food and water and air to breathe. Without a woman, he'd told her, he could not function.

There was no doubt in Julie's mind that David would turn to her now. Children could be a comfort, and friends, too, but a man like David needed a woman next to him in bed. He was a warm and passionate person who had been married to a cold, inhibited woman. If he'd made mistakes, as Didi Kravitz had intimated, it was because Lily Harpur had driven him out of the house. Julie herself had made countless mistakes, and if Dr. Rappaport hadn't forgiven her (the bastard had sent her a bill for his final telephone consultation), she was sure that David would.

For the three days following David's call, Julie anticipated the problems that would ensue once she agreed to change her station in life. David would almost certainly want to keep the townhouse on the East Side, and though Julie hated and detested East Side people, except those who had recently moved from the West Side, she supposed that she could adjust to it. Julie would have to learn how to live in a house all over again after having spent more than fifteen years in a cramped apartment. To occupy four whole floors of a brownstone without having a hippie upstairs with a leaky water bed (it sprung when he wrestled with his girlfriend), or Mexican hairless dogs yapping at her every time she stepped into the hallway, or bags of garbage sitting in front of every door like pagan offerings—well, it would be bliss. One could not get by anymore with a room of one's own. In a beleaguered city, one needed a whole house, a fortress.

She worried about trivial things. What would she do with the new drapes she'd spent almost two hundred dollars on just the spring before? And what about her furniture and her books? Good Lord, what about her cats? If Betsy had an allergy—small, patrician noses were easily irritated—would she have to have the cats put away? Nuts to that. If they bothered Betsy, she could wear a fucking gas mask. Or—and Julie considered how she would break the news to her new stepdaughter—she could be sent away to boarding school.

Then there was the Book of the Month Club, *Time* magazine, *Newsweek,* the *Atlantic, Ms., The New Yorker,* the *Manchester Guardian, Intellectual Digest,* and the three cat magazines she subscribed to, all of whom had to be notified. Also Sam Goody, Stern Nurseries, Marboro Books, Bloomingdale's, and Macy's. Also the Block Association (who would *they* get to sit at the goddamn candy apple booth next year?), and Zabar's. Or was there a Zabar's on the East Side?

She hadn't yet mentioned anything to her mother, who called once a week from Ohio to tell her how much she and Sol worried about her.

"So what should I tell your father?" Rheba Silverman always said before hanging up.

"What do you mean, tell?" Julie inevitably replied.

"Should I tell him you're thirty-nine years old and still living like a gypsy?"

"Mama, I'm all right."

"You call it all right, you live with nothing only police dogs?"

The last time Rheba had spent a night in Julie's apartment, she said that she woke up at three in the morning, looked out the window, and from one end of the block to the other all she'd seen were police dogs.

What would Rheba say when Julie told her about David Harpur? Would she at last be happy? Would she tell all her friends at the temple in Cleveland that Julie was no longer living in a dog run, shared by junkies, deviates, and muggers? Would she and Sol give up worrying about her?

No, they would not. They would worry even more, because Julie knew precisely what Rheba would say: "Harpur? Is that a Jewish name?"

A goy? What kind of improvement was that?

Julie didn't go into the office on Thursday because she wanted to tidy up the apartment. God knows, she wasn't much of a housekeeper—only the feeble-minded could actually enjoy it—but now, more than ever, she didn't want to appear slovenly. She washed and waxed the floors, ran the vacuum over the shag rug, beat the cushions of the sofa till they stood plump and erect, then fell to her knees and scrubbed the bathroom and kitchen floors. Finished, her face flushed from the effort, she prepared the lunch, dipping the boneless breasts of chicken (she touched them sensuously; they were like David's most private part, the very tip of him) into flour, egg, then bread crumbs and Parmesan cheese, page 271 of Julia Child, Volume One, open on the counter as she toiled. David had always said that he preferred to make love on a full stomach, and it was Julie's hope that Suprêmes de Volaille, herb rice, salad, Médoc, and strawberries with ice cream would drive him to a frenzy. Now that Lily was no longer fixing his breakfasts, she had a feeling that he would arrive with his stomach holding nothing but a pale English muffin swimming in tepid coffee.

She placed the Suprêmes in the refrigerator, then drew a hot bath for herself and sat in it for the next twenty minutes, a wet face cloth over her eyes to draw out the fatigue. Afterwards, she dusted herself with powder, made up her face, and dressed. At twelve o'clock—David said twelve-thirty—she opened the wine, a good one ("I'm not a profound judge of wine, but I'm a profound consumer," David once boasted), put the rice on, and removed the Suprêmes from the refrigerator. At twelve-fifteen, she dropped the latter into a pan of clarified butter, speaking tenderly to them as they sautéed (if plants could thrive on conversation, why not the mortal remains of chickens?). At twelve-twenty, she adjusted the gas under the rice to an almost imperceptible glow, gently turned the Suprêmes, and poured herself some Médoc.

The table was set, David's favorite *Der Rosenkavalier* was spinning on the phonograph, and the salad had just been dressed. Quickly, Julie ran into the bathroom for one final inventory of her face. She wished for the thousandth time that she was prettier

("I am big. That is my chiefest asset"), but knew that no amount of hoping could rectify a bad thing. David had said that he liked a big-boned girl because there was that much more to love. Women who were pretty were also inevitably shallow, she told herself. A good mind was worth a thousand nice faces.

At twelve-thirty, she turned off the gas under the rice and the Suprêmes and stood in front of the intercom box in the wall, her finger next to the button which read *Talk*. At twelve-forty, when no one had buzzed her yet, she covered the Suprêmes and poured herself another glass of wine.

By one o'clock, she began to worry. She could feel her face getting hot and reddish, possibly because of the wine. There were all kinds of reasons David might be delayed, she persuaded herself. For one thing, Con Edison was forever sending bulldozers to excavate whole streets in order to look for a blown fuse, and possibly David's taxi got caught in a traffic jam. Sometimes great, gaping holes dented the pavement or manhole covers would shoot thirty feet into the air, tying up whole neighborhoods. A bank might have been robbed. There could have been a shootout. Quite possibly, a group of protestors—pro-this or anti-that—had linked arms across Columbus Circle.

No, he must have been held up at the office, and what had happened was that her goddamn telephone was out of order again, and he'd been trying unsuccessfully to reach her for the last hour. Julie bounded for the telephone, picked it up (not really expecting a dial tone), called the trouble bureau of the telephone company, and asked them to ring her immediately to see if she was receiving incoming calls.

When, a half minute later, it rang, she spoke into it, "David, is that *you*? This goddamn telephone . . ." but it was only the woman from the trouble bureau.

So Julie called David's office and talked to his crosspatch of a secretary. Had he *left* yet? she asked.

"Mr. Harpur left for an early lunch today. Is there a message?"

"Did he say where he could be reached?"

In a moment, the woman replied, "Yes, he's at the Four Seasons."

Julie poured a bit more of the wine into her glass and tried to understand what might have happened. He *had* said Thursday, hadn't he? Julie consulted the calendar on the back of her kitchen door, then got out last night's New York *Post* just to make sure. No mistake. It was Thursday.

The Four Seasons? Why would he be there if he was in mourning? But of *course*, Julie said, he simply lied to his secretary because he didn't want her to know he was having lunch with me. Or would be? If he were, that is.

By one-thirty, Julie was in a state. Overheated and exasperated, she pulled at her blouse to cool herself off. She stood by the intercom box, waiting for the buzz from the foyer, then David's manly strides in the hallway, and she was so rattled that when the telephone rang, her first impulse was to release the lock on the front door in the lobby.

Then she was at the phone. "Hullo, hullo! David!"

In the background at the other end, Julie heard what sounded like silverware meeting china, glassware meeting teeth, and the humming voices of people chatting. Then there was labored breathing, and finally David's hesitant voice. "I've been trying to call you," he said.

"I knew you had!" she exclaimed. "I'm so pissed off with the telephone company, David. Honest to Christ, pretty soon nothing is going to work in this goddamn city. I just called them and those liars said nothing was wrong with my phone."

That wasn't what he meant, he said slowly.

"Just hurry over, will you please?" she interrupted. "I have everything ready. It'll take me about five minutes to warm things."

"Look, Julie," he began, speaking with more authority now. "I don't think I'd better see you again."

Julie sank into a chair.

"I said, I don't think I'd better see you again. Did you hear me?"

Julie felt something begin to push against her forehead from the inside of her skull. It was an effort to breathe. "I don't . . . understand. Do you mean because of Lily?"

It wasn't exactly that, he answered. "It's . . . well, you'll never believe it, but I've met this fantastic girl. She teaches at the Brearley School—that's where Betsy goes—and she's been marvelous through everything. She's . . . I just can't begin to describe her."

Julie let the telephone sit on her shoulder as she looked vacantly through the grimy windows at the buildings on the other side of the street. There were windows just like her own, and people behind them were just like her, she supposed: waiting for telephone calls, getting them, then wishing they'd never been made.

"She's only twenty-four," David continued, "and I feel as if I'm corrupting a minor, but you have no idea how she's changed my whole attitude toward life. I feel so young and animated again, Julie. Do you understand what I'm trying to say?"

Outside on the street, the maniacal whine of a grinding garbage truck—condoms, fetuses, yesterday's hypodermic needles—drifted upwards, and Julie held the telephone toward it so that diners at the Four Seasons could hear, too. Perhaps complain to the headwaiter.

"It's too early to know how serious it is," David said, "but this time I have great expectations. I really do. I just hope you'll understand." He waited. "I'll always think nothing but the best of you, I want you to know that. Knowing you has been one of the . . ."

Making a superhuman effort, Julie moved her finger to the phone button, depressed it, then heard a dial tone. In a minute, a recording told her that her phone was off the hook. Then there was nothing.

All afternoon, she sat on the chair listening to the nothing. It was, she imagined, how God would talk if she ever tried to strike up a conversation or seek counsel, as she did with Dr. Rappaport. There was a kind of language perhaps, but Julie could not get the hang of it.

At five-thirty, she replaced the receiver, and fixed herself a drink. She sat on the sofa in the soft November twilight, trying to match footsteps on the stairs with faces she occasionally saw in the halls or in front of the building. Dogs shrieked as people returned to them after a day spent in midtown or on Wall Street, then there were sounds of stereos and TV's, followed by pungent ethnic smells as mean little West Side suppers were prepared.

Suddenly, she was famished. She reheated what was on the stove and ate all of it directly from the pans: almost two pounds of chicken, a half pound of rice, two salads, a pint of Häagen-Dazs vanilla ice cream, and the whole container of frozen strawberries.

Finished, she pulled the bentwood rocker in front of a window and watched people pass up and down the sidewalks on the street below. Some, before the night was over, would be pushed out of their minds if they weren't already, some would find temporary solutions to intolerable situations, and others would be defeated beyond repair, perhaps even with their consent. Julie watched with fascination.

At eleven-thirty, she fed the cats, then set the alarm for six so that she would have time to jog in the park before she went to work. From past experience, she knew that the fatigue that followed running was sufficient to cauterize most wounds. If some were still left, a good breakfast—didn't she still have a pan of Sara Lee croissants in the refrigerator?—would numb them.

She couldn't sleep for the loneliness. At two o'clock,

she turned the TV on for company. John Saxon and Dennis Hopper in a movie she'd never heard of. She left the bed to go to the kitchen, then returned with a bag of potato chips.

As she watched TV in the darkness, she said from time to time, "What do they know about it anyway?" Somewhere in her head, an old dream was enkindled —she had been here before, she thought, or a place like this—but she soon lost interest and concentrated instead on the movie.